DESTINY

A BRIGHTEST KIND OF DARKNESS NOVEL

BOOK THREE

P.T. MICHELLE

Print ISBN-10: 1-939672-09-0
Print ISBN-13: 978-1-939672-09-4
Kindle ASIN: B00FVGCXKI
Nook BN ID: 2940148697626

Published by Limitless Ink Press

Cover design by Kim Killion
Book design by E.M. Tippetts Book Designs

Printed in the Unted States of America

When destiny is on the line, will love be enough to light the way?

In order to save Ethan, Nara gets pulled deeper into his dark world, where everything she thought she knew about Ethan and herself turns on its head.

Ethan and Nara turn up the heat with bone-melting seduction and heart-rending moments, but surprising revelations, lies, treachery, betrayal, and unimaginable evil will challenge their relationship and their future together.

As the stakes rise, encompassing more than just her relationship with Ethan, will Nara make the ultimate sacrifice?

CHAPTER 1

Nara

"*Did you find the feather I left for you?*" *Ethan's deep blue gaze holds mine as he hooks his fingers in my jeans' belt loops and tugs.*

I bite my lip and take a step toward him, loving how such a simple thing can ramp my heart rate just because it's him. "Yes, exactly where you left it."

He slowly wraps his arms around my waist and pulls me into his personal space. "And?"

The second my palms land on his hard chest, my knees wobble. Why does he do this to me every time we touch? *Cool wind whips through the frozen trees all around us, popping their ice-coated spindly limbs. My hair stirs, exposing my neck, but Ethan's heat flows through my veins, warming me, setting my heart racing like a hummingbird's. The last time we were together, while I'd slept in his arms, he'd tucked a raven's feather where my underwear curved along my hip before he left town; it was a promise of his return...and so much more we'd yet to explore with each other. I smile as I grasp his muscular shoulders, my breathing matching my quickening pulse. "Your promises are very memorable."*

He inhales deeply and places his hands on my waist. His deep blue irises darken, churning in a swirl of blue-black intensity as his thumbs run along the top of my jeans, then slide inside the material. "So you remember my promise?"

My fingers curl on his shoulders. So much pent-up emotion is run-

ning through me, I just nod.

"I want to fulfill this one, Nara." His fingers tighten, flexing against the back of my hips, pulling me forward ever so slowly. "Very much. Will you let me?"

His thighs brush mine and with each rise and fall of his chest, I feel his heart. Thump, thump. Then nothing. Thump, thump. Then nothing. I burn everywhere we touch, but I hate when his heart leaves mine, even for a second as he breathes. I rise up onto my tiptoes and clasp his neck, pulling his ear down to my mouth. "There's nothing I want more."

Ethan exhales a harsh, trembling breath, then yanks me against him until our bodies fully connect. Thump, thump, thump, thump, thump, thump. He disappears so quickly I'm left standing, hiked up on my toes, arms holding nothing but wisps of morning fog.

Where did he go? The icy landscape quickly thickens, eerie creaking sounds splintering along the branches. Frigid cold rushes my lungs, and I turn in the arctic, seemingly endless woods, panic surging.

"Ethan! Where are you?" While my voice echoes, I clench my teeth to keep them from chattering so I can hear his response. Nothing. No, he can't be gone.

I turn to call out in the opposite direction, but a sudden, ear-piercing sound echoes through the forest. I cringe and cuff my ears, squeezing my eyes shut against the jarring noise.

My eyes fly open to my darkened bedroom, a shrill sound grating in my ears. My cell phone's trilling on my nightstand, an unrecognizable number on the display.

Is Ethan finally calling? Five a.m. glows on my phone. *Just thirty-six hours after he was supposed to call me. Maybe all those freaked out texts I'd sent finally went through. Whose number is this? Danielle's? She's probably the reason he's late.* Annoyance briefly flits through me as I lift my phone and hit the Answer button. "Hello?"

"Nara? I'm sorry to call so early."

I don't recognize the voice, but the man's tired, worried tone makes me sit up. That, coupled with the fact I'd just been dreaming—yet another normal, inexplicable dream, where fantasy, reality, and deep-seated worries converge—jolts me straight up in bed. "Yes, this is Nara? Who is this?"

"It's Samson. I just wanted to let you know that Ethan's in the hospital and—"

"Hospital?" Blood rushes in my ears and my chest suddenly feels too small for my lungs. *Is that why I'm having* any *dreams at all right now...because something's happened to Ethan?* I push away my frantic thoughts and concentrate on what Ethan's older brother is saying.

"—found your number among Ethan's things. I thought you'd like to know." The sound of something opening then closing floats across the line.

"Which hospital?" I whisper, my throat raw and voice hoarse as tears gather.

"He's at Jefferson. I've only come home long enough to shower and get a change of clothes. I want to get back before my parents arrive. I'll be heading there soon. They're only letting family in the room right now, but I thought if you came with me they'd let you see him—"

"Yes!" I say, quickly. "Oh God, Samson—"

"The doctors think he's going to be okay, Nara. They're working on getting the swelling to go down."

"Swelling?" My voice pitches higher. I no longer feel my fingers wrapped around the phone.

"I'll explain on the way," he says. "Oh, I don't know where you live. Want to give me directions to your house?"

"I'll come to you. I can be there in fifteen minutes."

"All right. See you then."

Houdini crawls and stretches his muscular dog body across the covers, nudging his wet nose against my open palm. "Not now, Houdini. Mom'll take you out later. I have to get dressed."

When Houdini glances at the window, my gaze follows. Patch leans heavily against the glass, his black head tucked toward his chest. He's usually pecking at the window insistently and peering at me with that white patch of feathers around his dark eye. I've never seen the raven so subdued. His despondency spurs me into a flurry of frantic motion. Dumping all my books out of my backpack, I run to the dresser and grab any clothes I can find.

Nara

Samson's passenger seat is freezing, but I ignore the leather's biting cold seeping into my jeans. He'd gestured for me to go ahead and get in his car while he pushes the holiday garland and white lights out of his way to slip the house key up high onto a jutting eave. *Why doesn't he have it on his keychain?* The answer comes to me as I tuck my backpack at my feet. Probably so Ethan doesn't have to carry one.

Samson slides into his seat and I twist my fingerless gloved hands in my lap. I itch to pepper him with questions, but I hold back and wait for him to speak. Instead of providing immediate answers, he infuriatingly reaches over and cranks up the heat. As he pulls out of his driveway, I take in his tense profile. Normally he looks every bit his twenty-three-year-old age, but with a couple days' scruff on his cheeks and worry lines creasing his brow, he looks much older then five years Ethan's senior.

As soon as the warmth starts to chase away the cold in the car, he runs a hand through his close-cropped blond hair and exhales deeply, turning light blue eyes my way. "When Ethan didn't show up on Monday night like I expected him to, I went looking for him." He pauses, then plunges on, "If it hadn't been for the tracker I'd placed on his car, I'd never have found it halfway between here and D.C."

When I just stare at him, he shakes his head. "Don't look at me like that. I didn't put it there to keep tabs on him, but his car's a classic. If it ever got stolen, I wanted to be able to get it back."

"No, that's not it. It's Wednesday. Ethan's been in the hospital since—"

"Since one a.m. Tuesday morning after we found him."

My chest cinches with worry and relief. Ethan hadn't forgotten to call or gone quiet again like he had before he came to Virginia this past weekend just for our school dance. My brow furrows. "D.C.? I'm confused. I thought he was in Michigan with your parents."

Samson presses his lips together and turns onto the highway. "He must've left there and gone to D.C. for some reason, but I have no idea why. We don't have any family there."

Why did Ethan take a detour to D.C.? "What happened?" My voice is barely above a whisper while images from horrific car accidents I've seen on the news pop in my mind.

"I found his car flipped over in a ravine. Because of icy roads that night, they can't tell if he just lost control or what happened."

My eyes widen. "They don't think it was an accident?" Please let this have been just a freak accident. Please don't let this have anything to do with the changes I'd seen in Ethan before he left my house to collect his things back in Michigan.

Samson flicks on his blinker and takes the exit, his hand gripping the steering wheel tighter. "When I got there, I found Ethan along the edge of the woods about thirty feet from his car. He'd been thrown through the windshield. According to the police report, they're calling it an accident. They say there was too much sleet to determine otherwise."

"Through the window?" I touch my lips with trembling fingers. "Oh, God. It's his head, isn't it?"

He nods solemnly and pulls into the hospital parking lot. "He's heavily sedated until the swelling goes down, which kind of makes it hard to ask him why he was in D.C. If that's where he was coming from." He blows out a breath of frustration. "I'd just settle for him recovering right now."

Samson and I are quiet as we walk down the hall toward Ethan's hospital room. I can't enjoy all the Christmas decorations and blinking lights that decorate the nurses' station. Instead I look away and grip my backpack's strap tighter on my shoulder while my stomach roils with nausea. Before I'd left the house, Mom didn't say anything to me about skipping school once I told her about Ethan. She'd just written me an excuse note and hugged me, her perfume tickling my nose as she whispered in my ear, "I'm so sorry, Inara. I hope he'll be okay. Text me with updates."

Right before we walk into the room, Samson grips my arm, his expression grim. "He's banged up a bit. I just want to prepare you, okay?"

I fight the new level of worry and nod mutely, then follow Samson into the room.

It takes everything inside me not to cry out when I see Ethan: his bruised left eye, cuts on his face, the bandage on his left arm, the repetitive whooshing sound of the ventilator machine connected to the tube taped to his mouth. But it's the belted straps holding him down that send alarm bells clanging through my mind. I can't tear my gaze away from them. "Why is he strapped to the bed?"

"It's for his own safety. Ethan fought the sedation, but he needed to stay still to heal. Apparently it took three nurses and a doctor to finally secure and settle him." He releases a strained chuckle. "Ethan's a fighter even in an unconscious state."

I can't form a response; my chest hurts too much.

A warm hand covers mine. "Breathe, Nara. He's going to be okay."

Uncurling my fingers from his coat sleeve, I smooth out the wrinkles and take a couple of deep breaths. I didn't even realize I'd grabbed him. "Sorry."

Samson squeezes my hand, then uses his hold to pull me forward toward the bed. He nods to Ethan. "Talk to him. They claim he can hear us." A remorseful look crosses his face. "I kind of hope he didn't hear everything I've said to him. Some of it was pretty harsh."

I move to the side of the bed, then glance up when I see his brother opening the room door. "Where are you going?"

He lifts his phone up. "To check in with work and let them know I'm taking a couple more days off. Be back in a few."

Nodding, I wait for the door to close before I move closer and clutch the covers next to Ethan's hand, my whole body trembling. I'm afraid to touch him. I'm convinced I'll fall apart if I do. "What happened?" I ask, my gaze traveling over his battered face.

Nothing.

Maybe he just needs me to talk to him. Taking a deep breath, I say, "I was worried something might not be right when my dreams came back so quickly after you left on Sunday. You know how it usually takes a couple of days of being away from you before your ability to take my dreams wears off? Well, this time they came back right away. What's weird is that I didn't start dreaming about my entire next day again like I usually do—er, which kind of makes it easy *not* to piss Fate off, since I can't meddle in what I haven't seen yet. You'd be thrilled at that." I snort, knowing how much Ethan hates that I've challenged Fate enough times in the past to garner the vaporous entity's cold, vengeful hatred. "Do you know what kind of dreams I've had instead?" Leaning close to his ear, I whisper, "Normal people dreams." I quickly straighten to watch his face, hoping that revelation would evoke some kind of response.

He's so still. I swallow back the sob rising in my chest, but I can't resist any longer. I reach over to brush his hair with my fingers. "I'll stop rambling now. I just wanted you to know I'm here. Just get better, Ethan." *Please, please get better.*

"Hello?" a voice calls from across the room, sounding surprised.

An attractive blond woman in a navy designer dress and cashmere coat slung over her arm stands in the doorway with a questioning smile. A dark-haired man moves from behind her, his brow furrowed. "Who are you?" he demands.

The man has Ethan's intense deep blue eyes. And the woman's smile is definitely Samson's. I slide my hands into my hoodie pockets and offer a shaky smile. "I'm Nara Collins, a friend of Ethan's. You must be his parents."

"We were told no outside visitors." While Mr. Harris speaks, his wife quickly moves to the other side of the bed and touches her son's forehead, murmuring his name. Ethan's father takes up residence at the end of the bed, an unfriendly look pulling on his mouth. "How did you get in here?"

His brusqueness makes me tense. I start to speak when Samson says from the doorway, "She's here because I brought her, Dad. Stop being a jerk."

Mr. Harris stiffens his overcoat-clad shoulders and shoves his hands in his trouser pockets, cutting a narrowed gaze to Samson. "I'm tired and not happy you waited as long as you did to call us. We've driven all night. Go get the doctor. I want to hear his prognosis."

"He's doing rounds and said he'd check in soon," Samson says, folding his arms over his thin light blue sweater. "Do you have any idea why Ethan would've gone to D.C. after leaving Michigan?"

Ethan's mother gasps, her gaze watering as her pale blue eyes lock on Samson. "He was in Michigan? Why didn't he come see us?"

Samson's arms fall to his side, confusion flickering as he glances at Ethan, then back to his mom. "He's been in Michigan with you two this past month."

"No, he *hasn't*," Ethan's father bellows. "A whole damned month?"

"Gerald—" his mother hisses. "Keep your voice down."

"The hell I will. What in God's name is going on, Samson?" He drills a furious gaze on his oldest son, hands balled into fists by his sides. "You're supposed to be his guardian. *You*, who claimed you'd do a better job raising him than *us*."

"He's been calling me from Michigan. At least that's what he told me." Samson looks so betrayed and bewildered, my heart aches for him.

My gaze slips back to Ethan, stomach pitching. Ethan has been lying to me this whole time too. I glance at his slack features, seeking answers. *Where have you been?*

"That's it. As soon as Ethan's better, he's coming back to Michigan."

Samson's shoulders snap back and he gets right in his father's face. "No, he *won't*."

Ethan's mother squeezes Ethan's hand, looking worried and a bit righteous. "This wouldn't have happened under our watch, Samson.

There are other treatments—"

"Screw your treatments, Mom." Samson rounds on her, his shoulders stiff. "Ethan didn't want me to tell you he'd gotten his act together. Turning a blind eye the way you did, that's how bad you've *both* hurt him. You don't know him at all."

"Does he look 'together' to you?" Gerald slices his hand toward the bed, brows pulled together. "We see how well you know your brother."

"Stop it!" I snap, fury rising inside me as my gaze locks on the red scar along Ethan's neck—a lingering reminder he'd tried to commit suicide when he was still living with his parents. No matter how upset I am with Ethan, he doesn't deserve this. His family turns to me, eyes wide, but I'm past the point of caring what they think about me.

I clasp Ethan's hand in a tight grip, unshed tears suddenly blurring my vision. I quickly blink them away. "None of you really knew Ethan." I look at his parents. "According to him, you were too busy trying to fix him with pills and psychiatrists, like it was easier just to subdue him than try to understand him." *He's not mentally ill. He figured out that he absorbs people's negative energy whenever he touches them, but all that dark energy gives him horrific nightmares. He's worked so very hard to overcome how that impacts him.* I ignore his mother's gasp of outrage and glance at Samson.

"I know you love Ethan, Samson, but you haven't looked deep enough to really *see* him. Your brother is truly unique." My gaze flits to the bandage on Ethan's forearm and I briefly wonder if Ethan's parents know about the dragon tattoo under that gauze. I'm certain Samson doesn't know the true reason Ethan got that tattoo is to help him cope with his dreams. *I'll bet you still don't know about the sword tattoo that recently appeared on Ethan's back, do you, Samson? You know why he didn't tell you? He said you wouldn't accept a mystical tattoo and he couldn't risk losing your support too. Changes are surging through Ethan. He's trying to accept them, trying to cope, even though he has no clue why this is happening.*

I want so badly to say everything that's burning through my mind, but I understand why Ethan has held back. His parents aren't the open-minded type, and it's not like I've told my own mom about my ability to dream my next day. Instead, my gaze pings between his family members as I say something they all need to hear. "And now that he needs you most, you're pointing fingers and handing out blame? What he needs is for you to accept him just as he is, regardless—"

"Listen here, young lady." Ethan's dad's angry stare cuts me in half. "This is a family matter. You don't belong here."

Ethan's heart monitor starts to rise as his father speaks. I worry his father might kick me out, so I take a calming breath and gently lower his hand back to the bed. "If you want to know where he was, just ask Danielle."

"Danielle?" Samson asks.

I nod. "Your cousin. Ask her."

"That's just great!" Ethan's dad throws his hands up, sarcasm written on his face. "Looks like you didn't know my son any better. Ethan doesn't have a cousin named Danielle. He only has two *male* cousins."

My face heats and my attention snaps to Samson for confirmation, who swivels an annoyed gaze from his dad to me. His light blue eyes fill with an apology as he slowly dips his head in assent.

Ethan's dad turns to his oldest son, his tone building in force once more. "This is how things are going to go, Samson—"

"Excuse me," a man in a white coat says forcefully, but calmly from the doorway. "I want you all out of this room right now. Ethan doesn't need this arguing. He needs peace and quiet so he can recover."

Ethan's dad cuts his gaze the man's way. "Are you his doctor?"

The silver-haired man nods. "I'm Dr. Hammond. If you'll follow me into the hall, I'll go over your son's current condition. The swelling has already gone down. I'm very happy with how quickly his body seems to be healing. We shut off the meds a while ago. I'd hoped he would be awake by now, but sometimes it can take a little longer."

"How much longer?" his mother asks, clutching her hands.

"He'll be okay, Sherri," Mr. Harris says gruffly.

"Let's give it another hour or so." The doctor offers an encouraging smile. "We're going to take him off the ventilator soon. In the meantime, let's talk about what you can expect during his recovery."

The doctor's voice fades as Ethan's family files out of the room after him. No one notices that I don't follow, as if my presence is of no consequence whatsoever. I stare down at Ethan's hand resting on the bed, my eyes burning. I'm starting to feel like they might be right.

My phone beeps in my backpack. Probably my mom checking on me. I quickly retrieve it and read the text.

Lainey: Where are you? Are you sick? You never miss school. This must be life or death or something. Did Ethan finally come back?

Me: He's back. Finally.

Lainey: Is everything okay? I know you were worried. Why was he late getting back?

My best friend's question knocks the self-pity right out of me. I quickly type a response.

Me: Will fill you in later. Got to go. Have something important to do.

When a text immediately comes back from her, I turn off my phone. I'll talk to her later. For now I need to redirect my energy to something constructive.

Where have *you been, Ethan?* His relaxed features tell me nothing, so I start searching the room, looking for the clothes he'd been wearing when he wrecked.

CHAPTER 2

Ethan

Cold, wet darkness surrounds me. Sounds echo but they're muffled, distant. Something slithers close, displacing the water; that sound is crystal clear. I look left, then right, tracing the long, thick eel-like bodies that curve back around, hissing and bumping against me like they're testing to see if I'm edible. The creatures' scales reflect bits of elusive light, allowing me to briefly catch a glimpse of long, razor sharp teeth, spiny fins, and jagged tails meant to inflict pain. My eyes burn from trying to peer through the murky saltwater to determine how many creatures are lurking in the dark depths.

Seaweed tangles around my waist and arms. Every so often the movement of the water seems to loosen their clingy hold; I kick hard, trying to bring myself to the surface. Wherever that is. I'm confused as to which way is up. It's pitch dark, so watching for bubbles doesn't help.

Even though I taste the salty water, I can see the creatures' shadows without goggles. But taking a breath is hard, despite the scuba regulator I'm wearing. The tank must be empty. *Why am I scuba diving?*

My lungs are fiery with the need for oxygen. The pressure on my chest grows heavier and heavier as my last bit of oxygen evaporates. Dark spots fill my vision. *I'm going to pass out and finally be eaten by these hungry snakes.*

Right before I lose consciousness, air whooshes into my lungs, pushing them out so far and so fast, I wonder if they'll burst. I gulp and gulp, taking in as much life-giving air as I can while tracking the creatures' steadily aggressive movements.

As soon as my lungs are full, one of the eels bumps me hard. Excruciating pain slices through my ribcage and the water grows darker, clouding with my blood. The salt water stings my wound. I grit my teeth around the mouthpiece. Squeezing my eyes shut, I try to mentally distance myself from the pain, but another bump slams into my shoulder. I can't move, can't flinch away from the slow, torturous movement of a jagged tail slicing along my back. All I can do is endure.

I can't catch my breath again. The suffocating feeling is coming faster, and this time my vision turns fuzzy. I know before I pass out, this whole process will repeat all over again. Like it has a hundred times already.

The only difference is where I feel pain and how long it takes for the air to fill my lungs once more.

Is this what hell feels like? A constant, pain-filled loop? Never dying, but feeling like you're on the edge of death?

Nah, you're not in hell, a grating voice says in my head.

I grind my teeth. *Well shit, he's back.* And here I'd thought with the change of venue—suffering repeated hell in the freaking ocean instead of my usual monstrous nightmares—I'd left that gravelly-voiced bastard behind too.

You're just tired of the bullshit, the voice says. *Give in. Once you do, no more voices, no more images, no more questions. Stop fighting so hard. I told you I'll always be with you no matter where you go.*

As soon as he finishes speaking, an invisible clamp closes on my lungs, pushing every bit of the air out. This time I'm going to lose consciousness. Exhaustion overwhelms me. Do I really want to repeat this same scenario endlessly? What would it feel like to welcome the blackness and total oblivion? Where would I go? I'm so tired.

I'm ready for you, Eth—

Gravelly Voice is cut off as a trickle of light bleeds through the dark depths, and I'm suddenly rising in the water. I shake my head and focus on the pinpoint of light, ignoring everything around me. Humming! I hear a girl humming.

Then a soft hand takes mine and pulls me higher. All I can see is her hand, but I stare at the pale skin and fine bones and cling to it.

We've moved higher in the water now, where light shines through from the surface. Now that my mouthpiece has disappeared, I bite my lips a couple of times, enjoying the freedom from having to hold it in place.

Nara's suspended in the water beside me. Seaweed wraps her naked body like a bikini. Her green eyes shine emerald bright and her gorgeous blond hair floats around her in unruly waves. "What's it like, Ethan?" she asks, her brow furrowed.

I want to pull her close, but the only control I seem to have over my limbs is where we touch. I slide my fingers through hers. She talked through the water, so I answer the same way, surprised I'm able to without gulping in salty sea. "What's what like?"

She tilts her head slightly. "Dying."

My heart judders. "I'm dead?" Deep regret punches my gut as I sweep my gaze over her. The seaweed shifts with the water, moving just enough to tease me with a glimpse of her cleavage, the curve of her hip.

"Do you want to be dead?"

Her question jerks my gaze back to hers. "I'm not dead?"

Muffled, watery voices sound above my head. It can't be Nara. She's right here with me. Is that my brother? And my dad? I can't make out what they're saying, but I don't care. Even in this watery grave, Nara holds my rapt attention. If this is death, I'll welcome this version.

She runs her thumb along mine, her touch sending heat flowing through my arm, chasing away the water's cold grip. A small smile plays on her lips and she lowers our hands to her side. "I'd rather you not be. You're kind of important to me."

The seaweed buffs around her, drawing my attention to our clasped hands. Something dark shines through the green seaweed curved around her hip. I move our linked fingers toward her and hold my breath, my hand trembling as I brush the edge of the seaweed aside with my thumb.

A tiny black feather has been tattooed where her underwear would normally lie across her hip. Pleased shock shoots through me and my gaze snaps to hers. "When did you get this?"

Her laughter sounds like bells jingling in the water. "I've had it all my life, Ethan."

Nara's so nonchalant, my gaze drops back to her hip. Where the feather had been, another mark is there instead. It's faded and light. I tilt my head so I can see it better. It looks like an upside-down—

"...None of you really knew Ethan. It seems like you never tried..."

I jerk my head upright when Nara's voice slams through my consciousness, loud and clear. It's not musical. It's not watery. It's *real*.

Who's she talking to?

"...According to him, you were too busy trying to fix him with pills and psychiatrists, like it was easier to just subdue him than try to understand him."

Shit? My parents are here? Why is she talking to my parents about me?

"...I know you love Ethan, Samson, but you haven't looked deep enough to really *see* him. Your brother is truly unique."

She's talking to Samson too? What's going on?

"...And now that he needs you most, you're pointing fingers and handing out blame? What he needs is for you to accept him just as he is, regardless—"

Why do I need them?

A man's voice rumbles, low and angry. Definitely sounds like my dad.

"Ethan," watery Nara speaks to me as real Nara's voice fades into the background once more.

"Where am I, Nara?"

Her lips move, yet no sound comes out. I shake my head to let her know I can't hear her, but her body begins to fade too. "No!" I call out, trying to clutch her fingers tight, but they pull from my grasp as darkness surrounds me. Seaweed curls around my waist and arms, tugging me deep into the cold darkness once more.

CHAPTER 3

Nara

I find Ethan's clothes stashed in a closet in a plastic bag marked with his name.

Casting an apprehensive glance back to the closed door, I quickly empty his army jacket and jean pockets looking for some clue as to where he's been. His cell phone is missing, so I stare at the sparse items. Bewilderment builds and my heart sinks with each new item I inspect: a napkin from a nightclub, a matchbook from another nightclub, a wad of dollar bills, receipts for gas from various places in and around the D.C. area, and a hotel receipt.

My hand pauses over the smaller hospital baggie with his wallet and the red and black bracelet Ethan had been wearing when he'd been home a couple days before. It's the red ribbon and black rubber band he'd taken from my hair the day before he left to go back to Michigan a month ago. He'd said he needed to make things right with his parents before we could move forward in our relationship. At least that's what he'd told me. I close my eyes, picturing the sincerity in his eyes.

Was that a lie too, Ethan? The thought tears at my heart.

I pull the bracelet out of the baggie, then quickly retrieve my phone to take pictures of all the stuff that had been in his pockets before putting everything back in his clothes where I found it. Once I return the plastic bag of clothes to the closet, I move over to Ethan's side and slide the bracelet under his right wrist.

My hands shake as I try to tie it back together. I fumble several times trying to make a knot, but it's just too short now. My chest burns and pent-up tears trail down my face as I let the broken bracelet fall to the bed. I rub my shaking hands on my jeans and a sob wrenches from my throat as my gaze shifts to Ethan's face.

"Why were you in D.C.? What were all those items for? Does your trip to D.C. have anything to do with the sword on your back?"

Ethan's dad's deep voice echoes outside the door and my heart races. I reach over to slide the bracelet out from underneath his wrist, but pause when I see a curved black line along the underside of his wrist. Clutching the rubber band and ribbon in my fist, I start to touch his hand to turn it over when his parents enter the room.

Gerald Harris presses his lips together in a thin line and drills his gaze into me. His eyes are just as expressive as Ethan's, speaking without a word; right now they seem to be saying, "Are you still here?" I grab up my backpack and mumble the need to go to the restroom. As I pass his father, he says, "Nara, is it? I resent your earlier comments—"

I pause, my stomach bottoming out.

"Gerald," Ethan's mother cuts in, reprimand in her tone.

"I'm not going to let some seventeen-year-old kid think she can tell me how to be a parent."

She presses her lips together and shakes her head at her husband.

His father clears his throat and appears to count in his head for a second before he speaks to me once more. "I appreciate you caring about my son, but I think it's best if you wait until he's awake and the doctor allows friends to visit before you return."

His banishment sends a jolt of pain into my chest. I don't say a word, but just nod as I hold back the wail building inside me. Walking out of the room, I head straight for the bathroom. It's as good a place as any to bawl my eyes out.

I've just turned the corner when I see Ethan's doctor talking to a younger doctor while the other man studies a chart. "The medicine should be out of his system at this point. I'm not sure why he hasn't woken up yet."

Are they talking about Ethan? I swallow back my emotions and slow my steps, craning to hear what the other doctor says.

"You know how head injuries can be. The only thing you can depend on is their unpredictability."

Ethan's doctor gestures to the chart. "But this Harris kid is healing

miraculously. I expected him to be awake by now. Some of his respons-
es are like he's sleeping, but then others are as if he's still under. It's
baffling."

The dark-haired doctor shrugs and passes the chart back to him.
"Have you taken him off the ventilator then?"

The older man nods. "They're heading in to do that now. He doesn't
need it anymore."

"Then give it another couple of hours. I'm sure he'll wake soon."

Ethan's doctor sighs as I pass behind them. "If he doesn't, I'll be
ordering more tests."

Why isn't Ethan waking up? I tense as I push the bathroom door
open. At the sink, I turn on the tap and splash cold water on my face,
hoping to clear up my puffy eyes and settle my nerves.

When the jarring cold sets off a round of shivers, I turn the faucet
and grab several paper towels to dry my hands. I grimace that water
has run down my sleeve. I quickly push the wet material back to dry
my arm as well. As I run the scratchy paper across my skin, my mind
skips back to Ethan and the bandage on his forearm.

Oh God…what if his tattoo has been damaged too? Ethan depends
on that dragon and all the religious symbols he's added to it to help
protect him from the evil that permeates his dreams and the darkness
that's constantly pulling at him.

Dropping the towels, I grab my backpack and run out of the bathroom, glancing up and down the hall for Ethan's doctor. When I see the
man at the far end of the hall, waiting for the elevator, I hurry toward
him. "Excuse me, Dr. Hammond?"

He pauses and waits for me, silver eyebrows raised.

"I was in the room with Ethan Harris, the boy with the head injury,
when you came in earlier. I saw he had a bandage on his left arm. He
has a tattoo on his forearm. Can you tell me if it was damaged?"

The older man frowns in irritation as the elevator doors slide open.
"The boy has a head injury and you're asking about a tattoo?" Shaking
his head, he walks into the elevator, muttering, "What is wrong with
today's generation?"

What did I expect him to think of such an odd question? When the
doors start to shut, I block them with my foot and force a polite smile.
"Please. It really does matter. Ethan went through a lot of pain to get
that tattoo." *You have* no *idea.* "I wouldn't ask otherwise."

The doctor slides his hands in his coat pockets. "He sustained several glass cuts on his forearm, but nothing life threatening like a blow to the head can be." When I hold his gaze, refusing to react to his annoyed comment, he sighs. "I'm sure once the stitches do their job, his tattoo will heal without too much damage, Miss?" He eyes me, eyebrows raised.

"Inara," I say in a trembling voice. It's not good that Ethan's dragon is damaged.

"Ahem, well, Inara, if that's all, I'd like to be on my way."

I pull my foot back and nod my thanks. As I turn and lean against the wall, the medallion on the necklace Ethan gave me before he left a few days ago shifts between my breasts, reminding me of his insistence that I wear it and never take it off.

Is it possible that Ethan's tattoo isn't protecting him right now? Could he be stuck in his dream world? Is that why he's not waking up? In the past, whenever he touched me, he would absorb my dreams about my entire next day. He said watching me go through my day was a bright light shining through all that darkness in his dreams. But I haven't dreamed my next day for four nights now, so even if I touch him, I can't help him fight his way through the darkness.

I clasp the medallion through my shirt and rub its raven yin-yang design under my fingers as I whisper, "This necklace might be protecting me, but what's protecting you, Ethan?" As soon as I voice my worries, an idea comes to me.

Nara

"Your mom texted me this morning that you were here, something about Ethan being in a car accident? Is he doing better?" Aunt Sage's curly red hair is a brilliant contrast peeking out from under her black knit cap as she glances my way when I slide into the passenger seat of her car.

"No, he hasn't woken up yet." I shut the door, then hold my cold fingers against the heat blowing through the air vents.

My aunt's brow pinches as she presses on the gas and pulls out of the parking lot. "Then why are you asking me to pick you up? Your mom said you packed a bag. I assume so you can stay?"

I meet her questioning hazel green gaze. "That's why I asked you to come get me. I need your help with Ethan."

Her eyebrows raise. "My help? Yes, of course anything, sweetie. But what can I do to help Ethan?"

"I'll explain once we're back at your house. Do you mind dropping me off at Ethan's house first? I've got to grab my car, then run and let Houdini out. I'll follow you out to Barboursville after that."

After I give her directions to Ethan's, my aunt's gloved hands grip the wheel tighter, the only indication she's worried. "Does this have anything to do with your ability, Nara?

When she learned about my ability to see a day ahead in my dreams not too long ago, Aunt Sage had been adamant that I not interfere in the natural course of nature. Other than my great aunt, Gran (who learned about my ability years ago), Sage is the only other family member I've told. At the time, I'd thought her adamant warnings were because she was following her new-agey-and-in-tune-with-nature instincts.

"Please tell me you're not interfering," my aunt continues, her tone tense. "After seeing the videos your father left you before he disappeared, I can't imagine you defying his request to stay out of people's lives. My brother's missing. I don't want to lose my niece too."

"I'm fine, Aunt Sage."

And that's the real reason she's concerned. I'd inherited my ability to see my next day from my father, whom I'd recently discovered hadn't abandoned us years ago. He'd left to protect us because he believed our family was being punished for the thousands of lives his ability allowed him to save while working for a secret government division that prevents major disasters. Unfortunately I learned the truth about my dad on the same day that I found out he'd gone missing. *Where are you, Dad? I need to tell you so much. Starting with the fact that Fate is responsible for all the "accidents" that happened to our family.*

"That's not an answer. Are you using your foresight to help Ethan?"

The tension in my aunt's voice pulls me out of my worried musings. I can't let renewed concern for my dad overshadow my current fears for Ethan. Right now I need to focus my energy on helping him wake up. I meet her stern gaze and shake my head. "It has nothing to do with my ability to see ahead. If there's something I can do to help Ethan, I have to, Aunt Sage." She nods, apparently satisfied with my answer for now.

We grow quiet in the car and I stare out the window, thinking about something Samson said to me before I left the hospital that made me question if the people in our lives happen randomly or if their existence has a more meaningful purpose.

I went looking for Samson as soon as I formed a plan to help Ethan. I found Ethan's brother sitting in a chair in the hall outside Ethan's room. Head in his hands, elbows on his knees, with his fingers digging deep into his blond hair, he looked as beat down as I felt.

He must have sensed my presence, because he said quietly, "What did I miss, Nara?" His light blue gaze lifted to mine, full of doubt. "You said I didn't look deep enough. What didn't I see that I should have?" Rubbing his forehead, he rushed on, "I was told to go to Ethan once before. Thankfully I was able to be there for him then, but this time I'm right here in front of him, yet I'm powerless to reach him."

His cryptic comment surprised me. "What do you mean you were told to go to Ethan?"

Samson blew out a harsh breath and shoved a hand through his hair. "I got lucky with my government job. They didn't seem to care that I only had two years of college. I worked hard and was already moving up within the company, despite my dad's belief that I'd fail without a degree hanging on my wall," he said, curling his lip derisively. "I knew Ethan had been having trouble at home, but I thought, 'how could I help'? I'd made my share of mistakes and was still kind of stumbling my way through life. What could I offer him? I mean, that's what *parents* are supposed to do...be there for you. Give you direction."

Samson lifted his shoulders, then let them fall with a heavy sigh. "While on a weekend trip to visit old friends from my early college days, I chatted with the man next to me on the airplane. He asked if I had family and I mentioned Ethan, saying I wished I were older and more established so I could help him. Do you know what he said to me next? He looked me directly in the eyes and told me to go get my brother, that he needed me to be there for him. He was so intense, insisting that I follow through."

"What did you say to him?"

"I didn't know what to say. Other than to promise him I'd go and to thank him for his concern." Samson's lips crooked briefly as if reliving the surreal moment all over again in his head. "He could've been totally crazy for all I knew, but the seriousness and empathy in his expression made me think he must've lost someone close to him; that there were things he would've changed in his past if he could have. Even after I landed, I couldn't get the look in his eyes or the passion in his voice out of my mind. Suddenly I was worried. I immediately booked a flight to Michigan." Samson's eyes watered and he exhaled a shaky breath. "I barely made it, Nara. If I hadn't listened to him…"

"But you did listen." My heart ached for the pain and guilt in Samson's gaze. When I shared Ethan's dreams in the past, I experienced one of his painful memories. I saw Ethan attempt to hang himself; I felt his despondency over his parents' inability to understand what he was going through, and then his relief when Samson came bursting into his room to save him. Samson didn't judge Ethan, didn't scream that he was crazy. He just grabbed him in a bear hug and accepted his brother. He and Ethan left that very day. "You saved Ethan, Samson. *You*, not some stranger on a plane."

He blinked and brushed away the mist in his eyes. "But I don't know if I would've gone right then if that man hadn't made me promise not to delay." Samson glanced away, embarrassed. "I don't want to fail my brother again. I couldn't bare it if I lost him."

Kneeling, I put my face in front of Samson's. "You asked me what you *didn't* see. You know what that is, Samson? Ethan might be surrounded by darkness but he craves the light. He seeks it out. He's a good person."

Samson straightened his spine. "I know he's a good person. I've never questioned that. I just feel like he confuses his awful dreams with reality sometimes, you know? That he lets them own him. I know they trouble him, but dreams are dreams. They aren't real."

I tilted my head and held his gaze. "Are you saying that things in life are always black and white? That dreams can't have a measure of truth in them, or mean more than just a series of made up images we see while we're sleeping?"

Samson frowned. "What are you getting at?"

I rubbed my sweaty palms down my jeans, then offered a half smile. "You listened to a stranger's insistence about Ethan and even acted on it. If that's not believing without concrete proof, I don't know what is."

"That was different." His frown shifted to a scowl. "If there was even an ounce of truth to his words, my brother was in trouble. Ethan needed me. I couldn't take the chance he was wrong."

"It was a leap of faith for you then. Have you told Ethan about your experience on the plane? About why you came home when you did?"

Samson slowly shook his head, his voice hesitant. "Do you think

I should?"

"Yes, I do. Let Ethan know you're open to…possibilities. I think he'd feel better knowing you believe that not everything can be easily brushed aside as impossible." I held my breath and hoped that I helped. Ethan would never want his brother to torture himself like this.

Samson smiled and gently tapped his knuckles on my chin. "Now I know why Ethan likes you so much. You truly are a ray of sunshine."

I smiled, my eyes wide. "He said that to you about me?"

Samson waggled his eyebrows, looking smug. "Nah, he'd never share. I overheard him call you Sunshine one day while you were on the phone with him."

You're not the only one he hasn't shared with.

I pursed my lips ruefully and shifted my gaze to the floor. "I doubt your parents will ever think very highly of me. I've been banned from seeing Ethan until visitors are allowed."

"What?" Samson jumped up, hands fisted by his sides, outrage spreading across his features. "They don't get to decide what's best for him."

I scrambled to my feet and gripped his arm. "Calm down, Samson. I need to leave for a little bit anyway. Maybe that'll give them some time to reconsider."

He scowled. "Ethan would want you with him."

I applied pressure to his tense forearm. "Please don't fight with your parents because of me."

Inhaling deeply through his nose, Samson took a few calming breaths. "I'll talk to my parents, civilly. I'm sorry, Nara. My dad can be such an ass."

"Well, I did pretty much insult their parenting." I dropped my hand and shrugged. "I get them being offended."

"Their pride only punishes Ethan." Shaking his head, he shoved his hands in his denim pockets. "I'm still in the dark as to where he's been. I checked his car for his phone before they towed it to Mike's Body Shop, but couldn't find it. I even checked his computer, but he'd wiped all the history from his recent web searches. I only found school projects on his hard drive. Who do you think this Danielle person is?"

Just hearing the girl's name stiffened my spine. "I have no idea—" I paused and my heart suddenly raced. "Wait. Is it possible to find out where he's been from the tracker you put on Ethan's car?"

He grimaced. "Unfortunately, no. I paid for the bare minimum, low-tech device. It doesn't track where his car has been, just its current location."

"Nara, we're here."

My aunt's fingers on my cheek draw me out of my thoughts. "Are you okay, sweetie? You seem really preoccupied."

"Just thinking about Ethan," I say as I push the door open and hitch my backpack on my shoulder.

She offers an encouraging smile. "He's going to be okay."

I blink against the sleet that's starting to fall and shove my hands in my leather jacket pockets. "I'm going to do whatever I can to make sure of it. I'll see you at your house in a half hour."

CHAPTER 4

Nara

"Down, boys," I say affectionately. The smell of fresh pine hits me as I pat my aunt's dogs' heads and instantly seek the source.

My aunt always buys a live Christmas tree and every other year she changes the theme. This year's theme is apparently silver and blue: blue lights, silver and blue bulbs, silver icicles and blue crystals hang beautifully on the tree sitting by the front window. The dogs are sniffing my jeans and shoes so hard, I smile and say, "You guys smell Houdini. Maybe one day I'll bring him."

"Can you imagine the mayhem with four beasts tearing around this small house?" Aunt Sage shakes her head and chuckles when Bo, the Jack Russell, pings off the furniture to take a fast nip at Luke's back leg, before zooming off down the hall with the offended Rottie in fast pursuit. Duke races behind the rambunctious duo woofing deeply, his Shepard's tail wagging in excited swoops. Bells jingle with their antics, since each dog has one on his collar. The constant sound would drive me nuts, but Christmas is my aunt's favorite holiday so even the pets have to get into the Christmas spirit.

I smile after Duke, pleased to see him so happy. He has an extra special place in my heart, since Ethan and I rescued him from an abusive owner. "Yeah, good point. I'll wait until the spring when they can play outside."

Shrugging out of my jacket, I lay it across the couch's arm and immediately walk over to my aunt's shelf of New Age books, my gaze scanning the titles. "Remember that crystal necklace you created to help me get my dreams back? You said that you chose the Celestite because it was known for its dream recall property. What about metals? Do you have a resource in here that says which metal conducts psychic energy best?"

My aunt reaches for my hand as I trace along the titles and turns me toward her. "Psychic energy?" Her gaze searches mine, apprehension evident. "You told me you weren't planning on using your dreams to help Ethan, Nara."

I shake my head. "I'm not going to use my *foresight* to help him. That's what you're concerned about, right? But I am going to use my dreams."

She grips my shoulders. "But your foresight is part of your dreams. Which makes me wonder...don't you already know if he wakes up or not?"

Taking a deep breath, I ponder how much to tell my aunt. She doesn't know anything about Ethan's issues or his ability. When her hold tightens and her face sets in a stubborn line, my stomach knots. What if she refuses to help? I can't do this part without her, so I tell her the one thing that will blow her mind while also ease her worries. "I can't use my foresight from my dreams to help Ethan, Aunt Sage, because he doesn't show up in them. He never has."

"But..." Her hands fall away from my shoulders. "You're with him all the time. How is that possible that he's never in them?"

My lips quirk. "Crazy, huh? Remember when you first met him and you said, 'he's an old soul'?" I pause and spread my hands, shrugging. "Maybe that's why."

She narrows her gaze doubtfully. "That makes as much sense as—"

"The fact that I can see my entire day through my dreams the night before?" I arch my eyebrow.

A smile flickers and the tension in her face eases. "Okay, so you can't see his future. I get it, but then how will your dreams help him?"

There's no way I'm telling my aunt that Fate is a very real entity who has attacked me outside of my dreams several times in the past for interfering with other people's fate. If she knew that Ethan and I combined our powers through our dreams in the past so I could confront Fate and get him to back off, she would flip. But even Ethan doesn't know just how much power Fate wields in the dream world—that if

I die there, I'll die in the real world too. And Fate would like nothing more than for that to happen. My abilities are a prickly thorn the vengeful entity wants to permanently extract from his shadowy hide.

My aunt can't know any of this or she'd shut my plan down, cutting off my chance to try to help Ethan.

Fortunately Fate can only get to me through my dreams if Ethan and I touch while we sleep and *only* if I'm wearing the crystal necklace my aunt gave me. And since I haven't been having my dreams about my next day lately, I feel pretty confident that Fate can't show up. At least I hope he can't. On the other hand, the evil Ethan experiences in his dream world makes your skin crawl and is freakishly real, like walking through an endless, interactive haunted house. I don't want to go into his dreams without some level of protection.

This is where my aunt's expertise as a jewelry designer is crucial to making my plan work. So I tell her the parts she needs to know. "Remember when I wore the crystal necklace you made to help me get my dreams back but it didn't work?"

She nods. "But you did eventually get your dreams back."

I only got them back because Ethan stopped touching me. He had my dreams the whole time. I'd never "lost" them like I thought. "I did dream that night I wore the crystal, just not my dreams. I had Ethan's dreams. I don't know how. Maybe it's because Ethan and I have a strong connection, or maybe our dream abilities, even though they're different, somehow allow us to bond that way. All I know is, I was able to project myself into his dreams. It's a horrible, monster-filled dreamscape, Aunt Sage. When I asked him how he handled them, Ethan says the dragon tattoo on his arm helps protect him. Unfortunately his arm was wounded in the accident and the tattoo is damaged. I'm worried that… well, that he might be stuck in his dream world and that's why he hasn't woken up. I overheard Ethan's doctor talking to another doctor. He says Ethan should've woken by now."

Aunt Sage pulls me over to the couch. Her brow creases as she sits down beside me. "Why do you think he has such awful dreams?"

I shrug and gloss over answering directly. "His dreams don't define who he is, Aunt Sage. They just give him horrible insomnia. He sees my dreams too and they've helped him deal with the darkness."

She rubs her temples, squinting. "So wait…are you saying he sees your future? He knows about your ability?"

I nod, then snort. "Yes, he does, and you'll be thrilled to learn he agrees with you. He doesn't want me to get involved or change anyone's fate. Ever."

Aunt Sage beams. "I knew I loved this boy for a reason."

"So you'll help me?"

She cups her hands around mine. "I want to know more about why he has these dreams. There might be something we can come up with to block them."

Unless Ethan locks himself away in a room and never touches another person ever again, then nope, he's stuck with them.

Everyone has some kind of negative energy: bad pasts, sad home lives, all kinds of crappy baggage they carry around with them. My boyfriend just happens to be a magnet for it. Everything he absorbs morphs into vicious monsters acting out violence and mayhem in his dreams, and he feels and fights against all of it every single night.

"Maybe," I say, hedging. "But for now, we need to try to help him wake up. I can't imagine the torture he's going through." My eyes tear up as memories of his past dreams rush to the front of my mind.

Aunt Sage nods, her gaze taking on a committed gleam. "What do you have in mind?"

Nara

While I wait for my aunt to finish up the piece she's working on, I check my phone. Immediately several texts come through, one after the other from Lainey and Drystan—an exchange student from Wales I'd become friends with recently. I also have a couple of voice mails, one from each of them.

Once I send my mom a text with an update on Ethan, I scroll through the other texts.

Lainey: Where are you??? WTH, Nara? What is the important thing you needed to do?

Drystan: Lainey said you had something important to do today. Is Dark Boy the reason you're not here?

Dark Boy? That's how he sees Ethan? When Ethan had shown up at the dance late on Saturday, Drystan and Ethan had instantly disliked each other.

Lainey: Check out this Virality page link. That's the sophomore locker hall. Must've happened during the dance or on Sunday. Bet the teach-

ers are glad the students had Monday and Tuesday off.

I don't have to click the social media site link to know how bad the hall looks. I open Drystan's text next.

Drystan: School was a disaster zone in the sophomore locker hall. Whatever happened, it was violent. You need to get back to training. Where are you? Get your arse out to the park after school today.

Lainey: Drystan's being such a grouch to Matt and me. I know it's because D's worried about you. Text me back and tell me what's going on. Throw me a bone so I can keep this rabid dog from snapping our heads off.

Drystan: If you don't let me know you're okay, I'm going to show up at your house.

Ugh, and those are just the texts. I'm afraid to listen to the voice mails, but I do anyway.

Lainey: "I broke down and called your house before dinner. Ethan's in the hospital? Something about a car accident? I'm so relieved you're okay. How's Ethan doing?" Sighing heavily, her tone softens. *"I'm so sorry, Nara. Sending healing vibes Ethan's way. I'll let Drystan know. Just call when you can, okay?"*

I'm somewhat relieved to see Drystan's voice mail didn't come through until fifteen minutes after Lainey's. That meant he wouldn't bite my head off like he'd done in his texts. I click the button to listen to his Welsh lilt across the line.

Drystan: I know Dark Boy's in hospital and all, but I'm serious about continuing your training as soon as possible, Nara. I don't want that to be you in a hospital bed. Ring me!

I text Lainey first and update her on Ethan. Instead of texting Drystan, I call. He picks up on the first ring. "Hey. How's Dark Boy—"

"Don't, Drystan," I snap, feeling every bit as tired and tense as I sound.

"You ah, don't sound so good. Want me to bring you some take-away?"

"Take away?"

"You call it carry out and sometimes fast food here, I think."

"Oh, no. I'm fine, but thanks. You're going to have to back off on the training stuff, Drystan. Ethan takes priority right now."

"You didn't see the school, Nara. It felt very wrong to me."

Oh, I saw it. Got to witness the whole violent mess happen in real time during the dance. Drystan's feelings are "spot on" as he'd say in that accent of his.

I sigh. "I agreed to self-defense training, but we just need to hold off for a bit until Ethan's better. That's all."

"Promise?"

"Promise."

"You sure you're fine, Nara?"

I nod, then realize he can't see me. "I'm good. I'll see you at school soon."

He blows out a frustrated breath and I know he's probably shoving his fingers through his messy, blond-streaked hair. "Right. See you then."

Before I can reply, he clicks off.

I turn to my aunt who's coming through the door from her shop. "Ready?"

She walks up to me and sets a heavy silver ring in my palm, her face pinching in concern. "Are you sure this is safe?"

Possibly not. Fate may well kick my ass all over Ethan's dream world. I force a confident smile. "Of course. I'll be fine, Aunt Sage."

She presses her lips together as she sets a smaller version of Ethan's ring on my palm. "Since you'll be in there too, it's better for you both to have one. I'm coming with you."

I quickly shake my head, grabbing her arm when she turns to reach for her coat. "You can't. It's going to be hard enough to sneak back into Ethan's room."

"What?" Her hazel gaze swings back to me, narrowing. "Why would you have to sneak in?"

I curl my fingers into a fist around the rings, hoping the metal absorbs some of my positive thoughts for Ethan's recovery. "I um…kind of insulted Ethan's parents when I was in the hospital room with them, so they banned me."

"Nara! Why would you do such a thing?"

I shrug and release her arm. "They deserved it. Trust me. There's a reason he lives with his older brother."

"Oh." My aunt's tense shoulders slump a little. "That's sad."

"It is, but I'm not going to let their pride stop me from helping Ethan."

My aunt's fingers brush my furrowed brow. "Is it safe for you, Nara? You can't get stuck in Ethan's dream world too, can you?"

Get stuck? I hadn't thought of that possibility. When I walked in his dreams in the past, Ethan's presence had pulled me out of each nightmare I experienced, and a few times when things got really extreme a sudden soft darkness had folded around me, shielding me completely from all the violence. Ethan had been surprised when I told him about the dark comfort. Nothing protected him from the violence in his dreams but himself. So even if Ethan's incapable of helping me, I have to trust that the comforting darkness will be there, obliterating the horror. I nod with confidence. "I'm not worried, Aunt Sage."

"That makes one of us."

I grip her hand. "I promise I'll call you as soon as I wake."

Her gaze holds mine for several seconds, then she nods, pushing me toward the door. "It's late. By the time you get to the hospital it'll be ten."

"I'm hoping the late hour means his parents have already gone to their hotel for the night," I say as I shrug into my coat. "I seriously doubt they'll stay with his brother."

Nara

As I enter Ethan's floor via the stairs, the two nurses sitting at the station across from the lobby don't notice me walk up behind the standup, life-size animatronic Santa. They're watching Samson sleep in a wooden backed chair, his head propped up by his hand and elbow on an end table next to him. I'm so relieved he's not in Ethan's room, I give myself a second to calm my thumping heart after running up five flights of stairs and listen to the nurses talking about him.

"Poor guy," the young, redheaded nurse says to the older woman who's filing paperwork away in a lateral file. "He looks so uncomfortable. Should we get him a blanket?"

The older woman pulls her half-moon glasses down and observes Samson with a stern look. "He wasn't happy I kicked him out of his brother's room, then he refused to leave when I told him he should go home and get some rest. Said he wanted to be here when his brother woke up. I told him to come back fresh in the morning, yet there he sits, sleeping fitfully."

The younger nurse's face softens. "He has such love for his brother. I think his dedication is admirable."

The older woman snorts and quietly shuts the filing cabinet. "Won't do his brother any good if he gets sick from exhaustion. At least the parents have more sense. They left for their hotel a couple hours ago."

As the nurses continue to discuss Ethan and his family in low tones, I creep down the hall away from the station. At least the nurses confirmed what I needed to know; Ethan still hasn't woken up.

I reach Ethan's room and quietly enter. The room lights are off, but parking lot lights outside the window allow enough illumination to make my way through the room.

I quietly unzip my backpack, then slip the crystal necklace on over the medallion necklace. Once the cool crystal is nestled inside my shirt, I move over to Ethan's bed and am relieved to see they've removed the straps. Slipping out of my shoes, I gently ease myself into the bed beside Ethan and lift his hand toward my mouth.

Pressing my lips to his knuckles, I slide the ring my aunt created onto his ring finger, then slip the smaller ring just like his on my own hand. My fingers lace with Ethan's and I clasp our hands together. Ethan's masculine smell washes over me, reminding me what it felt like to fall asleep with his arms wrapped around me just four nights ago.

Before I found out he'd lied to me.

No matter what secrets he's kept from me this past month, I can't turn off my love for him. He affects me deeply. And he always will.

What if I never get to feel his touch again? A sob gathers in my chest, vaulting its way to my throat. I swallow back my swirling emotions and tighten my grip on his hand. When he wakes up, he'll explain everything.

Once my churning stomach settles, I lay my head on the pillow beside him and lean against his shoulder. Closing my eyes, I whisper, "Please let this work."

CHAPTER 5

Ethan

The massive lion-headed creature digs unforgiving claws into the dirt, its angry roar reverberating off the tall stone walls boxing us in. I yell and wave my arms in wild abandon, putting on as fierce a show as I can in the hopes I'll fool it into thinking I'm as big as he is.

Other battles echo all around, sounds of unknown creatures' claws scraping and jaws snapping before a huge body slams into stone walls elsewhere in the maze. At least those beastly fights have some semblance of fairness. My only weapon is my mind, but even if my spirit continues to fight like a junkyard dog, my body can only take so much before these never-ending scenarios infect my mind like a gnawing disease.

A huge light roams across the top of the maze's stone walls, like a prison guard's spotlight highlighting every hiding space. The creatures seem to have terrible vision and instead depend on their sense of smell and hearing to hunt.

Apparently my movements only manage to piss this particular beast off.

He dips his head and snarls, then whips his scorpion stinger tail back and forth. Poison spews with each thump against the narrow walls, leaving melting singe marks on the rough stone's surface.

When the creature pounces, I dodge, taking off down the narrow corridor. The ground shakes from his pounding weight, and the hair on the back of my neck rises with each expelling snort from his snout. I approach a T in the corridor, then take a left. Relief washes through me that this new path seems to go on for a while.

The beast slams into the T, shakes its head, then snarls his fury before bounding in my direction. I turn right down another path, my chest burning. Thankfully, I'd made the right decision. A long corridor with many branches sprawls ahead of me.

The lion-scorpion shortens the distance between us rapidly. I glance back to gauge how close, then dig my shoes deeper in the dirt. Tensing my thighs, I ramp up for a burst of speed. When I face forward once more, the layout before me changes, shortening to less than twenty feet with a dead end straight ahead.

"Unfuckingbelieveable!" My shoes skid on the dirt floor and my legs strain and flex as I dig my heels in to avoid slamming into the wall. I finally stop, just inches from the unyielding stone surface. I curl my hands into tight fists. Another change with no rhyme or reason. No way to determine a pattern. The only consistency in this world is inevitable, torturous pain.

My hand suddenly tingles and I glance down to see a silver ring appear on my finger; the dragon with symbols along its back reminds me of the tattoo on my arm. Well, the one I used to have. My forearm's a blank slate now. Seeing the ring makes me believe I'm not alone, like someone's watching over me. I'll be damned if I'll go down without one hell of a fight this time.

Clenching my ring hand closed in a tight fist, I whirl to face the creature thundering toward me and raise both fists, snarling, "Come on, you overgrown cat. You're going to have to work harder than all the bastards before you for this kill."

The lion comes to a lumbering stop. Pawing the ground, he lets out a low, threatening *rowrrrr* that sounds both leisurely and amused. He rolls his head slowly from side to side, an indication he plans to toy with me before he deals the killing blow.

My chest expands with fury. This repeat nightmare has the same ending—me in pieces on the ground, blood everywhere, my muscle and sinew flossing some random beast's teeth. I refuse to let him enjoy it. This time I don't wait to be attacked first; I jump onto his massive head before he can lunge.

He roars and tries his best to fling me off, but I use my hold on his mane to pull my legs away from his snapping teeth, dragging myself onto his back. He tries twice more to reach me with his mouth, but fails, so his barbed tail arcs, its poison arrow zinging for me. Keeping my grip tight on his mane, I swing myself down his other side at the last second.

The stinger barely misses me and enters his shoulder. The beast screams in pain. I don't have much time. He'll pull the stinger free of his muscle any moment. I move quickly, wrapping his long mane around and around the temporarily stuck barb.

The lion finally yanks his tail out of his shoulder, but growls furiously that his hair is now tangled in the barb; each swishing tug causes him to yowl even louder. I flip him off and smile, then turn to run. Before I take two steps he throws his hindquarters sideways and slams me into the wall.

Pain explodes along my spine; my breath propels from my lungs. As my vision blurs, I'm close to losing consciousness. I hammer my fist against his hipbone and kick hard, aiming for his groin. There's no room for honor when your life hangs in the balance.

Somehow I blindly manage to hit home, and as soon as the creature screeches, I shove his body away and slide free.

I run faster than I ever have before, but I refuse to celebrate that this is the first time I haven't been cornered and devoured by whatever new creature the never-ending maze conjures. I've only temporarily put off gasping painfully back to life, my splattered guts and dismembered limbs magically intact once more. A temporary reprieve from a torturous death is the sickest kind of torment; it allows the mind more time to dwell on the upcoming, inevitable agony. Even knowing this, I still fight.

The lion roars as he struggles to turn his massive body in the narrow space. Edging around, he vaults after me in fierce pursuit, but I tune out his loud fury when another sound captures my attention, striking true fear in my heart.

"Ethan! Where are you?"

Nara's terrified call sends a cold chill slicing through me. "Nara, keep talking so I can find you!" I smack the side of my fist against the stone wall as I run. The thought that any of these creatures could do to her what's been happening to me fuels my speed. I have to get to her, to protect her. Zooming around the corner, I look left and right as I listen for her voice.

"I'm in some kind of maze. What's that roaring? Ethan, oh God, are you in there with it?"

I follow the echo of her last words while trying to keep worry from my voice. "I'm coming, Nara. Keep talking."

"I've been looking for you. Ugh, the sounds and smells…it's like this place is feeding on your fears. The flashing light is giving me a headache." As darkness consumes the space once more, she grows quiet, then shrieks, "Aack! Something just slithered past. Ethaaaaaan."

For whatever reason, I'm able to see in the darkness. The lion had gone in the opposite direction earlier. I shut out the concern he'll find us and keep talking. Nara takes priority. Dashing around another corner, I call out, "Follow my voice. As soon as the light strobes back through, run toward it. I'm coming."

"Following," she says as the sound of her feet hitting dirt floats my way.

The moment I see her, my heart jerks. I pull her shaking body into my arms and gather her close, breathing into her hair. "You're okay, you're okay," I say over and over. I stroke her soft hair, cup her jaw, then run my thumbs along her cheeks. I can't stop touching her.

Nara clings to me, her hands tight around my waist. For several seconds, I tune it all out and just experience how much she makes me feel. I inhale her floral scent and revel in her soft frame pressing against me. My body has a mind of its own, wanting to mold to her every curve. It takes supreme effort, but I resist pressing my hips against hers. *She shatters me. Every damned time.* Exhaling harshly, I shake off the shudder rippling through me and take a deep breath to regain my senses. This is not the place to lose them.

My gaze snags her worried green one as I clasp her face a little tighter. I can keep fighting in this godforsaken place when it's just me, but if something happens to her here, I wouldn't bother fighting anymore. I'd be done. Gravelly Voice can have me once and for all.

"What are you doing here?" I demand, my voice cold, harsh, but I can't help it. I'm scared out of my mind for her.

Nara stiffens and pulls my hands from her face, her fingers gripping mine. "I'm here for *you*, Ethan."

I shake my head. "You shouldn't be here."

"Neither should you. You're—"

An ear-deafening roar vibrates the walls just around the corner. It's way too close. "Come on," I call over the din and clasp Nara's hand. Dragging her behind me, I run, my feet kicking up dirt.

We turn down another path, the unseen lion quickly gaining. He'll be able to see us soon. If I can find a dark space to hide, hopefully he'll pass by while the lack of light works in our favor.

I run down the darkest passage I can find, then back into a corner and wrap my arms around Nara, holdng her tight against my chest. She's breathing heavily, her body quivering as she grips my arms around her and looks over her shoulder at me in the darkness. "Ethan, we need to—"

"Shh," I whisper in her ear as I listen for the lion's heavy-footed approach.

Just when the lion starts to pass our area, the slow moving spotlight quickly swings back, zeroing in on our hiding place. The beast stops and follows the light, his huge head curving around the corner.

"Sonofabitch!" I quickly push Nara behind me and take several steps away from the corner, creating a buffer for her.

The beast narrows his dark gaze on us and I let out a steady stream of curses. We're trapped, completely and utterly at his mercy. His sudden low, steady purr says he knows it too. He takes his time, slowly stalking down the long, narrow passageway, his shoulders rising and falling, each pounding step vibrating the ground under my feet.

Nara claws at my shoulder, yelling something. All I can hear is the rush of blood in my ears. I try to think my way out of this, but I have no clue how to get us both out of this situation unharmed. If I attack the lion, that'll distract him, giving her time to get away. But what happens to her once the ravenous beast is done with me? How long do I stay dead before I come back? The idea I might not come back in time to save her makes it hard to breathe.

She grabs my shoulder again and this time her words spear through my rambling thoughts. "Use your sword, Ethan."

Nara

Ethan looks at me as if I've lost my mind, but I smack at his shoulder and repeat myself, "Use your sword!"

He shakes his head and reaches back to grip my waist, keeping me behind him.

If I don't do something soon, we'll both be lunch. I shove Ethan to the side and step in front to face him. The malice dripping off the stalking lion behind me sends a wave of nausea rippling through my belly, but I swallow the fear pounding my chest and keep my focus on Ethan as I cup my hand over his right shoulder. "Ethan, you need to use your—"

A whoosh of displaced air blows my hair forward and Ethan suddenly flickers as a wave of blackness begins to circle me, creating a veil between us. *No!* I push my hand against the softness. This time I can feel its solid strength as I shove it out of the way, mentally continuing, *Don't try to protect me. I'm here for Ethan. To help him.* He *needs your protection. Why have you never tried to help him like you do me?* Ethan suddenly flickers back in my line of sight at the same time the lion's swiping paw snags my jacket.

"Nara!" Ethan grabs my waist and yanks me behind him with lightning reflexes. "Don't ever do something so insane again," he grits out. "I won't lose you. I can't." A fierce look crosses his face, his gaze never leaving the lion. "When I take him on, I want you to run like hell. Got it?"

"What?" I grab the back of his shirt when he takes an aggressive step toward the creature.

"Come on, you sick bastard!" he yells, raising his clenched fists in the air.

My fingers twist in his shirt, holding tight. "I'm not running."

"Damn it, Nara! He'll kill me like he always does. I'll come back just so one of these sadistic beasts can tear me apart all over again, but I can't watch that happen to you. I won't."

Like he always does? He's been dying over and over in these dreams? I've got to get him out now.

Glancing up at the tall walls, I desperately wish some of the stones would come loose, slowing the creature's advance, giving us a chance to get away. The walls begin to vibrate and a few of the stones at the top of the wall shake free. As they slam into the lion's head and then hit his hindquarters, the lion rears up on his back legs and turns around, roaring his fury at the unknown source of his pain.

Ethan tries to yank free of my hold. His fists curl tighter, his shoulder muscles tense; he's going to strike out at the beast, hoping to attack while the lion's distracted. I grind my teeth and eye the stone wall next to us, directing more stones to fall. With each big boulder that rains down on him, the lion grows angrier. We have to get out of here. If I can make stones fall, can't I find a way to leave? I reach for a small rock jutting out of the wall next to me and imagine that it's a doorknob.

When the rock turns, I exhale a surprised breath of relief and push harder, welcoming the sound of stone scraping against stone.

Ethan jerks wide eyes my way as I push the stone door fully open. Before he can hesitate, I grab his hand and tug as I cross through, but he bounces off the doorway as if an invisible force won't allow him passage. Only our connected hands hang across the threshold.

Amazement flickers in his eyes. "How did you do that?"

The lion shakes his head and stumbles groggily. When he realizes his prey is escaping, he snarls and takes a running leap for Ethan. Long claws curled in shredding mode, he opens his mouth wide, aiming his sharp teeth for his victim's head and neck.

"Believe, Ethan!" As I tug on his hand, the lion's downward arc slows to a stuttering frame by frame pace. While the beast falls toward Ethan, I continue, frantic, "You need to believe you can come through."

Ethan blinks and shakes his head. "How?"

The frames start to speed up, the lion falling faster and faster; his claws curve viciously, a maniacal snarl lifting his open snout. Unsure how to reach Ethan, I realize our connection is the key to getting him through and jump across the threshold straight into his arms. "No, Nara!" He tries to set me away, but I wrap my legs tight around his hips, locking myself to him.

"Together 'til the wheels fall off. Remember?" I pant out, then press my mouth to his as if it's our last kiss. I pour every ounce of passion, worry and intensity I feel for him into my lips on his. If he's going to die, then we'll go together. I won't leave here without him.

Claws slice along my arm, splitting the muscle all the way to the bone. Tingling numbness sends a shock of cold shooting through me while warm blood spurts across my skin. As that arm goes limp, I sob against his mouth and clutch him harder with my uninjured arm, then pull him with me as I lean backward with all the strength I have left in my body.

We stumble against the threshold, passion and fear coalescing into a frenzy of pounding hearts and strong emotions. The second we slide along the stone wall and clear the doorway, the lion screeches and tries to jam his massive body through the small opening.

We fall to the ground together at the same time the lion shoulders his way through the doorway, stones exploding off the opening in his furious wake. The fall knocks the wind out of me, sending pain down my spine, but I squeeze my eyes shut and ignore it, focusing only on

Ethan.

As the lion rears his head back and opens his maw wide, then slams his massive teeth toward our heads, I grip Ethan's face, forcing his blue eyes to connect with mine and say forcefully, "Wake up, Ethan! I don't want to die here."

Ethan and I sit up together, gasping in the darkness. My hand supporting his back stings painfully and I yank it away. As I glance at his back, peering past his hospital gown opening, his sword's cold metal has already started to meld into his skin once more. A few seconds more and it'll turn back into a sword tattoo slashing diagonally along his spine from shoulder to waist.

"Nara?" Ethan says, bewilderment creasing his brow. "What's going on? Where are we?"

His voice sounds scratchy, probably from the tube they removed earlier. I take calming breaths and pull my sweatshirt over the cut on my palm, curling my fingers against the material to soak up the blood. Once his breathing evens out, I say, "You're at Jefferson hospital. Welcome back to the land of the living."

His eyebrows pull together. "A hospital?"

I nod. "I have several burning questions, but I'll ask the most important one first. Where have you been for the last month?"

Deep brackets form around his mouth, disbelief filtering in his expression. "I've been asleep for a month?"

My heart jerks and something close to panic grips my chest. "Uh, no. You've been in a drug-induced coma for a couple of days to reduce swelling in your brain from a car accident. I'm asking where you've been for the past few weeks prior to your accident. You certainly weren't working things out with your parents like you told me you were."

Ethan rubs his hand down his face, looking thoroughly exhausted. "I have no idea what you're talking about, Nara. The last thing I remember is driving you to a special place for a picnic..." He pauses, then looks at me. "Was it an early birthday surprise?"

CHAPTER 6

Nara

Istare at him with wide eyes. *Oh God. He doesn't remember any of it?* Ethan's deep blue eyes shift to a darker shade, reflecting confusion and worry. He really doesn't remember. His heart monitor goes off, beeping like crazy. We stare at each other and as each beep comes faster than the last, my nerves ratchet even tighter.

"Nara?"

He lifts his uninjured hand toward my face, but I slide off the bed just out of his reach. The second my feet hit the floor, Samson bursts through the door. The light flares on as the younger nurse quickly follows him into the room.

"You're awake. Thank God." He gives me a quick, surprised glance before rushing to the other side of the bed and addressing his brother in a mock stern tone. "'Cause it's hard to kick your ass when you're sleeping."

"He doesn't remember." My tone is flat as I move to the foot of the bed so the nurse can check Ethan's vitals.

Ethan's dark eyes burn into me, but I keep my attention on Samson and nod to acknowledge his worried gaze as it flicks to me.

"What don't I remember? What's going on, Nara?"

Ethan's tense tone wills me to look at him, but I can't.

The younger nurse fluffs Ethan's pillow behind him, her voice upbeat, "Temporary memory loss is normal after a head injury. It may take time, but your memory usually returns."

"Head injury? What *don't* I remember?" Ethan repeats, his voice harder this time.

"We don't know. You've been gone a month, Ethan," his brother says quietly. "Do you know a Danielle? Nara says you were with someone named Danielle."

I lower my gaze to the ring I slid on Ethan's finger. A dragon circles the entire ring's surface with religious symbols etched along his side and down his tail. The symbols are exact replicas of the ones in the flames around the dragon tattoo on his arm.

Ethan's fingers twitch, the only indication he notices the ring on his hand. "Who's Danielle?"

Heart racing, I lock my lips and shake my head as I stare at the pillow behind his head. Ethan shifts until he's in my line of sight. "Who is she?"

"You told me she was your cousin," I say, the unspoken accusation burning in my throat. I want to yell at him, to demand answers, but the pucker on his brow and the slight downturn of his lips tells me what he can't.

Ethan starts to speak when the older nurse pushes through the door, the attending doctor one step behind her. She instantly frowns in my direction. "What are you doing in here? No visitors allowed, young lady." Grabbing my shoulders, she turns me toward the door.

"She stays," Ethan says in the firmest voice I've heard since he woke.

The woman's hands on my shoulders tighten. "It's hospital policy, Mr. Harris. Miss Collins has to leave. Your parents insisted she not be allowed in."

"They banned Nara from seeing me?" He turns angry eyes to his brother. "How could you let them do that?"

"Calm down. I planned to talk to them," Samson soothes.

"It's fine." I shrug the nurse's hands off. "I was just leaving, anyway." I have to get out of here before I break down. Ethan's dream world exhausted me. My head hurts and the cut on my palm burns as if it's on fire. Before I turn away, I glance Ethan's way and the second our gazes meet, the bewilderment, confusion, and yearning flickering in the blue depths sends deep pain shooting to my heart. "I've got school tomorrow. I'm so glad you're awake. Means you're getting better. I'll see you…later, I guess."

"Nara!" he calls, but I force myself to walk out the door, my back ramrod straight.

The second the door closes behind me, Ethan freaks. I hear him thrashing around, yelling my name. So many emotions rush through me, I can't process them. I bolt down the hall and fling open the stairwell door. As I take the stairs, I try to hold back the sobs, but they come anyway.

It's probably for the best that I'm not allowed in Ethan's room right now. I'm angry, resentful, furious, heartbroken, and sad; the rapid spiraling of feelings is so mired I can't separate them. Seeing me this upset would only aggravate him more. At least I think it would.

Then again, the Ethan I thought I knew isn't the Ethan who'd shown up at the dance a few days ago either. The Ethan at the dance had been much darker. That night he'd been dangerous, but also thrillingly protective and intimately possessive, and he'd branded his mark on me in a way that left me eagerly anticipating his return.

I bite my lip as I reach the main floor and shove the exit door open. Running into the parking lot, I gulp in the frigid night air. I'm scared by how attracted and deeply connected I felt to that Ethan, whose bold touch set my body on fire, and who left me wanting to take our relationship to a whole new level of intimacy.

Is the Ethan from this weekend gone? Was all that we'd shared a lie too?

Will the answers that connect me to Ethan through the ravens be lost forever if he can't remember?

I get in my car and crank the engine, my body shaking from more than just the cold.

As my gaze strays to the fifth floor where Ethan's room resides, I set my jaw and suppress my emotions. What if Ethan's car wreck wasn't an accident? What if he was pushed off that road? Without his memory, he has no clue the kind of evil that's out there waiting for him. I'm not even sure what that evil is—only he seemed to know. That knowledge might be locked away with his memory, but it doesn't change the fact he's still in danger. That we both are.

Regardless of how mad I am that he lied to me about his whereabouts the past few weeks, I have to help him get his memory back. The ravens still connect us. And I need to figure out why I was led to a book about ravens with a secret compartment. I'll paint the broad picture for Ethan, then guide him into filling in the details. We both need answers, and the only way we'll get there is if he can remember what he'd planned to tell me when he returned.

"I can do this," I murmur. Exhaling a harsh breath, I ignore the hurt squeezing my chest and grab my steering wheel with a firm grip.

Nara

"You look like shite." Drystan leans against the locker next to mine as I spin the combination. "I take it since you're here, Dark Boy's awake."

"I didn't sleep for *shite* last night." I cut a quick glance his way, only catching a glimpse of his leather jacket before shoving several books in my backpack, then zipping it closed. "And yes, Ethan woke up."

A low chuckle erupts from his mouth. "Is that how I really sound?"

Just as I meet his green gaze, Lainey wraps her arm around my shoulders. "Yes, that's exactly how you sound, Drystan. Nara has you down, boy." Turning to me, she says, "You going to see Ethan now?"

"I've got too much school work to catch up on. Plus, his parents are there. I don't want to intrude."

"Huh?" Lainey says. "He's your boyfriend. You wouldn't be intruding."

"Yeah, I'd want Lainey smothering me with all kinds of extra attention if I were in the hospital." Matt buries his nose in Lainey's auburn hair as he wraps his arms around her waist and pulls her back against his chest.

While Lainey laughs and ruffles his short blond locks, I start to lug my backpack up on my shoulder and wince.

Drystan grabs my hand and tugs it toward him, frowning at the bandage I'd wrapped around my palm. "What'd you do to your hand?"

I pull my hand back. "Nothing. Just a cut." Before I can hike my backpack onto my shoulder, he grabs it from me and slides it onto his. "Come on. I'll walk you to your car."

Lainey nods to me, pleading in her eyes. She's telling me Drystan needs to talk, so I shrug and fall in step beside him. I know she'll call me later.

After Lainey and Matt head off to talk by his car, Drystan strolls slowly beside me, kicking up the remnants of ice left over from last night's sleet. "It's supposed to warm up later this week. Maybe by then your hand will be better and we can get back to training."

"Sounds good." I grin at him as I cut my gaze his way. "So who'd you end up hooking up with after I left the dance? Last I saw, the new Welsh exchange student had plenty of girls hanging on him to choose from."

He digs his hands into his dark jeans and flashes a wide smile. "I don't kiss and tell."

"Fair enough," I say, borrowing one of his favorite phrases.

"You really do have me down." Drystan snorts out a laugh, then halts beside my car. Glancing back toward Lainey and Matt leaning against Matt's car, he rubs the back of his neck. "Indoor practice starts soon. Lainey says you two usually play in the coed league, which is the one I'm signed up for, but I didn't see your name on the roster. You going to play indoor football—uh, damn I'll never get used to that—I mean, soccer this season?"

I'd spent the last few weeks so absorbed in the journal I'd been working on for Ethan, filling it with research information about ravens, raven tattoos, sword tattoos, yin-yang raven symbols, and raven lore, I'd completely forgotten about indoor soccer season starting. "Oh no! Yeah, I'd planned to play. Just so much going on lately." I let my shoulders slump. "So much for staying in shape. Guess it's too late to sign up now."

"Lainey was going to give this to you, but I needed to talk to you anyway." Drystan pulls a folded piece of paper from his coat pocket. "The coach says you just need to drop it off with your payment by tomorrow."

"Thanks." I start to take the form from him, but he holds on to it.

"You and Lainey getting attacked in the bathroom at the dance by that girl—what was her name? Harper?—has set Matt on edge. He's watching Lainey like a hawk. Lainey swears the girl hasn't come back to school, but you need to be careful, Nara."

I'd gotten so caught up in spending Saturday night with Ethan after the dance, then anxiously waiting for him to return on Monday night, freaking out all day Tuesday when he didn't, then Samson's call yesterday and the hospital…I'd completely forgotten about the attack. I nod numbly as I take the form and my backpack from him. "So much has happened, Harper's the last thing on my mind."

His steady gaze locks on me. "The fact that she's out there in the wind should be enough to get you back to training."

I heft my backpack onto my shoulder, smiling. "You know, if it weren't for your training, I'm not sure I would've been able to fight her off Lainey. Been meaning to thank you for that."

Drystan nods, but keeps his gaze focused on mine. "What aren't you telling me? Do you know why she attacked you?"

I shake my head, suggesting, "'Cause she's crazy?"

His mouth tightens. "Not buying it."

I spread my hands. "All I know is she was jealous of my friendship with Lainey. Maybe it was because she was new at school and didn't have any other friends yet. I guess she saw Lainey as competition for my friendship and wanted her out of the way."

His gaze narrows. "Lainey said she attacked you too."

"I'm telling you…" I pause and twirl my finger close to my temple.

"You've been attacked too many times." Drystan folds his arms, his open expression shuttering. "I learned a long time ago coincidences don't exist, random happenstance is bullshit, and people lie. A lot."

With that philosophy, maybe he could accept the existence of Fate as an actual entity, but the fact he knows about my dreams is as far as I plan on sharing with him. And I'd only done that because he'd told me about his own special ability to find lost things by holding something connected to it. As for Harper, I have an idea why she attacked Lainey and me, but I don't have any proof at this point. As much as I hate how wronged Drystan must have been in his past to be so mistrusting of others, I shift my gaze to Matt and Lainey chatting by his car and pile on yet another half-truth. "All I know is that Harper said 'Lainey was in the way.'"

Drystan snags my chin, pulling my gaze back to his. "I want to help you, Nara, but you have to tell me what's going on so I can."

"You already are helping." I back away and open my car door. Moving behind it, I continue, "I might never learn all your parkour moves, but teaching me how to defend myself on your own time is more than enough. I wouldn't ask for anything more."

"You could ask…" he begins, green eyes seeking answers. Sighing, he finger-combs his hair. The blond streaks flip through his fingers as he nods to the paper in my hand. "Don't forget to turn in that form."

As I wave the paper, relieved he doesn't push for more answers, it suddenly occurs to me that Drystan can help with something else. "Actually, Dryst, there is something you could help me with if you're willing."

He shoves his hands in his pockets and rocks on his heels. "I'll help you if you'll pitch in with a project I have to do. I need an assistant to get me started."

"Sure, I'll help with your project." It makes me feel less guilty asking for his help when I can return the favor.

A pleased smile plays at his lips. "Right then. What can I help you with?"

"I need to find a cell phone."

"Yours?"

I shake my head. "Ethan's." When his smile fades, I rush on, "The accident has erased some of his memory." I can't explain everything so I tell him what I can. "He doesn't remember this past weekend or some time before that. His phone might help him retrace his steps."

Drystan's eyes narrow and his lips twist mockingly. "Convenient how he can't remember the part about where he's been."

"It's not like that, Drystan. He really can't remember. Trust me, I know for a fact he's not lying."

He shrugs. "Whatever you want to believe. For the record, I'm only doing this for *you*."

Exhaling a sigh of relief, I pull out my phone and scroll to Ethan's phone number. When I turn my screen toward Drystan, he shakes his head. "I'll get a better connection if you write his number down on a piece of paper."

I quickly fish a pen and scrap of paper from my backpack. Once I've written down Ethan's number, I start to hand it to Drystan, but he wraps his hand around mine and crushes the paper in our palms as he tugs me into his personal space.

Why does it always feel so intimate when Drystan uses touch to mesh his psychometry ability to find things with mine? I tense. I can't help it. With his leather jacket's scent tickling my nose, all I can think about is Drystan's mouth on mine in that dream I'd had the night before Saturday's dance. I'd been so freaked out that he kissed me, I'd somehow rewound my dream and changed my future to where the kiss never happened. Fate truly hates me now. Changing my dream on the fly—and therefore my future—was totally new and beyond blasphemous territory.

"This works better if you relax," Drystan whispers in my ear while he closes his eyes and rubs his thumb along the number on the paper.

I haven't told him that my dreams have disappeared yet, but I exhale slowly and hope that maybe he'll get a connection anyway.

After a few seconds, his grip on my hand tightens. "I can't see us retrieving the item like I've been able to in the past…" he trails off. Guess it was too much to hope he could pick up on my powers even though I seem to have lost them. A couple seconds later, his green eyes fly open. "It's totally dark, but I can make out cars up on hydraulic lifts. A garage maybe?"

Samson mentioned that he'd had Ethan's car towed to Mike's Body Shop. He must have missed the phone when he looked for it before in Ethan's car. I smile as I take a step back. "Thank you. That's an important clue."

Disappointment reflects in his eyes. "Why couldn't I see us retrieving it?"

I inwardly grimace. I'm not ready to admit my dreams might be gone for good. Like somehow saying it out loud could make it permanent. "My dreams have been sporadic lately."

"Is everything okay, Nara?"

No. It's not okay. My life's a freaking mess right now, but I'm determined to fix that. I nod and force a confident smile. "Yeah, I'm good, Drystan. Thank you for helping me and let me know when you need help on your project."

He searches my face for a second, then glances at the piece of paper in my hand, a slight frown creasing his brow. "Would you like me to come with you? We have no idea if you'll be able to find it based on what little I gave you. Maybe together we can find it."

I shake my head. "That's okay. I know exactly where to start looking now."

Drystan sighs as Matt calls his name, waving for him to come on. "Guess that's my cue." He backs away several steps. "Ring me if you need anything, yeah?"

I nod. "I will, thanks."

Nara

There's a flurry of activity at Mike's Body Shop when I arrive. Six men are working on Ethan's car at once. They remind me of a very efficient pit crew working an Indy 500 race. An older man is standing off to the right, looking baffled but impressed. I approach, unsure of how I'm going to get permission to search inside Ethan's car.

"Hi!" I say, smiling broadly.

His warm eyes flick my way. "Can I help you with something?"

"Actually," I pause and point to Ethan's car. "I'm looking for my boyfriend's cell phone. Ethan thinks he left it in his car and asked me to get it for him."

Concern fills the older man's gaze. "How's Ethan doing? His brother told me he's in the hospital."

"Yes, he's awake now and starting to recover. Thank you for asking." I smile and gesture toward the car. "Would it be okay if I looked for it?"

The older man scratches his head. "Uh, sure…if you can get this crew to stop long enough. They've been working like crazy fiends ever since they showed up this morning."

I skim a confused gaze across the men. "These guys don't work for you?"

He snorts. "Think I could afford to pay this many employees? Nah, it's just me and George," he says, gesturing to the young dark-haired guy sitting on a stool drinking a soda.

"Then who are these guys?"

"Beats the hell out of me," he says, expelling a harsh laugh. "Said they were sent to move things along. All I know is…they really know their stuff, so I'm letting them do their thing."

How am I going to get into Ethan's car if these guys never take a break? Ethan's parents probably sent them. The last thing I want is for these mechanics to call Mr. and Mrs. Harris to ask them if they can let me in the car. I'm pretty sure I know what the answer will be. Frustrated, I chew my lip.

The sound of a soda can hitting the metal trash bin draws my attention. As George celebrates his two-pointer, an idea suddenly hits me. I turn to the older man. "How do you like your pizza?"

CHAPTER 7

Nara

Turns out, six hardworking men are easily distracted by the lure of free pizza. While they devoured the three pizzas I'd ordered and had sent to the break room, I snuck into Ethan's car and searched until I found his cell phone jammed between the damp carpet and the metal leg under his front seat.

Once I get home, I have to let Houdini out. First, he barks at the Nativity scene Mom has set up in the yard—like he's done the last six times he's seen it. Once he comes to the conclusion his yard's not being invaded, he runs around in the icy grass looking for a spot. I glower at all the dead leaves crunching under his paws.

Mom's only going to have so much patience if I don't get this chore done soon, but first I have to put Ethan's phone in some rice. The people at the electronics store where I'd stopped to buy a charger told me to put the phone in a sealed container of rice to absorb any moisture that might have gotten inside before I attempt to turn it on. In case that fails, they also sold me a SIM card reader.

Just as I snap the rice filled plastic container closed around Ethan's phone, a text comes through on mine from Samson. Heart racing with worry for Ethan, I slide the box of rice under my bed and hold my breath as I open the message.

Samson: Ethan's recovering quickly, but he refuses to speak to our parents. Unfortunately, his silence isn't helping them believe he truly doesn't remember anything. I talked to my parents. It's okay for you to come visit any time you'd like.

I could hug him for standing up for me. Even though I'm still upset with Ethan, excitement races that I'm allowed to see him. I want to go, but then I picture his father's tense face and regretfully type back a response.

Me: Thank you for letting me know Ethan's doing well. I appreciate the invitation, but I think my being there will cause problems with your family. Try to get Ethan to talk to your parents. I think it will help him to deal with the issues between them. I'll talk to him once he's back home from the hospital.

My hands shake as I hit the send button. I don't like bailing, but I need time away to think and decide the best way to help Ethan remember. I'd been too upset to do any kind of rational, reasoned thinking last night beyond sending my aunt a text to let her know Ethan had woken up. Once I finally did fall asleep, I dreamed of endlessly running through a snowy forest looking for Ethan.

With guilt weighing my shoulders down, I scan my phone for the right number, then call Bright Blooms before I start toward the garage. I'd just picked up the leaf blower when *Witchy Woman* rings on my phone. The song always makes me smile. Just like my aunt.

"Hey, Aunt Sage."

"How's Ethan?"

"He's doing well. His brother just texted me that he's recovering quickly."

"That's great to hear. I want to talk more about Ethan's dream issue later, but that's not why I'm calling. You mentioned wanting to go through all the paperwork I brought back from your dad's place in D.C."

I set the blower back down. It can wait. If I can help find my dad, I will. "How about I come over now."

By the time I get home from my aunt's, I'm bone tired. My aunt and I went through every single receipt, letter, and bill. We scoured over everything twice, looking for anything that would give us a clue and take us beyond my dad's last steps before he disappeared.

He'd gone to a café for coffee every other day around the same time. My aunt had already talked to the people at the café. Based on receipts, my father had coffee and read the paper that day like he always did, then the trail just stops. Whatever happened to him, happened after two o'clock, but before seven when the shift changed with the doorman at his apartment. He never returned.

Mom looks up from typing on her phone as I walk through the door. "Oh, I was just getting ready to send you a text before I left."

I sweep my gaze over her dark green cashmere sweater and black dress pants. "You're going out with Mr. Dixon…er, I mean David?"

Mom nods, a soft smile tilting her lips. "He wants to make up for being busy all weekend tutoring so he's taking me to a holiday party. Your text said Ethan's doing well…" She pauses, a pucker creasing her forehead. "I'm surprised you were at your aunt's and not the hospital. Is everything okay between you and Ethan?"

"Ethan's parents are there, so I wanted to give him time with them," I say before I pull open the fridge and retrieve a plate of leftovers from the night before.

I jump slightly when my mom's hand lands on my shoulder. "Are you sure everything's okay? I can stay home if you'd like me to."

I shake my head, then lift a piece of pizza from under the plastic wrap. "Go enjoy yourself. Tell David I said, 'hi.'"

"You can tell him yourself when he comes to pick me up."

I take a big bite of the pizza and mumble around it as I start to back out of the kitchen, "Got too much homework to make up since I missed yesterday."

Before Mom can answer, I bound upstairs and nudge Houdini to my other side with my knee. He's hoping I'll drop a pepperoni and his tail keeps hitting the garland decorated with white lights and holly Mom has draped along the handrail in beautiful drooping loops.

Just as I reach the top of the stairs, the doorbell rings. I exhale a sigh of relief that I avoided seeing them together. Now that I know the truth as to why my dad left, I can't watch Mr. Dixon wrap his arm around my mom's waist or even give her an innocent kiss on the cheek without feeling tremendous angst. I might have set them up before I learned about my dad, but guilt completely obliterates any rationalization pep talks I try to give myself.

After Mom and David leave, I crawl into my bed with my books and settle down to do homework. That hadn't been a lie. Now that I don't see my next day in my dreams, I have a ton of work to catch up on or my grades will nosedive.

Two hours later, once darkness descends, I take a break. Just as I start to plug in some tunes, someone knocks on the front door.

Houdini instantly jumps into major bark-defense mode. Hackles raised, he takes off down the stairs and throws his big body against the front door.

"Houdini!" I call out sharply as I descend the stairs.

My dog settles somewhat. He might be a mutt with a Labrador look, but his Rhodesian Ridgeback lineage shows through in the barrel chest and dark brown line of hair standing high along his back. When I try to use the peephole, he thrusts himself between me and the door, ready to protect.

"It's me," Ethan says in an even tone.

My heart instantly ramps. I flip on the light switch and yank open the door. "What are you doing here?" Ethan looks a bit pale as he leans against the doorframe, his hair damp and slightly disheveled. His army jacket is pulled on one arm, but drapes his other shoulder, leaving his bandage-wrapped arm hanging loosely by his side.

"You sent flowers? I wanted to see you, not flowers. What the hell, Nara?"

Whether he realizes it or not, the deep scowl and tension on his face is more like the darker Ethan who'd left an indelible imprint on me a few days ago. I haven't been able to get that version of him out of my mind. These traitorous thoughts instantly raise my defenses. "You lied to me for a month, Ethan. What the hell *back*."

Houdini whines, drawing my gaze to the tight grip I have on his collar. "Sorry, boy." I ease my fingers away and pat his head. "You remember Ethan, don't ya?"

As soon as he's free, Houdini instantly jams his big head against Ethan's thigh, demanding to be rubbed.

A brief smile flits across Ethan's face as he looks down at Houdini. "You got a dog?" he says in surprise, scratching behind Houdini's ear. "This big guy's got a scary bark. I like him already."

When his gaze meets mine once more, I see total nonrecognition of Houdini, which reminds me how pale he'd looked when I first opened the door. "I can't believe the hospital let you out so soon." I glance around for Samson's car. "Where's your brother?"

"At the hospital, sleeping in a chair in my room."

My gaze jerks back to Ethan's calm one. "What? How'd you get here?"

"I walked."

"You walked five miles? In the freezing cold?" I stare at the frost coming out of his mouth, yet he seems completely unaffected by it.

He shrugs, his expression resolute. "You said you'd talk to me when I'm home, so I came home."

"Are you crazy—?" I start to say, then quickly move to the kitchen to grab my keys and wallet from the island. "Meet me at the garage. I'll take you back to the hospital before they discover you've gone AWOL."

Ethan's face sets in stubborn lines. "I came here to talk to you. I'm not leaving until we talk."

"Fine." I point to the garage, trying hard to contain my composure. I'm scared for his health, angry with him, frustrated, and hurt. When it comes to Ethan, I'm so emotional it's hard to think straight. To keep from freaking out, I focus on maintaining a tough stance. "You want to talk. The only way that's happening is while I drive you back to the hospital."

"Nara—"

"I mean it, Ethan."

Without another word, he turns toward my driveway.

I don't say anything at first. I just drive with both hands gripping the wheel tight so Ethan can't see just how shaken I am.

"What happened to your hand?" Ethan brushes his fingers across the back of my hand. His light touch sends heat to my face, making me grip the steering wheel tighter.

I barely hold back the wince of pain lashing across my palm. "It's nothing. You wanted to talk, so now's your chance. You have four miles."

Heavy wet snow starts to fall as I pull onto the main road. The fat white flakes splatter on my windshield, scattering into feathery patterns that remind me of the white feather tattoo that appeared on my shoulder blade the morning after Ethan had left me this past weekend.

The feather looks like the one he had on his shoulder before it transformed into a sword, except mine is white, not black. Why isn't it black? And why had he marked me like that? I can only assume the feather came from him. I'd been waiting for him to come back so I could demand answers.

Ethan exhales a sigh and rakes a hand through his hair. "I don't know why I left town. I remember having a driving need to, but not why. If I didn't tell you, the only reason I can think I'd do that is to protect you."

Once I turn onto the interstate, I snap my attention his way. "Protect me from what? The truth?"

Ethan starts to say something, then sets his jaw and glances out the window. "I don't know. Maybe once I get home I can see if I left anything behind to give me a clue."

I snort. "I doubt that. You were too good at covering your tracks. Erased everything on your hard drive that would give your brother any bread crumb to follow as to where you might've gone." *Come on rice, do your job faster!*

As a look of anger flashes in his eyes, I continue as I take the hospital exit off the interstate. "Don't you even think about getting mad. The only reason Samson did that was because he loves you, Ethan. He cares what happens to you. Just like I do."

A sudden smile appears on his face and he brushes his fingers down my cheek in a soft caress. "Glad to see you admit you still love me. That kiss you laid on me in my dream would've singed that lion to ashes if he'd actually bitten down on us. But after the way you acted in the hospital when we woke up, I was beginning to wonder."

The arrogance flitting across his handsome face mixed with his teasing makes me want to hug and smack him at the same time. Instead, I grind my teeth to stay focused. "I'm *mad* at you. And..." I smack his hand away. "Stop trying to distract me. The only reason I'm talking to you right now is because this isn't just about you anymore. I need answers and you're going to deliver if I have to drag them out of you."

"The only reason you're talking to me?" His brow furrows. "Wait... not about me anymore. What are you talking about?"

Tension creeps into my shoulders and I shrug to ease my muscles. I pull into a hospital parking spot and cut the engine. Facing Ethan, I exhale slowly. "It's too long and involved to get into here. You told me some stuff, showed me a couple of things. Anyway, once you're officially released by your doctor, I'm going to do my best to help you remember the parts you didn't tell me."

"I told you stuff? Showed you a couple of things? So I wasn't completely absent for the whole month."

Ugh, how much do I share right now? As far as Samson knows, Ethan's been gone the entire time. "You ah, called a couple of times and came home this past weekend to take me to the school winter dance." I search his expression for any recognition of our time together and just how far our relationship had progressed.

Frustration fills his face. "Why can't I remember? A dance, huh?" His eyebrows suddenly shoot up. "Did we—?"

"You told me you'd tell me everything when you got back," I jump in, cutting his question off. "And then you were in the accident before you could make it home."

He slowly shakes his head. "Right now nothing makes sense, but one thing I'm certain of..." Ethan touches my injured hand, then lifts it from the seat to press his lips softly to the bandage on my palm, his dark blue eyes holding mine. "We're connected, aren't we, Nara? I've always known that, since before we officially met."

Even through the gauze, his warm mouth sends electric tingles racing down my arm. Memories of all the intimate moments we recently shared return. I can't resist reacting to them and a shiver races through me. "It's freezing out here. You need to sneak back inside."

I try to pull my hand away, but Ethan tightens his hold. "I'm not letting go until you at least admit *that* about us."

I nod. "Yes, we're connected." As a smile of male satisfaction starts to form on his lips, I pull my hand from his. "But not in the way you're thinking."

I open my car door and dash through the snow, heading toward the building. Ethan quickly catches up, demanding in a harsh tone, "What do you mean by 'not in the way I'm thinking'?"

Stepping into the main doorway so the automatic sliding glass doors glide open, I sweep my hand out. "Take the back stairwell. You can get up to your room without the nurses seeing you. Hopefully your brother is still asleep."

Flakes of snow quickly salt Ethan's pitch-black hair as he stares at me stubbornly, unmoving.

"Focus on getting better, then I'll do what I can to help you remember." When I turn to walk away, Ethan's question—and the sadness in it—halts my steps.

"Why weren't you in my dreams last night?"

The snow pelts my skin with cold, wet kisses as I turn to face him. I bite my lip and shake my head. "I'm not dreaming my next day anymore. I haven't been since you left on Saturday. I'm having 'normal dreams' and sometimes weird, out-there dreams, but they have nothing to do with my next day."

His lips press together for a second, then he steps close. "I've been meaning to ask you...when did you learn to manipulate your dream world? Creating an escape door in the wall from that lion was sheer genius."

I shrug and try not to let his closeness affect me. "It's only happened in extremely emotional circumstances. I seem to have some control over manipulation in your dream world and in Fate's, but in mine it was entirely out of my control. It just happened."

His eyes widen. "You controlled your future inside your dream?"

I lower my eyes to his chin, unable to meet his gaze. "I didn't plan it. It happened by accident, and of course now that I've done so, I've moved to number one on Fate's enemy list."

"What were you thinking?"

I stiffen and look up. "I said it was an accident."

He holds my gaze for a couple seconds, then he lifts a strand of my snow-coated hair and says in a low voice, "You wear snow well." His gaze settles on mine, searching deep. "You'll always be my light, Nara. Whatever is coming, whatever truths we uncover, please don't let it change us."

I can't promise him what we'd always said to each other in the past: "together 'til the wheels fall off". The fact he lied infuriates me. Even if he did it to protect me, I believe we're stronger *together*. Pushing up on my toes, I whisper close to his ear, "Together 'til".

As I lower myself to the ground, then take a step back, Ethan frowns. "What about the rest of that promise?"

I spread my hands wide and start walking backward toward my car. "That's up to you."

CHAPTER 8

Nara

I drag myself in from school. Mondays are usually hard, but today was killer. I haven't slept well the last few days, and having little sleep has finally caught up with me. Houdini plops down on my bed beside me, resting his chin on my ankle. I throw my arm across my eyes and give in to my exhaustion, where I dream of looking endlessly for Ethan all over again.

Except this time, I'm running through a frozen forest that grows colder with each step I take. Just when I feel like I'm freezing to death someone grabs me from behind and wraps strong arms around my waist. I'm pulled back against a hard frame, and I scream and kick until Ethan whispers in my ear, his breath warm and inviting. "I'm here, Nara. You've found me. All you have to do is turn around."

"Ethan," I gasp in happiness and turn...

My eyes fly open and Ethan's leaning over me, hands pressed into my bed, his dark hair slightly flopped to the side instead of spiked. As my eyes lock with his deep blue gaze, a cocky smirk lifts his lips. "If you're going to have normal dreams, it's good to know I'm in those."

"How'd you get in here?" I quickly scramble back and lean against my headboard to put space between us at the same time I search for Houdini. My dog's laying in the doorway, facing outward in "guard" position, just like Ethan had him do on Saturday night when he'd stayed over. I stare at Houdini's rump accusingly. "What kind of watch dog are you?"

Ethan chuckles. "An excellent one. He let me know right away that you're his number one priority. Made me an instant fan." Returning his gaze to me, he continues with serious eyes, "You should change the code on your garage every once in a while."

Lainey said something similar. I've got to change that code! Grabbing my hot pink pillow, I wrap my arms around it to put another buffer between us. Or maybe it's because I don't want Ethan to hear how rapidly my heart is beating. In my own ears it sounds like one of those huge band drums being hit by a mallet. *Bong, bong, bong, bong.*

He looks more like his old self today…except more muscular, his gaze sharper, more intuitive. I wonder if he's noticed the changes in himself. It's been a few days. Surely he's looked in the mirror by now. "What are you doing here?"

"I'm here to help you find answers. That's what you said you wanted from me, right?"

The sharp bite in his comment makes my stomach clench, but I refuse to feel guilty for upsetting him. "Are you officially released from the hospital this time?"

Ethan flicks his hands from his head to his thighs. "Do I look injured to you?"

Unlike the cut on my palm that's definitely going to leave a scar, no cuts or bruises mar his handsome face. He's wearing his army jacket over a navy Henley-style shirt, so the wrap on his arm must be gone. He might appear healed on the outside, but he certainly came filled with sarcasm. Great. Now I know how he reacts when he's really upset. "I'm serious."

His expression settles. "Yes, I've been released."

"Did you finally speak to your parents?"

Surprise flickers. "How'd you know—?" He cuts off, then sighs, rubbing the back of his neck. "Samson told you. I told them enough to get them off my back." Shrugging, he grunts. "And now they've decided to rent a place in Blue Ridge to watch over me for a while."

I sit up straighter, brightening. "That's great. Maybe then they'll see—"

"I don't want them here."

He sounds so annoyed, I smile. "Well, too bad. Maybe they really do care and you're going to have to accept that."

"Why are you defending them? I heard what you said to my parents while I was under."

He did? What else did he hear? My hands curl tight on the pillow. "That wasn't my best moment."

A grin flashes. "I thought it was great. Finally they heard the same truth from someone other than their screwed up son. Thank you for that." He pauses, sincerity creeping into his expression. "And thank you for talking to my brother. He told me about the guy on the plane. How weird and random is that?"

Drystan's comment about randomness comes back to me and I blink to clear away the creeping suspicion. "I'm glad he told you. Maybe now you'll be more comfortable telling him about the tattoo on your back and how it appeared."

Ethan snorts. "It's bad enough I can't explain to him why I cut my hair or what I've been doing this past month." He lifts his arm and flexes, the bunched muscles pulling tight against his jacket. "Something physical obviously." Lowering his arm, he continues, "But I don't think my brother's ready for the full truth of my overall inexplicable weirdness."

I press my lips together in annoyance, thinking of this unknown Danielle girl and his "physical" comment, but something in his deprecating tone distracts me. Is he talking about more than the tattoo, more than his ability to absorb negative energy? "Is there something else, Ethan?"

He jams his hand through his hair and blows out a frustrated breath. "That's what I'm here to find out." Blue eyes hold mine with mesmerizing intensity. "Seems you know far more about me than I do right now."

Not everything. *Who the hell is this Danielle chick?* I want to demand. Instead, I inhale deeply and scramble off the bed to grab my laptop. Queuing up the Virality link that Lainey sent me, I sit down and turn the laptop toward him. "Okay, let's start with this. Check these pictures out of the sophomore locker hall. Someone anonymously posted these. The school has been making students pull down all of the ones they can find, but they haven't found out about this link yet."

Ethan's blue eyes flash with emotion as he scans the horrific damage to the ceiling, the dented and claw-marked lockers, the broken floor tiles. He jerks wide eyes my way. "That's at school? What happened?"

I point to the screen. "You happened."

Denial flares in his eyes and he shakes his head. "I didn't do that."

I nod slowly. "Actually, you did. You were fighting a guy named Drake who attacked me in the hall when I was on my way back to the dance from the bathroom."

"He attacked you?" Fiery fury spills across his face. "Why?"

I point to my laptop. "Look at it again. Try to remember."

"That's not a fight scene, Nara." Ethan jams his finger toward the screen, his face stiff with disbelief. "That's a war zone."

"If you hadn't stopped him, he would've killed me. He'd already killed an old man I knew named Freddie, and he planned to do the same to me when you showed up."

Ethan's shoulders tense and his hand fists on his thigh. A lethal calm rolls through his features. The coldness is scary. "He planned to kill you? My God, Nara! Why didn't you start with that?" Ethan slides close, his thigh brushing against mine. "Why did this guy want to kill you? And why did he kill an old man? What happened while I was gone?"

"A lot." I exhale in a fast breath. "I met Freddie while researching ravens. He was a local author here in Blue Ridge. Drake killed Freddie because he was looking for a book Freddie had about ravens. But Freddie didn't have the book any more. He'd given it to me. That's why Drake came after me."

"Why did he want a book on ravens?"

"We'll get to that later. First I want to help you remember." His dark gaze narrows. "There's no way you told me any of this. Otherwise nothing could've kept me away."

Ethan's dead-on statement, combined with his piercing gaze and appealing smell of spicy deodorant and outdoors makes my heart race. "You told me you were making things right with your parents. I didn't want to screw that up for you," I say quickly before I slide off the bed and glance at the computer. "I'd hoped the pictures would help trigger your memory. But maybe something closer to home will."

A stubborn look settles on his face, as if he planned to push me for more answers, but as I pull the long silver chain from under my shirt, Ethan quickly stands and approaches. I turn the medallion so he can see it. "Look familiar?"

He stares, his gaze transfixed in excitement. "That's the same symbol on my sword tattoo. Where'd you get it?"

"You gave it to me and told me to never take it off. That it would protect me."

I turn and quickly rifle through a box of papers under my bed. I start to pull out the letter he'd left me that Sunday morning, when the ring my aunt had made to keep me safe in Ethan's dreams drops on the floor.

Ethan quickly picks it up before I can and looks at me. "Why aren't you wearing this?"

My gaze flicks to his hand and my stomach twinges; he's still wearing the ring I put on his finger in the hospital. I can't tell him it hurts to wear something I might have to take off later, that I'm holding on to it until he can tell me everything, so I take my ring from him and say lightly, "Your tattoo was damaged. I worried it wasn't doing its job and that you were stuck in your dream world." A wry smile twists my lips as I slip my ring back in the box. "Since that lion nearly bit our heads off, I'd say it didn't work so well." Straightening, I hand him the letter. "Here, read this."

Ethan takes the letter, but doesn't read it yet. "Thank you for having it made. It did help, more than you know."

I smile and then nod for him to open the letter.

> Nara,
>
> I'll be back by Monday night. Don't take off the necklace I gave you. It will keep you safe. I might not know how I know that, but I just do. Please trust me on this. Stay safe, and...no more Internet searches, library research or interviewing people about ravens, swords or tattoos. I promise to share what little I know when I get back. I have more questions about your connection to ravens too.
>
> Happy birthday, Sunshine! I hope you enjoy your present.
> TTTWFO,
> Ethan

His eyes snap to mine, acceptance reflected in the deep blue depths. He can't deny his own handwriting. "Where'd I get the necklace? And protect you from what? Did I give you your present already?"

"Yes, you gave me my camera. Thank you for such a great gift." I smile, continuing, "You said you found the medallion in a turn-of-the-century house. That you were drawn to it." I step closer and grab his hand. "Watch this…" I lift his palm and lay the medallion against it.

The moment the metal touches his hand, he clasps his fingers around it, awe in his voice. "It's warm."

I nod. "You have some kind of connection with it."

He slides the medallion into my shirt, then rolls the chain between his fingers, his knuckles brushing my neck as he says softly, "Just like us."

Ethan's magnetic presence takes up the whole space in my room, his warmth sliding over me in pulling waves. I lean into his touch, feeling absorbed by him; my traitorous heart ignores my resolve to stay focused, yearning to fall into him.

Shaking my head, I take a step back and rub my suddenly sweaty palms on my jeans. "I read last night that sometimes going back to a place you've experienced but can't remember might trigger memories." I pretend not to hear his regretful sigh as I grab my keys from the desk, then head toward my doorway.

"Guess I'm up for that." Ethan's fast on my heels, following me so closely down the stairs, I swear I can feel his warm breath on my neck. I pick up my pace, almost tripping over Houdini in my haste to get to the bottom floor. I'll have to keep Ethan at a respectable distance. Every time he steps into my personal space, he slams against my emotions like a gale force, quickly eroding all my carefully erected layers of resistance.

As soon as we get to school, I jump out of my car and start walking briskly. "The locker hall is still under construction, but hopefully just seeing it might help," I ramble as Ethan walks along beside me through the mostly empty parking lot, hands pushed in his jean pockets.

"Nara!" Drystan looks me up and down, a slight scowl on his face as he approaches. "You're going the wrong way for practice. You're coming tonight, right?"

As he halts in front of us, I take in his athletic fleece, shorts and soccer flops, and grimace. "Crap, I forgot about indoor. Looks like I'll have to miss the first practice, Drystan. I have something to do."

"The coach should be okay with it since we have practice again tomorrow." But Drystan's not looking at me anymore. He's eyeing Ethan with a hard gaze. Ethan's returning it, his whole frame suddenly tense.

"Drystan, you remember meeting Ethan at the dance," I say in a light tone, then glance at Ethan. When Ethan starts to shake his head, I step a bit closer to tell him, "I told Drystan you lost your memory in the accident. He's here on the exchange program."

Ethan takes advantage of my sudden closeness and slides his arm around my waist. Pulling me against his side, he dips his head in a curt nod to Drystan. "How long you here for?" Instead of curiosity, Ethan's question sounds more like an irritated demand.

Drystan tugs his duffel bag up on his shoulder, a challenge in his eyes as he slides a smirk my way. "Long enough to do some damage."

When Ethan stiffens and his arm cinches around me, I pull out of his tight hold. Right now I want to choke both of them. "Just be sure not to slide tackle anyone at practice, Drystan. It's illegal in indoor league. Ignoring the rules will get you kicked off the team faster than it'll take for your check to clear."

Drystan's attention flicks to me. "I've been looking forward to playing with you, so I'll be sure to be on my best behavior." Saluting us, he continues on, heading for Matt's car, but pauses to call over his shoulder once he's several feet away, "By the way, our first game will be at that school adjacent to our park." Pausing, he ignores my narrowed gaze and gives me a thumbs up. "It's going to be a brilliant season."

"*Our* park?" Deep creases form around Ethan's mouth. "What's he talking about, Nara?"

Drystan had recently been training me in self-defense at the Stonehaven park, but I'm not ready to talk about that yet with Ethan. Irritated that Drystan peppered the conversation with double meanings, then left me to deal with the heat, I shove my clenched fists into my coat pockets. It's the only way I won't pick up the closest pebble and chuck it at the back of the boy's head. Drystan doesn't know about the tension between Ethan and me, nor does he know anything about Ethan's abilities, but purposefully antagonizing Ethan doesn't help matters. I'm so going to kick that Welsh boy's ass the next time we meet for a training lesson.

For now, I shrug off my annoyance. "Ignore him. He's trying to yank your chain."

"It's working, *brilliantly*." He glares after Drystan as he drives away. "Where's he from, Ireland? I really don't like his accent."

Even meeting Drystan the second time around, Ethan hasn't changed his opinion. Not that Drystan makes it easy. I resist the urge to roll my eyes. "He's from Wales." Drystan and Ethan are sparks in their own puddle of gasoline; the question is, which one will ignite the explosion first. "Come on. Before we check out the locker hall, maybe if we retrace a few steps from that night it might help you remember."

Once Ethan and I reach the gym entrance, I say, "We stood out here talking for a bit. Do you remember anything?"

He glances around, then shakes his head. "Nothing."

I sigh and head off down the path that leads from the gym. I keep my gaze away from the field house as we start to pass it.

Ethan catches up and glances down at me, warmth seeping into his gaze. "What did you wear?"

I wasn't expecting him to ask that. My voice shakes as I stare forward and describe my dress. "I wore a strapless white dress with a silver beaded bodice and a matching silver shawl."

"I hate that I can't picture you in your dress. I'm sure you took my breath away." Recognition sparks in his eyes and he pauses. "Did you wear your hair up?"

I stop and face him, elation filling me. "You remember that?" His eyes light and he touches my hair. "I just got a quick flash of curls around your face." Stepping close, he slowly wraps a blond strand around his finger, continuing in a softer tone, "Like this." A second passes and his unfocused gaze shifts back and forth as if sifting, rewinding. Then he closes his eyes and inhales. "I remember the smell of menthol and rubbing alcohol." His nostrils flair. "And your floral shampoo. A dark room. Light coming through half-closed blinds. Trophies." He tightens his eyes and shakes his head. "I'm furious, jealous. Both. Did we fight? I'm kissing your neck. Your skin is so soft; I'm running my hand along your leg. Your bare leg, back of your thigh—"

My stomach flutters and panic sets in. I take a step back. Now isn't the time for him to remember the hot kiss we'd shared in that coach's office. I need him to stay focused on remembering everything else. The second I pull away, his eyes snap open, frustration and dark desire swirling in the deep blue pools. "What happened between us, Nara?"

You kissed me with a hunger and passion you never have before. You made me not care who discovered us. All I wanted to do was drown in you, but we were interrupted and ended up hiding in a closet. I straighten my shoulders and shrug off the emotions. "Nothing more than that." I take a few steps away and turn back to him. "Focus, Ethan. Your life. *Our lives* are in danger until you can remember more about what happened while you were gone. Walking around blind isn't good for either of us."

"What else happened?" he repeats, his expression resolute. He starts to take a step toward me when a blur cuts between us.

"Where's Drake?" Harper's bony fingers clamp painfully on my shoulders like eagle talons. As she aggressively shoves me back toward the storage building in a mere flash, I'm shocked by how fast she moves and how completely different she looks. Black leather and mesh have replaced her preppy clothes, and her once long silky dark hair now stands in pixie-cut spikes.

But it's her eyes that render me immobile; they're dead, evil. Just like Harper's boyfriend Drake's were when he attacked me in the locker hall. The Harper that had gone after me and Lainey in the bathroom had been crazed and vicious, but not like this. Something else is spewing in my face; her strength, the sounds she's making, and the sheer depravity in her expression project something not quite human. Not anymore. "Actually, all I really want is that book he'd bragged about finding. Where is it, bitch?"

As she focuses her dark gaze on me, a chill—colder than the air around us—whips through me, making me shiver. At the same time I try to twist from her vice hold, Ethan tugs hard on her shoulder, commanding, "Let go of her!"

Harper swivels a hateful "drop dead" look Ethan's way, and an otherworldly snarl erupts from her throat as she swings her arm wide, knocking him in the chest. Her powerful hit sends him soaring across the walkway and into the field house building twenty feet away.

My worried scream for Ethan dies on my lips as Harper turns her attention back to me. Tilting her head, she studies me with detached interest, like I'm a piece of gum she got on her shoe and she's not quite sure how to remove me.

"What *are* you?" she asks, shaking me until it feels like my neck might snap. Certainty quickly fills her expression and she sneers, "You're too weak to be Corvus." I don't get a chance to answer before irritation settles in her features. "This is taking too long. I'll just take the information from you."

The second she looks deep into my eyes, a surge of dark energy thrusts against me, making me cringe. I grit my teeth and fight the skin-crawling sensation of worms squirming along my skin, seeking an entrance to invade my body and mind.

"You're blocked!" she snaps, her black eyes full of wrath. "Where do you have it on you?" She roughly skims a hand down my arm and pushes my sleeve back, then does the same to my other arm, looking for something.

I have no clue what she's talking about, but before she can touch me any more, I take advantage of her arrogance that I won't fight her and drill my fist into her throat as hard as I can. "Here's my block!"

While Harper gasps for air, I don't wait for the evil inside the girl to recover. Past experience has taught me that they bounce back far faster than a normal person. Grabbing her jacket lapels, I jerk her sideways to send her off balance. The second she stumbles, I pull her toward me and jam my booted foot against her stomach, sending her into a set of prickly bushes next to the storage building.

"Come on, Ethan!" I run toward him, my breath coming out in frosty plumes.

Ethan is just getting to his feet as I reach his side. His stance is a little unsteady and he's rubbing his shoulder as if he's in pain, but his expression is one of vengeful concentration. "Go now, Nara!" he commands, his posture straightening.

His eyes might have turned the color of coal, but he still seems a bit conflicted. The Ethan who fought Drake that night had focused, deadly intent in his eyes—a sense of calm righteousness that couldn't be denied. In my gut, I know this isn't good. As Ethan's hands bunch into fists and he starts toward the bushes where Harper landed, I step in front of him and grab his arm, whispering frantically just for his ears, "You need your sword!"

He jerks his gaze to me, brows pulling down. "What are you talking about?"

A furious growl shakes the bushes. Branches begin to break inside the greenery.

Oh, God. He doesn't know about his sword. He must be going after Harper purely on instinct, which means he doesn't remember how to defeat her. He has no idea how strong she'll be with that evil inside her.

When Ethan dodges around me, I do the only thing I can to save him. I turn and jump onto his back. Wrapping my arms and legs around him in a tight squeeze, I scream in his ear, "No, Ethan!"

Harper crawls out of the bushes. Once she stands to her full height, she sends an angry, eerie snarl in our direction. Ethan tenses and grips my arm in a painful hold, continuing forward with determination.

Harper bares her teeth once more, then she takes off running.

Ready to spring after her, Ethan's breathing ramps and tension ebbs through his muscular body. As she disappears around the corner, he takes several steps, his pace increasing, frame coiling tighter like a winding spring. At any second he'll toss me to take off after her. Despite the pain he's inflicting on my arm, I speak forcefully in his ear. "You need your sword to defeat her. Please stop before you get us both killed."

Ethan halts and takes several deep breaths. Once his breathing settles, his grip on my arm loosens. I slide to my feet and absently rub my arm as he turns to face me, his expression far from calm.

"I had every intention of ripping that thing to pieces. What is she? Was she talking about that Drake guy I killed? And what book is she looking for?" His brow creases as he thinks out loud. "I thought I heard her say Corvus, which is the technical term for raven. And that's the second time you've brought up a sword. When you mentioned a sword in my dream I thought you were speaking symbolically." Clenching his fists, he works his jaw. "The sword, the ravens…this is all connected to me somehow, so why did she attack you?"

"It's about both of us." I push my hair back and exhale deeply. "I think she attacked me because she thought *I* was Corvus. She doesn't know that you are."

"*I'm* Corvus? What does that even mean?" He takes a deep, calming breath, then pins me with an intense stare. "I need you to start talking right now, Nara. No more scenic routes. I need the express lane to yank my memory back to the present. Your safety depends on me remembering what the hell is going on."

CHAPTER 9

Nara

"You said the locker hall looked like a war zone, which is a very apt description." I pause and slide my gaze to Ethan sitting in my passenger seat as I drive back to my house. "You didn't just fight Drake that night. You obliterated him."

Ethan winces briefly, then deep furrows form around his mouth. "What do you mean obliterated him? I didn't kill the guy or the police would've arrested me at the hospital. You said he intended to hurt you, so I'm not sorry if I did take him out, but I'm just trying to understand what you mean."

"I mean, you *decimated* him, as in *poof*, turned him into ash."

He shoots me a "that's bullshit" look and I glare at him. "Do I look like I'm trying to screw with your head? Your dreams do a good enough job of that. You obliterated him with your sword."

He crosses his arms, his face turning to stone. "What sword?"

I turn into my neighborhood and glance his way. "There's a reason that sword on your back looks so real. It has the power to turn a person to nothing but ash."

Ethan swallows several times, his face turning pale. "This is all so unbelievable, I—"

"Look. I know it's a lot to take in. And maybe if you remembered part of what you learned while you were gone for a month this wouldn't sound so...well, crazy."

"What did I learn while I was gone?"

I turn into my driveway, then pull into the garage, cutting the engine. As I get out of my car, Ethan quickly follows suit and holds my gaze across my car rooftop. "Well?"

"That's just it. You didn't tell me much while you were gone this past month. As far as I knew you were camping, snowmobiling, and going to concerts with your dad."

Ethan's cheeks flush slightly, but he keeps his gaze locked on my face. "How did you learn about me being this…Corvus? Did I tell you?"

I use the excuse of shutting my car door to glance away as I answer. "Fate told me."

Ethan's behind me in a nanosecond as I open the house door and step into the kitchen. "When did you *talk* to Fate again?" he asks, disapproval dripping in his tone. How hasn't he noticed the changes within him, how fast he moves? It's beyond normal.

"Why would you do that when you know he wants to kill you?" Ethan continues, following right behind me.

Houdini jumps up on Ethan and me as we stroll through the kitchen toward the living room. I pet my dog's massive head, then scrub his neck fur. "It wasn't intentional. Fate zapped me into a conversation while I slept."

Ethan's warmth envelopes me from behind as his hands land on my shoulders. "You've only been able to speak to Fate if I held you while we were asleep," he says near my ear in a low, rumbling register. "I stayed here Saturday, didn't I?"

My heart pounds and my pulse races. I want to lean against him. My legs are still shaking from the run-in with evil-Harper, but I take a step away and face him, adopting an even tone. "That's not important right now. You wanted the express lane, so let's stay on it."

He holds my gaze for a second, then nods. "What did Fate say about me?"

"He said you're Corvus, a kind of enforcer who keeps balance."

Ethan's dark eyebrows lift. "Balance of what?"

I shrug. "I don't know. He told me you exist outside of our realm, and that he can't see your fate, but you have a destiny."

"That doesn't make any sense," Ethan grumbles, eyes narrowed in disbelief. "I eat, breathe, sleep, and bleed. I exist like everyone else."

"Since you came back, you move much faster, you're more muscular, and you've grown at least an inch. Your body has changed. *You've* changed, even if you don't remember why."

When Ethan suddenly stills, I soften my tone. "Think about it. You've never been in any of my dreams about my next day, even though I spend hours with you. Why do you think that's the case? Fate said if I wanted to know more about the Corvus I should ask the Order."

His eyebrows shoot up. "*The* Corvus? As in plural?"

I nod. "Apparently there are more like you."

Wonder flits through his eyes before he scrubs his hands down his face, growling in frustration. "What's this Order?"

"I didn't run across anything about your kind of Corvus or the Order in my raven research."

"Why were you researching ravens?"

"I figured while you were gone I'd work on a journal, collecting every bit of information on ravens, swords, tattoos, basically anything I could get my hands on to help you come to terms with your tattoo. I planned to give it to you when you came back." My lips twist downward. "Of course, I had no clue you were out discovering who and what you are on your own."

"Nara." Ethan reaches for me, but I step back.

"I gave you the journal on Saturday, but you left it behind. I'll get it for you."

As I turn toward the stairs, Ethan falls into step behind me. I stop and gesture to the couch. "Wait here. I'll be right back."

Before he can say anything, I bolt upstairs, Houdini in fast pursuit behind me.

Once I'm upstairs, I take a few minutes to calm down. I can't let Ethan touch me and draw me in. For both our sakes, I have to stay focused until he remembers and can tell me where he was and what he was doing. Keeping things platonic is for the best.

The sad look Ethan gives me from his position on the sofa when I come back downstairs sets me on edge, but I shrug off the tension and set the books in his lap.

His big hands instantly grip them as I sit down, leaving a cushion between us. "Two books?"

"That's the journal I worked on." I nod to the leather bound book. Pointing to the other book, I continue, my voice turning husky with sadness. "And the blue one with the metal corners and spine findings was Freddie's."

Ethan reads the title out loud: *Ravens*. He glances my way as he flips through it. "A book all about caring for ravens? This is the book Drake killed Freddie for? Why?"

"Yes, he killed Freddie for this book. I'm pretty sure he wanted the book because he was looking for this..." I trail off as I hold up the silver triskele necklace my grandmother left for me. Then I lower the charm near the identical symbol on the book's spine until it suddenly adheres. As soon as the charm locks to the book, the metal finding on the bottom of the spine pops open.

"What the—?" Ethan lifts the book and peers into the empty space behind the print and the spine's binding.

While Ethan pokes his finger inside, I nod to the book. "This is how we're connected, through the ravens. My grandmother saved this necklace for me until I turned seventeen. Freddie had kept this book safe for almost thirty years. Both my grandmother and Freddie were given these items separately and at different times, but each item came from a mysterious blond man who told them to keep them safe and they would know what to do with them when the time came."

Bafflement travels across Ethan's features before he returns his gaze to the book and shakes it trying to see if anything falls out. "This hiding spot is empty. Was there something hidden inside?"

I nod. "It held a small scroll of parchment paper."

Ethan lowers the book, excitement in his gaze. "What did it say?"

"I can't remember."

"What do you mean you can't remember?"

I twist my lips and pick at the seam on my jeans. "As soon as I looked at it, the paper disintegrated in my hands. It literally turned to dust."

He blinks, then shakes his head slowly. "And you really can't remember what was on it?"

"I know it had something to do with ravens." Sighing, I worry my lip with my teeth. "I've tried to remember, but I can't picture what was on the paper at all."

"So it's lost forever then."

His obvious disappointment tightens my chest. "I believe I was meant to see it, since I was led to it. Hopefully I'll be able to remember what it said when the time comes." I spread my hands wide and shrug. "Whenever that is."

Ethan raises an eyebrow.

His skepticism makes me doubt myself. I grip the couch cushion.

"I have to believe that, Ethan. I couldn't live with myself if I thought Freddie kept the secret within that book safe all those years, then lost his life for nothing."

As my lips start to tremble, Ethan grips my shoulder. "I'm just trying to process all the strangeness, Nara. If I only had one person I could depend on, I would choose you. No matter who the stranger was who gave your grandmother and Freddie these items to keep them safe for you, one thing I know for sure is that he picked the very best person."

When I dip my head, appreciating the fact he still believes in me despite the tension between us, his hand falls away and my gaze shifts to Freddie's book. "The question is…who was that man and *what* did he pick me for?"

Ethan grins. "When the time comes, you'll know."

I snort, warming to Ethan's amused response. "Well, others obviously want Freddie's book. They don't know I've discovered its secret. You heard Harper. She wants it and that guy you fought in the hall wanted it too. That's why he attacked me. He planned to give it to someone he said would 'be my worst nightmare.'"

His gaze locks with mine. "You said Drake wasn't entirely human. I got that same sense from that girl today too. Pure evil rolled off her. I've never wanted to hurt another person as much as I did when I saw her grab you."

He appeared to be acting on instinct earlier. *What drove that?* "What did you feel when you thought she would hurt me?"

"Dead calm, then cold fury. An absolute knowing that she must be eliminated." He seems a little surprised by his response, but plunges on, his tone building in assurance, "Whatever that evil is…it should never have gotten so close to you, let alone attacked you. I wasn't going to let her walk away."

There isn't an ounce of hesitation in his statement now. His unyielding "must be eliminated" viewpoint instantly reminds me of the enforcer label Fate had given the Corvus. I blink as I realize the changes that'd happened to Ethan while he was gone haven't left him; the base instincts are just simmering under the surface, muffled by his memory loss. That means he's not totally defenseless. I just need to figure out a way to help him tap into them again. "Those were your thoughts, but what did you physically feel?"

Ethan rolls his right shoulder. "After she knocked me back, my shoulder burned as if it was on fire, which is weird because I hit my back on the building, but I just ignored the pain and followed the tightness in my gut. It felt like a rope had been lashed between us. Each time I took a breath, my lungs burned and the rope tightened, tugging me forward. It took everything inside me not to attack that thing as soon as I saw her. If you hadn't been standing in the way, I would've gone after her instantly."

If I helped trigger this feeling before, maybe I can again. "I have an idea that might help you remember." I scoot close, then lean across him and curl my left hand over the top of his right shoulder. Tapping his back, I hold myself still and try not to react to him leaning closer to me. "Is this where your shoulder burned?"

Ethan rests his cheek against mine for a second, then he suddenly stiffens and grips my wrist. "You're touching my tattoo. I thought you were talking about a real sword earlier."

When he starts to get up, I clamp my fingers tight to keep him seated. "Close your eyes and picture what happened with Harper. Think about how you felt when she attacked me."

Ethan sets his jaw, but closes his eyes and takes a deep breath. A second passes, then two. His breathing increases and he rolls his shoulder like I saw him do by the field house. I thrum my fingers on the back of his shoulder. "You're burning here, aren't you?" When he dips his head once, I say, "Now imagine if she'd thrown me like she did you. Hold on to that thought."

Ethan hisses out in pain, then jumps up and quickly tugs his jacket and shirt off. As he drops his clothes, I stare in amazement at the sight of the hilt of his sword tattoo sliding over the curve of his shoulder, then turning, the raven-feathered blade following around the bulge of his bicep.

"What the hell?" he grates while the ink continues to snake around his arm at a rapid pace. He turns his hand to the ground, palm down and flexes his fingers. When the point of a very real sword starts to emerge behind his fingers, Ethan dips his head back and a moan of pain erupts from deep in his throat.

By the time I reach his side, he's holding the sword decorated with a raven's feather along the blade and a raven yin-yang symbol near the hilt. His arm flexed inward, the blade's tip touching the floor, Ethan lowers his chin and exhales deeply, his once blue eyes pitch black. His face is pale, and shock reflects in his expression, yet his grip on the sword is tight with instinctual confidence.

"I'm so sorry, Ethan. When you let me feel it forming right on your back before, you didn't act like you were in pain."

Ethan swallows a few times, but doesn't speak. *Did I push him too far, too fast?* Guilt knots my stomach and before I realize what I'm doing, I lay my hand on his chest. "Are you okay?"

His gaze slowly comes into focus, natural blue starting to swirl with the black color. "Nara?"

With that one word, he's asking a zillion questions I can't answer. I shake my head slowly and curl my fingers into a fist on his chest. "That's all I know."

I shift, intending to step back, but Ethan grasps my waist in a tight hold. "Stay."

How is he holding me with both hands? I start to glance down, but the sword is already returning to his body; the tattoo is curling back up his arm, sliding around the defined muscles, moving toward the slope of his shoulder.

Once the hilt disappears over his shoulder, Ethan pulls me forward and touches his forehead to mine. "Please, Nara. Just for a minute." His grip might be firm, but his body quakes under my palms. I stay put.

A full minute passes as we breathe in and out, then Ethan exhales deeply and slides his nose along my cheek. His intensity and appealing smell wreak havoc on my resistance. My hands itch to run along his warm skin, to explore the bulk of his muscles. It takes everything inside me not to press against him.

Ethan's fingers dig into my spine, pressing me closer. Before we connect fully and I lose total control, I force myself to step out of his hold. Picking up his shirt and jacket, I adopt a crooked smile. "At least now I know how you retrieved your sword when you were dressed in a suit jacket. Been wondering about that."

Disappointment is evident in the wry twist of his lips, but he takes his clothes and shrugs into them. "I hope you're right and that gets easier. Felt like my arm was turning inside out." Sliding his hands in his jacket pockets, he asks, "Do you know where this Harper girl lives?"

"No, I don't. And she doesn't know where I live either. For now we need to focus on your memory."

His body tenses. "When I find her, she'll tell me who wants that book and why."

I shake my head in fast jerks. "Ethan, whatever Harper is, you're not ready to face her yet. I saw you fight Drake and how inhumanly strong he was. You need to regain your memory first."

When his face sets in stubborn lines, I cross my arms, refusing to back down. "Speaking of memories, why don't you try to remember Danielle? You know, your supposed *cousin* you spent the last few weeks with."

Lines crease around his mouth as he shakes his head. "Bits about you are coming back, but nothing about anything or anyone else."

"If your memory doesn't return, this Danielle person might be the only one who can fill in the blanks." I square my shoulders, my tone hardening. "I might not like all the answers I get, but at least we'll have them."

Ethan pulls his hands out of his jacket and takes a step toward me. "Nara—"

The sound of the garage door opening draws our attention. I pick up the books from the coffee table, then hand him the journal. "Mom's home. Flip through the journal tonight so you can catch up on all things raven. I have one more thing I want to show you tomorrow after school that also might help jog your memory."

Ethan reaches for the leather book, but clasps his fingers around mine, holding me captive. "Tell me you believe we were meant to be, Nara. That more than this..." He glances from Freddie's book in my other hand to the journal between our fingers. "Is keeping us together."

My heart races as I stare into his eyes. I'm not ready to answer the emotional part, so I answer the best way I can. "Fate told me that everyone has a fate, and he's the one who keeps us heading toward our destination. We're on the same path, Ethan."

Worry flickers in his eyes, making my heart ache. "He said he can't see my fate. *Are* we on the same path?"

"But he said you have a destiny and so do I. All we can do is keep moving forward."

Frustration reflects in his gaze and his mouth thins to a grim line. "So, together 'til?"

I nod just as Mom walks in and calls from the kitchen doorway. "Oh, hi, Ethan! I'm so glad to see you're okay." After she sets the groceries on the counter, she strolls into the living room smiling. "Inara was so worried."

Ethan's blue eyes flash to me, a slow smile tilting his lips. "She was worried about me?"

Thanks, Mom. How will I keep him at a distance with you saying things like that? Mom nods, oblivious to the look I've shot her way. "Of course she was. You should've seen her—"

"I've got to take Ethan home, Mom."

Ethan's smile broadens as he turns toward the front door. "That's okay. I'll walk, but I hope you don't mind being my ride to school, at least until I get my car back from the shop. What do you say? Will you be my wheels, Nara?" he asks, eyebrows raised innocently.

I narrow my gaze. I'm just about to tell him that the couple miles to school is not a big deal to walk when Mom pipes in, "Of course she'll be happy to give you a ride."

Ethan flashes a brilliant smile. "Thanks, Nara. I'll see you tomorrow morning."

I follow him to the front door and as he walks out, I say, "I can take you in the morning, but you'll have to find a ride home. I just remembered that Drystan reminded me we have indoor practice after school."

He turns to me, all amusement gone. "I thought we had that thing after school tomorrow."

I'm too irritated at how easily he's twisted my emotions into knots to think about taking him to the raven sanctuary right now. I shrug. "It can wait a day. I'm sure you have a ton of homework to catch up on anyway. My guess is it'll feel like a whole *month's* worth."

"Nara…" he begins.

I plaster on a smile. "I'll pick you up at seven forty-five tomorrow. Be ready bright and early."

CHAPTER 10

Nara

"Lainey!" I quickly wave to my friend over the crowd of students milling about in the locker hall.

She pushes off Matt's locker, kisses him on the cheek, then heads in my direction.

I've just spun my combination lock when she reaches my side and immediately spouts in my ear above the end of the day noise. "Why did I have to find out from Drystan that Ethan's lost his memory?" Folding her arms, she leans against the locker next to mine. "I shouldn't have to remind you of the best friend 'no secrets' code."

I'm stunned into silence and for a couple seconds I imagine wringing Drystan's neck. How did he tell her without revealing why I told him about Ethan? The fact she chose to yell at me about this issue means he didn't share the real reason I told him. If she knew the truth about either Drystan or my abilities, she'd really flip. Lainey can only handle certain truths and my ability to dream my next day—well, my past ability—isn't one of them. "Sorry, Lainey. I only told Drystan because I thought he might have ideas of other places a guy might keep his phone that I hadn't thought of."

Her bottom lip pokes out. "Still, you should've told me. Poor Ethan." Pausing, she glances around. "Where is he anyway? Isn't he back at school? I thought I saw him in the hall earlier today."

I nod. "He's here. I was his ride to school since his car's in the body shop. He's probably busy trying to catch up with teachers, homework, and stuff."

Lainey nods, her long red hair falling into her eyes. Pushing strands behind her ear, she says, "So catch me up. Drystan was stingy on the details."

"Important things first. I ran into Harper yesterday afternoon on the school grounds."

"What?" Lainey's eyes go wide as she presses her hand to her throat. I can tell by her expression she's reliving Harper choking her in the bathroom. "What'd she say? What'd she do? Did you—?"

"Lainey." I grip her wrist. "If you see her, don't confront her. Run as hard and as fast as you can in the opposite direction."

"But—but she needs to be arrested for attacking us."

I squeeze her wrist tight. "Please, Lane. Trust me. She's changed her hair, her clothes, her entire look. It's like she's gone truly crazy. Her eyes are even wilder than they were that night in the bathroom. Maybe she's on drugs or something. If you see her, *run*. When you're far enough away, call the police. Got it?"

When Lainey bites her lip and nods, I pull a piece of paper from a slot in my backpack. "Can you do me a huge favor? Do you think you can get your dad to look up who this phone number is registered to?"

Lainey glances at the paper I slip into her hand, then shifts her brown gaze back to me. "Where'd you get this?"

"Off Ethan's cell phone." Unfortunately I couldn't get Ethan's phone to power up, which meant I couldn't check for photos—the first thing I'd planned to do. I had to resort to using the SIM card reader. All I could get from the SIM reader were his contacts: Samson, me, and one other number I didn't recognize. It had to be Danielle's. "I'm hoping that number will lead me to the person who can tell me where he's been," I tell Lainey.

Her eyes widen. "So it really is true. He can't remember anything from the past few weeks?"

I shake my head. "Pretty much. He's had glimpses about us at the dance, but nothing that explains where he went or what he did while he was gone."

She holds up the piece of paper, eying the number. "Well, obviously he was in D.C. and not Michigan."

My heart pinches at the reminder. "Maybe. But that's probably a cell phone, which means the person who owns it can live anywhere.

That's why it's important to learn the name and hopefully the address tied to the number. It'll at least give us a place to start."

"What did Ethan say about it?"

"He doesn't know I found his phone, and until I can get a solid answer, I don't want to get his hopes up. Can you keep this just between us?"

"I'll see what I can do. Speak of the devil," Lainey murmurs, then quickly shoves the paper into her jeans front pocket as she looks over my shoulder and calls out, "Hey, Ethan. So glad to see you back at school."

"Hey, Lainey."

Lainey backs away, waving. "See you at practice in a couple hours."

"A couple hours? That's plenty of time for a trip down memory lane."

Ethan's voice is directly above my head. How does he manage to sound both annoyed and pleased at the same time?

"The place I plan to take you is a half hour away," I answer, resisting the urge to look over my shoulder. Grabbing several books, I shove them into my book bag. "Add the half hour back and time spent there and I'll be late for my practice if I go today."

"We can make it back in time. I think you're bailing because you don't think you can handle an hour alone with me."

The teasing confidence in his tone is driving me crazy. "You're so sure of yourself." I reach up to grab my locker door with every intention of slamming it shut.

Ethan's hand lands on mine on the locker door as he whispers next to my ear, "I remembered more last night, Nara. You and me, in a very small, dark closet. I lifted you up against me and kissed you in a place I've wanted to for a long time."

I swallow a couple of times to calm my racing pulse. Even though he's behind me, I sense his gaze has lowered to my chest. My whole body tingles with the attention. *Why'd I have to wear a fitted sweater today?*

"I said something about fulfilling a promise." His fingers flex against mine, tightening. "Despite what I can't remember, I'm very sure about us, even if you aren't."

I close my eyes and try to calm my pounding pulse. His seductive reminder of our time together in the closet yanks at my heart.

"What other promises did I fulfill that night, Sunshine?"

The velvet purr in his tone rocks me all the way to my toes.

At that moment, Drystan's voice breezes by as he walks down the hall. "Hey, Nara, did you find it?"

I inwardly tense even though I'm thankful for the distraction. I'd hoped to find out more about the number I gave Lainey first before letting Ethan know about the phone. "Yeah. Thanks for the tip."

Drystan turns and walks backward, a cocky grin on his face. "Anytime. Don't forget you owe me help on my project."

Ethan's fingers tighten on mine and I feel the heat in his palm shoot down my arm. "I won't. See you later."

As soon as Drystan turns the corner away from the locker hall, Ethan asks, "What'd he help you find?"

Pulling my hand from under his, I retrieve his phone from inside my backpack. "Your cell phone. He suggested checking your car. I remembered which body shop your brother told me they'd towed your car to, so I searched inside. It's pretty damaged. It kept shutting down when I tried to turn it on."

As I start to hand it to him, he shakes his head. "Trash it. You would've been the only reason I got a phone. Now that I'm back, it's useless to me."

"Don't you want to see if there's any information on it?"

He shrugs. "You said it's damaged."

"Maybe you can get it working. Or at least get it to stay on long enough to check who you called or texted other than me."

"I guess it's worth trying." As he tucks the phone in his back pocket, his gaze lands on the end of the hall where Drystan had exited. "He gives off a vibe that makes me think there's more to him than he lets on."

I'm pretty sure Ethan can sense Drystan's psychic vibe, even if he doesn't know that's what he's sensing. Drystan revealed his ability to find things to me in confidence, so I'm not going to say anything about it. "Drystan has layers, that's true, but he's a good guy. He watched out for me when everything went nuts this past month."

Ethan tenses. "How exactly did he *watch* out for you?"

May as well get this out of the way. "He's been teaching me self defense." I slam my locker shut, then turn back to him. "If you still want to go, we need to go now, but we won't have time to linger."

Distrust flickers in his eyes. "Has he hit on you yet?" Before I can answer, Ethan shakes his head. "I see the way he looks at you."

I roll my eyes. "Calm down. It's just self-defense."

His jaw hardens. "Don't think for one minute he's teaching you self-defense just to be nice. He's pushing my buttons by eyeing you like you're already his."

He's so intense my insides quiver, but my inner feminist shouts for me to defend her honor, so I poke him in the chest. "I'm not anyone's *possession*, Ethan. I have feelings and emotions and a mind of my own."

Ethan hooks his finger around mine and bends close. "I'm always aware of your strong mind, Sunshine. As for your feelings and emotions, I *want* to be the center of them."

My heart ramps. He's making it hard to think straight, but one of us has to keep on track. "Before you left you said we couldn't move forward until you worked things out with your parents." Let him assume that's where we left it. If/when he remembers everything that happened between us Saturday night, I'll deal with the truth then, but I'm not opening up any more crevices in my heart. He's wedged himself in so deep, it feels like any second the sensitive muscle will explode.

"I was an idiot, on all fronts." His deep blue gaze searches mine for a few heart-stopping moments, but when I don't disagree with him, he steps back with a wry half smile. "I suppose I deserve your silence. Let's hit the road."

Thirty minutes later, my hands grip the steering wheel so tight my fingers are numb as I turn into Freddie's long driveway. I haven't been back here since that night a couple weeks ago when Drystan and I found the sweet old man's body all broken and mangled up in that tree. Seeing Freddie's place again brings the horror and sadness of that night flooding back.

"Are you okay? You look pale."

Ethan's deep voice pulls me back to the present. I take a shuddering breath and focus on the house ahead of me, pushing the painful memory to the back of my mind. "Yeah, I'm good. I just want to get this done."

"Whose house is this?" Ethan asks as I park at the top of the drive.

Without answering, I jump out of the car and rush past the For Sale sign in the yard, heading straight for the backyard. The sight of that sign makes my heart hurt.

"Where's the fire?" Ethan says, rushing to catch up to me walking through the backyard.

"I just need to get back, that's all." My words rush out, sounding strained as I step onto the path in the woods behind Freddie's house.

Ethan grabs my arm and pulls me to a stop. "You didn't answer me...whose house is this, Nara? Do they know we're here?"

I feel like everything's in slow motion as I glance over my shoulder toward the deck on the back of Freddie's house. The shattered glass door has been replaced, the yard perfectly manicured. You'd never know a violent murder happened here. "This is Freddie's house."

Pulling away, I start up the path. Ethan is right on my heels. "Freddie? Did he live alone?"

I can only nod. The lump in my throat grows bigger as I get closer to Freddie's raven sanctuary. As soon as I see the thirty-foot-tall enclosure of chicken wire surrounding a cleared area with a few trees inside, I stop so fast Ethan slams into my back.

He grips my shoulders to steady me as I stumble forward. "Are you really okay? Whatever this place is, it's upsetting you. I don't know if this is a good idea."

I don't look back at him. My attention is frozen on the big oak tree in the middle of the sanctuary and the missing limb where Freddie's body had been impaled. The police and firemen had sawed it off in order to lower his body to the ground. I blink rapidly, trying to erase the image from my mind, but my hands start to tremble while my legs feel as if the bones are melting inside them. *Maybe I can't do this.*

Ethan squeezes my shoulders, then pulls me against his chest. "Let's leave. This is a bad idea. Seeing you like this...it isn't worth it. Not to me."

Familiar sounds suddenly erupt all around us as thirty or so ravens let out guttural calls and begin to swoop down from the trees, flying into the opening in the sanctuary.

The lump in my throat gets larger and tears form in my eyes, but this time for a different reason. The birds are welcoming us. They must have been the ones who protected Freddie's body that night. His own ravens had been taken to another sanctuary. I can't understand them, but I hear the greetings in their soft croaks and throaty *raaaaacks*.

"Amazing," Ethan whispers in my ear as more birds continue to swoop in by the dozens. The ravens find space in the trees, filling every branch. Others settle on the ground when no more perches can be found.

Once the horde of incoming birds slows to a trickle, one last black bird glides into the sanctuary and lands gracefully on the back of the circular bench surrounding the oak tree. He's massive and looks so familiar I hold my breath until he turns his one white-feathered eye toward us. "Patch!" I call out, releasing a happy laugh.

He bobs his head up and down, then flaps his wings, letting out a low guttural welcome. The birds' and Patch's warm presence is exactly what I need to help me through this.

"Patch? You've made a pet of one of them?" Ethan sounds dumbfounded as I pull away and rush inside the sanctuary.

"Hardly," I snort over my shoulder as I move toward the massive raven. "He just allows me in his personal space. I haven't seen much of him lately. I've missed his crazy antics."

Ethan starts to follow me, but I hold my hand up. "No, stay out there for now."

When his mouth turns down, I spread my hands toward the birds. "This is what we're here for. I didn't know if they'd come. I'd hoped they would, but…"

Ethan leans against the sanctuary's doorway, shaking his head. "I don't understand, Nara. How did you get all these ravens to follow you here?"

I hold my hand out to Patch, who pecks at it. "Hey, be nice," I say softly. He dips his head and puffs up his neck feathers, making me laugh. "Show off."

As soon as I turn to address Ethan, he pushes off the doorway, alarm in his gaze. "Nara, watch out."

A flutter of black appears in my periphery right before Patch lands on my shoulder, his bird feet gripping my jacket. I smirk and fold my arms. "It's all right. He would never hurt me."

Ethan's forehead crinkles. "Ravens can be unpredictable."

"Not as much as you might think." I gesture toward Patch, who's currently swaying back and forth on my shoulder. "Think of Patch…of all those like him as an extension of you."

He crosses his arms and shakes his head. "I know I have a connection to ravens, but they're just birds."

"Oh really?" The one way I know we've connected in the past was when Ethan thought about me. I bite my lip and tell myself this is to help him remember. "Think about touching me."

A sensual smile tilts his lips. "I'd rather *do* that than think."

Okay, maybe this isn't the best idea, considering I'm supposed to be keeping my distance from him. Then again, it's the only one I've got.

I purse my lips. "Just do it."

"Fine." His lips quirk, and as I see all kinds of sexy thoughts scrolling across his face, the birds begin to titter and hop around as if agitated, but nothing else happens.

"Concentrate." I huff, setting my hands on my hips. "Walk outside the sanctuary behind the wire."

Ethan grunts, but does as I ask. "Why am I out here?"

I nod to the fence between us. "Pretend you can see me but you're unable to reach me."

"How is this any different from reality?"

"*Ethan*. Now, think about what you'd do if nothing stood between us."

I ignore the scowl on his face. "Close your eyes."

As Ethan let's his eyes slowly close, I do the same.

"I don't like this."

The hurt in his voice pulls at my heart. I can tell he's talking about more than this exercise.

"Just…think about me, about us," I say. "Imagine what you'd think about if we could only talk on the phone. What would you wish for?"

"You. With nothing between us."

His wish, full of heat and want, carries on the sharp cold wind whipping through the bare trees. The longing wraps me in a layer of warmth, tugging at my heart, making my body tingle.

A sudden rush of softness blows past my cheek, whipping my hair around my face. The earthy scent of pine and wintry air fills my nose, and a dark wall of warmth blocks the afternoon sun, providing its own protection against the crisp air stinging my cheeks.

I smile when I feel Ethan's fingers softly running along my jaw.

"Is this really happening?" Ethan asks from his position on the other side of the fence. "Whatever I think, you can feel it through them?"

"Yes," I say over the swarm of ravens circling around me. Sighing, I give in to my own pent-up longing and lean slightly into the birds' wings so Ethan can feel me press against him. Here, with the wall of birds transferring our feelings while blocking Ethan's view, I take advantage of a chance to be close to him without risking my heart. "Do you feel me?" I whisper.

"Amazing," he calls over the rushing sound of bird wings, his voice full of awe. "I remember this part. Were we talking on the phone?"

"Yes," I say again, and try not to whimper when warm hands cup my face and gentle thumbs reverently trace along my cheeks. I inhale deeply and try to draw in Ethan's own unique smell. I've missed him so much.

The cyclone of circling birds pulls in closer until I can feel every part of Ethan's body pressing against mine, from chest to thigh. It's so real, I even feel his breath on my cheek, his fingers lifting my jaw.

"I miss you," I whisper just for my ears.

Ethan's lips press against mine in a soft caress, then his fingers slide along my jaw, threading into my hair. God, it's so amazing. I want it to be *real*.

My eyes flutter open for a split second, but it's long enough to see that Ethan's towering over me, his broad shoulders blocking the rest of the sun as ravens continue to fly around us.

I gasp, but before I can take a step back, Ethan hooks a hand on my nape in a firm grip, locking me in place. "Not as much as I've missed you, Sunshine."

"Ethan, that wasn't the point," I say, pushing on his chest to create space between us.

As our connection breaks and the birds began to scatter, I'm stunned by the heat and desire swirling in Ethan's deep blue eyes. "I'll never accept a substitute for you, Nara."

My face flushes even as my heart clings to the belief he's speaking about something much deeper than the ravens; he's talking about us. I pull out of his hold and take a step back to raise shaky hands to my face. "I think it's best if we stay focused on getting your memory back for now."

Ethan's hand falls to his side, frustration in his gaze. "You're punishing me for something I can't remember. I'm still stuck on trying to remember a picnic, where all I can picture is you and me alone in the woods, the warm sun and a blanket. I would've finally been able to kiss you in all the places I've wanted to for as long as I wanted."

You did kiss me in several intimate places. It just wasn't during that picnic. While the enticing memory flickers through my mind, I'm careful to keep my face neutral as I tilt my head. "You're forgetting that I still have my memory. Regardless if your reasons were to protect me, you still lied and that is very real to me. Let's keep this—" I draw my hand back and forth between us "—on a friend level and work toward finding answers until you can tell me everything."

"What if I never recover my memory?" Ethan steps close and

touches my cheek. "Is being friends going to be enough for you? It'll never be enough for me."

It takes all my willpower not to lean into his touch. Instead, I turn away and stare into the woods as I answer, "I'm not going there. You'll get your memory back."

"You're drawing a gray line with this 'friends' thing."

I stiffen at the tension in Ethan's voice. He's moved directly behind me and I can feel his heat seeping through my clothes, despite the cold air. If he touches me once more, I'm afraid I'll crumble. I jerk my chin higher. I need to remain strong. For both of us.

A strand of my hair lifts and the sound of him inhaling sends a shiver through me that only intensifies as his deep voice resonates next to my ear. "I've always been black and white, and when it comes to you, I'm all in. I'll do whatever it takes to get my wheels back, Sunshine. Whatever it takes."

The predatory promise in his vow winds its way straight to my gut, sending a whole horde of butterflies scattering in frenzied nervous excitement. I straighten my spine and force an "all business expression" as I spin to face him. "Then focus on remembering. We need to get back or I'll be late for practice."

Ethan

I ask Nara to drop me off near the downtown mall. I figure walking off my frustration might help. As soon as she drives away, I head up a side alley. I know something more happened between us this past weekend. I feel it in my gut.

My faulty memory had continued to spoon feed me glimpses of an erotic puzzle with all the important pieces stripped to teeth-grinding G-rated images. It had gotten to the point where I was beginning to wonder if it was all just a fantasy I'd concocted in my mind.

Until Nara took me to the raven sanctuary.

That place blew me away. I'm still not sure how we synced like that with the ravens. Nara seems to think it's all me, but I honestly believe our connection made the ravens react to my thoughts about her. As the birds swirled around her and I began to feel her presence and smell her girly scents as if she were standing right next to me, that's when a sliver of a memory started to bleed through—something about a phone call we'd had while she was at the sanctuary. But then I heard her whisper that she missed me and nothing could have kept me away. I didn't give a damn that she'd probably get mad. I had to touch her face, to press my lips to hers and breathe her sweetness in. She quiets all my worries and fills my heart with pure happiness.

It's sad when you're jealous of a bunch of birds, but there was no damn way I was letting them touch her in any kind of intimate scenario, even if they were acting on *my* desires. I'm the only one who will fill her needs. She can't have the birds. She has me, and I plan to spend every day reminding her of that until she lets me back in. I've missed seeing her "I'm so happy to see you" smile ever since I woke up in that hospital bed.

You really screwed up, didn't you? Gravelly Voice interrupts my train of thought. *You don't deserve her, you know. It's probably for the best. Might as well let her go and stop holding onto something you're obviously losing. Then, it'll just be you and me, like always.*

As much as he's grating on my nerves, it occurs to me he *is* always with me. I turn onto the brickyard mall. *Shut up. Since you're so chatty, why don't you fill me in on where I've been for the last month?*

I don't recall.

Bullshit. I shove my hands deep in my pockets and set my jaw, waiting for him to respond.

You were digging. I told you not to. You don't want to know me. See where it got you? Empty-headed and well on your way to losing the one good thing in your life. When he lets out a knowing laugh, I roll my head from one shoulder to the other. I have to work hard to keep the anger from showing on my face as I pass a mother strolling her baby. *If you're not going to tell me where the hell I've been, fuck off!*

Gravelly Voice begins to laugh. His laughter continues, growing so loud, I find myself heading toward McCormicks. I'm not sure what kind of reception the Irish pub's house band Weylaid will give me since I've been MIA for a month, but I really need a distraction right now. Anything to muzzle the stupid voice in my head and hopefully also tamp down this desperate need for Nara. The more time I spend near her without being allowed to touch her is pure torture. I have to keep clenching my hands to stop myself from pulling her close.

"Adder!" Ivan calls, pulling me out of my musings.

He stands behind his drum set and points his drumsticks in my direction like double exclamation points, then waves me toward the stage in the corner of the pub.

I wind my way past the partially filled café tables and wave to the redheaded bartender, who finally stopped carding me once the leader of the band, Dom, told him to "Let down your dreads and stop being such an Irishman."

Several of the bar patrons begin to clap as I pass them, but then the four band members join in—with much louder and slower, smartass claps. I roll my eyes and resist the urge to flip them off as I try to ignore how self-conscious they're making me. The band doesn't know my real name. Add's just a name I gave them when I stumbled across the group and fell into practicing with them not long before I met Nara. Ivan had changed it to Adder. I'm not sure where the name Add came from, but at the time it seemed to go with the musical talent I didn't know I had until I picked up one of their bass guitars for the first time a while back.

I still don't trust or understand the hidden musical talent, but all I know is, just like when I sketch the monsters I see in my dreams, playing music helps me escape from all the crap plaguing me. So every so often I show up and join in on a jam session.

My preference is to just practice with the band, not perform with them, but it's late in the day and their gig for the evening is about to begin. If I want the escape of music, then I must perform.

Just as I reach the stage, Ivan sits up from pulling something out of a duffle bag sitting against the back wall. "It's about damn time you showed up. I finally got my shit together to have this made for you and then your sorry ass disappeared."

Dom, Chance, and the lead bassist, Duke, laugh when the black T-shirt smacks me in the face before falling into my hands. The shirt reads *Bringing the "A" to Weylaid* in bold white lettering.

"Thanks, dude." My voice is gruff with guilt as I start to roll the shirt back up.

"Oh hell, no!" Ivan's pierced eyebrow shoots high. "I've been carrying that around for a month. Strip and put it on, kid. You're wearing it tonight just for ditching us for so long."

While I do as I'm told, Chance sets his guitar next to the stool he's pulled up for me, then plugs in the keyboard in front of his own stool. A couple of girls whistle in the background as I yank off my shirt and call out, "Looking buff there, Adder."

Duke's auburn eyebrows pull down in irritation. "Put your shirt on."

Duke's real name is Wey, and I smirk as I tug the new shirt on, because I know just how much he hates the groupies' attention being pulled away from him. He's the reason the band's name is Weylaid. As Ivan put it, "A twist on the actual word, because it's ironic and sex sells."

Dom's dark hair looks even more clean-cut than usual. Must've just gotten it cut. He laughs as he reaches over and ruffles Duke's surfer-messy hair, irritating the guy even more. "That's rich coming from you. I've seen you coming out of your room naked more than I've seen you dressed. You can't possibly have all the girls."

"One day that bed is going to fall through the ceiling."

I grin at Chance's smartass comment.

Duke gestures to the guitar leaning against my stool and grumbles, "Just grab the damned guitar and let's get playing."

While the stage lights grow brighter, I quickly grip the guitar's neck and savor the feel of the strings under my fingers.

We play hard for two hours, and I'm coated in sweat by the time we take a break, but at least my shoulders aren't tense anymore.

Just as I'm walking off stage to get something to drink, three college-aged girls walk up. The thin blonde starts to speak, when a wiry, slick-muscled arm cuts between them and grabs my wrist, then a head of curly brown hair dips between two of the girls.

"Sorry, ladies, but *Adder* and I need a minute."

The girls murmur their understanding and head off to the bar, leaving me with Shaun.

"Nice gig you got going here, Ethan," he says, giving a snarky smile. "Why the hell didn't you tell me you'd joined Weylaid?"

I haven't seen Shaun since he and a few other guys I hung with at my last school helped me deal with two assholes who were giving Nara a hard time at Blue Ridge.

I pull my arm from his hold and try to play off how much it bothers me that he's seen me performing. I don't want to have to explain my surprising new talent. Hell, *I* can't even explain it. The reason this gig has worked so well for me is because no one knows me here. "I'm not a member of the band. I just fill in from time to time."

Shaun eyes my shirt with a cocked eyebrow. "You're the "A" aren't you?"

I'd forgotten about the stupid T-shirt. Rubbing my hand on my neck, I change the subject. "I thought you'd been banned from this pub for fighting."

He flashes a grin and tucks his hands in his jeans pockets. "I snuck in the back door when someone walked outside to grab a smoke. Old Red Dreads doesn't know I'm here—"

"Hey, you there!" the bartender says as he rounds the counter, a scowl on his face.

Shaun quickly glances over his shoulder, then back to me. "Well shit."

The bartender grabs hold of Shaun's arm, and I shake my head and hide my relief behind a grimace of sympathy. "Sorry, bud."

As Shaun's getting hauled away, he shouts, "See you later, Eth...er, Adder. The boys aren't going to believe this shit!"

Before I can dwell too much on Shaun's parting comment, Dom calls me back to the stage to discuss upcoming songs.

Ethan

My dad's BMW is parked on the road in front of our house when I pull into the driveway. I shake my head and pretend like I didn't see my parents as I get out of my car. Unfortunately, my dad's not about to be ignored.

"Why are you getting home so late on a school night?" he demands as he walks up the driveway, his expensive trench coat flapping in the cool wind.

I slip my keys into my pocket along with my hands and turn to face him. "Eleven's not that late."

A scowl creases his brow. "Where were you? We've been waiting here for two hours!"

I shrug and watch my mom close the car door with a quiet click, then button her cashmere coat around her as she heads up the driveway. "I didn't tell you to wait."

Dad leans toward me slightly and sniffs, wrinkling his nose. "You smell like smoke. Where have you been all night?"

I bristle at his probing questions. "Where I've been and what I do are none of your business."

"Do not speak to me like that—" my dad starts to say, but my mother puts her hand on his arm.

"What your dad is trying to say is that he's concerned for you, Ethan. We've found a doctor who's agreed to work with you to regain your memory."

"Another shrink?" I laugh and shake my head. "Sorry, Mom, but that's not happening."

"You don't have a choice, son."

I turn a bold gaze my dad's way. "I absolutely have a choice and the answer is never again."

My dad's face turns to stone in the darkness, his tone low and harsh. "If I have to, I'll call the police and haul you back to Michigan."

I snort and shake my head. "What judge would give you any say-so over me after this much time?"

"You're still underage, Ethan," he snaps.

I adopt the same hardass look he's given me over the years and step close to him. "Try it and I'll file for emancipation. I don't want you in my life. You weren't there for me when I needed you back then, and I sure as hell don't need you now!"

As I step back, my dad slides his hands in his pockets, a smug smile tilting his lips. "You have to have a job for that."

I smile back, but mine is cold, detached. "I do have a job, which is where I was just now."

"Who do you think is paying your medical bills?" my dad sputters. He never has liked being one-upped. "Or do you want your brother going into debt over something you did that you *supposedly* can't remember?"

I clench my fists in my pockets to keep from punching the triumphant look off his face and turn to my mother. "I'm sorry, Mom, but until he can admit that he screwed up, I don't have anything else to say to him. There's nothing he can teach me, nothing he can give me, and definitely nothing I want from him. Ever."

"He's your father, Ethan." Her voice trembles and she glances between us as if her quiet statement should mean something to me.

What kind of father turns his back on his own son the way mine did? I face my dad, my whole body stiff with renewed resentment. "What do you *want* from me? I left so you wouldn't have the embarrassment of a screwed up son around. Why are you hounding me after all this time? Are you feeling guilty that I was in the hospital? If that's the case, I'll let you off the hook. I'm good."

I start to walk away, but my mom speaks up once more, her voice imploring. "You're our children. We aren't perfect. We know we've made mistakes. We just want to be a part of your lives."

I whirl back to them, addressing my dad, so he can't possibly miss the look of angry frustration in my eyes. "If you really want that, then for God's sake, stop being such an ass to Samson. As far as I'm concerned, he's the only one I owe anything to." My gaze swings between my parents. "Does he even know you're here?"

When they don't say anything—just look at each other—I shake my head, then strengthen my tone, directing it at my dad once more. "Let me give you some facts about your oldest son. He knows me better than you ever did. He's been there for me every step of the way, seeming to know exactly what I needed even when I didn't. Did you know that he has enough money in the bank to buy a second home if he wanted to? Just because he didn't finish college doesn't mean he's a failure. Make amends with him. Seriously make the effort and not some half-assed attempt just for show, then *maybe* I'll talk to you. Until then, back off."

My dad's gaze narrows.

I stiffen and mentally prepare for another arrogant tirade of threats.

"When did you become a man?"

I'm so surprised by his question, I answer honestly. "When I had to take on everyone else's crap and figure out how to remain sane."

I don't stay to watch my parents dissect my comment. Instead, I turn away and call over my shoulder as I head for the front door. "I've got school tomorrow. Good night."

CHAPTER 11

Ethan

Other than driving to school together this morning, Nara has managed to avoid me all day. I know she's doing it on purpose, which drives me freaking nuts. It's like she doesn't want to be alone with me.

As soon as the thought hits me, my fingers dig into the locker door, denting it slightly. Then I remember her whispering how much she missed me yesterday…and the heat of our kiss…and my grip on the metal eases. She doesn't *trust* herself to be alone with me. That I can work with.

My lips curl into a pleased smile as I grab a couple of books from my locker. Since I'm hitching a ride home with her, she'll have to talk to me. It's not like she can kick me out of her car once we're in my driveway. My brother had told me in the hospital it would be another week before my car's ready. That's plenty of time to bring Nara back to me.

"Hey, Ethan." Lainey walks up behind me, her boyfriend in tow. "Nara has to stay after and talk to her teacher about an upcoming project. Since Matt passes right by your neighborhood, he'll be happy to give you a ride home."

My gaze shifts past Matt's blond head to the Welsh guy Drystan, who'd stopped to talk to a couple of cheerleaders in the hall. I've seen him hanging with the basketball player after school, which means he's probably living with Matt's family. The idea of sharing a car with the guy sets my nerves on edge, but for a split second I actually consider accepting the ride. It would be the perfect opportunity to brush against Drystan and see what kind of negative stuff I absorb. My gut tells me he has some baggage. As soon as the thought flickers through my mind, I dismiss it. I know he's hiding something beyond his agenda to win Nara over, but I'll figure him out later. Alone time with Nara takes priority right now.

I close my locker and nod my appreciation to Matt for the offer. "Thanks, Lainey, but I'll just wait for Nara."

"Are you sure?" She waves to Matt. "He's happy to drop you off. It's no problem."

Lainey seems especially accommodating. This feels like a Nara set up. I grit my teeth and smile past my annoyance, shaking my head. "I'm good."

She sighs and tilts her head, looking at me with sympathy. "Any more memories coming back?"

I hold her steady gaze, a challenge in mine. "You mean other than the one where you sent me a picture of Nara dressed up for the dance and told me 'This is what you're missing?'"

Lainey giggles sheepishly as she flips her long hair over her shoulder. "Well, it all worked out, didn't it?"

"It's going to." My lips curl in a determined, wolfish smile. "That's all that matters."

"Nara will be out soon," Lainey tuts and waves, tugging her boyfriend behind.

I wait until the hall clears out, then stroll toward the atrium area where people often hang out after school. As I reach the open space, a strong buzzing rings in my ears and the hair on my arms rises.

I grip the books in my hand tighter as I glance around, looking for the source of the sudden sensitivity flowing through me. No one stands out. The harder I scan, the stronger the sensation grows until I feel completely on edge. My muscles twitch all over. I shift forward and roll my head from one shoulder to the other, trying to alleviate the tension, but the closer I get to the huge picture windows, the stronger the feeling becomes.

Whatever it is, it's outside and getting closer. I don't feel threatened like I did with that Harper girl, but my body is amped and I can't shake the feeling of strong familiarity. I move to the doors to look outside. Everyone appears to be going about their normal routine of hanging in groups and talking.

I hear it first, a car rumbling into the entrance of the school. It's a Mustang, the same year as mine, except its black paint job shines.

Without thinking, I walk outside and watch the car with tinted windows pull up to the curb in front of the school.

Like me, everyone has turned to stare at the gleaming classic car.

When the door opens and a girl with long black hair stands up and turns to stare at me over the roof, my heart suddenly jerks with odd familiarity. She's exotic looking, with olive skin and dark brown eyes that appear much older than her face, even though she can't be more than a year or so older than me.

"Danielle," I breathe out. As soon as I see her face, the name pops into my head, but the rest is a blank. I frown and move closer to the curb. Nara told me I'd been with a girl named Danielle for the past month. *Why? Who is she to me?*

"Hey, Ethan. Good as new, yes?" Her eyes gleam with pride as she slides her hand across the roof of the car like it's precious glass. "Well, with an upgrade here or there."

I shake my head, completely baffled.

"Come on," she says, waving to the passenger side. "We have a lot to catch up on."

Whoever she is, this girl has important answers I need. I don't hesitate. I pull open the passenger door, but before I slide inside I scan the parking lot until I find Lainey leaning against a Jeep with Matt. I wave to get her attention, then call out, "Tell Nara I found a ride and I'll call her later."

Nara

Once Lainey let me know Ethan planned to wait for me, I linger in Mr. Gillespie's class sorting through project paperwork as long as possible. But my attempt to delay facing Ethan's intense magnetism gets cut short when she sends me another text twenty minutes later.

Lainey: You need to get outside ASAP!

Me: Coming.

As I hurry down the hall, I wonder how long I'll be able to stay away from Ethan. His comment about how much he enjoyed our kiss in the car this morning only reminded me how little sleep I got the night before. I tossed and turned all night, thinking about the very same thing. The attraction between us is so strong, the thought of never touching him again makes it hard to take a deep breath; all I seem to manage around him are short, choppy ones. Ugh, wouldn't that be pretty if I hyperventilated and passed out? The last thing I need is to confirm that his plan to wear me down is working.

He did have a valid question yesterday though. What if he never gets his full memory back? Will I be able to forgive him for lying to me about something he can't even remember? Can I trust that he'd tell me if his memory does return? What if he thought the truth might destroy us? My instincts say he'd tell me if he remembered, especially since there's more than our relationship on the line; our lives are at risk. Then again, maybe that's my heart overriding my ego.

My pulse races as I approach the entrance. Ethan's out there waiting to drown me with his piercing stare and strong presence. As much as I plan to maintain our "friendship" status, I'd be lying if I said I didn't enjoy being the recipient of such fierce attention. I crave it like a junkie. Every time he brushes close, the brief connection sends indescribable tingles shooting from my head to my toes. I have welts inside my cheeks from biting them to remind myself to move away.

I know Ethan. He won't give up on this mission. And truly, I don't want him to because it means no one else is on his mind. Taking a breath, I step outside into the brisk air and immediately slam into Drystan.

"'ello," he says, green eyes bearing down on me.

"Oh, hey. Sorry about that. Didn't mean to run into you," I say as I quickly scan the empty courtyard for Ethan. "Have you seen Lainey? She sent me a text."

Lainey steps beside Drystan, Matt right behind her. "I'm here. Hey, um…who the heck is Danielle?"

"Danielle?" I squeak the name out. I haven't mentioned anything about Ethan's time away to her so I'm shocked to hear the name.

"Yeah." Drystan thumbs back over his shoulder. "The hot girl Ethan just drove off wi—*ooouf*."

Lainey turns from elbowing Drystan in the side. "I've never seen her before, but Sophia told me she heard Ethan say the name Danielle before he left with her."

Of course Sophia would make sure to share this juicy bit of information with Lainey. She'd always enjoyed taking jabs at me, on and off the soccer field.

"She drove up in a shiny black '69 Mustang with tinted windows,"

Matt offers, as if that might jog my memory.

"Tinted?" I vaguely respond. Could Danielle have been the one who sent that slew of mechanics to work on Ethan's car? I'd assumed his parents had. The fact that she'd changed the car's original look sets me on edge. I grind my teeth as my mind whirls. *Who is she? How can she afford a team of mechanics? What had Ethan been doing with her for a whole month?* My stomach churns. I haven't even met this girl and I hate her already.

"Nara? Are you okay?" Lainey asks, concern in her tone.

I lock gazes with her. "Did your dad find out that information yet? I really need it, please. She might be connected."

Understanding dawns and Lainey touches my shoulder. "You think this girl is the one Ethan talked to while he was gone? The one from his phone? Who is she?"

"I don't know, but I'm going to find out. Can you ask your dad again?"

She bobs her head. "Absolutely. For what it's worth, Ethan asked me to tell you he caught a ride and will call you later."

As the thought *He'd better!* flits through my mind, Drystan throws his arm across my shoulders. "Don't worry about her. She's no Nara."

"You just said she's hot," I grumble.

He shrugs. "So. Lots of girls are hot. But hot isn't the whole package."

The thought of Ethan with this Danielle person still knots my stomach, but I force a smile, appreciating his effort to try to make me feel better. "Thanks for the ego boost."

He hooks his arm tighter around my neck. "You can return the favor any time you want."

"Are you kidding me?" I poke him in the ribs and pull out of his hold. "You can hardly fit through a doorway as it is with all the girls here inflating your head on a daily basis. 'Oh, Drystan, I can listen to you read a phone book. Say something sexy, Drystan.'" I mimic things I've heard them say.

A cocky grin rides his face. "I love America!"

Snorting at Drystan, Lainey rubs her arms and stomps her feet, then glances up at the puffy clouds. "Looks like more snow might be on the way. We're going to go for some coffee. Want to come?"

The alternative is I'll go home and have more time alone to worry about Ethan spending time with this *hot* girl. My chest aches. Has seeing her brought his memories back? Ugh, I don't know if I want him to remember *everything* if it pertains to the same girl who'd answered his cell phone and casually told me he was in the shower like it was no big deal. Like hell it isn't a big deal, especially now that I know she's not his cousin! A distraction is definitely what I need to keep me from inventing all kinds of horrible scenarios in my head. At least until Ethan calls me later.

"Sure. But I can't stay long. If we really are getting more snow, I have to get the leaves in the yard cleared up or Mom's going to kill me."

Nara

The leaf blower's shrill high-pitched noise helps drown out my worried thoughts of Ethan that returned the moment I pulled in the driveway. As I push all the leaves into a tall pile in the yard, Houdini bounds around the stack barking and pouncing on it.

I snicker, letting him have his fun. In a couple of days I'll have to take him back to the shelter to be fixed; it's a rule at the Charlottesville Animal Shelter where I volunteer—any animals adopted from CVAS must be sterilized to help prevent the constant cycle of animals being born without homes. Because I'd fostered Houdini, he'd temporarily avoided the procedure, but now that I've officially adopted him, he's getting it done. While I watch Houdini romp, I realize he's about to undo all my hard work. "Okay enough, boy."

When he pounces onto the mound once more, I shake my head and put him inside the house, then grab several black bags, some gloves, and a rake.

Now that the blower's grating noise isn't invading my mind, I scrape the rake hard against the dead grass, hoping to create another noisy distraction, but it's not loud enough and my thoughts quickly return to Ethan. *What is he doing right now? How long will it be before he calls me? What are they doing? No, don't go there, Nara!* So far I've miraculously managed not to glance at my phone every five seconds, even though I wanted to the whole time we were at the coffee shop.

I wince at the pressure of the wooden handle against my hand, but shrug off the pain and continue on. Ethan's sword has left a raised scar across my palm that's sensitive to any kind of pressure. Maybe over time it'll toughen up. While I rake loose leaves, several birds settle on the ground just beyond the main leaf pile, their fluttering and sleek black feathers catching my attention. I wave to them before transferring the mound of leaves into several trash bags. I'm sad that Patch isn't among the birds like he was at the sanctuary. He still hasn't shown back up at my window yet. He might be unpredictable and make a mess at times, but I really miss that crazy bird.

By the time I finish the leaves, I'm tired enough that my brain doesn't automatically switch back to Ethan. I'd just tied the last bag closed when someone speaks behind me.

"I see you finally got around to using your blower."

I glance at the older man standing on the sidewalk. "Hi, Mr. Wicklow." Wind ruffles his gray hair while his hands are tucked in his wool overcoat pockets. His formal English accent makes me think of drawing rooms and afternoon tea. My lips tug into a self-deprecating smirk as I sweep my hand toward the frozen ground. "And I only waited until it's about ready to snow again to do so."

He laughs, his salt and pepper goatee stretching with his smile. As his amusement settles, his gaze sweeps the yard behind me. "I've never seen so many birds hanging out so calmly before."

I take in the hoard scattered across my entire lawn and realize it probably does look strange. Even more had gathered while I worked. I've gotten so used to them being around, I find their presence oddly comforting, especially when Ethan isn't with me.

"They usually scatter at the first sign of anyone coming near," he says, stepping off the sidewalk onto the grass as if to prove his point.

Instead of taking off, several of them flap their wings and let out low *raaaaaackkkks*, then hop a bit closer. A few more birds join in the chorus just before Patch swoops down to land right next to my feet.

Even I recognize this as odd behavior, so I don't express my excitement to see Patch or call his name. "They probably like the sound of the rake," I say and scrape its thin tines across the grass several times with rapid movements.

His gaze strays from the birds to me before he clears his throat and takes a step back onto the sidewalk. "This kind of closeness isn't common for ravens. I should know. I've studied them."

I pause and turn his way. "You study ravens?"

He smiles and rocks on his heels. "I shadowed the Ravenmaster at the Tower for a week when I was a young boy. Got to see his every day interaction with them. They're incredibly smart, resourceful birds."

My fingers grip the rake's handle and I return my gaze to the leaves to hide my excitement. "I think ravens are fascinating. I'd love to hear what you learned."

"You should come for tea some time, since that's the order of things."

My heart skips several beats. He didn't actually say it like "The Order," yet I can't keep my gaze from snapping back to his. "The order of things?"

"Yes," he nods, smiling as he slides his hands into his pockets once more. "It's how we Brits converse…over tea."

"Ahhh." My shoulders slump slightly. He didn't mean anything more by his comment, which is probably for the best.

"Any time you're ready, I'll be happy to discuss ravens and their purpose in our world."

"Ravens' purpose?"

His attention shifts to my shoulders briefly, understanding in his gaze. "Has it changed yet?"

Is he asking about the feather? I work hard to keep a neutral expression. There's no way he could know about the one on my shoulder blade. Unlike Ethan's, my feather hasn't changed. It's still just a white feather. My fingers grip the handle and my stomach clenches. "Has what changed?"

"It's okay, Nara. I don't mean you harm." He strokes his goatee and smiles gently. "It's the Order's mission to get to know Corvus. To be there when they need us."

The Order's mission?

My pulse whooshes hard. I hadn't misunderstood him. *What are Corvus? What is the purpose of the Order? Am I Corvus and don't know it? Why is my feather white? Why hasn't it changed like Ethan's did?* I want so badly to ask all these questions and more, but I don't want to expose myself or Ethan. Enemies seem to be springing from every corner lately. Fate had told me to ask the Order if I wanted to learn more about Corvus, but then Fate hates me. Did Fate encourage me to seek out the Order for answers to set me up? How has this man found me? What if the Order is a group of hunters, and the moment I admit to knowing anything about the Corvus he'll attack me?

Patch has made several agitated sounds since he landed. The racket draws my attention. The fact that he's just now shown up after being mostly absent makes me wary. He's protected me before, and even though the bird's not attacking Mr. Wicklow, he's also not sitting idly by. If he got any closer, he'd be on top of my shoe. Better to err on the side of caution.

I shake my head in fast jerks. "I'm sorry, Mr. Wicklow. I'm confused by what you're saying. Are we still talking about ravens?"

He holds his hands up and smiles, taking a step back onto the sidewalk. "My apologies, Nara. I can see you're not ready to talk yet," he says in a calm tone as if he's trying to gentle a spooked horse. "You know where I live. If and when you're ready, do come for tea. We have a lot to discuss."

CHAPTER 12

Nara

"That's her," Lainey whispers in my ear as I'm pulling books from my locker the next morning. "What the hell? Is this girl attending our school now?"

It's hard, but I don't whip around. Instead I slowly close the metal door and lock my gaze with Lainey's narrowed one. "Please tell me your dad came up with a name for me."

Lainey continues to check out the girl over my shoulder, while at the same time typing in a message on her phone. "My dad got home late last night and didn't give me this until the morning. It seems like a dead end, since it's some guy."

I stare at the name William Gaston that pops up in the text from Lainey. His name seems familiar somehow. Tucking my phone away, I casually slide my gaze in the girl's direction, whose midnight black hair flows halfway down her back. She's wearing tight jeans, tall brown boots, and a matching buttery-soft cropped leather jacket. And several guys in the hall are nudging their friends and staring at her. Even Matt and Drystan have stopped talking and noticed her.

I take in her shapely figure, then shift my gaze to her strong profile of high cheekbones, full lips, and chocolate-brown eyes. I want to strangle her when she smiles and makes bold eye contact with several guys before walking off. It's the kind of smile that says, "I'll probably ignore you, but you can try if you want."

As her swinging hips sets a few football players shuffling, bumping, and nudging each other down the hall to be the first one to open the door for her, I press my notebook tight against my chest and try to suppress my anger. There's nothing shy, innocent, or otherwise cousin-like about her. And this is the girl who spent at least one night very late with Ethan?

The fact that all I got last night was a voice mail from him saying he was sorry he'd missed me and we'd talk tomorrow at school—he'd called after I'd finally fallen asleep—didn't help. Where had they gone yesterday? His message had been short and to the point. It was hard to tell if he remembered anything after seeing her. I hadn't seen him yet, but seeing Danielle only fueled my anger and amped my determination to get to the truth. All of it.

"I dislike her even more than Harper," Lainey says, cutting an annoyed huff Matt's way.

I'd intended to snort at her comment, but it comes out more like a snarl.

Lainey nods, a glint of sheer dislike in her eyes. "Good to know we're on the same page. I'm suddenly very curious about this chick myself. Damn she looks way too mature to be walking these halls. She's practically shooting laser pheromones with her eyes. Doesn't that take like 'til you're in your early twenties to perfect?" She gestures after the football team crowding through the doorway. "Apparently drool-stupid is the result. Hopefully you can get something out of that name I gave you."

"Oh, I intend to."

"You intend to what?" Ethan's deep voice floats over my shoulder.

Lainey narrows her gaze and gives Ethan an "I'm watching you" hand signal before walking off. I snicker, but turn to him with a determined look. "What happened to calling me last night?"

Surprise flickers. "You didn't get my voice mail?"

"Yes, but I was already asleep."

His lips turn down in annoyance. "I got dragged to a dinner with my parents and brother. We didn't get back until late."

"You uh, don't sound too thrilled."

"It was my dad's way of trying to mend things with my brother, but then he said something that ticked Samson off and dinner turned into a tense deal. It's like being home all over again."

My heart twinges for him. "Maybe one day your dad will figure it out."

"The man thinks all he has to do is show up with a credit card. He needs to forget the money and remember he has a heart."

I wince. "That's tough."

Ethan shrugs. "I only went for my brother. Are you done avoiding me now?"

"I wasn't avoiding—" When his eyebrows shoot up, I flip my hand. "I'm serious Ethan."

"So am I." He ignores the bell signaling time to head to class and takes a step closer until we're almost chest to chest. "My memories about us have been coming back fast and furious. That's what happens when you spend all your time *wanting*."

The gruffness in his voice reminds me of the night we spent together. Strong emotions bubble up, and without conscious thought I lean a bit closer. The pull I feel for him grows stronger each time we're together. It consumes my thoughts, takes over my body and makes me forget why I'm mad at him. I start to glance away, but he touches my chin, pulling my gaze back to his.

Has everything that happened between us come back to him? Panic sets in. I wasn't ready for that. Not when I feel so vulnerable and insecure about Danielle. "What do you remember?"

"Enough to know by the way you've been acting that more happened between us than you're sharing. What I don't understand is why you won't tell me?"

How am I supposed to tell you that we had some kind of epic connection in the coach's closet, and oh, by the way, I'm pretty sure that's the reason a white feather tattoo suddenly appeared on my back? "I—I've got to get to class."

I start to walk away, but Ethan captures my arm. "Why, Nara?"

The steely confidence I'd seen in him during the dance is back, full force.

Apparently some memories are returning. "Because you lied to me about everything, about Danielle, where you went. How can I trust you or anything that comes out of your mouth?" I stiffen my spine. "At this point, I'm not even sure I want to know where you went yesterday."

"For the record, you're a terrible liar." He sighs and his fingers ease a bit on my arm. "Remember when you kept trying to avoid your dad's texts and I told you that if you have the opportunity to find out more about your powers, you should take it? That's what I did, Nara. I went to find out more about what was happening to me. To understand what I'm becoming. If I'd told my brother the truth, he probably would've had me committed. And as much as I believe you would've understood, I know you. You would've tried to stop me from going."

I open my mouth to deny it, but can't. "You still should've told me. So that girl you rode off with yesterday is Danielle. I take it Samson still doesn't know about her. Who is she and why did you continue to lie to me about being with her for a freaking month?"

"No, my brother doesn't know Danielle's here and I'd prefer to keep it that way. He definitely wouldn't understand this." He exhales heavily. "Danielle doesn't matter, Nara. What she knows does. She had the answers and would only tell me if I went to her, alone. She doesn't trust many people. That's why I had to go."

The feeling is definitely mutual. "*Who* is she?"

"She's the one who posted on that forum asking a question about a black feather tattoo forming on one's shoulder."

A thick weight hits my stomach. I gave Ethan that information I'd found while researching about his tattoo. "Is she Corvus too?" I hate how my voice cracks. I couldn't compete with that kind of connection.

"It's not my place to say," he says, glancing into the crowd behind me.

Hurt ripples through my chest all the way to my heart. "You're not going to tell me?"

His deep blue gaze shifts back, full of determined challenge. "I will if you tell me about Drystan. I *sense* something's different about him, and I think you know what it is."

I can't betray Drystan's trust just because Ethan's giving me an ultimatum. When I press my lips together, disappointment flickers across his features and his shoulders tense. "I'll tell you everything else I know." Glancing around, he tugs me through the nearest door, which happens to be the teacher's lounge and thankfully is empty. Once the door closes, he says, "Danielle's the one who trained me, Nara. She taught me how to kill demons like that one inside of Drake."

"Demons?" My eyes widen and I shudder. "Before you just said they were pure evil. Somehow it seems so much worse now that they have a name that comes with all kinds of history. So Corvus keep balance by eliminating demons. Would've been nice if Fate had told me that. Do you remember everything now? How does she know how to kill demons? And where do Corvus come from?"

He shakes his head. "I haven't remembered everything yet. Danielle has had special defense training. When I asked her about Corvus and realms, she explained that there are three realms: Celestial, Mortal, and Under and that Corvus is a spirit whose sole purpose is to maintain balance in the Mortal realm by sending demons back to the Under realm. She said that once the Corvus spirit merges with a human body, the Corvus' purpose overrules the human's fate. I guess we finally have an answer why Fate couldn't see mine."

My chest tightens. "You mean you no longer have control over your own path?"

He shrugs. "I'd like to think so, but the spirit's instinct is strong. When I saw Harper attacking you, the driving need to kill her rose up in me. It's instinctual, so the Corvus is definitely driving some of my reflexes. I told Danielle about Harper attacking us here, and that's why she enrolled in the school. She said demons can change human bodies, so it may or may not be inside Harper the next time."

My eyes widen with worry. "If Corvus can sense demons inside people, can demons also sense Corvus? Are you a target now?"

Ethan flashes a confident smile. "Corvus actually *see* the demon inside people, not just sense them. And no, demons can't see us, because Corvus is always spirit, whereas demons are forced into a spirit form once they enter the Mortal realm. Demons can't exist in corporeal form here. In the veil—a kind of safety zone that exists around the Mortal world—angels constantly battle demons in their physical forms, keeping the demons from entering, but sometimes demons break through. The moment they do, they become non-corporeal and will take over humans."

Chill bumps rise on my arms despite the morning chaos and chatting going on just outside the door in the hall. Is that what I saw that day the sky appeared to rip apart while I was driving to school? Now it makes sense why that fast-spinning ball of smoke, fists, scales, feathers and blood vanished the moment it hit the top of that car, leaving the vehicle completely undamaged; the fighting angel and demon had changed to non-corporeal forms. Why could *I* see that when no one else could?

Could the demons really not see Corvus? That would definitely give Corvus the advantage. Harper might not have been a demon initially, but she had tugged my jacket and tried to look at my back when we were working together at the animal shelter. Not to mention that creepy guy's reaction in the library when he saw the raven symbol I'd drawn in my journal. "But if a demon saw your sword tattoo or anything related to Corvus like the raven symbol on the sword, that would give you away, right?"

Ethan nods, his face suddenly tense. "That's why I asked you not to research ravens anymore in that letter I left behind. You'll draw the demons to you, Nara."

That's exactly what I'd done. I fold my arms against my chest and try to ignore the sudden burn in my stomach. Guilt and worry for Ethan bubbles up and won't subside. "Why don't angels battle the demons in their spirit forms? Why are Corvus even part of the equation?"

"My understanding is that angels have the ability to manifest in their physical form in the Mortal realm, but they can't hold it long enough to battle demons who've possessed humans. That's where Corvus fit in. I'm pretty sure it'd be bad for PR in the Mortal world if angels went around taking over human bodies just so they can fight demons. They're supposed to take the moral high road after all," he finishes, smirking.

I shake my head, trying to absorb all this new information. As overwhelming as it is, at least it answers a lot of questions. Of course the researcher in me is astounded. "There is nothing about Corvus as a spirit in any research I've done, Ethan. Yes, ravens feature in many religions, even from a creationism perspective, but nothing like what you're describing."

He nods, his lips quirking. "How does that saying go…something about a 'grain of truth'? I'm sure they all have pieces of the real story buried within them. Why else would ravens show up so prominently in drawings and many origin stories so far back?"

Now my aunt's comment about Ethan being an "old soul" and Ethan telling me how he sometimes feels "so over stuff, like an old geezer" makes complete sense. The spirit inside him *is* ancient. I grip my books as worry washes through me. "But why does my boyfriend have to have the deadliest job *unknown* to man?"

"So you're admitting I'm your boyfriend now." His expression instantly brightens.

I roll my eyes. "You know what I mean."

Ethan shrugs. "The Corvus is the best secret 'unknown to man' for a reason. Being that way has kept the human world balanced since the beginning of time." He spreads his arms wide. "That's the extent of my knowledge on the Corvus, Nara. Danielle wants to help me find Harper and find out about this raven book the demon is after, so until I'm fully retrained, she'll be around. I know there's tons more for me to learn about Corvus, but right now training is most important."

I really don't like the idea of Ethan spending any more time with Danielle than necessary. "Why don't we contact the Order? Since they supposedly know all about the Corvus, they can tell us how they fit into the picture. They might also know why the demons want that raven book of Freddie's."

Ethan shakes his head and grips my shoulders. "No. We can't go looking for the Order."

I raise my shoulders. "Why not?"

"When I mentioned their name to Danielle, she flipped and said the Order had betrayed the Corvus in the past and I shouldn't trust them."

"But Fate said—"

"Why would you trust anything Fate says?" he asks, releasing me. "You're his enemy number one, remember?"

It's on the tip of my tongue to tell him about Mr. Wicklow just to see his reaction, but instead I take a breath and hold his gaze. "How do you know you can *trust* Danielle?"

"I just do. She only cares about helping me embrace my destiny."

"And what is that, Ethan? A couple days ago, it seemed like we agreed we were following the same path."

Ethan expels a low sound of frustration before pinning me with an intense look. "You drive me crazy, you know that?" He thumps his chest, then gestures to mine, drawing a line between us. "*We* haven't changed, Nara. I didn't choose this Corvus life. The spirit chose me, but I refuse to let what I am redefine us. I'm sorry I didn't tell you everything before, but I didn't know what I was getting into until Danielle told me what I was. Once I learned my path involved very real, very deadly demons, I wanted to keep all of that as far away from you as possible. I want to keep you safe. The idea of you being attacked by another demon terrifies me."

But you're forgetting we've always been better together, Ethan. We're intricately connected, through our dreams and the ravens. Why can't you see that? Yes, his logic makes sense. It's not like I'm strong enough to fight demons, but I didn't like being shut out from helping where I can. It should be my choice. And really, did I have one? *My* path has led me here too. "I don't want to be attacked by a demon either, believe me, but...wait...are the demons that were inside of Drake and Harper the same demons you've been seeing in your dreams? Are there that many demons residing inside of people?"

He shakes his head. "I think my nightmares were my mind trying to interpret what few demons I'd seen in random people in the past and then meshing those images with all the negative stuff I absorb on a daily basis brushing against people. Because I didn't understand what I was seeing, it became mired and twisted in my dream world. When I explained how my mind had tried to decipher things, Danielle was amazed I hadn't lost it already. That's what happens to some people who can't handle the Corvus inside them. They go crazy."

"Thank goodness for your dragon tattoo."

When he smiles and nods, my stomach pitches. *Danielle must not know how I help him cope then. Ugh,* had *helped!* I'm not sure how I feel about the fact that Ethan hasn't shared our special connection with this girl. A part of me is glad he's kept our bond a secret, but the jealous, possessive side wishes he had shared just a little. "Can you see the demons in people now when you look at them? You didn't mention seeing the one in Harper."

He slowly shakes his head, his brow creasing. "I have to really concentrate. It's like my mind gets in the way of the Corvus, who should see the demon instantly through the human face its hiding behind. Danielle believes I was really close to embracing my Corvus before I left D.C., but now my mind is distracted because it's working overtime trying to remember everything. Even calling my sword is painful, when it should be as smooth and natural as breathing."

"Mr. Harris and Miss Collins. Would you care to join the rest of the students in class, please?" Mr. Wallum speaks to us from the open doorway.

Oops. Guess we weren't as quiet as I thought we were. "Sorry, Mr. Wallum. We're coming," I say.

Ethan nods to the scowling principal and we exit the lounge, following slowly behind. Once our principal turns the corner, Ethan stops and steps into my personal space, his warmth and inviting smell enveloping me. "All I want is to hold you close and remind you how perfect we are for each other. You're the one who took my wheels away, Nara."

I don't miss the irony that Danielle is the one who gave Ethan his wheels back, all shiny and purring to perfection. I start to speak, but he steps back. "Don't say anything right now. Just think about us while I get through this training over the next couple of days. I think my memory will return sooner this way."

As he walks off down the hall, I stare after his broad shoulders and want to scream, "Don't trust her, Ethan!" But I can't deny that Ethan needs this girl's expertise to remember how to fight demons. I grit my teeth through the idea of them working together now, while I try not to think about the fact that they've spent this whole past month "training." *Trust, Nara. You've got to trust him, but there's nothing stopping you from following your instincts and doing what you can to protect him.*

Squaring my shoulders, I pull my phone from my pocket and glance over Lainey's text.

Nara

After school, I drive into the Brick Café's parking lot, my tires disturbing the thin layer of light snow coating the asphalt. Inside, Winter Wonderland is playing, and Lainey and Matt look all cozy huddled in a cushy corner booth drinking lattes and chatting.

As I approach, a pang of jealousy twinges; they look so into each other, as if nothing could tear them apart. I miss having that feeling of security with Ethan. "Hey guys," I say, smiling despite my worried thoughts.

Lainey waves to the waitress to bring me the same drink she's having, then pats the empty space next to her. "Where's Ethan?"

I notice the sympathy in Lainey's eyes and know she saw Danielle follow Ethan after school today. I swallow the pang and make up an excuse. "Danielle knows classic car engines, and since his isn't sounding quite right, she's following him to his mechanic to get the glitches worked out."

"That girl knows cars?" Matt's eyes light up. "Wait'll the guys hear—"

"Matt!" Lainey cuts him off, then turns to me, tension in her expression. "I figured you were in the library researching when I didn't see you in study hall. What'd you find out?"

I nod and slide into the seat beside her. "The library computers are much easier to research on than my phone's small screen."

Matt glances at the smartphone clasped in my hand. "So, what's the verdict on the new girl? She's all the guys could talk about today."

Wonderful. Not only is the football team bewitched, the basketball team is too? I swallow my grimace, then pull up the news video I'd found to share with Lainey. "I knew that man's name looked familiar." Turning the phone so Lainey and Matt can see it, I hit the play button.

As soon as the news announcer ends his story bit, I hit stop and Lainey snorts in annoyance. "She's a freaking heiress? Well, this gets better and better!"

Matt laughs. "That just makes her even hotter." When Lainey swats his arm, he sobers, but continues to chuckle. "Sorry, Lane, but it'll be true for all the guys at school at least. Not that this information should surprise any of them. She did drive off in a Jaguar."

"Did both of you miss the part where she's only an heiress because she inherited this William guy's entire estate when he died?"

Lainey shrugs and looks perturbed. "No, I got that."

As the waitress sets my latte down, I scroll to a tabloid picture from three years ago of Danielle with William at a charity event. The title reads *Rare photo of reclusive Billionaire William Gaston with his newly adopted daughter, Danielle.* "He's what, maybe eight years older than her in this picture. The article says he adopted 'orphan Danielle' when she was fifteen and became her legal guardian."

"Oh, I assumed he was much older." Lainey twists her lips. "He's so young. How'd he die?"

I point to another article I'd bookmarked. "He died in a fire last year, and at the young age of seventeen, Danielle inherited everything."

Matt shrugs. "Guess this means she's the luckiest girl alive, while also proving she's not too old to be in high school."

"Whose side are you on?" Lainey scolds him, before asking me, "How come I've never heard of this William guy?"

Scowling at Matt for poking holes in our distrust of Danielle, I put my phone away. "The only reason I remember his name is because I happened to be translating a website in Latin when the news flash about the D.C. billionaire's death popped up in the feed."

"Why are you taking Latin?" Matt asks.

"I'm not."

His brows shoot up. "You translate things in Latin on your own?"

When I nod, Matt looks at me like I'm some kind of alien. But if I rubbed car grease all over myself, dressed in fitted clothes and grew a few inches, suddenly I would turn him and the entire guy population at school on? *Grrrr.*

"She's weird like that." Lainey flicks her hand before returning her attention to me. "I'm confused. If this girl's home is in D.C., what's she doing here? And how does Ethan even know her? I thought he was in Michigan with his parents?"

Since telling Lainey the "Corvus/trainer/whatever-Danielle-is" truth isn't possible, I spin a backstory my friend will accept. "Supposedly Ethan knew her from middle school before she switched to a foster home in the D.C. area, which is apparently where she eventually ended up becoming William's adopted daughter."

"Wish some rich dude had adopted me. I sure as hell would love to be driving a Maserati right now."

I roll my eyes at Matt and keep talking. "Ethan stopped off to see her on his way back from Michigan. He said she wants to go to Central and decided since she has a friend living in the area, that she'd rather finish up school here, where she has easier access to the campus for interviews, tours, and such." The entire time I'm weaving this fantastical tale, bile is rising in the back of my throat.

"She'll be going to my college too?" Lainey sighs her frustration, then looks at Matt. "How about let's keep Danielle's rags-to-riches story between us. No reason to give this girl a leg up at school any more than she's already got with her sex-on-a-stick curvaceousness."

"You said it, not me," Matt snorts, smiling.

"You must be talking about the new girl," Drystan says before dropping into the seat practically on top of me. "Sounds like the same thing all the ladies said about me when I started at Blue Ridge. Well, at least the 'sexy stick' part."

While Lainey and Matt laugh at his misinterpretation, I say, "That's 'sex on a stick,' Welsh boy." Tilting my head, I tug at my ear. "Do I detect a bit of jealousy? Are you worried your limelight's dimming?" I snicker as I grab my latte and we all slide over to give him room.

"How'd you get here, dude?" Matt jerks his head toward the entrance of the café, confusion in his gaze.

"Maddie and Megan dropped me off." Drystan grins as he glides close once more. Pinning me between his thigh and Lainey's, he amps up his Welsh accent. "And, no, I'm not worried. It's not like I'm interested in the population she's attracting."

Matt snickers. "Point taken."

Drystan grins and shakes his hair, spreading snow all over the table and me, then leans back against the seat. "All these stupid blokes are so sodding gobsmacked by her, their girls are turning to me. Suddenly my end of the pool just got a lot more crowded."

Brushing the snow off my jacket, I take my irritation with Danielle's presence out on Drystan with an elbow to his ribs. "Scoot over. Your bloated ego is suffocating me."

He rubs his ribs as he moves to give me room. "You're growing soft, Nara. That barely hurt. We need to get you back to training."

"It's *snowing*, Drystan." If I went toe-to-toe with him in the mood I'm in, I'd leave more than a few bruises behind.

The look I give him must convey that, because he holds up his hands and chuckles. "Okay, okay. We'll take a pass on training today."

As his laughter subsides, Drystan's green gaze holds mine and I realize he's trying to give me an excuse not to wallow at home. If Lainey and Matt saw Danielle follow Ethan today, then I'm sure Drystan did too. Then again, if a little snow isn't stopping the destruction of pure evil, why am I being such a wimp?

"You know what?" I point to him, my gaze focused. "I think training is exactly what I need. Fierce exercise would do me a world of good."

A broad smile brightens his face, erasing the cocky arrogance. "How about a compromise? You promised to help me with my project, which also involves hard work and exercise. You ready to give it a go?"

When I nod, he grabs my keys from the table and jumps up. "Hope you got your training gear in your car. We only have an hour to take full advantage of it before class starts."

"Class?" I ask, waving to Lainey and Matt as I follow after him.

"Yeah." He opens the door and a gust of snow slams him in the face, making me laugh. Unperturbed, he smiles like he's truly happy. "You'll see. It's everything you asked for and then some."

CHAPTER 13

Nara

"Well, what do you think?" Drystan asks, sweeping his arm wide. The entire basketball court is full of gymnastic mats, ramps, springboards, odd-shaped walls with cutout windows sprinkled between the mats, random sets of stairs along the edge of the mats, and of course a very long, extra-springy slackline strung between two hooks on a far wall for balancing. Anything a parkour lover would want was here in the school's gym right next to the park where we normally work on defense training and some parkour moves.

I take it all in, grinning as I stand in my workout T-shirt and shorts and run my hands up and down my arms to ward off the chill in the air. "Wow, how'd you find this place?"

"Actually, the guy who started this program found me. He saw me outside in the park doing my thing and asked if I wanted to teach a couple days a week. This gym is usually used for basketball practice, but for a couple afternoons a week, it's mine." Drystan wraps an arm around my shoulders and rubs his hand up and down my arm quickly. "Don't worry, once we get going on those parkour moves you've been too afraid to try, you'll warm up fast."

I start to shake my head, still unsure if I'm limber enough to execute the crazy kind of inhuman twists and turns Drystan does effortlessly, when he says, "Oh, and check this out."

I follow him up a ramp and around a wall with several cutout windows, then stare at hundreds of blocks in rainbow colors piled up to the edge of a squared-off pit below the ramp and right next to a set of stairs. "What is it?" I ask, shaking my head in confusion.

"Your favorite part."

"Drystan!" I scream as he shoves me off the ramp. I roll in the air to protect my arms and face from the blocks' sharp corners and tense my back, preparing for impact, but gasp with laughter when I'm swallowed in a soft mound of squishy foam.

"Padding!" Drystan roars right before he dive bombs straight for me.

I scream again and try to roll out of his way, but the blocks are like mini springs. I get thrown right back and end up as a landing pad for Drystan's antics.

Air whooshes out of my lungs and I shove at his shoulders, wheezing, "Get *off* me, you goof."

He quickly rolls away and rubs his chest. "What the 'ell are you wearing under your shirt, a plate of armor?"

I clamp my hand on the medallion. "No, just a necklace."

Drystan leans over me and pulls the medallion out before I can stop him.

"Ravens? Why am I not surprised?" Laying it back on my chest, he shakes his head. "Take it off. It's dangerous to wear jewelry while doing parkour."

I wrap my fingers around the disk and try to ignore the dull throb of pain when the metal pushes against the scar on my hand. "I can't take it off."

He scowls. "Why not?"

"I just can't," I say as I turn over and try to swim/walk to the side of the foam pit.

Standing in the middle of the foam blocks, Drystan releases a breath of frustration. "Then find a way to bind it to your body so it's not swinging around on your neck, Nara. The whole purpose of this—" He sweeps his arm to encompass the equipment in the gym "—is to make parkour as safe as possible for those who want to try it."

"Fine. I'll put on an athletic top under my T-shirt. The spandex should hold it against me. Happy?" I jump when he grips my waist, his thumbs digging into the base of my back.

"You're going to get hot in all those layers," he whispers in my ear right before he lifts me over the pit wall.

I ignore his teasing and move to pick up my sports bag. "I'll be fine. Where's the bathroom?"

Drystan hops over the wall and spreads his arms. "All locked up. You'll have to change right here."

I roll my eyes and glance over at the bleachers pushed against the wall to accommodate all the equipment. "I'll change beside the bleachers. You stay here."

As I'm changing, Drystan shouts from across the room. "Hurry up, Nara. Class starts in forty minutes. Stop hiding back there like a chicken."

"Chicken?" I say as I struggle into the fitted spandex top. "You do realize those are fighting words, right?"

A low chuckle echoes in the gym. "I'm counting on it, right 'nuff."

Jamming my T-shirt over my head, I pull my ponytail free of the shirt and step out from behind the bleachers. "Why do I get the feeling you're intentionally trying to antagonize me?"

Drystan runs full speed across a matt before jumping up the side of a wall, monkey-climbing to the top. Once there, he springboards from the top of that wall to a higher wall before diving straight through the small cutout window of a third adjacent wall, where he executes a perfect landing roll on the matt. He glances up at me with an innocent smile. "Because you need an outlet, and I'm willing to be your punching bag."

I approach him on the matt and grunt my disbelief. "You're nobody's punching bag."

He straightens to his full height and shrugs. "Maybe I just like to see you get all riled."

As he speaks, he punches my upper arm with a fast right hook, then takes off up the ramp we'd been on earlier. I stumble back and rub the sore spot, before chasing after him. "That was a cheap shot, Drystan. I thought this was about me learning parkour."

Drystan's waiting for me, hands raised in battle mode, feet bouncing on the platform. "You'll get all the parkour you want being my assistant in this first class and any others you decide to attend, but you need to be ready for anything, Nara. I'm just making sure *you're* not being anybody's punching bag or doormat or any other euphemism for that matter."

I realize he's referring to Ethan and Danielle. Drystan doesn't know everything that's at stake and the secrets I have to keep, but the implication still stings, especially since there are things *I* still don't know.

Anger wells so fast, my face flames. "I've never been, nor will I ever be the kind of girl who let's people run all over her." Before he can move, I spin into a roundhouse kick and slam him in the chest, sending him flying back into the foam pit.

"Good to know," Drystan says in a wry tone as he stands among the colorful squares and pounds his chest as if trying to regain his breath. Moving to the edge of the pit, his eyes glitter with respectful amusement as he folds his arms on the pit wall. "Now that your claws are out, the gloves are coming off."

My jaw slacks a little when I think of all the bruises I'd acquired while "training" with him. "You've been holding back on me?"

"Hope you don't plan on moving fast during soccer practice." Drystan lets out a pleased laugh right before he grabs my ankles and yanks, tumbling me back into the pit.

Nara

"What's the Dark One doing here?" Drystan sounds annoyed as we walk into the gym ten minutes late for soccer practice.

The last person I expect to see is Ethan, but there he is, dressed in a blue T-shirt, black track pants, and soccer shoes, passing the soccer ball to a guy in the middle of the gym. I smile at him despite the tension between us. It makes me happy to see him dribbling a soccer ball again. I know how much he misses playing.

Five girls from school had shown up for Drystan's parkour class. None of them liked the fact that he used me as his assistant to demonstrate the parkour moves he planned to teach over the next several classes. The girls' tittering appreciation of Drystan prior to class had annoyed the six guys who'd shown up, but as soon as the boys saw Drystan in action, they were all in and pretty much ignored the girls the rest of the class. Once the session was over, Maddie and Megan stayed after to praise Drystan's athletic skill. I stood by the door, sports bag in hand, and kept pointing at my watch to let Drystan know we had to go.

Between the physical sparring session with Drystan and demonstrating parkour moves I've yet to master, I'm absolutely beat. The last thing I want to do is spend forty-five minutes running around in yet another school's gym, but Drystan needs a ride and Lainey has given me a hard time about missing soccer practice, so I have to come to this scrimmage the coach has set up.

I sense Ethan's intense stare while Drystan and I sit on the bench to pull on our indoor shoes, but I pretend like it's no big deal. Let him notice that I have other people in my life to keep me preoccupied. I don't want Ethan to see how much the idea of him spending his afternoon with Danielle bothers me.

I'd just laced my second shoe when a shadow hovers over me.

"Didn't know you played," Drystan says to Ethan in a dry tone as he rises to his feet.

Ethan stares Drystan down. "I only came for Nara, but your team was apparently down some players and the coach asked me to step in to warm up for the scrimmage."

Drystan shrugs off Ethan's dig about our tardiness, then glances at me. "Looks like the scrimmage is about to start."

I don't like Ethan towering over me with that tense look on his face, so I stand too as Drystan trots off. "How was training?"

"Training went fine. I got your message, so I stopped by your house, but you weren't home."

"I was helping Drystan demonstrate moves for his new parkour class. That's the project he asked for my help on."

Ethan's mouth hardens when I mention Drystan. "Parkour?"

"It's a type of exercise that involves jumps and twists across obstacles. Parkour utilizes moves and fast thinking to help you push beyond your limitations."

Ethan crosses his arms and watches Drystan warming up with the ball. "I don't trust him, Nara. I don't think you should either."

I sigh and readjust my ponytail. "While you were gone, he saved my life more than once, Ethan, so he's definitely trustworthy. Speaking of trusting..." I wait until Ethan turns back to me. "That's why I called. I think you should be careful around Danielle. Did you know her adoptive father, or whatever she called him, recently died in a fire that left her inheriting his entire estate?"

His expression hardens. "You've been investigating her?"

I raise my chin. "Someone has to be objective."

"I told you to stop researching—"

"You asked me not to research ravens." I hold his gaze with a bold stare. "And I haven't been."

"Nara?" Lainey calls.

"You coming?" Drystan follows up, kicking the ball in my direction.

Nodding, I trap the ball, then send it back to him.

"Yeah, I see just how objective you are," Ethan says, jaw muscle twitching.

When the coach blows the whistle, signaling the beginning of the scrimmage, I'm surprised Ethan runs back onto the court, but I shake off my unease and try my best to focus on playing.

Of course our coach assigns Ethan to the opposing team, putting him and Lainey on one team and Drystan and me on the other. We play hard and manage to score right away. I'm impressed by Drystan's ball handling skills, but then I shouldn't have been; he grew up playing this sport.

As Ethan shoots for his team, the strength behind his shot makes me cringe for the goalie. I'm thankful I'm not playing goalie tonight.

Each team scores two more shots in rapid succession. Now it's tied, three-three and the competition gets fierce. Ethan and Drystan trade shoulder jabs and hip checks that the coach just ignores most of the game, but near the end of the scrimmage, Drystan rips a shot that curves unexpectedly, and Ethan has to twist sideways to avoid getting smacked in the head.

Thankfully the coach blows his whistle about something else, which gives both guys a few seconds to cool down. But the minute the game starts back up, I swear I hear Ethan say "bite me" and Drystan reply "piss off" the next time they pass each other.

I try to ignore them and keep my focus on the game. Finally an opportunity opens up. I get to the ball first and make a quick pass to Drystan, hoping he'll score the winning goal.

Just as Drystan's about to take the shot, Ethan comes at him from the side. It's a clean slide tackle, knocking the ball away first, but Drystan's legs get tangled in Ethan's, and he goes down hard.

As soon as the coach's whistle shrills, Ethan tries to help Drystan up, but Drystan knocks his hand away and scowls.

"What was that about?" Lainey asks.

The game had gotten pretty intense with lots of players getting physical, but not as much as Ethan and Drystan have with each other. I shake my head. "Proof that pride and testosterone don't mix."

"Slide tackling is only legal outdoors. Ethan had to know the coach would call him on that," Lainey whispers.

Sure enough, the team coach pulls Ethan out, but when Ethan just shrugs and walks straight out the door instead of sitting on the bench, I throw my hands up. "Ugh, guys!"

The scrimmage ends ten minutes later. Everyone probably had homework or dinner to get to, because Lainey, Drystan, and I are the last ones to leave. I'm so beat, I don't say much while I stuff my soccer gear into my bag. Drystan and Lainey follow behind me as I push the gym doors open and walk out into the crisp night air.

"At least it quit snowing," Drystan says, glancing up at the clear sky.

I pause when I see Ethan leaning against my car. I hadn't expected him to wait for me. I look for his car but don't see it. Did he walk here?

Lainey sees my hesitation, then notices Ethan and quickly hooks her arm through Drystan's. "I'm giving you a ride home. I want to hear all about this new parkour class you've started up before you get home and fill my boyfriend's head with bone-breaking ideas."

As she steers Drystan toward her car, I mouth, "Thanks," to her, then call out, "Night, you two. See you tomorrow at school."

Once Lainey and Drystan drive off, my heart starts thumping. Ethan's expression is hidden in the shadows. I'm not sure what to say, so I delay saying anything and instead beep my car. When Ethan doesn't move to let me open my door, my heart starts to race even more.

"I don't like what's happening between us."

His words hurt because they echo my own thoughts. He's feeling the distance too.

Since I can't see his face and mine is bathed in the glow of a nearby building's neon sign, putting my emotions on full display, I shift my attention to the hood of my car. "You said you needed to train, so I'm giving you that time."

He steps close and speaks in a low rumble. "By spending it with the one guy who wants to replace me in your life?"

My gaze jerks to his. "Drystan is just a friend. At least I've taken the time to introduce him to you. I still haven't met the girl who answered my boyfriend's phone and told me he was in the shower…at ten at night!"

Ethan pales a little. "Danielle answered my phone?"

"We've already had this conversation, but apparently you haven't remembered that part yet. By the way, that came before the 'closet scene,' where you told me she was your cousin.'" I don't care if I sound snarky. My nerves are coiled so tight I can't help it. Sighing, I step around him to beep my car again. "It's been a long day. I need to go." As I start to pull open my door, Ethan's hands land on the doorframe and he pushes it shut.

"This memory thing would go a lot faster if you'd stop holding back on me. I sense you're not telling me everything."

I tense at the frustration in his voice, and Ethan leans close, his hips pressing against my butt. "I'm sorry, Nara. Please, don't go." My gym bag drops to the ground as his muscular warmth cocoons my back. "It feels like you're leaving me, and I can't bear the thought. It might be slowing me down, but I'm doing everything I can to remember."

I don't want to be the reason Ethan gets hurt. Guilt makes my hands shake, so I press them to the car's window to hold them steady and bow my head. "This is just so hard. I'm trying to be understanding."

Ethan's warm hands cover mine, and he whispers in my ear, "It drives me nuts to see you with another guy, even if it's just something as simple as riding together to play soccer. I know exactly what he's thinking. I know, because I can't help but want you more when I see you all sweaty and running your heart out." He pauses to press his lips to my throat, murmuring, "Mmmm, salty and sweet."

Tilting my head, I give him access to my neck. I absorb the feel of his hard frame behind me, holding me up and supporting me, even for a few seconds. This isn't full on intimacy. At least I tell myself that as my body yields to his.

"I miss touching you so much." His lips slide up my throat and his fingers fold tight around mine, locking our left hands against the cold glass. I swallow hard, my heart hammering when his other hand falls to my hip to press me closer.

Running hard has intensified Ethan's appealing smell. Or maybe it's hearing him say how much it bothers him to see me with someone else that amps my attraction. All I know is…I don't notice the cold air or the thin layer of snow beneath our feet. His heat and intensity seduce me, making me want him so much my insides quiver and my nerves tingle with excitement.

I press my free hand to his jaw, enjoying the feel of his five o'clock shadow against my fingers. Ethan whispers my name and slides his hand up my shirt. My muscles flex as his fingertips trace slowly along my belly until they come to rest over my thrumming heart, and his thumb slides under my bra clasp. Skin to skin. Warmth melding into warmth. "*My* heart," he rasps before kissing my jaw and pressing his fingers closer, locking me against him.

The pressure intensifies each beat of my heart, making me feel it flow from the front of my chest to my back. But it's not my heart I feel against my back. As Ethan's lips trail along my cheek, I count the beats. Ethan's heart is pounding just as hard as mine. I know it's my imagination, but it almost feels like they're in sync. My heart beats a little faster at the thought.

Ethan's hold tightens on me and just before his lips capture mine, I realize I let this get too far. Why can't I keep my wits whenever he touches me? Gripping his hand, I pull it away from my heart and say in a breathy voice, "What have you learned about our connection when you talked to Danielle?"

He takes a deep breath and shakes his head as if clearing it. "Connection?"

I stare straight ahead and try to calm my racing heart. "Yes, the ravens. You've told Danielle about our connection, right?"

When he stills behind me, I realize he hasn't shared anything about us with the girl. Turning to face him, I hold his gaze. "I think you should tell her about our dreams and our connection through ravens. She might have some insight."

"Answers are really all you want from me?"

He looks so incredulous, I lift my hand to touch his arm. "No, I didn't mean it like that." *Danielle needs to know what you and I have is beyond special; it's a deep, emotional connection. And if she has some knowledge to share that can help us learn more, then great.* But how can I say that without sounding insecure? Before I can say anything, he steps back.

"Then you'll get your wish." His voice sounds flat, his expression shutting down. "See you tomorrow."

"Ethan wait, I—"

But he takes off running and is quickly swallowed by the night.

CHAPTER 14

Nara

You know that roiling, anticipatory feeling you get in the pit of your stomach? That's how mine feels as I stand in the atrium at the front of the school, hanging with Lainey, Matt, and Drystan this morning.

My dreams used to tell me everything that would happen. Now they're nothing but a strange mishmash of worries, fears, and hopes in moving imagery each night.

Last night I dreamed I was running around the frozen woods again, looking for Ethan. I'd call his name and every so often I'd hear him respond, saying, "I'm here." Once I reached the area where I heard his voice, Danielle would pop out from behind the tree, laughing.

From the moment I woke up, my stomach's been wound tight. I'm not sure what I'm feeling, just that my gut's telling me something's in the air. Maybe intuitiveness never goes away; it just adapts to its new environment.

I arrived early, hoping that chatting with my friends would help take my mind off Ethan. I'd been so spoiled when he had that phone. It would've been easy to send a message, saying, "You took what I said the wrong way. That's not what I meant at all." Then again, Ethan's personality is so strong, it's better to have a conversation like that in person, which I plan to do as soon as I can get him alone.

A sudden hush rushes over the crowded atrium. Even Drystan, Lainey, and Matt seem spellbound by something at the front of the school. I glance toward the entrance to see what has caught everyone's attention.

Ethan and Danielle are chatting just inside the door. The breathtaking sight of them, like the same half of an alluring, dark-hued coin, slams my chest as if someone has just clotheslined me.

Standing a few inches shorter than Ethan, Danielle's dressed in all black: fitted jeans, moto boots, and a side-zip leather jacket. Ethan's wearing a black sweater and dark jeans over his boots. While Danielle's hair flows in black silky waves down her back, Ethan's is a mess of spiked sloppiness that opens his face and enhances his chiseled bone structure. They both exude seductive confidence as they pause and scan the crowd.

Had they finally noticed the effect they were having? All I can think is…they look like they belong together. Apparently the crowd shares my thoughts, because several people cast sympathetic gazes my way.

A couple girls stroll past, blocking my line of sight to the front of the school. The dark-haired one glances my way over her shoulder, saying, "Looks like you've been traded up, Nara. Ah well, better luck with the next guy."

I glare at Miranda—the captain of our soccer team—as she turns to Sophia and laughs at her own wittiness. Once they walk off snickering, and the people in the atrium start to buzz and move around the crowded area once more, a warm hand squeezes my shoulder.

"Damn, you weren't kidding about those two, were you?" Drystan whispers in my ear. "If you want, I'll invite them to my parkour class and throw in a self-defense lesson right up front so you can use them as volunteer dummies." The idea of knocking the wind out of them under the guise of self-defense is so appealing I can't help but laugh.

"Nara." Ethan's deep voice floats my way. His gaze immediately snaps to Drystan's hand on my shoulder and his jaw tightens. As Drystan's fingers slip away, I let out an inward sigh of relief and start to respond when Drystan moves closer, his chest brushing against the back of my right shoulder.

"You going to introduce your new friend, Ethan?" he says, laying on his Welsh accent.

Danielle stands beside Ethan, all tall, curvy, and gorgeous, eyeing us with avid curiosity. Her gaze quickly sweeps over Drystan's proximity to me, then a perfectly plucked eyebrow raises in knowing amusement.

Ethan ignores Drystan and steps forward to grip my hand. Pulling me toward him, he turns to Danielle. "Danielle, this is my girlfriend, Nara."

Danielle swings a contemplative gaze away from Drystan, and I shiver as her dark eyes lock on to me. She's beautiful and coolly unreachable, yet at the same time magnetic. She might be smiling, but her eyes are so dark it's hard to read her.

"Nice to meet you, Nara." Sweeping her attention to Lainey, Matt, and Drystan, her smile broadens. "And what are your names? Any friends of Ethan's are friends of mine."

"These are my friends…" I begin, but pause when Ethan tucks me by his side and slides his hand deep into my jeans' back pocket.

"Go on, Nara. Introduce them," he says in a light tone even as his deep blue eyes challenge me to balk.

Apparently I'd flipped his patience switch last night and he was done giving me my space. He's never been so openly possessive before. While a part of me feels relief that he's making it clear to Danielle we're a couple, another part of me wonders how much of this move is for Drystan's sake. Nothing in Ethan's expression tells me that he'd learned anything from Danielle about us.

But he did tell her. I can tell by the way Danielle's sizing me up as I lift my hand toward Lainey and continue, "This is my friend Lainey, her boyfriend Matt, and Drystan, who's here from Wales and living with Matt and his family."

While Danielle nods to them and Matt asks her questions about being new to Blue Ridge, I speak to Ethan in a low tone as I start to slide out of his hold. "You took what I said yesterday the wrong way."

His hand curves in my pocket, cupping my butt and locking me against him. "I don't think I did, but if you want we can talk about it at your house after school."

My heart thumps at the idea, but being alone with him isn't the smartest move right now, especially after yesterday. I can barely think with him touching me. Drystan's "doormat" reminder bolsters my resolve to keep things as uncomplicated as possible between Ethan and me right now. "Did you learn anything about us from Danielle?"

"Just that our connection surprised her. She's never heard of Corvus having the kind of relationship we do." A cocky smile flashes. "Told you, Sunshine."

"How does she know so much about Corvus?" I ask as Danielle

weaves her charisma around Matt, Lainey and Drystan like a spider's sticky web.

"She was trained."

"By whom?"

"Her adoptive father."

My eyebrows shoot up as my friends listen intently to Danielle talk about working on a NASCAR pit crew for six months. At least Matt now knows where she learned about cars. I glance at Ethan, who's watching her too, which makes me grind my teeth. "What is she?"

His mouth presses into a thin line and he nods to Drystan. "What is he?"

Stalemate. This sucks. I sigh and shake my head. "You can't come over later, I have to stop by CVAS to take pictures of the pets who've been there the longest. After Sally saw my pictures of Houdini, she asked me to take ones of the other older dogs romping in the yard for the website. I've got soccer after that. Coach wants us there early for our game. What about later?"

The first bell rings, indicating we have five minutes to get to first class, and as our friends start to leave, we follow behind at a slower pace, entering a side hall that leads to the lockers. "I can't meet later," Ethan says. "We're training 'til late."

I frown. "How late?"

"Not sure yet. Danielle was able to learn information from some guys here at school about Harper. They mentioned places they saw her hanging out recently...some dive bar and a couple clubs. We plan to check the bar out tonight. We'll keep looking until we find her."

I shake my head. "I don't think you should go looking for a demon while your memory is faulty and your training is rusty. That's just crazy."

Confident arrogance tilts his lips. "The Corvus instinct is very strong. I know how to call my sword now. It's getting easier and faster each time I practice. If the demon's still inside her, we'll find out why she wanted that book, and since the book is tied to you, we might learn more about how you and I are connected. That's what you wanted, answers."

"Not like this, Ethan. Wait until your memory returns, then all that training you've had will come back to you."

His face hardens. "If this helps my memory to return faster, I'm all for it."

"Why are you being so stubborn?"

"Because *you* are." Frustration stamps the hard lines around his mouth, but it's the vulnerability banked in his gaze that holds me in place as he reaches for my hand. "Even though I'm the one with the memory loss..." He swipes his thumb across my palm in a slow, leisurely caress. "Why does it feel like I'm the only one fighting for us?"

"Ethan..." That really hurt—a deep in my chest kind of pain. As I close my eyes to hold back the emotions, his finger moves higher, brushing the edge of my scar, and my legs nearly buckle. Instead of the dull pain whenever anything comes into contact with the raised line of skin, a jolt of pleasure shoots down my body.

I swallow my gasp, but can't help the shiver that runs through me as he steps so close I feel his breath stirring my hair. I don't move away. I can't. I inhale deeply, calming my reaction before I open my eyes. "I'm worried for you. Last night I dreamed I was looking for you in the woods. It's a dream I've had several times, but in this dream every time I run toward your voice calling me, Danielle would pop out from behind a tree and laugh, like it was some kind of twisted game."

His lips bend in a smug smile. "You sure you're not just jealous?"

"I'm serious." I grip his hand. "My dream might've been weird, but I woke up anxious and tense."

"I don't want you to worry." Pressing his lips to my temple, he says huskily, "I just want you to love me."

I never stopped loving you, I want to scream, but I'm so afraid he'll break my heart when his full memory returns. As his thumb starts to slide across my palm once more, I look down at our clasped hands and notice he's not wearing his silver ring anymore. I take a step back, untangling our fingers. "Where's your ring?"

He flexes his hand. "I had to take it off during training. I can't grip the sword right with it on."

I nod my understanding, even though not seeing the ring on his finger makes me sad. I lift my gaze to his. "Ethan, it's because I care that I'm worried. Why can't you see that?"

"All I see is you pulling away." Irritation flashes in his gaze as it snaps between our separated hands.

"That's not fair. You know I'm here for you."

Glancing around the cleared hall, he expels a resigned sigh. "I'll be fine, Nara. We need to get to class. I'll let you know when I have answers."

Nara

My phone rings as I drive past Ethan's house.

"Hello?"

"Inara, sweetie. What have you been up to?"

"Hey, Gran." I make a U-turn at the end of the street and then park in the darkest area I can find that'll still give me a good view. *Not much. Just stalking my boyfriend's house at eleven at night.* "I'm just getting back from hanging with my friend Lainey after our soccer game. What are you doing up so late? Aren't you usually in bed by nine?"

My great-aunt Corda—who I've called Gran since I was little—sniffs into the phone. "I can't sleep. I'm worried about Clara. She might drive me crazy at times, but she's like a buckshot of morphine right to my taillight; she keeps me hopping."

A hilarious image of Clara chasing Gran around the Westminster retirement community with a shotgun-sized syringe and a gleeful grin instantly pops into my head. I press my lips together to hold back the chuckle. The subject isn't supposed to be funny, but half the stuff that comes out of my gran's mouth usually is. Both ladies are full of life, yet the fact her friend isn't feeling well is also a reminder that they're in their late seventies and won't live forever.

The thought of something happening to my great-aunt instantly sobers my amusement. "Oh no, Gran. What's wrong with her?"

"She felt a sharp pain in her chest, so they're keeping her in the clinic overnight for observation and tests. I should know more tomorrow before I come over to your house."

"You're coming over?"

"Yes, dear. Didn't your mom tell you she invited me to dinner? How do you not know this already, Little Miss Dreams-a-lot?"

"Um, I haven't been sleeping so well the past few days, Gran." Mom had mentioned that Mr. Dixon was coming over tomorrow. She didn't tell me she'd invited Gran. Introducing the man she's dating to her deceased mother's sister is a big deal. This dinner says Mom's relationship with him is moving to a whole new level. Ugh, I wonder what Aunt Sage will think. Not that telling her will do anyone any good. We may never find my dad. Guilt tugs at me for introducing them, but I can't begrudge my mom happiness. It has been wonderful to see her bloom after so many years of being alone.

"Hmm, that seems to be happening a lot more to you lately," Gran says, pulling me out of my musings. "Make sure you drink warm milk before you go to bed. That'll help. Now, about dinner. I warned your mom that I hope she's ready for an honest opinion. I have no problem telling her if he doesn't measure up to your dad."

From what I can remember, Gran and my dad got along great. Maybe having her over for dinner to meet Mr. Dixon isn't such a bad thing. Then again, as far as Gran knows, my dad just up and left us without a word. I grimace at the conclusion my great-aunt will come to in that area. Mr. Dixon seems to worship my mom already. I wonder what he'll think of Gran's unique way of saying things. "I'm sure Mom will appreciate your opinion, Gran. It'll be like her own mom meeting him." *That's how I feel at least. Corda's my Gran just as much as my mom's mother.*

"Well, I don't know about that. Your grandmother was much more open-minded when it came to men, which is why she got married and had a family. 'Live your life so you never leave regrets behind,' that was a motto my sister lived up to the day she died. Sometimes I wish I'd listened. I remember this one fellow from school chased me all over the place. Who knows what might have happened if I'd let him catch me. He was such a bad boy though. I didn't think I could trust that one with my heart..." She trails off wistfully, then her tone turns upbeat. "I haven't thought about that boy in years. He's just the distraction I needed to get my mind off Clara. Going to try and get some sleep now. Good night, Inara. See you tomorrow."

"I'm so glad you're coming, Gran. Night."

As soon as I hang up, I start to hit the button for my aunt's number when I remember how late it is, so I send a text instead.

Me: Hey! Been busy with school and soccer, but wanted to touch base. Have you heard anything more about Dad?

Aunt Sage: I got one more box from his secretary yesterday. Nothing in it worth having you go over with me, but there's something I want to give you. Am running errands tomorrow and will stop by your house later. Ok?

Me: Sounds good. See you then.

As soon as I set my phone down, my gaze tracks back to Ethan's house. Both his and his brother's cars are in the driveway and the house is dark. How had Ethan's training gone? Had he and Danielle found Harper at that bar?

Ethan's comment that he felt like he was the only one fighting haunted me all day. He's right. I haven't done anything since he returned. I've been too freaked out about his memory loss, worried about the whole Danielle thing, and too scared to make a move for fear of making things worse. But I plan to fix that.

It will definitely be easier to sneak into the house later without waking my mom with Houdini at CVAS for the night. When I went to take pictures earlier, I took him with me. Sally had asked me to bring him so she could take some pictures of us for the "success story" board. He had such a good time playing with the CVAS mascot, Roscoe, she begged me to let him stay overnight. At least he'll be there on time for his appointment the next day.

I start to unbuckle my seatbelt when Ethan's front door opens, snagging my attention. I blink rapidly as he gets in his car and pulls out of the driveway, but doesn't turn on his lights until he's on the street that leads out of the neighborhood. *Where is he going this late?* Of course my mind conjures all kinds of bad scenarios: the whole nightclub thing was just an excuse to party with Danielle, or they're grinding their hot bodies together on a gritty dance floor in some seedy dance club, or she's living in some swanky hotel and Ethan's heading over to do all kinds of kinky things to her perfect body on thousand dollar satin sheets. My heart lurches at any of those options.

Stomach churning, I set my jaw and start my engine. As soon as I put my car into Drive, intending to follow, I get a text from Lainey.

Lainey: Didn't get to talk to you after the game. You feel better after meeting Danielle?

I'm following my boyfriend like a total stalker. What does that tell you? Putting my car back in Park, I shut off the engine and take a deep, calming breath.

I type out: Right now I'm thinking she's a boyfriend-stealing ho-bag. Then hit the delete button.

Me: Not sure. What did you think of her?

Lainey: I don't like how the guys drool all over her, that's for sure.

You and me both, sister.

Me: But what do you THINK about her?

Lainey: She seemed nice enough. Told me she'd come watch us play soccer some time.

Bet she's a star athlete too. *Bleh.* Even though texting Lainey a bunch of symbols, asterisks, and exclamation points would explain my feelings much better, I type my response.

Me: I don't trust her.

Lainey: Ethan seemed more PDAish than usual today. That should make you feel good. Wish Matt would be intense like that every once in a while.

If only I knew for sure that Ethan's PDA wasn't mostly for Drystan's benefit. And that I hadn't just seen Ethan skulk out of his house, especially knowing he had plans to visit a dive bar with Danielle tonight.

Me: Yeah, he was in rare form today. Jury's still out on Danielle.

Way the hell out!

Lainey: She hasn't hit on our boyfriends yet. Seriously, I see the way he looks at you. I have an idea that might help you and Ethan get back in the groove. Matt, Drystan, and a couple friends of his are checking out this newly renovated club Mindblown downtown tomorrow night. Meet us there and bring your man.

Me: I can't. Mr. Dixon is coming to dinner tomorrow and so is my Gran.

Lainey: That would be SO weird having dinner with my teacher. Bet your Gran will liven up the table. She cracks me up! You can still come with us. Most clubs don't get hopping until at least 10pm. Say you'll come and don't forget your fake ID.

As soon as I read Lainey's text, I look up at Ethan's dark house and realization dawns. If he really is looking for Harper, or those who might know where to find her, it makes sense that he would wait until the bar is mostly crowded. Most places like that stay open pretty late.

I bite my lip, mulling it over as I type a message back.

Me: Put me down for a maybe. Might be fun.

Lainey: Good, you're coming.

Me: I said, "maybe."

My phone goes silent after that. Which is probably for the best. No point in arguing with her. I stare at the clock on my dash and wonder how long I'll have to wait for Ethan to return. It might be the wee hours before I get home. Thank goodness my mom's a heavy sleeper.

Nara

After I'd put the key back under the eve on the front porch, I slip inside Ethan's house. I'd waited another forty-five minutes once Ethan arrived home—two hours after he left!—before entering. My heart races as I tiptoe up the stairs to his room.

A board creaks halfway up, and I freeze, holding my breath. *Please let the Harris boys be heavy sleepers.* Several seconds of silence pass before I exhale and continue up the stairs.

Dim light from some lamppost outside highlights Ethan in his bed. He's sleeping face down on top of the covers; it's as if he'd fallen into bed in exhaustion the second he got back to his room. My pulse amps as I admire his broad, shirtless back and his muscular arms; one curves over his head and the other rests by his side. His fitted black boxer briefs outline his nice butt and hard-muscled thighs. My gaze lingers on his legs. I'm stunned by the corded strength of his thighs and his thick calf muscles. This is what I missed out on Saturday night? I swallow a sigh of longing and shake my head to clear it of sexy memories.

Focus, Nara!

Shrugging out of my shoes and leather coat, I pull off my sweater and remove the medallion necklace, laying it on the pile of clothes on the floor. I know the exact formula for seeing Fate and I don't want to screw with that one. My crystal necklace swings as I move, so I tuck it inside my shirt, then set the vibrate timer on my phone before returning it to my jeans' pocket.

I try to move the bed as little as possible as I settle next to Ethan. Exhaling an unsteady breath, I roll onto my side and lay my hand flat on the only part of him that's clothed. My fingers want to cup the hard ball of flesh, but I keep them relaxed and I close my eyes.

If my phone doesn't wake me in time, I hope you'll pull me out, I mentally whisper to the Corvus inside Ethan, praying he can hear me.

My eyes float open briefly and skim over Ethan's dark hair, then down to his handsome face as he sleeps. I hate sneaking in here like a sleep-thief in the night, but I know he wouldn't let me do this. I'm determined to do my part to find answers.

Ethan fights his way, I'll fight mine.

CHAPTER 15

Nara

I squint and raise my hand to block the bright sunlight shining through the floor-to-ceiling glass windows.

Dark wood gleams under my feet and ornate, cushioned window seats line the wall of windows. I'm drawn to the French doors; a massive manicured lawn, sporting benches and its own maze hedge blends into a huge forest surrounding the property. Even though I can tell it's cold outside, I touch the door handle, ready to open them and run down the stone stairs, past the huge columns. I want to explore this peaceful, tranquil place.

A vibrating sensation behind me draws my attention. I turn to see Ethan and Danielle in T-shirts and shorts facing each other. Standing in a battle stance on the room-wide workout mat, her fists in a defensive pose, Danielle says something and waves him toward her. *Why can't I hear her?*

Ethan lowers the wooden sword he's holding and shakes his head. As soon as he takes a step back, Danielle charges him and hits him with such force, he's knocked on his ass. Before he can recover, she's pinned him to the mat with the flat of her wooden sword across his neck.

Scene after scene repeats, Ethan and Danielle working out during the day. Sometimes with a sword, sometimes not. It's hard for me to watch, but I do even as the knot in my stomach grows tighter. Their clothes and the training exercises they perform change, but their expressions only become more fierce, their fighting more dangerous. As the scenes progress, the bright light in the room grows dimmer until they're combating each other in the dark.

I blink, confused by the darkness consuming the room, because I can still feel the sun at my back, warming the top of my head. I glance over my shoulder, and the sun is there, but it stops where I stand, like the wall of darkness they've created is too thick for the light to penetrate.

As I realize I'm seeing what Ethan did this past month he was gone, worry grips my stomach. It might just be a dream, but my concern is real. I call Ethan's name, but nothing comes out. That's why I can't hear them; it's like they're in a dark void and I'm on the edge of it. I step forward onto the mat, intending to bring the sunlight to them, and I'm suddenly swallowed by the darkness too. I turn and try to step back, but the sunlight stays just out of my reach. Coldness seeps through my bones, surrounding me in its frigid grasp. I shiver and my eyelids grow heavy as sleep beckons. I try to fight it, but it's too cold and my legs buckle.

Sudden softness glides around me, surrounding me in silken warmth. As I'm carried away by its comfort and security, I nestle against the warm darkness. When my body starts to warm, I grumble, "I'm such a lightweight" and I could have sworn a rumble of suppressed laughter vibrates against my cheek.

My feet are righted and the softness fades away. My eyes adjust to the bit of light in the darkened bedroom. Ethan leans over a dark-skinned man while he sleeps; the tip of his sword is a hair's breath from the man's chest. Firm resolution sets in the lines on Ethan's face, and I gasp as he whispers, "For Marcus," before he plunges the sword into the man.

The man's body bucks once, then a cloud expels from him. As soon as the cloud dissipates, his body instantly relaxes back onto the bed.

When Ethan withdraws his sword, I ask, "Is he dead?"

He doesn't look up, but the air grows thick with tension. I start to say, "Can you hear me—?" when my world begins to spin; I'm yanked into black nothingness. As soon as electricity crackles in the air, I know this is Fate's doing and not one of Ethan's dark dreams.

"If you can't see, you can't mess," he hisses next to my ear.

His cold breath makes me want to shiver, but I don't give him the satisfaction.

"Too chicken to show your face?" I snort. His body might be nothing but morphed smoke, but I hate being at a disadvantage when it comes to dealing with Fate. Not seeing is a huge drawback.

The sound of a match being scraped echoes, and then a small flame glows near his face, like a kid getting ready to tell a ghost story at camp.

I roll my eyes. "Who knew Fate needed to depend on the dramatic for effect?"

Fate lets out a growling *tsk* and tosses the match behind him. In the blink it takes for the empty space to illuminate all around us, he's towering over me in his shadowy-smoky humanoid form, the dark sockets where eyes should be narrowed in suspicion. "Before I snuff you out for good, I'm curious why you'd risk your life to come here again."

I tilt my chin higher. "I need answers."

Fate throws his head back, laughter echoing in the void. It goes on for so long, I set my jaw and raise my voice over the annoying sound. "I don't care if this doesn't concern you. It concerns me."

Fate's mirth dies, but he smiles, a cold, calculating, deep crescent moon. "It really doesn't matter now." He spreads his arms wide. "You have nowhere to go. Nothing to manipulate. You're all mine."

As a chill starts to rush over me, the first icy tendrils snaking around my body and moving toward my neck, I shrug off the cold as best I can and blurt out, "Can you see demons inside of people?"

"Demons!" Fate spats the word and releases me to fold his cloudy arms. "They're the bane of my existence. And that's saying a lot, considering my present company."

As I rub my arms to ward off the chill, I pause as what he's implying soaks in. "Are you saying that when a demon hijacks a body, the demon changes the person's fate?"

Fate flicks his hand as if batting a fly. "*You* are chaos and will, bundled in a stubborn package." His smoky hand curls into a fist by his side and he spats a loogie of wet smoke by his feet. "A demon-inhabited human is nothing more than a puppet on a string."

He has to hate that more than me. Demons have been around forever. And there are far more of them. Give him a reason not to kill you. Maybe then he'll negotiate. "You said Corvus are none of your concern, but if they keep balance in the mortal world by killing demons, then they're a necessity, even for you. I'm connected to Corvus somehow, but I don't know why."

Fate grunts, but doesn't answer, so I throw my hands wide and huff. "Well? Do you know why?"

"Where your path connects to Corvus, sometimes it's clear, other times it's a void, but I do know—"

When he cuts himself off, I grit my teeth. "What do you know?"

Fate holds a finger up. "Give me something worth this information you seek. Your powers are still on the table. I'll happily take them now. And no more deceit, little girl."

He's willing to deal, which means he's not going to kill me, yet. I tilt my head and stare him down. "Will this information you provide send me into dangerous territory? I was told the Order can't be trusted."

Fate shrugs, unconcerned. "You asked about Corvus. The Order is the authority."

I can't decipher Fate's expression to determine if he's being deceitful or sincere, but I have to find answers, and he knows *something*. He wouldn't be dangling it like a lifeline if he didn't. I think about my missing father and all the lost years I'll never get back, about all the heartache our family went through because of Fate's hatred of our ability. My dad's heartfelt request in the videos come back to me. "Please don't follow my path, Nari…Live *your* life and only yours."

I snap my chin up and lock gazes with Fate. "Fine. I promise never to take a job that uses my unique ability."

"Not good enough! I want you to give it up," Fate demands.

I shake my head. "You asked for a promise. You got one. Your turn."

"Give me your ability, Nara." Fate starts to vibrate at a rapid pace, moving up and down, then back and forth. When a shrill sound I've never heard before rings in my ears, I realize he's beyond losing his temper; he's going to explode.

My insides pitch and churn, but I hold my ground and shake my head. "I answered honestly and sincerely. A deal's a deal."

Words gush from Fate's hyperactive body like spewing vomit, as if he can't control them. His pitch is up and down, flat and shrill, but I hear them. "The answers start and end with the raven book. Go back to its creation."

Fate suddenly stops in front of me and lets out a horrific roar. "You didn't give me what I wanted!"

Before I have a chance to move, he dives into me. Fierce, devastating pain rips a blood-curdling scream from my lips. He's never gone inside me before and the sensation is both excruciating and violating. I can't move, can't breathe. All I can do is absorb the agony of his cold energy spreading through me like fast growing kudzu, flash-freezing my body from the inside out.

I've never felt so cold. My teeth clack together as Fate quickly stretches through my arms and down my neck, his glacial touch solidifying the blood in my veins. As the frost moves down my limbs, I fall to my knees, my body so cold I don't feel the pain of hitting the floor, but I do wonder…*when the ice reaches my toes, will I fall over and shatter into thousands of pieces?*

Fight him, Ethan's voice, full of fear and rage, penetrates my sluggish mind. Warmth radiates from a hard band around my stomach, and begins to penetrate the frozen skin along my spine, shoulders and neck.

"*Wake up, Nara. Wake up now, damn it!*" The command rushes in my ears right before glossy, dark warmth wraps completely around me, breaking me from Fate's cold grasp.

I gasp awake and am thankful I'm on my side as I draw in gulps of air, taking the warmth into my frozen lungs.

"Jesus, Nara. You're freezing. What were you thinking?" Ethan growls from behind me as he throws his bare leg over my jeans and rubs his hand briskly up and down my arm.

"Doing…my…part," is all I can get out through chattering teeth.

"Don't ever do that to me again," he says in a hoarse voice as he slides his leg between mine and moves his hand to my chest to rub the chilled skin in fast circles, creating wonderful, warming friction. Laying his cheek against my neck to give me warmth, he continues, "I tried to shake you. I took off that damned crystal—which you're not getting back. Ever! Nothing that worked in the past, worked. I couldn't wake you. I was out of my mind."

Heat starts to spread through my body, and the more places he touches, the harder my heart pumps. I inhale deeply as his hand slips under my thin button down shirt to rub along my belly in brisk strokes, but when his movements slow to a gentle, caressing glide across my skin, my heart trips and nervous excitement flutters in my stomach.

"You're warming up some. Can you talk now?"

He sounds relieved, his hard body relaxing, melding more fully around mine. I hold my breath and close my eyes while his fingers spread wide and travel up my ribcage, the pressure of his fingers gentle, exploring. "I—heard you yelling for me to wake up. Your voice pulled me out," I finally answer, releasing my breath.

He lets out a frustrated grunt as he cups his hand high on my rib-cage, his thumb rubbing my back. "I don't know how…I've never been able to intervene with Fate before, but I was frantic, Nara. As in ape-shit, freak out mode. It's a good thing Samson sleeps like the dead." Taking a breath, he settles. "I'm just glad something worked. You kept getting colder and colder in my arms." Leaning over my shoulder, he runs his nose up my neck and inhales along the way. Once he reaches my jaw, his fingers tighten on my ribcage, clasping me against him. "Why did you do it?"

He's obliterating my ability to stay unaffected, making it hard to concentrate, but I force myself to focus. "I told you I was doing my part. You said I had stopped fighting."

"What—?" Rolling me onto my back, he lifts my chin, eyes blazing. "That's not what I meant and you know it." His voice softens and his fingers trace the soft skin under my chin in a tender caress. "You've been so distant, it felt like you were giving up on *us*."

Hearing his thoughts voiced rips at my heart. I swallow the sob that wells in my throat and wrap my fingers around his wrist. "Ethan, that's not—"

He captures my lips in a hungry kiss, his fingers sliding into my hair, clasping against my scalp to pull me closer. His kiss is so pas-sionate and fierce, full of worry and love, yearning swells and my body responds instinctively. I press my hand to his warm chest and kiss him back with all the pent up desire I've felt but couldn't express since he woke up in that hospital bed.

Ethan breaks our kiss and moves over me, pulling my hands above my head. "Since you can't believe anything that comes out of my mouth, I only know one way to show you how I feel. And tonight you're going to let me."

His intensity leaves me speechless, and when I don't answer right away, his hold on my hands tightens. "Say yes, Nara."

An arousing jolt of pleasure/pain steals my breath as it ripples down my arm, then shoots straight to my belly and below. I gulp back the shock that Ethan's barest touch along my scar evokes such a primal response. It wasn't just me wanting him so desperately the other day. I hadn't imagined it.

Ethan's lips curve in a wry, pained smile. "I'm tired of seeing flash-es of things that might've happened between us that Saturday night. I'm done trying to decipher what's a lost memory and my own personal fantasies about you—of which there are *many*." His fingers dig into mine, burying our hands deeper in his pillow as he lowers his mouth to my ear and slowly hitches his hips higher. "Ever since I woke up, I've been in a constant state of pained arousal whenever you enter the room. It's like my body knows more than I do."

We were so close that night, Ethan. I bite my lip and try to keep the answer off my face.

Pressing his hardness against me, his voice drops to a deep rasp. "I know you want me too. I hear it in your breathing and feel it in your thumping heart every time we touch. Stop torturing us both."

I love the rough feel of his overnight beard running along my cheek as he pulls back to wait for my response. It feels so good, I whimper. I can't help it. The strong, confident Ethan from that night is back, demanding acceptance. He still hasn't recovered his full memory and probably won't be happy with me for holding back when he does, but my Gran's comment about taking a chance echoes in my head over and over. *Live your life so you never leave any regrets behind.*

I start to nod, but he shakes his head. "I want you to admit the truth about us."

Tears cloud my vision and I blink them away. "I never stopped wanting us."

His mouth hardens. "You said we needed to just be friends."

"Because you left me!" I hiss with renewed anger.

Ethan rolls to his side and leans on his elbow, stunned. "I never left you. Not in the way that matters."

"You didn't trust me to help you. You left me out and kept me in the dark. That hurt so much." There. It's out. The ache in my chest feels lighter, even if my heart still hurts.

He scowls. "I told you why. I wanted to keep you away from all the demon stuff."

I shouldn't have to *tell* him we're better together no matter the odds. He acted like he knew that before he left, but now…it's like that understanding has disappeared right along with his memory. I sigh and get up from the bed. "I know. It's late. I need to get home."

I kick my phone as I lean down to pick up my sweater. Great, so much for that idea. Must have fallen out while I slept. Rolling my eyes, I slide it in my back pocket, then start to reach for my sweater just as Ethan's voice, dark with anger, comes from directly behind me. "You took my wheels away, Nara. Ripped them right out from under me.

That fucking hurt."

I whirl and face him, sarcasm my new best friend. "At least we're both equally ticked. Got any news from your tryst with Danielle tonight?"

"Not yet," he bites out his annoyance. "Learn anything from your death wish visit with Fate?"

"Just that Freddie's book is important," I say, narrowing my gaze.

He clenches his fists by his sides, his eyes shining like obsidian in the dim light spilling into his room. "You almost died learning what you already knew?"

"God forbid I thought you were worth it." I lift my chin and hold my hand out. "I'd like my crystal back now."

"Screw this!" Ethan grips my hand and yanks me forward. The second I slam against his chest, he clasps the back of my neck and captures my lips in a primal, heated kiss.

Gripping his shoulders, my head reels as every emotion I'd held back flows out and I surrender myself to his kiss. The pressure of his lips lessens, but the tension in his arms remains as he murmurs against my mouth, "I love you, Sunshine. Even the stubborn parts."

"Just remember you said that," I pant back and run my nails down his back.

Ethan's chest rumbles with a groan as he slides his tongue sensually past my lips, enticing a deeper intimacy. When I stand on my toes to wrap my arms around his neck, he clasps my hips and presses against me, sending goose bumps spreading across my skin.

"My life is never worth risking yours for, Nara," he says as he grabs my rear and lifts me into his arms. "When are you going to get that through your head?"

Wrapping my legs around his waist, I press a chaste kiss against his mouth and pat his jaw. "The second you get it through yours that we're a team…we're stronger together."

Defiance flashes in his eyes, then he takes a couple steps and drops me onto the bed. Before I can recover, he's hovering over me, his strong shoulders blocking me in. "I'll never willingly put you in danger. It's not in my DNA."

I pull my phone out of my pocket and set it on the bed next to us as I sit up to lean close, almost touching my lips to his. "Is that Ethan or the Corvus in you talking?"

My teasing question makes him frown. "This is all me, Nara.

There's no room for the Corvus between us."

I put my hand on his cheek, surprised by the sudden fierceness in his tone. "But you said the spirit is part of you."

"I don't share you," he says, shaking his head in three quick jerks. "Not with it, not with anyone." Pushing me back onto the bed, he drops his knee between my legs as he plants a slow, worshiping kiss to my chest. "Not now." Another heated kiss sears my skin a bit lower as he releases the first button on my shirt. "Not ever."

While his fingers undo the buttons down my shirt, he feathers light kisses along the swell of my breast above my bra. I try to remain focused, but he's quickly hijacking my ability to think. Before I lose my thoughts completely, I say, "It's totally my choice to share...or not. No one owns me. Remember?"

He finishes the last button, then flips the bottom flap back to press a lingering, reverent kiss to my belly button before he looks at me, a dark, knowing smile curving his lips. "You won't want anyone else, Sunshine."

"Arrogant much?" I say even as my skin tingles from his warm kiss.

Ethan settles beside me and clasps my hand. "I just know we're deeply connected. Tonight will prove just how deep that connection goes," he continues, absently sliding his thumb across my palm.

Unable to stop myself, I moan and arch my back, completely undone by the sensation of his thumb pressing on my scar.

"Are you okay? I'm sorry. I didn't mean to hurt you." Concern etches into his expression as he turns my hand over, inspecting my palm. "Is this what that gauze was covering the other day? What happened?"

His worried gaze locks with mine. If he knew the truth—that this scar is like his own personal aphrodisiac shot for me—his arrogance meter would explode. I start to laugh, but cough, catching myself just in time. "It's just a scar. I cut my hand on your sword."

Confusion flickers on his face. "But you never touched my sword."

"Actually, your sword touched me. Remember when we woke up in your hospital bed and we jerked upright together?" As he nods, I hold my hand up and fold my fingers over the scar. "It must've been forming on your back as you were coming out of the dream. That's when my hand brushed it."

"I'm sorry I hurt you." Ethan clasps my hand and turns my palm toward the light coming in the window, his brow furrowed. "But I don't understand. A Corvus' sword can't hurt a human. They're meant for demons."

I snort. "Are you forgetting you turned Drake's body to ash?"

Ethan folds his fingers around my hand. "That's only if I turn my sword while it's buried in the person. If I just plunge it in their chest, it kills the demon inside, but leaves the person unhurt."

"Then why didn't you just kill the demon inside of Drake?"

"Because he'd killed once that we knew of and he tried to kill you. The evil residing inside him wasn't just below the surface, it permeated his whole being. He was just as guilty. Most of them are."

Another question pops into my head, but Ethan gently tracing his finger from my nose, down my throat, to the top of my shirt erases all thoughts of demons from my mind.

My skin prickles as he brushes my top back, exposing my bra and bare stomach.

"I've dreamed of this so many times," he whispers huskily as his fingers gently trace the sensitive swell of my skin above my bra. When his hand reaches the bra clasp in the center of my chest, he pauses, quiet sincerity in his voice. "I don't ever want you to regret anything that happens between us, Nara. Are you sure?"

I touch his jaw and smile. "I've never been more sure of anything."

Ethan presses a quick kiss to the inside of my hand, but just as he unsnaps my bra, his eyes flick to mine, recognition in his gaze. "This has happened before, hasn't it? But it was daylight, not night." His brow furrows. "I remember a ribbon." Frustration shifts in his eyes and his tone turns gruff. "How far did we go?"

I slide my fingers down his arm, not wanting to break the truce we'd managed. "Does it matter?"

His mouth sets. "Did we have sex? God, Nara, I deserve to know."

I shake my head, my lips twisting in a wry half smile. "You got to second, not third base. No home runs or grand slams. For the record, you were the hold out."

Ethan chuckles, touching my pouty bottom lip, then ponders for a second before nodding. "I never would've left you after that. It would've been too painful, like leaving a vital part of me behind."

Shaking his head as if to clear it, he kisses my forehead. "The only memories that count are right now," he says, before he slowly brushes my bra aside as if unwrapping a much-desired Christmas present.

My heart is pounding insanely fast, but Ethan surprises me in this "redo." He doesn't instantly go for the gold—I mean, come on, when guys think for one second they'll get a glimpse of your boobs, you won't see their eyes the rest of the night. Instead, Ethan lays his hand under my left breast and cups my ribcage in a firm hold, while pressing his thumb to the center of my chest. "I meant what I said that night by your car, Nara. This is *my* heart. Mine to love. Mine to cherish. I love you. I'll always love you. You make me better than I am."

Excitement and sheer joy thrum through me, but when Ethan leans over and presses a kiss where his hand had been and whispers, "You make me whole," tears trickle down my temples.

I slide my fingers in his thick hair and clasp his head, pulling him up until our foreheads touch. "I told you, we're a team."

"A *very* close team." He grins and moves his hand up to cup my breast.

I laugh and smack his shoulder. "You're such a guy."

He smiles and plants a lingering kiss on my lips, then trails his mouth down my chin and neck, making sure to kiss each collarbone before moving lower.

My breath catches in my throat and I clasp his head and press him closer, wanting him to hurry yet hoping he takes his time.

Ethan's mouth is warm, moist decadence as the heat moves down my chest in slow, torturously sweet kisses. The cool air hitting my breasts make them extra sensitive to the warmth of his breath as he hovers over them, so close but not touching. "Stop torturing me," I pant, then gasp when his hand cups the inside of my thigh and he slides me flush against his hard-muscled body.

"Shhh," he whispers as he massages higher up my thigh. "I want you as close as possible so I can feel every response."

"I can think of a few ways to get closer—*ahhhhh*," I exhale, my fingers digging deep into his scalp as his mouth finally connects. Searing warmth surrounds and pulls against me, sending waves of pleasurable tremors shooting out to every part of my body at once.

"So sweet," he murmurs against my chest. "And all mine," he continues as he slowly traces his thumb from the top of my thigh to the seam of my jeans.

Wonder and bliss spiral through me and I moan, arching against him, digging my fingers into his bicep.

I feel Ethan smile against my breast. The torturer. But when he quickly glances up at me, his gaze reflects recognition and his heart thumps harder against my side. Moving his thumb back to the top of my thigh, he presses against my jeans. "You have a birthmark here. It's white and in the shape of an upside down heart."

I shake my head. "But we never went that far. How do you know that—" As soon as the words leave my mouth, I realize how. He must have seen it when he slipped that raven feather between my underwear and hipbone while I was sleeping.

My phone starts buzzing beside me on the bed. I roll my eyes, thinking, *I'd be dead by now if I'd depended on my phone to wake me.*

"What?" He pauses and sits up, his brow creased.

I grab my phone to turn it off, but when I turn it over in my hand, I realize it's not my phone but Ethan's.

Danielle: See you at seven tomorrow. XXX

I must have picked up his phone from the floor by mistake. I instantly sit up and shove the phone into Ethan's hand. "This is yours. I have to go."

Ethan grips my hand as I try to get up. "Nara, wait. What's wrong?"

I pull my hand free and close my bra, nodding to the phone in his hand. "You told me you had no use for your phone now that you were home. Apparently Danielle gave you a reason."

He drops the phone on the bed and sighs. "It's the only way I could keep my brother from finding out about Danielle while I'm training. Having to explain her means explaining far more than my brother can handle."

"How do you know? Have you tried?"

"Have you told your mom about your dreams?"

I shake my head, annoyed that he has a point. "How does your brother think you got your car?"

"Samson thinks my dad took care of the bill."

Ugh, do guys ever communicate? "Whatever." I don't even bother buttoning my shirt. I just put the medallion back on and tug my sweater over it. Ethan's standing beside me as I shrug into my jacket.

"Please don't go, Nara. I've tried to explain. I don't text anyone on it. Just meeting times and stuff."

I step into my shoes and pull out my keys. "It's late. I have to go." Before I walk out of his room, I glance over my shoulder and say, "Oh, your *cousin* sends her triple-X love."

Ethan

"Shit!" I dig tense, shaking fingers into my scalp and welcome the pain as I pace the room after Nara leaves. It takes everything inside me not to go after her, to pull her close and press her heart to mine. To show her she can't deny what's between us no matter how mad she gets at me. I start to grab my keys and follow her, so I can make sure she gets home okay, but I know I'm the last person she wants shadowing her.

Finally being able to touch Nara, to be given that trust and have it yanked away, makes my chest ache. Her floral smell still floats all around me, the softness of her skin tingles my fingertips and her sweet taste lingers on my lips, but it was watching her react to my touch that made the whole experience with Nara pure heaven.

I never wanted it to stop. *Fucking hell.*

Now that I've had a taste of a deeper intimacy with Nara, I want her so bad I'm shaking with need. I clench my hands to keep from punching my bedroom wall and try to shake off the pent up yearning that's making it hard to focus my thoughts.

Being unable to think straight isn't a good place for me to be while hunting demons. It almost got me killed tonight, but I managed to keep my head in the game. Even though we didn't find Harper at that club, I learned a couple other places she might hang out, thanks to a guy who wishes he'd never met me. At least there's one less demon roaming Blue Ridge now.

I should feel good about that. A part of me acknowledges the accomplishment, but another part resents feeling conflicted and tense about all this Corvus stuff. Maybe once my full memory returns, my body won't feel like it's in a constant state of tug-of-war. As soon as Nara left, my entire frame started tensing up again. It's like she unwinds me somehow. I don't know how to put to words the calming effect she has. All I know is…I hate feeling like the darkness inside me is gaining major ground. I thought I had it firmly shoved away, but it seems to be claiming more territory lately.

You really didn't think you'd gotten rid of me, did you? Gravelly Voice laughs heartily. *You don't want to know or accept me. But I'll always exist. You live in the dark. Own it. Solitude is your only true companion, the only thing you can depend on. Everyone else will just disappoint you in the end.*

"Fuck you!" I growl and rake everything off my desktop, sending books, pens, papers, and cups to the floor.

I hate that even an ounce of what he says is true. And since Danielle didn't mention anything about Corvus having a constant "other" voice talking inside their heads, I never mentioned my persistent pain-in-the-ass companion. I only told her about my nightmares. She'd said when the Corvus spirit first merged with a body, the person would think they were losing their minds; they suddenly saw things that couldn't possibly be real, they had memories that weren't theirs and had talents they'd never been taught (at least that answered where my untrained ability to play guitar came from).

Once they learned that their Corvus carries memories of previous hosts before them, they had a much easier time accepting the spirit and eventually adapted. If Danielle knew about the voice, she really would think I've lost it. And she'd probably stop training me.

Danielle's the one who screwed up your reconciliation with Nara. Not me.

Raging anew, I quickly send a text back to Danielle.

Ethan: Do NOT text me any more. I'll text you when I need to know where to meet.

Danielle: Why is sending you a text suddenly a crime?

Ethan: No more XXX stuff. Nara saw it and flipped.

Danielle: At 3:00 a.m.? Tsk, tsk. Didn't think she had it in her. Color me surprised.

Ethan: I mean it. No more texts.

Danielle: Training and regaining your memory come first.

Ethan: I'll decide what's important.

Danielle: Do you want to die?

When I don't respond to her text, she sends another.

Danielle: Fine. Whatever.

Tossing my phone down with a grunt of frustration, I quickly pick it back up and send Nara a text.

Ethan: I'm sorry. That wasn't how it looked. That's just Danielle being Danielle. Let me know you got home safe. We can talk tomorrow, okay?

I pace and wait ten minutes. When she doesn't text me back, I send another.

Ethan: I'll keep sending texts until you answer.

I wait another ten minutes, and just as I start to type another text to her, Nara answers.

Nara: Home.

Just one word. The lack of any other response—not acknowledging my question or even just railing at me—says a lot.

Told you, solitude is your future. It always has been.

Gravelly Voice doesn't sound gleeful like I expect. He sounds resigned, almost sad, and for some reason that's even harder to swallow.

"Shut the hell up!" I fall into bed, knowing I'm in for a sleepless rest of the night.

CHAPTER 16

Nara

Patch's glass tapping wakes me late in the morning. I yawn, surprised he's here at eleven as I quickly step to the window to let him in.

"Morning, Patch. What have you been up to?" As he steps onto the windowsill, I glance outside and all traces of snow are gone, and gray storm clouds are brewing. "Wow, it's warm. This weather is so weird for December."

The bird's presence reminds me of Ethan and how angry I was last night. I'm still not happy, but while trying to fall asleep, it occurred to me that he was using "guy logic" in his need for a way to communicate with Danielle. I consoled myself with the fact that he'd kept his contact with her on his phone to a minimum in the past and finally fell asleep, just frustrated that our night together had been ruined.

Of course, all night long I dreamed about Danielle in the forest again. Then the scene switched to her standing next to my desk in my bedroom while I'm trying to translate a document. She flicked her long, gorgeous hair over her shoulder and lectured me about Ethan's training schedule. I might have woken up less upset with Ethan, but Danielle was definitely on my "I'm going to deck that girl sometime soon" list.

Patch hopping onto the back of the seat near the window pulls my mind out of the clouds. The raven pauses and turns his head back and forth, glancing around the room as though looking for something.

I smile at his head twitching. He's looking for Houdini. "Houdini's having a sleepover." I sweep my hand around the room. "See? Not here. You don't have to be on your guard as much today."

Patch bobs his head and makes several *tok, tok* sounds, then flies over to my desk to wait for me to give him some paper to shred.

I turn on my laptop and while it's booting up, I ball up a piece of paper and set it in front of him. When he looks at me like, "What am I supposed to do with that?" I snicker. "Since you ditched me for a while, I'm challenging you today. You'll have to figure out how to unravel it before you can shred it."

While Patch pokes his beak at the new object before him, I slide Freddie's book out from between my mattress and think about Fate's statement: *The answers start and end with the book. Go back to its creation.*

I flip through the pages, my brow furrowed as I read through it front to back once more. Unless the book is written in some kind of code, I'm not really sure how the pages on raising a raven can help me. Sliding my necklace over the spine, I watch the hinge pop open, then pull the necklace off so the hinge closes.

"Whoever came up with this design to hide that scroll was genius," I murmur.

Patch looks up from batting the ball of paper on my desk with his foot, letting out a frustrated *gronk*. "Fine. I'll give you a hint," I say and pull one corner of the paper out of the ball. As soon as I set it down, Patch dives onto the corner, attacking it in full shred mode.

I laugh. "You're welcome for unlocking the puzzle for you."

The raven completely ignores me, intent on his mission of destruction.

As my gaze swings back to the book, an idea forms. I quickly thumb to the front, looking through the acknowledgements and past the author and illustrator names to a listing for the book designer: Madeline Strauss.

I start to type her name into the Internet search engine when a breaking news alert pops up on my screen.

TRAIN DERAILS IN PARIS, FRANCE. CARS TORN IN HALF. *Hundreds are injured. The number of casualties are yet to be released. An investigation is underway as to the cause of the derailment.*

I click on the news feed to watch the reporter, but the video instantly cuts over to an eyewitness's cell phone that caught the accident on camera. As I watch the event unfold, my jaw falls open. All anyone else will see is the train jumping off the track and then ripping apart.

That's not what happened. I saw a huge ripple between our world and the veil push the train off the track. Then three balls of fighting angel-demon fury tore open the veil surrounding our world like a cheap zipper, ripping the massive train car in half. The opening they tore through, warbled, then it sucked backward, closing instantly as if it had never happened.

The screaming people are oblivious to the whirling dervishes that slam to the ground among the wreckage and smoke. If I had blinked I would have missed it myself; they turned to spirit form that quickly. I'm pretty sure Ethan would have brought it up if he had remembered me telling him that I can see this kind of anomaly happening. I transfer the video to my phone to show Ethan later; three demons coming through the veil at one time seems like a lot. Not to mention it wasn't that long ago that I witnessed a similar event on the way to school. This can't be normal for demons to fight their way into our world this often. Otherwise the angels aren't doing their jobs very well.

Shaking my head, I type in Madeline's name and discover there are seven Madeline Strauss' living in England, but none of them appear to have anything to do with publishing. I dig deeper and click on the website of Madeline Strauss, a designer of wooden puzzle boxes.

I glance at the book's clever concealment department and nod. This has to be her. Clicking on the contact form on her website, I compose an e-mail.

Dear Ms. Strauss,

I recently inherited a certain book with unusual properties that I think you were responsible for creating. I would love to discuss it with you. In case you're wondering, I also own the necklace that goes with the book.

Sincerely,

Inara Collins

I read over the email once more, making sure that I don't give anything away, but that I also included enough information so that Ms. Strauss knows I'm supposed to have the book. As soon as I send the e-mail, Patch squawks, demanding my attention. He's taken the paper ball to the floor, but still hasn't figured out how to pull it apart.

Laughing, I walk over and pick up the paper. "You want this? You're going to have to get it." As soon as I toss it across the room onto my bed, the bird quickly flies over and retrieves it in his beak, then flings it toward me. It lands at my feet and I snicker as I pick it up once more.

"Oh, you want to play, do you?" This time I toss it onto shelving behind my desk, where it lands on a pile of books. Patch starts to fly toward my shelf, but quickly lands on my desk where he makes harsh clicking sounds while bobbing his head up and down. He's scolding me for putting it where he can't easily fly to get to it.

I walk over to my desk and decide to try something I never have before. Sliding my hand slowly toward his feet, I say, "If you want it, you'll have to let me help you." Patch eyes my hand warily and takes a couple steps back. I inch my fingers closer. "How bad do you want it, hmmm?"

Fluffing his wings, he pigeon-walks toward my fingers, surprising me when he steps onto my hand. Amazed by his trust, I slowly tilt my hand so he knows I'm going to lift it off the desk soon. Patch quickly side-walks up my hand, to my wrist, then he moves to my arm as I raise it off the desk. "See that wasn't so bad, was it?"

The raven isn't looking at me though. He's eyeing the ball of paper and clenching his claws into my skin. "Okay, okay," I say, trying not to wince. "Here's your reward for trusting me." The second I get close enough to the books, he hops off. Watching him navigate over taller books, then shorter ones, fully intent on his quarry makes me laugh. I start to help him over an extra tall notebook when an incoming email beep pulls my attention away. I turn to check it out and quickly open the email, my heart racing.

Dear Inara,

I would prefer to video chat with you if possible. Do you have the capability on your computer? If so, use this email address and log in.

Excited, I send an email back.

Just give me a few minutes and I'll ping you.

Once I get the video program pulled up, I run a brush through my messy bed hair, then hold my breath while dialing the video call. A few seconds later, a woman with a soft gray bun and friendly light green eyes pops up on my screen.

"Hello, Inara. It's nice to meet you."

I smile and nod. "You can call me, Nara, Ms. Strauss. Thank you so much for taking the time to talk to me."

"It's no bother, dear, and please call me Madeline. I'd hoped I would get to meet the person whom the book was meant for. It has been so long, I'd almost given up." Pausing, she nods and smiles at the shelving. "I see you have a friend behind you."

Patch has finally gotten to his paper and figured out how to unravel it. Now he's walking back and forth across several books with the paper in his beak, shaking his head like a dog with a prized bone.

I laugh and return my gaze to the screen. "Meet Patch. He's been trying to figure that out all morning."

She chuckles, then her expression settles. "I'd like to see the book you e-mailed me about if you don't mind."

I retrieve the book from my desk and hold it up to the camera where I turn it so she can see the front, the spine and the back. "Here it is. I was hoping you could tell me more about it."

She pulls a pair of black half-moon glasses from the top of her head, dropping them to her nose as she leans close to her screen to peer at the book. Glancing at me above her frame's rims, she says, "You said you have the necklace too?"

"It was a gift from my grandmother. It's right here." I quickly lift the charm lying on my desk toward the book's spine. Once the charm attaches to the symbol on the spine and the metal piece at the bottom of the book pops open, Madeline presses her hands to her cheeks, her eyes glistening with unshed tears.

"I didn't know if I would get to see the two pieces come together in my lifetime. I'm so happy to see this, Nara. Truly happy. Please, can you tell me what was inside?"

Disappointment is so strong, my hands tremble as I set the book and necklace down. "You don't know?"

She smiles gently and shakes her head. "I have no idea. A young, handsome man with unusual eyes the color of a lion's came to me a long time ago. He asked me to create the book cover and hand paint everything you see on it. He gave me every detail. At the time I thought it was an odd request, but I love puzzles so I did as he asked. I truly enjoyed working on that piece. It was by far the most unusual item I've ever made. And it also came with such a huge reward and responsibility, I've never forgotten it."

"So you don't know anything about Corvus then?"

"I didn't say that." A mischievous sparkle lights her pale green gaze. "I said I didn't know what was eventually hidden inside the book. I do know, whatever it was, it's very important to the Corvus."

I grip my desk and lean forward in my chair. "You know about

Corvus?"

Madeline bobs her head. "Of course, my passion is history. I read everything, and I've always had a strong curiosity about ravens. Why do you think I was chosen to create the book? I'd been researching ravens' existence across various mythos and legends, their presence in battles and in all types of religions. I kept trying to connect the dots, but our world is too large, the references too scattered and seemingly as unconnected as the stars.

"As my reward for creating the book, I was told the story of how Corvus came to be. I'll bet you didn't know the real reason the raven didn't come back when it was sent out from the Ark after the great floods, do you? It wasn't because he was selfish. The raven was a messenger sent to let the Master Corvus know to get ready to start over." Flipping her hand, she makes a *pffft* sound. "The raven had *the* most important job, but the poor bird has been portrayed as untrustworthy in history, while the dove and its olive branch got all the glory." Pausing to shake off her frustration, she tilts her head and studies me. "Though I'll admit, I didn't expect someone so young to be the one responsible for unlocking the book's secret."

I grimace slightly, feeling inadequate for not remembering what was inside. "Can you please tell me more about the Corvus? I'm supposed to help, but I feel like I'm still in the dark. Where did Corvus come from? And do you know anything about the Order?"

Madeline lifts her finger. "I can answer your first question, but the second one I know very little about. All I know about the Order is that they were the overseers of the Corvus. The Order knows Corvus' history here in the Mortal world. I just know why Corvus exist."

I spread my hands wide. "Anything you can tell me would be helpful. I know I'm connected, but just not why."

Nodding sagely, she asks, "So you understand the existence of demons, yes?"

I nod. "I understand demons are real and not just fiction, and that they possess humans. I know Corvus' main purpose is to keep balance in the Mortal world by sending the demons to Under."

"Excellent." Madeline claps her hands like a proud teacher. "That's correct. Do you know the story of Lucifer, Nara?"

I start to nod, then halt. "Well, I know the version I learned in church. Lucifer was one of God's most powerful angels, but he felt that God favored his human children over his angels, so he rebelled. As punishment for his sins, God cast Lucifer from heaven, along with the legion of demons who felt as he did."

"That's correct. As it was historically written, God allowed Lucifer to roam free in the human world, because he believed in the ultimate good of his mortal children, and that they wouldn't be swayed by demon-whispered persuasion. But Lucifer's demons—known as Inferni or Inferi for a single demon—didn't stop at persuasion, they began to possess the bodies of God's children and make them do things against their will."

"Can demons possess anyone?" I interrupt as I suddenly realize that the evil presence I'd felt pushing against me when Harper attacked me was the demon trying to take possession. Now I know what she meant by, "I'll take what I want."

"Ah, possession." Madeline taps her temple. "A human with a darker mind is easier for a demon to possess than a person with lighter, positive inner strength. In other words, the weaker your will, the easier it'll be for a demon to break through it. They'll even mess with your head if they can. And if you can sense them, like some people have the ability to do, they'll appear monstrous. Evil and vengeance has twisted them so far from where they began as beautiful angels. So, the short answer is, it's not impossible for demons to possess just about anyone, but it's just not as easy. That's why they prey on the weak, seeing them as easy pickings."

I shake off a shiver; the idea of a demon trying to possess me makes me nauseous. I'm so glad it failed. Fate might hate my strong will with a passion, but that's probably what saved me. "Is demon possession why Corvus are so important? Can't priests or ministers or pastors cast demons out too?"

"People in certain religious positions can only cast out a demon from a person, and even then, not all of these men or women are strong enough to do that." Madeline's eyes glitter with excitement. "Corvus was the ace up God's sleeve, so to speak. As much as God believed in the overall good of his human children to resist evil's temptation, he wasn't just going to allow Inferni to roam the earth unchecked. He knows their nature, their jealousy, and their pride. They are, after all, fallen angels and far more powerful than humans. Mortals wouldn't stand a chance against them.

"Since the Corvus spirit considers the Mortal plane its territory to protect, it wants all aspects of our world to flourish. God struck a deal with Corvus to protect those who can't protect themselves until the fallen angels who betrayed God are finally judged."

"So that's how it all fits together," I say in wonder. "You're right, the pieces were all there."

She smiles, nodding. "So yes, even though their existence isn't known in our history, the Corvus play a vital role, sending demons that possess humans to Under. Unfortunately, unlike Furiae, Inferni can return if they can find a way back into this plane through the veil. Of course, God's angels don't make that an easy task, but the Inferni sometimes get through."

The recent train wreck pops into my mind. "How do the Inferni get through?"

"My understanding is that there has to be a weakness in the veil for them to even try to enter."

I lean closer to the screen. "What causes weaknesses in the veil?"

She purses her lips. "I believe natural disturbances beyond the ordinary can weaken the veil."

A warm breeze blows into my room and I glance at the stormy clouds. "Like crazy weather?"

She nods. "That's possible, I suppose, but think on a bigger scale, like an earthquake, a volcanic eruption, hurricanes or a tsunami...basically anything sudden and severe that disturbs our world's balanced, steady state. The more often that happens, the more cracks in the veil." She tilts her head, concern etching her brow. "Come to think of it, there have been a lot more natural disasters in the world news lately."

Ugh, which means more opportunities for Inferni to break through. The tiny hairs on my arms stand up with just how deeply the Corvus is ingrained into humans' overall existence. I don't think Ethan knows how far reaching his destiny is. He seems to be running mostly on instinct. "You mentioned Furiae. Are they demons too? Where did they come from?"

Madeline moves her glasses back to her bun. "Yes, Furia is a lower demon—or Furiae for more than one demon—that is created when a human is killed by a Corvus while possessed by an Inferi. That human's soul is bound to this plane and becomes a slave to Lucifer as a Furia; a demonic spirit that can possess a human body too. The difference is... when Corvus send Furiae to Under, it's permanent. Furiae can never return to the Mortal plane."

A book falls from the shelf behind me, making me jump and my heart race. "I think it's time for you to get down from there, Patch." I stand and put my arm up for him to hop on. Once I move him to my desk and he hops down, Madeline laughs.

"I've never seen a raven take to a person quite like that one has to you, Nara."

I twist my lips as Patch tries to remove my pencils from the holder. One of his feathers is sticking out from his wing, but I don't dare try to smooth it down. I value my fingers too much. "He's very entertaining company, that's for sure." Returning my attention to her, I try to think of as many questions as I can while I have a Corvus resource in front of me. "Do you know anything about the Corvus, like how its spirit chooses who to merge with?"

Madeline shakes her head. "I know very little about that. I just know that a child is somehow chosen—tagged—by one of God's angels as a candidate, but it's up to the Corvus spirit to choose who to inhabit. Angels cannot communicate with Corvus directly. The spirit is more evolved and operates at a much higher vibration than angels."

Fate had spoken about Corvus as plural, but she's talking about Corvus as a single entity in spirit form. "Isn't Corvus more than one? That's what I was told at least, but I don't understand how the Corvus spirit can exist in more than one body at a time. Inferi can only inhabit one body at a time, right?"

"Ahhhh." The older woman wags her finger at me, a knowing smile on her face. "You're a smart girl. I love that you ask such good questions. This is the reason the term Corvus is used for both a single Corvus or more than one—because they all come from one source. Remember, I said that Corvus is a highly evolved spirit, which is different from demons. To protect against demons, the spirit gives up a piece of itself for each Corvus that's created. There can only be as many Corvus as there are Inferni, which includes the Inferni in Under, since they don't really die and can return at any time. If a Corvus is killed while fighting a demon, then the Master Corvus creates a new Corvus to replace the one that was lost. It all comes back to balance."

Logically I know it's possible, but hearing about Corvus dying twists my stomach. I keep asking questions to get my mind off it. "But if there's only one Corvus for every one Inferi, doesn't the Furiae's existence create an imbalance?"

Madeline's lips dip downward. "Indeed, it does. While defeating Furiae is like swatting flies for Corvus, Furiae can still cause havoc and wreck lives in our world. It's a good thing Corvus try not to kill the person being possessed when they're battling an Inferi."

Ethan didn't stop himself from killing Drake. As worry sets me on edge, I rub my forehead and try to stay focused while thinking of more questions to ask. I really need to understand this. "If an Inferi can create a kind of lower class demon known as Furia to help do his dirty work, why wouldn't they create an army?"

Madeline raises her eyebrows. "Because everything comes with a price. For a Furia to be created, an Inferi has to be in possession of the body long enough to have fully corrupted the person when the person is killed by a Corvus. When a Furia is formed, the Inferi it replaced is shoved back to Under. Inferni don't often give up their place on this plane just to create Furiae, especially when doing so means they'll be sent to Under in an excruciatingly painful way. The Inferni who get thrust to Under heal very slowly, which means it'll take them a lot longer to try to fight their way back through the veil into our world."

"But if the Corvus are the ones sending them to Under, do Inferni have a choice about going to Under so painfully and creating Furiae?"

"Sure they do. If an Inferi *attacks* a Corvus, then yes, it's a conscious decision to make himself known; he knows what will happen to him if the corrupted human dies when the Corvus kills him. That's why most Inferni prefer to work their evil in a subversive manner, defiling humans' in stealth mode."

Does Ethan have any idea that when he kills the person being possessed along with the Inferi inside, he could be creating a Furia? Does he know Drake's spirit might have turned Furia and is probably out there right now taking over some unsuspecting person? I don't think he does. He would have mentioned something like that. And if Danielle knows so much about Corvus, why didn't she tell him this? Righteous anger starts to swell.

"Nara?"

"I'm sorry, Madeline. I was thinking about everything you've told me so far. Is there anything at all you can tell me about the Order? I know next to nothing about them."

Madeline's apologetic expression creases the wrinkles on her face even more. "All I know is that the symbol on your necklace and on the book's spine represents three arms: Corvus, the Order, and humans. The arms are the exact same length and curled in the same direction for a reason. Each part must exist for perfect harmony and balance. At least, that's the way it's supposed to work."

The odd inflection in her voice snags my attention. "Supposed to work?"

"Something happened about thirty years ago. I don't know what, but that's when I was asked to create the book. Maybe the book's a reminder of sorts…about maintaining balance?" She lifts her shoulders and sighs. "I'm sorry, dear. That's all I know."

"You've been so helpful. Thank you for talking to me, Madeline."

She nods, her features softening. "I'm honored to have played a small part. Good luck, Nara. You were chosen for a reason. And after talking to you, I have every faith you'll figure out the role you're supposed to play. I know that book will help you. Keep it safe until then."

Once Madeline logs off, I stare at the blank computer screen, worrying my bottom lip. Standing up, I pull out a huge map of the world that came in a travel magazine Mom gave me after her last trip.

I lift my laptop up and spread the map out on my desk, then set the laptop back down on it. I type in the search term, "natural disasters for this year" then hit enter. When the list pops up, I mark every single one on the map. Then I reset the year of the search term to the same year that the plane crash occurred when I was a little girl—the same day the blonde man gave my grandmother the necklace to give to me—and I mark all of those natural disasters on the map.

When I'm done, I sit back and stare at the marks I've made. There was a recent freak storm in France that spawned a massive tornado not far from the place that train crashed. And yes, we'd had an event here in Blue Ridge. An earthquake that registered 5.3 and was felt all the way to Pennsylvania and down to Georgia. That even happened just a couple days before I saw the battling angel/demon burst through. A hurricane blew threw D.C. just a week before that plane crashed when I was a child. Based on this tiny sample size, Madeline is probably right about the natural disaster correlation.

More disasters equals more rifts, which potentially allow more Inferni through. As I tap my pen on the map, my mind keeps going back to Furiae.

Is it possible that Ethan's not the only Corvus who doesn't know he's creating these Furiae? Could more Corvus be doing the same? And what happened thirty years ago? Madeline said the Order is part of the balance. If Danielle doesn't know about creating Furiae, should Ethan listen to her about the Order?

A part of me wants to take Mr. Wicklow up on his invitation, but for now I grab my phone and quickly type a text to Ethan.

Me: *We need to talk. This is important. It's about C stuff.*

Ethan: *I'm running errands with Samson for most of the day. Can we meet later tonight? I want to talk in person. I told Danielle not to text me anymore.*

I don't want to think about him with Danielle and her stupid XXX text, but he needs to know what I do before he kills another Inferi-possessed person.

Me: *I have a family dinner, but will be at Mindblown club later.*

Ethan: *Mindblown club?*

Me: *A new club downtown. I'm going with Lainey and some other friends.*

Ethan: *I'd rather talk alone.*

Me: *We need to talk before you do any more "club" hopping. I promised Lainey I'd come with her, so that's where I'll be.*

Ethan: *I'll find you.*

My phone starts ringing right as I read Ethan's text. It's Sally.

After Sally let me know the doctor came in late and Houdini's surgery had been pushed off until tomorrow morning, we hang up and I glance at my watch, surprised that it's already almost three, and Gran and Mr. Dixon will be here at five. Time to get a shower.

I gather up my necklace and Freddie's book. Once I put my necklace away, I slide Freddie's book inside the drawstring bag and start to hide it back between my mattresses when Madeline's parting words echo in my head, "Keep the book safe." With Houdini not here to guard my bed like he usually does, I'll worry about the book. I scan my room, looking for an alternative hiding place, when the answer hits me. Why not put it where it has always been safe?

CHAPTER 17

Nara

Oak Lawn Cemetery is quiet for a Saturday, but as I pass through the main gate I realize it's probably because the weather is so warm; everyone is outside enjoying the unusually nice day.

The ravens are loud in the trees today, and I can't help glancing up at them as I stroll through the cemetery. One croak stands out stronger than any of the others. Patch has followed me here. He didn't want to leave when I tried to get him to. Actually, he made so much noise, my mom called up the stairs asking me to turn down whatever wildlife show I was watching.

Thankfully she didn't come up the stairs or she'd have thought I was nuts—I had to use a small laundry basket to herd Patch toward the open window. So I'm not at all surprised to hear him announcing his presence as I make my way to the back corner where Freddie's grave resides. I'm thankful no one else seems to be around. I know there are laws against grave robbers, but I'm not so sure what happens to grave givers, and I honestly don't want to find out.

Warm wind blows through the bare trees, pushing my loose hair back from my face as I scan the graveyard once more. The clouds are getting darker overhead. Exhaling a sigh of relief that the caretaker must be running an errand or taking a very late lunch, I drop to my knees and pull a trowel and a brown paper bag from my backpack.

"I hope you're okay with this, Freddie." I direct my comment to

Freddie's headstone as I quickly dig a hole big enough for the bag. "But I can't think of a better place to keep your book safe than with you. See, even now you're still protecting its secrets. Well, whatever they are," I say as I lower the paper bag into the hole, then start to cover it up with dirt. Patting the newly refilled dirt, I glance up at the swirling gray clouds. "Don't worry. Your book is sealed inside two airtight baggies inside this paper bag, so even heavy rain won't harm it."

Once I'm done, I brush the dirt from my hands and cover the spot I've disturbed near his headstone with a new layer of haphazardly strewn brown leaves.

"Looks like it was never touched," a man says right next to me.

I let out a yelp and fling the trowel, losing my balance. As I start to fall to my side, the blond man crouched beside me quickly grasps my arm and pulls me upright with very little effort.

"Hello again, Inara." A dimple forms in his cheek and his golden eyes appear to sparkle with flecks of silver as he picks up my trowel and hands it to me.

"Hello *again*?" He might be wearing casual khaki pants and a navy blue Polo shirt, but the man is so beautiful, those are the only words I can muster. He smells amazing, like all the seasons, earth, forests, and the sea rolled into one. I inhale deeply and try to regain the ability to speak as I tuck the trowel away in my backpack. Once I zip the bag, I'm finally able to meet his arresting gaze. I'm dying to know how he snuck up on me without me seeing him, but instead, I say, "I met you when I was a little girl, didn't I?"

His smile deepens. "Do you remember?"

I shake my head. "My grandmother wrote about the necklace you gave her in her diary. You're exactly as she described." Nodding to Freddie's tombstone, I continue, "Freddie made sure to keep the book safe, but I'm not sure what I'm supposed to do with it. Are you here to tell me?"

"I can't stay long." As he speaks, he looks up and nods toward something.

I follow his gaze and blink rapidly. Ethan's sliding a piece of paper under something on top of a headstone closer to the front of the cemetery. Is it under a rock? *Who is he here visiting?*

"He's lost, Inara, like a compass spinning out of control," the man continues. "Be his magnet. Point him in the right direction."

The wind suddenly rushes, swirling the leaves everywhere at once in the cemetery. At that moment, Ethan looks up and snags my gaze across the distance. The wind ruffles his dark hair and pushes against his black V-neck sweater, outlining his muscular frame underneath. My heart ramps as memories of last night flush my face. Ethan doesn't take his eyes off me as he tugs on the paper to make sure it's secure, then strides in my direction, his expression resolute and assured.

"He looks pretty non-lost and confident to me..." I turn, speaking to the man, but trail off. He's gone.

Ethan stops on the other side of Freddie's grave and glances down at the inscription on the tombstone. "Were you talking to your friend Freddie?"

I stand and brush the dirt off my jeans, then tug my backpack up on my shoulder. "No, I was talking to the man."

Ethan's eyebrows shoot up. "What man?"

"The man squatting beside me," I say and gesture to the ground where he'd just been.

Ethan rubs the back of his head. "No one was there, Nara."

I point to the space next to my feet once more. "He was *there*. Maybe Freddie's tombstone blocked him from your view."

He holds up his hands. "Okay, I believe you. What were you talking about?"

I grasp my backpack strap and shrug. "He said you don't know where North is."

Ethan scrunches his face. "Huh?"

I wave my hand. "Never mind. What are you doing here?"

He glances over his shoulder toward the tombstone where he left the note, then shoves his hands in his denim pockets. "Keeping a promise."

If it has to do with a tombstone, I'm sure it's a sad story. He doesn't appear to want to talk about it, so I clear my throat and change the subject. "Well, since you're here, I may as well tell you what I wanted to talk about."

The wind is really starting to howl and Ethan squints against it. "Do you want to go sit in my car?"

I shake my head. "I can't stay. I have to get back to help Mom prepare for a dinner she's having."

Ethan tenses slightly. "Okay. What did you need to tell me?"

I nod to the leafy area where I've just buried Freddie's book. "I spoke to the lady who created Freddie's book. I thought you should know something I learned from her. Did you know there are two types of demons?"

"I know some are much harder to kill than others. Why?"

"So you don't know about Furiae or how they're created?"

Ethan's expression shutters slightly. "What are Furiae?"

"If a person has been possessed long enough by one of Lucifer's demons—known as Inferi or Inferni for more than one—when the person's killed by a Corvus, then the soul becomes a lower demon called a Furia or Furiae for plural."

"What?" Ethan pales slightly. "That can't be true. Danielle would've told me."

I shrug. "Maybe she doesn't know everything."

Ethan blows out a sharp breath, then shoves a hand through his hair. "How reliable do you think this woman's information is?"

I fold my arms, feeling as if Ethan's ready to reject what I'm saying. "Very reliable." As I quickly fill him in on the Corvus' origin story, Ethan's expression turns somber. Once I'm done, I ask, "Did you know any of this?"

He slowly shakes his head. "Apparently what I knew just scratched the surface."

"Madeline said she was told the Corvus' origin as a reward for creating the book. She doesn't know anything about the Order side of things, but she's kept the Corvus' secret and only shared it with me because of my connection through the necklace and book. She knows I'm supposed to be involved and hopes the book will eventually help me figure out how. She said the symbol on my necklace is in three parts because it takes all three arms to maintain balance in the Mortal world: Corvus, Order, and humans. She also mentioned that something happened thirty years ago, which was about the time she was commissioned to make the book and given specific instructions on what to include on it."

"Who asked her to create it?"

I laugh and swing my hand toward the empty space beside me. "Well, I'm pretty sure it was the man who was just talking to me. He also happens to be the same man who gave my grandmother the necklace to keep for me, and who gave Freddie the book that Madeline created."

"And he said I don't know where North is?" Ethan shakes his head. "Who *is* he?"

"I don't know. He was there before I looked up and saw you, and then he was gone when I turned back to speak to him. One thing I do know...the Order is part of this. I think we should try to talk to them."

"No!" Ethan barks out, then shakes his head as if surprised by his own vehemence. "What I mean is...I just know that the Order and Corvus' relationship didn't end well."

"What relationship was that? I still don't know."

"I think the Order acted in a kind of support role for the Corvus in the past." He shrugs. "I just know Danielle says the Order is not good for Corvus."

I throw my hands up. "But she also didn't tell you about creating Furiae either, which means she might've left a few other important details out."

"She would never do that." Frustration stamps creases around his mouth. "Putting me at risk defeats the whole purpose of training me."

"How would her not telling you put you at risk?"

"Because, beyond their vileness, another reason I take demons out is to make sure they can't reveal that I'm Corvus to other demons. Usually people who survive a possession don't remember anything that happened while they were possessed. If a Furia is possible, then this newly formed Furia might remember the Corvus who killed his human body and rat me out to other demons...or come after me himself. Danielle would've told me about that possibility."

My eyes widen as his comment sinks in. "Oh, God, I just realized... can't an Inferi you've killed come after you as soon as he makes his way back to our world?"

Ethan shakes his head. "That's my point. No matter how long it takes them to make their way back through, the veil part is key. After demons cross the veil to enter back into our world, they have no memory of their existence here. If Furiae are created here and remain here, they never pass through the veil, so their memories are never wiped."

"Have you killed every possessed *person* that you've run across?" I ask, my voice shaking.

Ethan presses his lips together. "I told you. The ones who died deserved it."

"How do you know they deserve it?"

"I can sense if the human's soul is evil through my sword."

"You mean once you stab the person?"

He nods solemnly.

"Can you tell if the demon corrupted them or not?"

"Evil is evil, Nara."

"What if what Madeline told me is *true*? If Furiae are being created by Corvus killing humans whose souls have been corrupted by Inferni, then yes it does matter. If you can't tell how dark the soul is, wouldn't it be best to kill the Inferi without killing the person? That way, the imbalance between Corvus and the Inferni won't grow larger by accidentally creating a Furia and exposing your identity."

Ethan pushes his hands deeper into his pockets and inhales in and out of his nose several times while his jaw muscle pops.

"Ethan?" When he looks at me, his eyes are pure black. "Are you okay?"

Expelling a harsh breath, he steps around Freddie's grave to stand in front of me. "I'd hoped we could talk about us, but I should go find Danielle. I need to know if she's aware of these Furiae."

I nod. "That's more important—"

Ethan presses his thumb to my lips, then lifts my chin up until I meet his dark gaze. "*We're* just as important, but I know you have to go, so we'll talk later."

I'm mesmerized by his closeness. All I can do is stand there as he slides his thumb slowly across my bottom lip, applying gentle pressure. The moment my lips separate, he presses his warm mouth to mine in a lingering, heated kiss, then turns and walks away, leaving me staring after him, my heart beating like a hummingbird's.

On my way out of the cemetery, I stop and look at the tombstone where Ethan had left a note under a toy truck. The inscription says: *For a loving wife and mother who left us too soon.*

Curiosity gets the best of me, and I pick up the truck and read the note Ethan had left.

> Marcus,
> Your dad seems calmer now. Guess that required counseling helped. I know he misses you. I talked to the police and told them it was a misunderstanding on my part. They've agreed to drop the charges against your dad, and hopefully you'll be able to come home from foster care soon. I know he regrets

hurting you, and I don't think he'll do it again.

Ethan

P.S. If you ever want to hang out, you can sometimes find me at this place (see other side). And if I'm not there, it's still a fun place to be. You'll make lots of friends there.

I flip the paper over and smile. It's a CVAS advertising flyer. *Marcus? Why does that name sound familiar?*

"Hey, that's my truck."

I turn to the boy standing to my side. He looks to be about seven, and is staring at me with suspicious chocolate brown eyes, his forehead crinkled in distrust.

"Oh, I'm sorry." I hold my hand out to give him the toy, but when he reaches for it, I tuck the paper into his palm along with the truck. "I believe this is for you. I'm Nara, a friend of Ethan's." *And you must belong to the sleeping man who Ethan saved from a demon.*

The boy's tightly pressed lips flip into a bright smile. "This is from Ethan?"

I watch his face as he slowly reads the note. It's hard not to choke up when he scrubs his short nails through his close-shaved hair and tears begin dripping down his brown cheeks.

I start to say something when he jerks his head up, eyes bright with happiness, and says, "I gotta go!" Then he turns and bolts from the cemetery.

"Bye," I call after him, smiling. *I'm so glad you can see that some people are worth saving, Ethan.*

CHAPTER 18

Nara

I'm running through the icy forest, desperately looking for Ethan, calling his name.

This time I run through a mowed down path and pop out in a clearing that looks familiar. Instead of ice, snow covers every pine surrounding the pond that takes up most of the open space. Moonlight sparkles off the snow, lighting up the idyllic scene.

Even though I'm cold, warmth seeps into my heart as I picture Ethan and I lying on a blanket kissing like we'd done that day by the pond before he left for a month. Back when my heart felt whole and happiness seemed to be my constant state of being.

Something disturbs the glass surface of the pond and ripples spill outward as Ethan slowly rises from the water.

"Ethan," I call, but he doesn't hear me. He's turned at a slight angle away from me as he continues to slowly move higher in the water, his gaze focused straight ahead.

I shiver at the single-mindedness in his dark eyes, but the whapping sound of a lone bird's wings draws my attention to the sky. A massive raven is heading toward us. He's gliding now, his black eyes locked on Ethan.

My heart races and I return my attention to Ethan as he lifts his arms out of the water, resting his palms on the surface. Tilting his head back, he closes his eyes and basks in the moon's glow. Everything about his pose reflects relaxed composure and full acceptance.

Does he know the bird is barreling right for him? It hasn't made a sound.

As the raven draws close, I clench my hands and wince, preparing for its massive body to slam into him. Instead, the moment the raven hits, he melds into Ethan's body, completely disappearing. The only indication Ethan felt the impact is the slight step back he takes in the water. His palms don't disturb the water and his head remains tilted back.

Several seconds pass and I hold my breath, wondering what just happened.

When Ethan lifts his arms wide, the muscles in his shoulders, chest and abs flexing with his movements, my gaze shifts to the shadow the moon reflects in the water behind him. It isn't a man's body with arms spread wide, but a raven about to take flight.

Water drips from Ethan's sleek arms and down his broad chest. The arch of his neck and set of his shoulders are proud, arrogant even as a cloud moves over the moon. He's brutally beautiful in his darkness: gorgeous, majestic, powerful and untouchable. Chills race down my spine just looking at him. I'm so overwhelmed with emotions of both awe and worry, my legs buckle and my knees sink into the deep snow.

Danielle's laughter suddenly echoes everywhere. She's standing beside me, hands on her hips, smiling. "Ethan's busy right now. Leave a message and he might return your call."

When I shift my gaze back to the pond, Ethan's gone and the moonlit water is smooth once more. I jerk to my feet and step into her personal space. "What do you want, Danielle? Why are you here?"

The clearing goes dark for a second, then tendrils of light start to bleed through. I'm in my bedroom now and the sensation of being watched is so strong, I quickly sit up. Danielle's standing beside my bed, staring at me.

I jerk back and look around my dim room. *Am I still dreaming?* Blinking my eyes, I repeat my question in a fast gush of air. "What do you want?"

"You need to cut Ethan loose," she says, her voice sounding older, harsher. "All this"—she lifts her fingers in air quotes—"'you need to remember' bullshit is messing with his training, and I won't have it."

She advances close to my bed until the outside light glitters in her dark eyes. "He needs to focus, to fully accept his Corvus. He'll never be as strong as he should be with you holding him back."

My heart aches with each jabbing word. She's saying everything I've thought but never voiced. I swallow the hot rush of guilt that lodges in my throat and sit up on my knees. "Ethan needs me. He needs the light or—"

"Or what?" she snaps.

My dreams flash through my mind. In them, at first Ethan disappears, then later he's missing or...no, lost, just like that man from the cemetery said. I'm looking for him, hunting everywhere, behind every tree and in every shadow, but it's so cold and dark that I'm never able to find him. In this last one, he didn't even acknowledge my presence. I lean forward on my knees and speak with conviction. "Or he'll be sucked into the darkness."

"You will—" Danielle begins, then gasps. I jerk back a little as she pulls the chain from my T-shirt. Holding the medallion in her palm, outrage fills her face. "This is mine! Where did you get it?"

"Ethan gave it to me." I straighten to my knees, the action giving me a height advantage. As the metal disk thumps against my chest, I lift my chin and stare her down. "I won't abandon him. He needs me or he won't be able to find his way. He's growing darker every day."

Danielle snorts. "You silly girl. His darkness is keeping him alive. How else do you expect him to fight demons? Like fights like. Your puny light only weakens him."

Is my light creating cracks in the dam of darkness protecting Ethan? The hole in my chest burns as my certainty starts to splinter, but I know one thing is true. "I love him."

"Are you really that selfish? This is bigger than you." Danielle curls her hands into fists. "Break it *off*. He needs to fulfill his destiny."

Sudden doubt grips my chest, but the fury swirling in my belly overrides it. "I'll make sure he's on the *right* path."

She lets out the same kind of laughter I've been hearing in my dreams, and a glint of silver flashes as she rushes me. I fall back against my headboard as she slams her fist into the wood right beside my shoulder, the jolt against the headboard rocking through me.

I'm frozen in place, my heart racing. Was that her fist or a sword drilling into the wood? I keep my eyes squeezed tight and try to shut out her spicy perfume as she leans in and hisses next to my ear. "End it!"

The two words echo in my head a couple of times before I work up the courage to challenge her. "Fuck. Off," I say forcefully and open my eyes…to an empty bedroom.

Heart thudding, I quickly turn on my lamp to flood the room with light.

Is she really gone? I lean over and look under my bed to make sure she's not hiding there. My gaze snags on the box my aunt had stopped by to drop off last night. Mom invited her to stay for dinner, and then right after, I left to meet Lainey at the club. There's no way I'm going back to sleep for a while, so I slide the box out and lift the lid.

Emotions swell as I pull a gray fedora hat out of the tissue with shaky hands, excitement coursing through me. Drystan could help me find—then I sigh when I remember Aunt Sage said she'd had it dry-cleaned, which would have washed away my dad's essence. Regret fills my heart as I run my fingers along the black band and short brim. I can totally see my dad wearing it. I love it too. Paper tucked inside the hat scrapes against my fingers. I pull the note out.

> Inara,
>
> I knew you would enjoy this. You definitely got your "love of things from the past" from him.
>
> Aunt Sage

Clutching the hat against my chest, I sniff back tears and glance over my shoulder to the headboard behind me. Nothing. Not a scratch. But it had felt so real.

A shudder ripples through me as I murmur, "It's official. I'm losing my mind."

Nara

Ding-dong.

Ethan's adamant words of distrust against the Order clang in my head as I lower my hand from the doorbell, but I know Danielle's behind his concerns, and right now, *she's* my biggest one. I'd checked my phone this morning on the way out the door and saw Ethan had sent a text late last night saying he was sorry he missed me at the club but that we'd talk later.

I never did fall back to sleep. I just laid there for two hours, staring at the ceiling and wondering if "dream Danielle" was right. *Am I holding Ethan back? Is he better off not worrying about us?* The thought of not being with Ethan hurts so much I shake my head and blow out a breath to settle the tension in my stomach just as the door swings open.

"Hello, Nara." Mr. Wicklow smiles broadly. "I'm so glad you finally came."

I'm still not sure if what I saw in the middle of the night was some kind of waking dream or real, but good, bad—or somewhere in between—the Order is part of the Corvus' history. I need to know what *they* know if I'm going to do...well, whatever it is I'm supposed to do.

Raising my chin high, I say in a no-nonsense tone, "I'd like you to answer one question, and please answer honestly."

His expression turns serious and he nods.

"What is the status of the Order/Corvus relationship?"

Mr. Wicklow grins, pride overshadowing something in his eyes. "It's a wonderful relationship."

My heart sinks and I give him a curt nod. "That's all I needed to know."

I start to turn, but he calls out, "Wait, Nara. Please forgive me. That was wishful thinking on my part. The general status of the Corvus/Order relationship is...tenuous, but it's getting better bit by bit, and my hope is that it will one day be back to the collaborative, supportive, and rewarding one it once was."

I stare into his eyes and try to validate the sincere look on his face. "What happened?"

"Why don't you come in and we can talk about it?"

I cross my arms and wait.

Exhaling a heavy sigh, he runs his hand through his close-cropped gray hair. "Honestly, I'm not sure. I was fairly new in the Order and didn't understand the politics going on at the time. All I know is that the Master Corvus went berserk and destroyed the sanctuary where Corvus and the Order have always found even ground with each other. Our leader, the only person who might've known what triggered the Master Corvus, was killed. That day, every Corvus around the world collapsed and the spirit inside them left their bodies."

Reaching up, he rubs the back of his neck. "We've been trying to recoup ever since and eventually we developed ways to discover newly created Corvus. We know there are many more out there, operating on instinct and without the one thing that grounds them to this plane. It's been slow and time-consuming to uncover new Corvus, but we are making progress so we can help them." He stops speaking and spreads his hands wide. "That has always been our only goal."

I blink several times, shocked by his honest answer.

His brow creases. "I really hope you'll come in and hear what I have to say," he says, stepping back to gesture to the foyer.

As if I really have a choice. Danielle keeps haunting my dreams. My effort at an appreciative smile feels more like a grimace. "Thank you for taking the time to talk to me."

He smiles encouragingly, pulling the door wide. As I step past the entrance, he glances outside. "Such odd weather for winter. I've never seen the temperature fluctuate the way it has here. Is this normal for Virginia?"

I shake my head. "Seventy degrees is definitely not normal for this time of year. The weather people are saying it might snow again in a couple of days, so…" Shrugging, I pluck at my cap-sleeved shirt. "I'm enjoying it while it lasts."

"Agreed. Why don't you come with me to the office?"

I follow him down the hall and as we enter the first room on the right, he says over his shoulder, "This is why I love this room." He walks right up to the blinds to quickly draw them out of the way. "Come closer and see."

I move behind the desk and stare out the window. The sloped backyard dips straight into the pine forest below, a sea of deep green treetops standing tall, defying winter's grip. "That's a great view. I knew there were woods behind this house, but I've never seen them from this perspective."

He tilts his head, eyeing me for a second. "You're unlike any Corvus I've ever encountered. Direct, but reserved. Open, yet closed." Clearing his throat, he gazes back outside. "The owners were very smart. This house's higher elevation really lets you get the most of that fantastic view. Makes me wish I could stay longer than a few weeks." With a regretful sigh, he spreads his hands toward the two leather chairs in front of the huge mahogany desk. "Choose whichever one you prefer. I'm going to put on some water for tea."

Before he walks out, I slide a suspicious gaze his way. "Are you really here on business with the university?"

My question makes him smile. "I am a professor, so the answer is yes, I'm here on business with the university, but you're the main reason I'm here."

He walks out, leaving me more tied up on the inside than I was when I walked in the room. I take the seat closest to the door, but I don't lean back. My nerves are wound so tight, by the time he returns and takes a seat across from me, I feel like I might throw up.

Sitting on the edge of his seat, he reaches out to touch my tightly clutched hands, but pulls his hand back as if I might bite him. "Why don't you say what's on your mind and we'll go from there, yes?"

I unlock my fingers and square my shoulders. "This is a big step for me to come here. For now, I hope you'll just tell me what I want to know."

Amusement glitters in his gaze. "You're such an interesting contra-diction. I hope I'll get to ask you some questions too, Nara."

"I'll answer if I can, but only if I can."

"That's fair," he says as he props his elbows up on the chair and folds his fingers together under his chin. "What do you want to know?"

"The other day you mentioned ravens, a feather, and the Order as if you knew I was aware of all of it. How did you find me?"

"Ah." Steepling his fingers, he nods. "Your Internet searches. We tap into the Tower of London's website and filter any keywords that fall under certain parameters. You'd be surprised at how many peo-ple click on the Tower of London seeking information about ravens. Considering the Tower's history of raising ravens and its old tale of the Tower falling if the ravens ever leave it, it makes sense so many search-es would reach the Tower's servers. But with the amount of traffic the Tower's website gets, it's been easy enough to use their website and add our own keywords. We just make sure certain search phrases that go to the Tower are then erased from their cache once they're rerouted to us."

He points to my shoulder. "That's how I knew. You typed in the phrase 'feather on the shoulder blade,' which routed you to the Tower. Sure you didn't find what you wanted, so you moved on to another website, but that was enough to alert us."

"The Tower doesn't know you're using their website? Isn't what you're doing illegal?"

"It's for the overall benefit of mankind. I sleep well at night." Shrugging, his lips twist downward. "This isn't the way we prefer to find new Corvus. We used to have a much easier method…" Trailing off, he points to me. "But if I found you, I guarantee demons will eventually find you too. Because you're fighting your Corvus and not accepting its knowledge, you've unwittingly painted a target on yourself. You might not think you need help, but let me assign you a Paladin to help you learn to accept the Corvus inside you."

"I'm not Corvus."

His eyebrow hikes. "Do you have a feather tattoo on your shoulder that just appeared from nowhere?"

"I don't have a black feather on my shoulder," I answer honestly.

He smirks. "I didn't say it was black. How did you know that it was?"

"You mentioned ravens, so a black feather makes sense." I barely resist drawing my finger in the air: Nara - 1, Order - 0. I sit up straighter, wondering about my own feather. "Are there other colored feathers?"

He chuckles. "No. Just black…well, until it changes. Has your feather changed yet?"

I don't want to discuss my feather. Its existence freaks me out. I'm glad it's on the back of my shoulder where I can't see it unless I make an effort to look. Then again, if it has changed to black that means I might be Corvus. Maybe it's best to let him assume what he wants for now. This Paladin sounds suspiciously like what Danielle is to Ethan. "Tell me more about the Paladins. How do they help a person accept their Corvus?"

His shoulders relax and he leans fully back in his chair, pleased I seem interested. "A Paladin is a person who has dedicated his or her life to the Order with the sole purpose of helping to keep the Corvus grounded to our world."

"How does this Paladin help keep the Corvus grounded?" I ask, my tone sharp, doubtful.

"Ah." Mr. Wicklow raises his finger, wagging it back and forth. "Not just anyone can be a Paladin. A Paladin has to also have some kind of special ability that's beyond the human norm. It can be anything: telekinesis, telepathy, precognition, automatic writing…just something that sets them apart. Otherwise, the Corvus will have a hard time accepting them because they can't relate. Due to their nature most Corvus just tolerate their Paladin, but they wouldn't even do that if the Paladin wasn't special in some way."

"That didn't really answer my question. Exactly how does a Paladin do that for the Corvus?" I can't believe how direct I'm being, but I'm anxious for answers.

By his chuckle, Mr. Wicklow doesn't seem surprised at all by my terse impatience. "They help the Corvus come to terms with the spirit inside them. They're there for them if they need someone to spar with, to debate with, have a pint with, whatever. The Corvus most likely won't become close friends with their Paladin—they're not wired to accept help—but their Paladin is there in whatever capacity they need. If the Corvus doesn't have human interaction from someone who understands what they go through, all the demons that the Corvus fight will eventually darken him or her, contaminating the Corvus."

"Contaminating?" That word jumps out at me, churning my insides.

He puts his hands together, then unfolds them like a book. "Think of the Corvus as two halves of a coin—light and dark. It's all about balance. As long as the Corvus maintains some human interaction via their Paladin, that helps keep the light and dark mostly balanced. If not, Corvus are like sponges. It's what makes them good at what they do, defeating demons, but it's also what can make them go dark. They absorb all that evil until their human body is so polluted it can no longer take it. If the Corvus goes too far down that path of darkness, they'll be lost forever."

I grip the edge of the chair. "What do you mean 'lost forever'? What happens?"

He shakes his head, his face sad. "The human dies and the Corvus spirit leaves the body, a broken shadow of itself where it's absorbed back into the Master Corvus. But the Master Corvus won't recreate a new Corvus to replace that one for a very long time. That poisoned part of his spirit has to heal first."

Worry for Ethan floods through me while hundreds of questions fly through my mind. I shove back my fear, determined to learn everything I can.

"Do you know how the Corvus are chosen?"

He shakes his head. "That's known only to the Master Corvus, and he's very picky. In my lifetime I've only seen him once."

"You can see the spirit? Is that *your* ability?"

"No." He gives me an indulgent smile. *This is my ability, Nara.*

My eyes widen. His mouth didn't move, but I heard his words in my head. "You can speak in people's minds?" Worry grips me. "Can you read my thoughts too?"

This time he laughs outright. "No, I can't. What I meant was that I saw the Master Corvus in a human. He usually only shows up once Lucifer has returned, remaining solo—no Paladin or Corvus to back him up—until his job is finished."

I grip my hands to keep them from shaking in my lap. "Return? I thought Lucifer ran free in our world."

This time his eyes widen slightly. "Can you imagine the chaos and destruction he would reign down on us if he were around all the time? No, Nara. The Master Corvus is the *only* Corvus powerful enough to cast God's fallen right hand angel out of our world. Do you really think Hitler killed himself in that bunker? Or Stalin or Vlad or Attila, or so many more before them?" He shakes his head. "That was the Master Corvus, sending Lucifer straight back to Under."

I blink in confusion. "But all those leaders reigned before you were born or when you were a small child. How could you have seen the Master Corvus then?"

"The one and only time I saw the Master Corvus was around thirty years ago. It was the only time he interacted with the Order, or humans in general. I'm honestly not sure why he appeared to us at the Order's sanctuary. Thinking back, there seemed to be no eminent threat, no leader in power who could destroy our world. The day we learned he wasn't just Corvus, but the Master Corvus, that's the day he destroyed everything."

"What happened?"

He lifts his shoulders. "I walked in on our leader and the Master Corvus arguing, and then he just lost it. We've been trying to pick up the pieces ever since. We've had to rebuild our network, and do our best to discover new Corvus being created so that we can assign them Paladins before they go dark."

The conversation swinging back to Paladins freaks me out. What kind of future will Ethan have if he continues to work with Danielle? Her views are completely skewed from Mr. Wicklow's way of thinking. "Do you know all of your Paladins personally? Have they been trained in the same way to help the Corvus?"

Mr. Wicklow laughs. "I know them all, and yes, they're all trained how to deal with Corvus."

"Have you assigned a Paladin named Danielle to anyone here in Virginia?"

His brow wrinkles. "There are no Paladins assigned here yet, and we don't have any named Danielle."

Then that means Danielle can only be one thing; she has to be Corvus, just like Ethan. The glint of silver I saw this morning must have been her sword slamming into my headboard. Though it feels like her sharp blade sliced into my chest instead. I'll never be able to compete with that kind of connection, but I have to confirm my suspicions.

"Why don't Corvus train other Corvus? I mean, wouldn't it be easier for one Corvus who's already made it through the transition to help another newer one through it?" I gulp, then twist the blade deeper. "Wouldn't they understand each other on a deeper level?"

Mr. Wicklow quickly leans close. This time he doesn't hesitate as he clasps my hands. "No, Nara. A Corvus training another is a bad combination. Think about what I just said. If one Corvus could grow dark fighting demons, imagine how two Corvus would be together. They would—"

"—pull the light right out of the darkness," I finish in a whisper.

A shrill sound pierces the air, making me jump.

"That's the teapot." He squeezes my hands. "I'm so glad you get it. You are truly unique. Corvus are usually so difficult to talk to. That's why it takes a special person to be a Paladin."

I tug my hands from his. "I need to go. Thank you for talking to me, Mr. Wicklow."

"But there's more you need to know."

The teapot continues to get louder, setting my nerves on edge. "I can't right now."

As I quickly stand, he follows. "You need help to accept everything about your Corvus. Let me assign you a Paladin." He pauses. "And I want to know why you asked about a Paladin already being assigned."

I take a deep breath, then slowly shake my head. "I'm not Corvus."

The wrinkles around his eyes deepen. "That can't be. You know so much." Waving to the chair, he says, "Stay so we can talk more. Let me get the tea."

I'm too anxious to sit, so I wander over to the huge office globe in the wooden floor stand next to the desk; it's one of those vintage old world kind that spins on its axis and makes me think of sea captains and pirates battling over treasure. Smiling, I spin the globe and watch the markings fly past. I lightly touch the spinning ball, and as it begins to slow under my finger, I think, *Were they adventurous enough back then to spin the globe and wherever it stopped, that's where they would go next?* When the globe stutters to a stop, I lift my finger and lean over to see where I would have taken my trip.

As soon as I get close to inspect the map, the medallion against my chest suddenly lifts toward the globe, T-shirt and all. It doesn't attach to it, just hovers very close. Fascinated, I pull the medallion out of my shirt and move it close to the top of the globe. It doesn't appear to be attracted any more. "Weird," I mumble as I slide it back to the first area, where I definitely feel a hard tug between the globe and the metal. Releasing the medallion, I stare in utter captivation as the disk not only hangs in the air pointing to that spot on the map, but the lighter raven on the medallion appears to be giving off a dim light.

Shattering china jerks me upright. I turn to see Mr. Wicklow standing in the doorway, broken porcelain and tea splattered around his feet, his face pale.

"Where did you get that?" His cheeks flush as he moves into the room, his eyes bright as they lock on the medallion now lying against my chest.

I clutch the disk in my hand, then tuck it back inside my shirt, tension creeping along my spine. "A friend gave it to me."

He licks his lips and takes a step closer. "I didn't think another one existed. This is amazing." Snapping his gaze to mine, he asks, "Can I see it?"

The excitement in his eyes makes me nervous. I step to the side, edging toward the door. "I need to get going."

He holds up his hands, his gaze imploring. "You don't realize what you have, Nara. This is important!"

I shake my head. "I really need to go now." Before he can move or say another word, I bolt, jumping over the mess he made in the doorway and heading down the hall toward the front door.

"Nara, please wait," he calls after me as I tug the door open.

The panic in his voice makes me glance back over my shoulder. He's standing in the hall, worry in his gaze. "You really aren't Corvus?"

When I shake my head, he steps closer to grab a pen and pad off the table in the hall. Scribbling something down, he tears off the paper and hands it to me. "Here's my number if you want to talk more. In the meantime, support your friend. He or she needs you to be there for them. And please keep the necklace safe."

I nod, then close the door behind me and take off running.

CHAPTER 19

Nara

I raise a shaky hand and knock on Ethan's door. I don't even know if he's home; I just know I need to talk to him. Now.

Instead of driving, I walked to his house. I don't want to take a chance Mr. Wicklow might follow me. If my Internet searches are being watched, who knows what else of mine is being tracked. I left my phone on the counter at home just in case.

"Come in, Nara," Samson says, his light blue eyes brightening as he pulls the door fully open.

As I step next to a duffle bag sitting in the foyer, he calls upstairs. "Eth, your Sunshine's here."

"Nara?" Ethan pokes his head out of his room, a look of surprise on his face.

While Ethan makes his way down the staircase amid Samson's laughter, his older brother shifts his gaze back to me. "Sorry, I couldn't resist picking on him. He's been so intense lately."

"Hey," Ethan says in a subdued tone as he joins us in the foyer. Questions reflect in his eyes, but he just shoves his hands into his pockets and turns to his brother. "I thought you were leaving to work out?"

"I can go to the gym later." Samson gestures to the living room. "Go on in and make yourself comfortable, Nara."

Ethan and I move into the living room, but as I sit on the couch, he turns and stares pointedly at his brother.

"Fine, I'm going." Samson raises his hands in defeat. Shouldering his duffle bag, he turns to us, a knowing look in his eye. "Be good."

When my face explodes with color, he laughs, then opens the door. "You're absolutely adorable, Nara. Be back in a little bit."

The moment the door shuts behind him, Ethan sits down on the couch beside me and mumbles, "Sorry about that."

My nerves are a jangled mess, and I instantly jump up the moment he reaches for my hand. Moving to put the coffee table between us, I say, "I—I have a lot to say, so I think it's best if I do it standing."

Ethan holds my gaze for a couple of seconds, then stretches his legs out and drapes his arms across the back of the leather cushions behind him. "Okay."

The action pulls his T-shirt up slightly and I shift my gaze away from the glimpse of flexing abs so I'm not distracted. "What did Danielle say about the Furiae?"

"She said this Madeline person doesn't have her facts straight. Corvus aren't creating Furiae."

I tense. "How does she know that for sure?"

He sighs. "She just does."

"*How*?"

"Trust me. She just knows."

Is it because she's Corvus too? I want to choke the answer out of him, but he isn't volunteering anything more. "Did you find Harper?"

His mouth tenses slightly. "We finally found her, but she saw me at the same time I saw her, and was able to get out of the club before we could make our way through the crowd to get to her." His gaze drops to my clenched hands. "Is this what you wanted to talk to me about—what Danielle said about the Furiae?"

I can't believe I forgot to ask Mr. Wicklow about Furiae. Ugh! But so much is going on in my head right now, it's hard to focus on just what to say. Ethan will freak out if I tell him about going to see the man, so I decide to start with Danielle.

"Danielle came to see me in the middle of the night."

Ethan sits up; his hands move to his thighs, gripping them tight. "What?"

"She told me that I'm holding you back, and that me pushing you to regain your memory is messing with your training. She wants me to let you go, Ethan. To end our relationship so that you can just focus on accepting your Corv—"

Ethan's in front of me before I can finish. "No, Nara! Danielle would never do that. She knows how much you mean to me." Clasping my face, he steps closer. "It had to be a dream, just another crazy dream. You told me she's been in several of your dreams lately."

His amazing smell invades my senses, making it hard to focus. As I step back from his hold, the memory of Danielle's perfume slams through my mind. In all the dreams I've had about her, I can't recall smelling her, but in my dreams she wasn't right up against me.

"She was there, demanding that I let you go."

Ethan pales and he grips my shoulders. "Are you breaking up with me?"

I gape, speechless, my heart twisting in two. "Is—is that what you want?"

Ethan jams his fingers through his hair and glances up at the ceiling, gritting his teeth. Returning his deep blue gaze to mine, he slowly exhales. "No. I'm just trying not to freak out here."

"She was *there*. And to make her point very clear, she jammed something…a knife or a sword…into my headboard right next to me. When I opened my eyes, it was as if she was never there. Even my headboard was undamaged." Lifting my chin higher, I offer him the chance to tell me once more. "What *is* she?"

His eyes lock with mine. "She's Corvus. Which does make her like a cousin to me." A brief smile tilts his lips, but when I don't return it, he continues on a sigh, "Corvus are sworn to protect, Nara. It's ingrained in us not to harm a person unless they're under the influence of a demon."

"Even if she thinks I'm keeping you from accepting your Corvus?"

He nods. "Even then. She's the one who taught me the code. And our swords *will* damage anything non-human. If you saw a sword, that's how I know for sure it was a dream."

His comment about the sword gives me pause, but my instincts are telling me otherwise. There's so much I want to tell him, but I feel like anything I say right now will fall on deaf ears, especially when he learns the source of my information. Taking a step back, I pull the necklace over my head and hold it out to him.

"What are you doing? I told you never to take that off."

"You can give this back to Danielle. She wasn't happy that you'd given it to me."

Worry fills his gaze and he shakes his head. "You need to wear it,

Nara. It'll keep you safe."

I set it down on the coffee table. "I can't. I shouldn't be the one to have it."

Ethan grabs the necklace and holds it out to me. "Please, put it back on."

Mr. Wicklow was really excited about the necklace. But since he knows where I live and he doesn't know about Ethan, the best place for the medallion is with him. I shake my head and back away. "Right now the safest place for it is with Corvus. Please Ethan, be careful working with Danielle." My throat burns with the need to say more, to tell him everything Mr. Wicklow said. God, could this *be* any harder? *I need to get out of here before I explode.*

As I turn to leave, Ethan grips my hand, his expression devastated. "Why are you leaving? Talk to me, Nara."

I close my eyes for a second, then meet his gaze. "I have to go pick up Houdini. Think about what I said. I know the difference between dreams and reality."

"The medallion isn't important, but you are. You need to wear it."

He looks so upset, guilt clenches my stomach. I press my lips together and swallow the need to spill my guts. Sliding my hand from his, I force an even look on my face. "I'll be fine. I have to go."

Ethan

My chest feels like it's being crushed as Nara walks out of my house.

Was I wrong to tell her it was a dream so quickly? She told me she'd had several dreams about Danielle. But the way she talked about this one, the look in her eyes, she's worried; she *believes* it was real.

Damn it! *Why do I keep screwing things up with her?*

I pace the carpet, the stupid necklace in my hand. It feels warm against my palm and I pause to look at it. The damn thing is glowing, which only irritates me. Nara will never wear it again. The look on her face; it's like I betrayed her somehow by not telling her it belonged to Danielle. Dream or not, she believes what she's saying. Did Danielle give it to me?

The carpet feels like it's dragging my feet under as I tear back and forth. I scrub my hand through my hair and pull on the strands, hoping the pain will help jog my memory. If I could just remember, I could give Nara answers.

The necklace grows ice cold in my hand. As I tighten my grip, its frosty bite sears my palm, setting me off. "Fuck it all!" I yell and throw the disk at the stone fireplace.

I jump back when the metal explodes off the stonework, raining silver all around me.

How did that happen? It was a solid piece of metal. My adrenaline pumps as I stare at the powdery silver mess all over the coffee table, the sofa, and the carpet. Samson's going to chew my ass if I don't get this cleaned up. I never remember him being such a pain about keeping things neat at home, but in *his* house, he's as anal as they get.

With a grunt of frustration, I head for the closet and drag out the vacuum. As the shrill whine of the machine drills in my ears, I keep thinking about Nara. I know she's bottling her emotions up. I can feel she's not telling me everything that's on her mind. When I'm done, Danielle and I are going to have a serious talk. Then I'll find Nara and get her to tell me what's going on.

Nara

Even having Houdini back with his tail wagging and licking me incessantly didn't stop me from crying myself to sleep last night, especially when I checked my shoulder.

My tattoo hadn't changed; it was still a white feather. I cried when I woke up this morning too. Not because I'd had another dream about Danielle, but because I didn't dream about Ethan. Actually, I didn't dream at all. Losing Ethan, even in my dreams weighs heaviest on my mind, and no amount of makeup can cover the puffiness that restless sleep and tears cause.

"I'm so glad winter break is almost here. I'm ready to go skiing," Drystan announces as he walks up and leans against the lockers. His smile falls as he tips my chin up to inspect my face. "You look like 'ell."

He'd said it without his normal acerbic bite, and the lack of sarcasm in his tone feels somehow harsher. Like I really do look like I've been run over. I wince and pull my chin away. "I'm good, Drystan."

He shakes his head and glances at Lainey over his shoulder. "No, you're not."

I'm too tired to put up a front, so I shrug. "I'm just working through some stuff."

"Hi everyone," A friendly smile curves Danielle's lips as she presses her backpack between her body and the lockers on the other side of me. "I'm sorry for hogging all Ethan's time lately, Nara. I didn't mean to take him away from you, but he's been helping me figure my way out around here."

"Seems as if you've learned your way around here pretty quickly," Drystan says. "Soon *you'll* be hosting new students."

"Yep, you're a fast study, Danielle," Lainey adds as she walks up behind Drystan, her eyes pinging from me to Danielle.

I notice sarcasm in Drystan's voice. My friends assume she's talking about how much time she and Ethan have spent together since she arrived. I hold Danielle's penetrating gaze, meeting the challenge I see in her eyes. Plastering on a smile, I say, "Ethan's good like that, always rescuing others in need."

Danielle's confident smile falters, turning downward. I knew that would get to her. The last thing a Corvus wants is to be perceived as weak. The way Mr. Wicklow treated me when he thought I was Corvus and the things he said about their acceptance of Paladins, not to mention the transformation I've seen in Ethan make that fact painfully obvious. I should feel better about that; it explains so much about why Ethan has done this whole Corvus thing on his own. Instead, it makes me feel like I did this morning when I woke up, like I'm no longer a part of Ethan's life. And just like that, my victorious moment quickly evaporates.

"I've got to get to class, guys. See you later."

"Nara," Lainey calls, but I don't look back. I just shoulder my way through the crowd.

Homeroom dragged by and I'm anxious to get to History. Even though I ran out on Ethan yesterday, I need to see him sitting in the back of the classroom. My lack of dreams really freaked me out. I didn't realize how addicted I'd become to seeing him in them until he wasn't. Even if my dreams are full of worry and fear...he's there, he exists. In them, he's a part of my life, and I'm doing everything I can to save him. Last night's nothingness scares me more than our fighting, more than worrying we're being torn apart. It's as if our connection never existed...and that terrifies me.

I quickly file into History class with everyone else and turn in my seat to watch the doorway for Ethan. When the bell rings and he still hasn't shown, I chew the inside of my cheek and open my three-ring binder. *Why isn't he at school? Has something happened to him?* I couldn't bear that, especially after the way I left things yesterday.

"Nara."

I jerk out of my worried musings to see Mr. Hallstead's expectant look. "Yes?"

"If you're done reorganizing, would you mind going to the office and getting this packet copied for me to pass out at the end of class?"

I glance down at my six-subject notebook and swallow. Not only have I completely rearranged the subjects in alphabetical order, but I've color-coordinated all the separator tabs within each subject. As snickers from students to my left and right bleed through, I mentally curse my tension-induced OCD and walk up to the front of the classroom to retrieve the packet from him.

He sets the stack of papers in my hand, then lays a key on top of it. "Please stop by the supply closet for a ream of paper. Ms. Cresh wasn't too thrilled the last time I requested copies without bringing my own supply."

The supply closet is right next to the teacher's lounge and thoughts of Ethan and the last tense conversation we had in there rushes to my mind as I unlock the door. Flipping on the light, I shove thoughts of Ethan away and try to focus on my task. Reams of copy paper take up the entire back wall of metal shelving.

Someone, in their infinite wisdom, has stacked the reams of paper so tightly together and all the way to the next shelf above and below that I can't easily pull a single ream out. Setting the paperwork and the key on a stack of pencil boxes on the shelving next to me, I tug with all my strength, but the paper isn't budging. I blow out a breath of frustration and crane my neck to see if the shelf above has a stack that's not packed like Lainey's suitcase after a trip to New York.

In the center there's a stack with only five reams. If I stand on my tiptoes and wiggle the bottom ream, hopefully I can get it out without tumbling the other four reams down on my head.

Just as I start to tug, warmth spreads across my shoulders and along my back. Grasping the top ream of paper, Ethan pulls it down and sets it on top of the stack of papers and the key, saying, "It's amazing how when you want something bad enough, it finally comes to you."

He's all right. I close my eyes and soak in the sound of his deep baritone. "*What* comes to you?" I say quietly as I grip the shelf in front of me, my stomach tensing.

Ethan bends close and whispers in my ear, his voice gruff, "I remember everything, Nara. Every breathy sigh, the curve of your back, kissing every bruise, waiting until dawn to untie the bow on your bra, and being in awe with how beautiful you are when I saw you for the first time. I remember wanting you so bad my body ached that next morning, and how leaving without kissing you awake was one of the hardest things I've ever done."

As my heart thrums, he runs his nose down my neck and lowers his hand to my hip, his fingers sliding inside the top of my jeans. "I know what your birthmark looks like, because I slid a feather here," he says, hooking two fingers where my underwear curves over my hip. "It was my way of telling you that we'd finally finish what we started when I returned."

My eyes flutter open and an explosion of raw emotion slams through me, making it hard to breathe. "I found it and knew what it meant."

Ethan moves his lips to my temple, his voice hoarse and tortured. "Then why would you keep such a precious memory from me?"

"Ethan, I—"

He turns me around. "I want to see your eyes."

He has his memory, all of it...and he's here demanding answers. That has to count for something. I can't help the tears that trickle down my face. My heart jerks when Ethan brushes them away with his thumbs, his tone softening. "Just tell me, Sunshine."

I search his deep blue gaze, hoping he'll see my sincerity. "I didn't know if you'd still feel the same way about us once you got your full memory back. You were changing. You didn't seem to want me to be a part of this new you. You kept things from me. You were gone longer than you promised. And when you woke up without your memory, I just didn't know. It hurt to think that I'd open my heart up, only to have you walk away once everything came back to you."

He cups my face and pulls me to him, touching his chest to mine. "I'm sorry I got delayed coming back, but Danielle insisted she needed help with a trio of demons she'd discovered. I couldn't let her go after them by herself. Anyway, that's not important. I told you why I kept my distance. I'll always want to protect you. What has changed is that I realize now that not telling you where I was going before I left was a big mistake. I own that. I should've trusted you would support me no matter what."

He bows his head, his dark bangs falling to the side. "I've been shit on so many times, it's hard to let go of feeling as if that might happen again at any moment, especially once I discovered my life had just changed in such a drastic and irrevocable way when I learned I was Corvus. I meant what I said that night I spent with you, every bit of it. I don't deserve you, and I really should break it off. It's truly the only way to keep you completely safe, but I can't. I love you too much. You are my light. Do you believe me now? Really believe that you mean everything to me?"

I nod and smile past my trembling lips. The weight pressing on my heart is lighter, but Danielle still hangs between us like a dark cloud ready to let loose her violent storm. "I believe you, but I need you to believe me about Danielle, Ethan. She really—"

"I do," he says, sliding his fingers into my hair.

"You do?"

He nods, his fingers moving to my neck. "I confronted her and she admitted she tried to get you to break it off with me because she was trying to protect me." His fingers tighten slightly on the back of my neck and his expression hardens. "I'm sorry she did that, Nara. Apparently Corvus can get hyper-focused on fulfilling their duties to the point they don't understand the purpose of anything else."

Mr. Wicklow's comment on the need for Corvus to have Paladins pings around in my head. I start to tell Ethan, but he continues, his expression serious, "I told Danielle my personal life is none of her business and that you're off limits." His expression softens as he massages my neck. "She was supposed to find you and apologize this morning. Did she?"

I shrug. "I guess you can call what she said an apology, but she didn't just talk to me last night. She used her sword to scare the crap out of me."

His mouth slants in a grim line and he shakes his head. "Danielle says she didn't pull her sword. She was very frustrated that you appeared half-asleep and groggy when she tried to talk to you. She seemed surprised that you even remembered the conversation."

"I saw silver, Ethan."

His eyes darken, then light up with understanding. "She wears a thick silver bracelet on her wrist. That's probably what you saw."

Now that he mentions it, I do remember seeing the bracelet on her before, but I still press my lips together.

His body tenses. "Did you actually see a sword? I need to know."

I open my mouth, but quickly close it. "Not exactly."

Ethan's tense face relaxes. "Don't worry. Now that I've talked to her, she won't ever bother you like that again."

There's so much I want to tell him. "I'd like to talk to you some more, but I have to get to the office for Mr. Hallstead—hey, why aren't you in class?"

Ethan pulls me close and presses his lips to mine, murmuring, "I was waiting for the perfect time to get you alone."

Wrapping my arms around his neck, I kiss him back, then smile. "Closets seem to be a thing with us."

"Are you *sure* you have to go back to class?" His grip on my waist tightens and a slow, devil-may-care smile tilts his lips as he sets me back against the reams of paper behind us.

The fluttering in my stomach stirs to a crazed frenzy. I'm thankful I'm holding on to him when he plants a hot kiss on my throat, but just as his fingers slide up the back of my shirt, I gather the strength to push on his chest. "I really do have to go. Can you come to my house after school?"

Ethan flashes his rare brilliant smile and all I can do is stare. He's so devastatingly handsome, so incredibly sexy, I'm stripped bare, as if every bone in my body has just taken a vacation. If he ever decides to use his good looks to his advantage, he'd be beyond dangerous for any female with a pulse. I have to force myself to step out of his hold. "I take it that means I'll see you this afternoon?"

His sexy smile turns tender as he brushes his fingers down my cheek. "Just try to keep me away."

CHAPTER 20

Nara

I offer Ethan an apologetic smile as I open my front door and say in a low tone, "Mom's home early. Try to pretend like you don't notice the explosion in the kitchen."

His dark eyebrows shoot up, but he grins and steps inside as I close the door behind him.

"Hi, Ethan." Mom glances up from rolling out her very first crepe. Jingle Bells is playing softly in the background, and the island is littered with baking items: a bag of flour, sifter, bowls and spoons, rolling pen, rolling mat.

"Hey, Mrs. Collins," he says, laying his jacket on the stool.

"I'm making crepes for dinner. Will you be joining us? I want to make sure we have enough." Pushing a strand of hair away from her face, she smiles. "Oh, Mr. Dixon will also be here."

Ethan acts like he doesn't notice the streak of flour she just rubbed on her forehead as he clasps my hand and pulls me to his side. "I'd love to stay for dinner if it's not too much trouble."

His deep voice must've finally overridden the lure of food scraps, because Houdini pokes his head around the corner of the island, then bolts toward us, his nose and paws sprinkled with flour.

"Whoa, sit, boy," Ethan says, holding his hand out to keep Houdini from throwing his hundred pound weight against him.

I laugh when my dog drops his butt to the floor, his tongue flopping out of his mouth as he waits for Ethan's next command. Though, he's only so obedient. His tail wags at a rapid thump, thump in his excitement.

While Ethan rewards him with a head pat and an ear scrub, I say to Mom, "We're going upstairs for a little bit unless you need my help with anything?"

She glances up, her furrowed brow smoothing briefly. "I'm just trying to make sure I do this right." Waving us on, she returns her gaze to the counter. "I'll call you if I need you."

"Okay, Mom." I smile at Ethan and tug him toward the stairs.

Of course, Houdini is right on our heels, but Ethan turns to him and says in a commanding voice, "Stay here. We'll be back."

Houdini lifts his big brown eyes to me and I nod, glancing back toward the kitchen. "Stay and keep Mom company, boy."

As we walk up the stairs, Ethan glances down at the garland and asks, "Why haven't you put up a tree yet?"

I laugh. "We usually buy a live one, but Mom's worried Houdini will think it's his own personal pee post." Shrugging, I pull him to the landing. "Plus, she likes to drag out the holiday, since half the time she ends up working late right up through the end of the year to close out her company's books. For us, Christmas just lasts longer; we usually celebrate and do gift exchanges on the first of January so Mom can relax and enjoy it."

His eyebrows shoot up as he steps close and rests our clasps hands on the small of my back. "So you want me to wait 'til then to give you your gift?"

"If you don't mind. Then you can celebrate with Mom and me. And maybe this year Aunt Sage will come and Gran too. My Gran's a... unique character. I think you'll love her." Smiling, I turn and lead him down the hall.

The second we cross the threshold into my room, Ethan tugs me into his arms and presses his mouth to mine. I laugh and thread my fingers in his hair, kissing him back.

"I can't get enough of you," he murmurs against my mouth, his hand sliding along the small of my back to pull me closer. "We have lots of lost time to make up for."

I curl my fingers in his hair and lose myself in Ethan's lips moving against mine, their persuasive warmth drawing me in. I've missed him so much. When our breathing starts to elevate, he lifts his mouth long enough to groan his frustration. "I wish we were alone."

I start to nod my agreement, but he kisses me again with a fierceness that slams straight to my belly. "I'll stop in a minute, I promise," he rasps against my mouth.

"I know," I start to say, but he cuts me off, his tongue sliding hungrily against mine while his hands glide down my back, curving along my hips as if he's trying to memorize every part of me. The thought seduces me even more, and I match his passionate kiss, clasping him against me.

"I've spent so many sleepless nights thinking about us, missing touching your face, your hair, the feel of your body locked close," he murmurs against my mouth. "I hated the distance that kept growing between us. I know it's my fault. I never meant to hurt you." A low rumble vibrates in his chest as he kisses me again, tangling his tongue with mine. Lifting his head, his deep blue eyes turn even darker as he cups my rear, his hold tight, possessive. "Being apart nearly killed me."

This is the Ethan who ignited a fierce burning need inside me that night—the Ethan who'd started to accept who he was and went after what he wanted, never backing down. I burn everywhere at once; his even stronger intensity leaves me unable to form a coherent sentence.

Ethan's fingers flex on my rear. "Do you forgive me, Sunshine?" he says in a low, tortured voice right before he pulls me fully against him.

The sincerity in his eyes melts my heart, while the feel of his hardness molding to me draws a gasp from my lips. Heat unfurls in my belly, spreading to my chest and thighs. "How's this for an answer?" I say, and I lift up onto my toes to get as close as I can.

Ethan's arms come around my back and our mouths mash together, hunger and need fueling our kiss. As we drown in each other, everything around us ceases to exist. I vaguely notice stumbling over a pile of clothes, bumping into my desk and nearly knocking over my trashcan, but I don't care.

Somewhere in the distance, someone's calling my name. I jump away from Ethan as my mom's voice finally bleeds through. We stare at each other, quietly panting as I turn and shout, "Did you call me, Mom?"

"Houdini's asking to go out."

"Okay, I'm coming."

When I turn back to Ethan, his sexy mouth is curved in a pleased, dark smile. "What?" I ask, my heart still thumping hard.

His grin widens. "It's just good to know I'm not the only one who has a hard time keeping my hands to myself."

I start to shake my head in denial, but Ethan raises an eyebrow as he slowly re-tucks his button down shirt back into his jeans.

Vague recollection floods my mind...my hands gripping his cotton shirt, the bottom button popping off as I yank it from his pants. Embarrassed heat shoots up my neck, but before I make it out of the room, Ethan's by my side, clasping my hand. Leaning close, his deep voice fills my ear, spreading through my insides like warm honey. "You didn't hold back. *That's* the Nara I want."

By the time I get back from taking Houdini out—and finally convincing Lainey that I really was okay by texting her a picture of Ethan's jacket on our kitchen stool with Mom in her flour-coated apron in the background, captioned: *He's putting his life in Mom's culinary-challenged hands. If that's not proof I'm good, I don't know what is*—my hormones have settled.

Ethan's sitting on my bed, holding the picture he'd drawn of me that day by the pond. He'd propped the picture against my birthday present as a surprise the morning he left to go collect his things from Michigan—well, D.C. He looks up as I step through the doorway, his expression subdued, contemplative. "I never did ask...does your camera take good pictures?"

I nod and try not to look at the box he'd taken the picture from under my bed. It's the same box that holds the silver ring and other memories I want to keep. Apparently I'd forgotten to put the lid back on and tuck it fully back under the last time I pulled it out.

"Yes, it takes great pics. I've used it to take snapshots of the animals at the shelter. Did I tell you the adoption rate has doubled?" I ask as I sit down beside him and use my foot to slide the box farther under my bed. Too many unfiltered, raw thoughts reside in its cardboard walls, jotted down on scraps of paper. Ethan doesn't need to see them.

He smiles and holds the picture beside my face. "It's not as good as the real thing. It's missing all the spark that makes you so unique."

His sweet compliment warms me as I take the picture and lean it against my lamp on my nightstand. "Thank you for remembering my birthday."

Turning back to him, I ask, "How did your memory come back to you? Did you just wake up and it was all there?"

"It was after you left yesterday. I was wrecked and reacted. After, I uh…had some cleaning to do. Once I started vacuuming, that's when it all came flooding back." Snorting, he shakes his head. "All that time I spent training, I thought for sure that would trigger my memories. Who knew all it would take was doing a simple, mundane task to unlock it. And when they started coming back, the memories gushed through in one big flood of images and emotions. Yeah, I had a hell of a headache the rest of the day."

I brush aside a lock of his hair. "I'm just glad they came back. You seem more…settled." Ethan clasps my hand and lightly touches his lips to my wrist. When his mouth moves higher, getting closer to the scar on my palm, I fold my fingers closed. "My mom's going to call us down in a little bit. Before she does, there's something I wanted to talk to you about."

Lowering our hands to his thigh, he threads his fingers with mine. "Fire away."

"How is Danielle so sure you're not creating Furiae?"

Hesitation reflects in Ethan's gaze, and my chest starts to ache, but this time I tap into that determined, passionate girl who demanded answers from Mr. Wicklow, and who just now got so lost in Ethan's arms she didn't hear her mom calling. I squeeze his hand. "No more holding back."

He nods, running his thumb over mine. "The reason I know we're not creating Furiae is because of Danielle. She'd told me she was special in the past and asked me not to tell anyone what she was, but when I told her what you said about the Furiae, she revealed something she hadn't before. She's the Master Corvus."

That's the last thing I expected Ethan to tell me. I'm so shocked I just stare at him. I'd planned to tell him everything Mr. Wicklow told me, but if Danielle really is the Master Corvus, now I know why she reacted the way she did when Ethan first mentioned the Order.

Ethan lowers his face to my level. "I can tell you want to say something."

What I *want* is to tell him to run away from Danielle and never look back. Instead, I swallow my fear and ask as calmly as I can, "Why is she here?"

Ethan shakes his head. "What do you mean?"

I stand and try not to show how much this news worries me. Why would the Master Corvus want Ethan to embrace his darkness, encourage it even? "What big event is getting ready to happen?"

"I'm not following you, Nara."

"The Master Corvus only takes over a person on our plane when our world is threatened."

His eyebrows pull down and creases form around his mouth. "Why didn't you mention this before?"

"Why didn't Danielle already tell you this?" I counter his question while sending a silent prayer of thanks that he didn't ask where I got my information. I meant what I said about "no more holding back." If he had asked, I would have told him. "It seems only fair that the Master Corvus should tell you what's coming since she's training you."

When Ethan doesn't have an immediate response, I sit beside him once more. "I didn't say anything before now because we've never discussed the Master Corvus. She knows the history, because she *is* the history. I can't understand why she's only told you surface stuff. Why have I learned more from others when you've been training with the source? Ask her why she's here. If you're expected to help, you have a right to know."

Ethan looks away, deep in thought.

Just as Houdini saunters into my room, Mom calls, "Nara, Ethan! Dinner's almost ready. Why don't you come on down? David will be here soon."

Ethan starts to follow me out of my room when he pauses and lifts my dad's fedora from the corner of my mirror. "This is new." Dropping it on my head, he nods. "Not many girls look hot in hats, but you rock it."

My smile trembles as I take the hat off and slide the brim through my fingers. "Thanks. It's my dad's."

Ethan's eyes light up. "Your dad's? Did you finally see him while I was gone?"

I shake my head and sigh as I hook my dad's hat back on my mirror. "My dad wasn't on an extended business trip like we thought. He's gone missing."

"He's missing? How did you get his hat then?"

Turning to face him, I quickly tell him about the videos my dad left behind, why he left Mom and me, and that Fate said my dad is still alive. "At this point, there aren't any leads from the people he works with. He's just…gone."

"Why haven't you told me about your dad?"

I shrug. "You had so much going on, the last thing I wanted to do was dump my issues on you."

Ethan spreads his hands, then lets them fall by his side. "So it's okay for you to expect me to share, but you get to keep everything to yourself? That's a bit of a double standard, don't you think?"

He's upset about my dad? That's the last thing I expected. Right now I'm emotional after reliving stuff about my dad all over again; I don't want to fight about this. "We should go downstairs."

I start to walk past him, but Ethan stretches his arm out, blocking my exit. When I try to push his arm out of the way, he curls it around my chest, pulling me back against him. "Your worries are mine, Nara," he says into my hair. "How can you expect me to think we're a team and that we work better together, when you don't?"

I hold back the sob that's trapped in my chest and rest my chin on his arm. "You're right. I'm sorry I didn't tell you."

Ethan wraps his arms around my waist, hugging me against his hard frame, his voice softer. "I'm sorry about your dad. Hopefully—"

The doorbell rings, sending Houdini down the stairs barking in full defense mode. As Mom fusses at Houdini to settle so she can open the door, I sigh and glance up at Ethan, waiting. The second Mr. Dixon's voice floats upstairs, understanding dawns in his eyes.

"That sucks."

I lift my shoulders, dropping them in defeat. "Knowing that my dad didn't leave us for some selfish reason is killing me." I pause at the sound of Mom talking to Mr. Dixon about dinner and his rumbling reply. "And now she's cooking something from scratch for him? Ugh, holding back the truth makes me want to pull my hair out, but I know it's for the best right now."

Ethan shakes his head. "It seems like nothing in either of our lives is ever simple." Kissing me on the temple, he nods to the doorway. "Let's go make the most of it for your mom."

I take a breath and nod, but pause to remind him before we head downstairs, "Mom seems to have conveniently forgotten her past cooking experiments. No matter how they taste, happily choke the crepes down, okay?"

Nara

Is there an early pep rally? I wonder as I slip through the school's main doors.

People are packed in the atrium, all bunched together, their voices raised in a fever pitch. Everyone's cheering and yelling. Then as I take in their raised fists and aggressive expressions, I realize there's a fight.

Apparently no teachers are around to stop this one. I roll my eyes and try to skirt past the rubberneckers, but someone calls my name.

Casting my gaze over the crowd, I seek the source. Lainey is standing on the square base of one of the columns flanking the atrium. Her arm's wrapped around its curved surface while she points to the center of the crowd. I've never seen her look so frantic.

Panic seizes my chest, and I move to the north stairwell curving around the outer edge of the atrium, pushing past people lined along the railing so I can see below.

Matt's standing to the side on the main floor, cradling his jaw. Danielle's a few feet away from him, watching Ethan slam Drystan to the ground with a pounding blow. Amusement glitters in her eyes and her arms are crossed as if she has no plans to interfere.

"No!" I scream, but the crowd is too loud. No one hears me. They're too busy yelling and encouraging the fight.

Drystan rolls to the balls of his feet and wipes the blood off his lip. Snarling, he springs up and twists in the air like a bullet, slamming Ethan in the chest with his feet.

Ethan stumbles back but quickly recovers, then storms after Drystan with clenched fists and renewed wrath in his eyes.

My backpack drops to the floor as I run down the steps and shoulder my way through the crowd entranced with bloodlust.

"Stop it!" I call out, but Ethan and Drystan have locked themselves together with one arm while delivering punches anywhere they can with their free fists.

I don't know what to do, so I run and jump onto Ethan's back, yelling in his ear, "Ethan, stop fighting!"

Ethan stiffens under me, and just as I look up to say something else to calm him down, I clutch his neck tight and cringe. Drystan's fist is slamming toward my face in a fast downward arc.

Ethan jerks upright, then captures Drystan's fist midair, stopping it as if there wasn't any force behind the flying fist. As a hush rushes over the crowd, a rumble of fury erupts from Ethan's chest right before he drops Drystan to his knees with a mere flick of his wrist. Bending close to Drystan's ear, he snarls, "Be glad I'm faster than you. If you had harmed her, you'd be dead right now."

A haze of pain blurs through Drystan's eyes, dissipating the blinding anger that had been there before. He blinks and stares at my face hovering close to his from my position on Ethan's back. "Nara?"

When Ethan grunts and straightens, flinging his hand down, Drystan falls back on his butt, his eyes never leaving mine. "I'm sorry. I didn't see you."

"I know you didn't." I sigh and release my death hold on Ethan, sliding down his back.

The second my feet hit the floor, Ethan quickly pulls me in front of him, scanning my face, his eyes full of frustration and concern. "Why would you do that? Are you all right?"

"What were you thinking?" While my gaze pings between them, Drystan slowly stands and clenches and unclenches the fist Ethan had in a vise hold.

Ethan narrows his eyes on Drystan. "He made one snide comment too many."

Drystan snorts and pushes on his lip to stop the bleeding. "He came looking for it."

"Mr. Harris and Mr. Maddox. My office, now!" Mr. Wallum's furious voice reverberates through the atrium like a sonic boom, scattering the students.

While Ethan and Drystan head for the main office, Lainey runs up and hugs my neck tight. "God, I thought Ethan was going to kill him." Pulling back, she touches my face. "Are you okay?"

I nod as I scan for Danielle. *Where'd she go?*

"I tried to stop them." Matt holds his chin, rocking it back and forth in his hand.

"Like you could've stopped them." Lainey sighs and turns from me to gingerly touch his jaw. "This has been brewing between them ever since that scrimmage."

"I'm just glad Ethan listened to me," I finally say, adrenaline still pumping through me.

"He sure as hell wasn't listening to me," Matt says. "I got an elbow in the jaw for my efforts."

"That's because you got in the way," Danielle says in a dry tone from behind me. "If he'd meant to hit you, you'd be hurting a lot more than you are right now."

Matt rolls his eyes. "Guess I'll count myself lucky then. Drystan's going to feel every punch tomorrow."

Danielle snickers. "It could've been much worse for him. He's lucky Ethan held back."

Lainey eyes Danielle, her brow pinched. "You talk like you've seen Ethan fight before."

Danielle brushes her long hair over her shoulder. "I have. We've trained together for a while."

"You can move like that?" Matt looks at her, awed.

Lainey shoots a cocked eyebrow my way. "Trained together?"

"Yeah, Ethan told me he and Danielle took defense classes when they were younger," I quickly say as I untwist Lainey's backpack strap on her shoulder.

"Yep, that's what we do, defend," Danielle agrees, a slight smile tilting her lips.

Before Danielle can say anything to unravel the story I've just made up, I gesture to the empty atrium. "We'd better get to class or Mr. Wallum will be after us next."

Lainey, Matt, and Danielle turn toward the main hall, but Lainey pauses when I don't immediately follow. "Aren't you coming?"

I nod to my backpack, relieved that it's still sitting on the staircase. "I have to get my stuff and head to my locker first. See you in study hall later."

The hall is quiet as I open my locker and switch out books for my first class. My hands are still shaking, but I manage to hang my backpack, then retrieve the books quickly. As soon as I shut my locker door, Danielle's standing behind it, her face bent to my level. I gulp back a yelp of surprise, then snort my annoyance.

"You're pretty good at making shit up on the fly," she says, grudging respect in her eyes.

I'm not in the mood to deal with her right now. "What do you want, Danielle?"

Straightening, she jerks her head toward the atrium. "You see what happened out there today. This is why you need to break it off. Things were getting heated fast and if you hadn't stopped Ethan…" She trails off, spreading her arms wide.

"You could've stopped them," I snap, angry she's trying to blame me.

She folds her arms and shrugs. "Corvus take care of themselves."

"Then why did you need Ethan's help to deal with three demons?" I swipe my hand between us as if brushing off a table. "The Master Corvus should've been able to wipe them up like yesterday's crumbs—"

"Do you want Ethan to die?" she cuts me off, her mouth set in a thin line.

"Of course not!" I grip my spiral notebook so hard the metal rings dig into my fingers. "What kind of question is that?"

"A valid one. You're a weakness, a liability for Ethan. He and I are the same. We welcome the rush and the risk, but we also have each other's backs as equals. You aren't Corvus. You don't understand us. We *get* each other. We're truly connected at a spiritual level." Smiling, she leans her back against the lockers and bends her knee, propping her booted foot against the metal. "Did you really think he could resist me?"

I narrow my gaze and turn to face her. "What are you saying?"

She tilts her head back and releases a low, throaty laugh, then crosses her arms and rolls onto her shoulder to face me. "You're so naive, Nara. Ethan and I are more than friends. God, his mouth is pure sin."

"You're lying." Before I realize what I'm doing, I've dropped my notebooks and am shoving her back against the lockers. "Ethan would never—"

"Lie to you?" She raises her eyebrow and easily unhooks my grip from her jacket, pushing me away like an annoying fly. "We both know that's not true." Her chin raises a notch. "Go ahead. Ask him. I'll even give you a hint. You talked to me that night."

Turning, she walks off as if she's just informed me I have pepper in my teeth, not delivered mind-rending, heart-ripping news.

Once she leaves the hall, I pull my phone out of my pocket and find Ethan's phone number, then scroll through our history to the date I called his phone and only spoke for a few seconds. As soon as I find the call, I quickly flip through my pictures looking for the one I took of the hotel receipt I'd found in his pocket while he was in the hospital.

My legs start to shake and I lean back against the lockers, sliding down the cold metal until my butt hits the hard floor.

The dates match.

CHAPTER 21

Nara

For the first time ever, I skip the rest of my day at school.
Actually, I skip the last two classes of the day once Lainey informs me in the hall that Ethan and Drystan got ISS (in-school suspension) for fighting. It's not like I can concentrate anyway. I didn't tell her about my conversation with Danielle, mainly because I'm holding on to the belief that Danielle's a lying bitch out to destroy our relationship.

Either way, whether she's lying or not, I fear for Ethan's future. How can the Master Corvus do this to him? What kind of agenda does she have…other than to *own* him body and soul? The thought burns my stomach.

I have no idea when I'll get a chance to speak to Ethan at school, so I get in my car and drive around until I find his. Parking next to the black Mustang, I drape my wrist over my steering wheel and settle in for the final bell.

After the last bell of the day goes off, I wait until every car in the student parking lot is gone but mine and Ethan's. When I see Matt's Jeep return to the school entrance an hour later to pick up Drystan, I open my door.

Five minutes pass before Ethan strolls out of the school. He's half-way through the parking lot before he looks up and sees me leaning against his car door. The warm wind blows my hair around my face, but I don't take my gaze off him as I push the strands out of my eyes.

Ethan digs his hands into his pockets and picks up his pace. Once he reaches me, his mouth sets in a stubborn slant. "I'm not going to apologize for hitting him. He deserved it."

His shoulders are tense, his expression unforgiving.

I just shrug. "I don't want to talk about Drystan."

Surprise flickers in his eyes, then he smiles and starts to step toward me, but I take a step back. "I'm going to ask you something and I want the truth."

Ethan gives me a wary look, then shrugs. "Okay."

"Did you sleep with Danielle?"

He scowls. "Hell no! Why would you ask me that?"

I press my lips together, thinking about that hotel receipt. "So you're saying you didn't share the same bed with her?"

His shoulders tense for a second, then he shrugs. "Once, while we were out hunting. We ended up having to share a room. We were dead tired and the hotel only had one left."

I clench my jaw. "Did you kiss her?" When he starts to shake his head, I hold up my hand. "Truth, Ethan."

Ethan rubs the back of his neck, then exhales. "I woke up to her kissing me, but once I realized she wasn't you, I pushed her away."

"But you kissed her," I say calmly while my body shakes on the inside.

Ethan lifts his hands. "Technically, yes, but on purpose, no. There's a *big* difference," he says, giving me a pointed look.

"What the hell, Ethan?" *I unwound* time *to stop Drystan from kissing me before the dance!* "Were you ever planning to tell me?"

"Were you?" he blasts back, fury stamped on his face.

"What are you talking about?"

He stares me down, the muscle in his jaw working, and I turn and open my car door.

"Nara, wait."

Ethan tries to clasp my hand, but I shake him off. "Don't, Ethan." Closing my door hard, I lock it and refuse to look at him. I don't let the tears fall until I can no longer see Ethan in my rearview mirror.

Nara

I've only been home long enough to let Houdini out when my phone buzzes with a text from Drystan.

Drystan: Today's the last day of this weird warm weather. Want to meet me in the park for a session now?

I consider refusing because my emotions are all over the place, but I haven't had a chance to talk to him since he and Ethan fought. Danielle was right about one thing; Drystan was lucky Ethan held back. I don't want him going after Ethan again.

Me: I'll change and meet you there in fifteen.

Apparently we're not the only ones taking advantage of the warm day. Several groups of people are enjoying the playground and picnic areas when I arrive.

I walk up to Drystan sitting on a nearby bench. It looks strange to see him in athletic shorts and a T-shirt while the grass is winter-yellow and the only trees with foliage are the pines, but I'm dressed the same way. We'd be sweating like crazy five minutes into training otherwise. The beginnings of a black eye are starting as well as a bruise along his jaw. Otherwise, he looks pretty good for someone who started his day with a brawl.

"You ready for a run first?"

Drystan glances up at me, squinting against the sun. "You know I'd never intentionally hurt you, right? I'm sorry it came that close."

"I know." I wave my hand. "Come on. Let's go."

"You don't want to talk about it?"

I shrug. "Only to say, 'don't ever get into a fight with Ethan again.'"

He scowls. "Protecting your boyfriend?"

I roll my eyes and shake my head. "No, I'm protecting you. Oh, and by the way, since you asked me to point it out, what you just now said, that was you being an 'arse,'" I say before I take off running toward the wooded path. I've already entered the cool forest of pines at the backside of the park when Drystan catches up.

"For the record, I've said more annoying things to him in the past."

I lift my knees higher to jump over a fallen branch lying across the path. "Apparently you reached your quota. Quit trying to antagonize him." I glance his way. "In case it wasn't crystal clear today, he can absolutely pound you into the ground if he wanted to."

"It's all that darkness," Drystan says on a snarl, clenching his hands tighter as he runs slightly ahead of me.

We run for another half mile before Drystan veers off into an open space we've used in the past. I smile at the slack line he's left stretched between two trees. "Why is it still up?"

He lifts his hand. "We haven't been on it in a while. I thought you'd enjoy doing some tricks on it before I took it down. Then we can work on some defense moves if you want."

I point to the tree. "But we didn't bring the ladder."

He bends at the knees and cups his hands together. "I'll give you a boost up."

Grinning, I step into his hand and wrap my arm around his neck to keep my balance as he instantly lifts me toward the slack line several feet above our heads. My fingers grip the inch wide flexible nylon, then I curl into a ball and try to pull myself up, but it's so springy and wobbly, I just end up upside down with my hips and thighs holding me on the line.

I laugh at my ineptness. Drystan would have monkey-climbed up on the thin line in five seconds flat. "This didn't work out so well."

Drystan's grinning like he's having a hard time not laughing. "I think you're doing great."

"Har, har. Tell me how to get up on this dang thing."

Moving beside me, he bends his knees slightly so his face is close to mine. "Straighten your body as much as you can. Pretend a line has been drawn from your head to your toes if you have to. I'll make sure you don't tip over. Once you're ready, I'll roll you over on the line, which should end up at your bum."

I hold my arms stretched out. "Like this?"

"You have to straighten your legs too." Grabbing hold of my thigh, he says, "Go on. Straighten. I've got you."

I take a deep breath and as I slowly uncurl my body, the line bounces. Drystan moves under the line and presses a hand to my stomach, keeping me balanced on both sides.

"I'm going to roll you now. You ready?"

When I nod, he starts to turn me. As I flip onto my back, the loss of balance sensation is so strange that it makes me instantly want to bend. As I yelp and start to curl inward, Drystan says, "Make yourself stiff."

I throw my arms out to the sides, making a big T. Suddenly I'm lifted off the line and shifted until I feel it pressing against my butt.

Drystan moves his hands to my lower spine and the back of my thighs. "Now you can start to sit up. Do it slowly and with as little movement as possible. Remember to keep your balance centered."

A few seconds later, he moves out from under me and grins, spreading his hands wide. "You did it."

I grimace. "You really don't expect me to bounce my way to a standing position on this like you do, right?"

He steps forward and grabs my dangling ankles. "Why not. You've got the ability. You just lack the confidence to believe you can do it." To prove his point, he pulls down on my ankles slightly.

I instantly lower my hands to the stretching line. "Don't you dare!"

"What?" A mischievous grin slides up his face right before he lets go.

As the line bounces upward, my body starts to lift off the thin seat. I yelp and almost forget everything I've learned, but then suddenly, I elevate my arms and tighten my stomach muscles, forcing my frame to remain centered as my butt reconnects with the line once more.

A few bounces later, the line settles. I glare at Drystan. "That was not nice."

He shrugs and steps closer, folding his arms. "You control your own center, Nara. Well, so long as you don't let outside forces influence you."

I can tell by his serious expression he's talking about more than slacklining. I open my mouth to make a snappy response but something pops and my seat suddenly disappears.

"Nara!" Drystan jerks forward, catching me on the way down.

We land in a tangle of limbs with me lying on top of Drystan. He quickly clasps my shoulders. "Are you okay?"

"I'm good." I roll off him onto my back, my breath sawing in and out as I stare at the broken slackline. "I'm really glad I hadn't tried any tricks yet. This is why you don't leave these lines out in cold weather."

Drystan's gaze locks on the broken line as he scrubs a hand through his windblown hair. "I'm sorry. I guess it can't handle the kind of extreme weather changes you have here in Virginia."

I shake my head. "This weather is not normal for us."

Rolling onto his side, Drystan leans on his forearm. "Speaking of 'not normal' there's something I've been meaning to ask you."

"Okay." I raise up onto my elbows and try not to look tense. There's so much that's "not normal" in my life lately, I have no clue which part he'll ask about.

"The last time you and I combined our powers—when I found Ethan's lost phone—I got this flash of me kissing you."

Despite the "Oh, shit! How can he be seeing that?" going on inside my head, I manage to laugh it off. "Ha, that's odd. Maybe it's from a dream you had."

His brow puckers and he shakes his head. "It was a bit like a dream in that it had a sort of surreal feel, but I haven't dreamed this. You're dressed up like the night at the dance, and I smell your shampoo and I remember the feel of your lips against mine."

"Wow, um…that's vivid." I sit up and brush the dead leaves off my elbows to keep from having to look him in the eyes.

Drystan blows out an unsteady breath and sits up too, staring into the tall pines. "I know this is going to sound crazy." His attention swings back to me, curiosity reflected in his green eyes. "But have you had a dream like this?"

I quickly shake my head and lie. "You know I only dream my next da—"

He touches my chin and shakes his head. "What I'm trying to ask in a round about way is…have you ever wondered about us?"

His mouth is curved in an adorably lopsided, sincere smile, not the sexy one he uses to entice the girls at school. I think of Ethan and how angry I am that he didn't tell me about that kiss with Danielle, and that I had to find out from her. The humiliation tightens my chest.

"I have." Drystan's fingers trace under my jaw. "Many times."

When he starts to lean close, I press my hand to his chest and push back slightly. "I won't do that to Ethan." *No matter how mad I am at him right now.*

Drystan cups his hand over mine, his expression serious. "Maybe it's time for you to start putting Nara first."

"There you are!" Matt bursts into the clearing, then leans over to catch his breath. Glancing between us with a raised eyebrow, he shrugs and continues, "If it hadn't been for some guy who remembered seeing you two head in this direction, I would've never found you. Drystan, your class was moved to today. The guy who runs the gym had to re-schedule. He called to tell you he's e-mailed the people signed up to let them know about the change. Most of them have already confirmed they'll be there in…" He glances at his watch. "Fifteen minutes. You can take my car. Lainey'll give me a ride back home."

I quickly stand and brush off my shorts. "Better get going, Drystan. By the time you get there, your class will be ready to start."

Drystan moves over to the tree and gestures for Matt to boost him up so he can take down the slackline. Casting a regretful half smile my way, he says, "Thanks for the run. I needed to blow off some steam." His eyebrows elevate. "You're welcome to come to class if you'd like."

I smile and shake my head. "Thanks, but I have some errands to do. I'll see you at school tomorrow."

As I turn into my driveway, Lainey pulls in right behind me. Before I can hit the garage door button, she's out of her car and standing beside my window.

"Oh no, you don't, Nara Collins." Pointing to the ground, she narrows her gaze.

Sighing, I step out of my car in the driveway. "What's wrong? Why do you look mad?"

Lainey huffs and tugs her purse higher on her shoulder. "Matt told me he walked up on you and Drystan kissing. Is that why he and Ethan were fighting this morning? And why the hell didn't you tell me you had a thing for Drystan? I feel like you're not telling me anything going on in your life lately. That's not what best friends do. They share things." Tucking a lock of hair behind her ear, she takes a deep breath after her tirade and softens her tone. "Don't you want to know if Matt and I have had sex?"

I grip her wrist. "Jared wasn't your first?"

"Nara! No, I never did it with Jared. Though not for his lack of trying." Rolling her eyes, she sighs heavily. "This is what I'm talking about. It feels like we've gotten away from sharing. That's the best part of being a 'best friend.'"

If only I could share everything, Lainey. Hooking my arm around her neck, I pull my friend toward my front door. "Come on. Let's have some girl time."

Houdini immediately greets Lainey with huge slobbery kisses. To her credit, my "easily grossed out" friend doesn't gag like I expect her to. Instead, she gets on her knees and hugs Houdini's neck tight. Then she grabs his jowls and baby talks to him.

"You're such a big cutie. I can't wait to bring Lochlan over to visit with you. You boys will have a blast."

I smile, picturing her father's Jack Russell and Houdini romping in the front yard.

Once Lainey settles on the stool next to me in the kitchen, I turn to face her. "*Have* you and Matt had sex yet?"

Lainey shakes her head. "We're close. It's a big commitment for me. It's why I never gave it up to Jared. As much as I had the hots for him, something just didn't feel right, so I held back." A look of evil triumph flits across her face. "It drove him nuts."

I nod, thinking about Ethan and me. "It's good that you're taking your time. I think it's a gut thing…that you'll know when it's right."

Lainey's smile brightens. "It'll definitely be with Matt. I just don't want to rush everything too fast." Tapping me on the nose, she says, "Now tell me about Drystan."

I shake my head. "Matt is dead wrong. Drystan and I weren't kissing. He was leaning close trying to convince me to kiss him when I told him that I would never do that to Ethan." Glancing away, I mutter, "Even though I'm really mad at him right now."

Lainey grabs my hand on the counter, her eyes wide. "What did Ethan do?"

"It's not what Ethan did. Technically he didn't *do* anything."

Lainey jiggles my wrist back and forth on the smooth surface. "The suspense is killing me. Just spit it out, Nara."

I hold her curious brown gaze. "Danielle told me in the hall today that she and Ethan kissed."

Lainey frowns. "Wait, how can Ethan kissing Danielle technically not be 'doing anything' in your eyes?"

Ugh, I didn't think through how I was going to explain this without revealing Corvus related stuff. "Because she kissed him out of the blue, surprising him. He didn't kiss her back."

"Ahh, I see. If Ethan's innocent, it sounds like Danielle was trying to crawl under your skin and make you question your relationship."

I grimace and draw figure eights with my finger on the counter. "Well, it worked. Ethan and I just had the biggest fight we've ever had."

"Because he *didn't* kiss her?"

"No, because I had to find out it happened from *her* and not him."

"Whoa!" Lainey raps her knuckles against my knee. "I admit Ethan should've told you. That was definitely a screw up on his part, but are you really going to let her win?"

"What do you mean 'let her win?'"

Lainey scooches her stool closer until her knees touch mine "Don't you see…if she can't have Ethan, she's making sure you don't either."

"But you don't understand. There's just a lot—" —*you don't know.*

My friend clasps my face and presses her forehead to mine. "Do you love Ethan?"

I cup shaky hands over hers and nod, a hard lump in my throat.

Releasing me, Lainey squeezes my hands. "Then talk it out with him. How else are you going to tell me about the great sex parts later?"

When I sob out a laugh, she smiles and hops off the stool. "I'll bet he's left you a zillion messages. Have you even checked?" Before I can move, she pulls my phone out of my backpack and turns it toward me. "Mmmmm hmmmm."

I have several missed calls and a couple of texts from Ethan's phone.

CHAPTER 22

Nara

So far Mr. Wicklow hasn't tried to contact me, which I'm thankful for, but since I'm still not sure if my phone's being monitored or I'm being followed, I wait until it's dark to leave and take a long, meandering path to Ethan's, entering his neighborhood the back way.

Ethan's backing out of his driveway as I turn down his street. Disappointment grabs my chest and I let off the gas a little. Where could he be going? He hadn't tried to contact me since his last text several hours ago. My fingers grip the steering wheel tight as he turns out of his neighborhood. Pushing on the gas, I follow.

The last place I expected to end up is the downtown mall. I park my car on a lower level in the parking deck and keep my distance as Ethan makes his way up the alley and into the brickyard area at a brisk pace. I follow, but quickly step into the entrance of a card shop when Ethan pauses and glances over his shoulder.

Taking cover behind a card carousel, I'm surprised to see him enter an Irish pub called McCormicks. Based on the people entering behind him, it's a college-aged crowd. Is he meeting Danielle here? Is this another hunt to find Harper? I hang out in the card shop, pretending to browse for another five minutes before I decide to go get my fake ID.

By the time I return from my car, the line waiting to get inside McCormicks is now several storefronts long. I wait for a half hour in the long line before I get to the entrance and pay my cover charge.

The place is packed with people trying to find a seat or wall space to lean against in the dim light. Everyone's apparently here to listen to the band Weylaid, which I'd heard several guys and girls talking about in line. The band is warming up on the stage in the low light.

"We're just about ready," a dark-haired guy says into the mic. "Oh, and we have special guest Adder here tonight as well, so get ready for a rockin' evening, folks."

Several girls yell out Adder's name and a few even scream. I'm standing on my toes trying to scan the crowd for Ethan, but it's just too dark to see anything but shadows. The drummer begins tapping his drumsticks at the same time the stage lights start to slowly brighten. The crowd goes crazy, clapping, whistling, and hollering, and I'm relieved too. At least I can see better now.

The loud music starts up, guitars, drums, and keyboard melding together in perfect harmony. I find myself tapping out the beat with my toe as I start scanning heads down in the far corner, looking for Ethan's broad shoulders.

The lead singer begins the song and my gaze is drawn to him briefly. He has a nice voice and I really like the Southern rock feel of this music. It's exactly the kind Ethan would like. I continue my search through the crowd while enjoying the lyrics. I've made it halfway through the room when another voice joins in the chorus. The deep resonance gives me chills and feels strangely familiar. My attention instantly snaps back to the stage, pinging to each of the band members, looking for the source.

When my gaze lands on Ethan sitting on a stool playing the guitar and singing, my knees give out. A guy behind me grabs my arms before I make it all the way down. Hauling me upright, he yells over the music, "You okay?"

I nod and thank him, but quickly return my focus to the stage. Even though I try to hold them back, tears trickle down my cheeks as deep hurt swirls. Why didn't Ethan tell me about this part of his life? He's so talented, his voice sending goose bumps across my skin and chills down my spine. I would have come to every event. Every damned one!

My emotions ride the full gamut as I shoulder my way a bit closer to listen to Ethan sing backup and play so fiercely: sadness, pride, excitement, happiness, joy, elation, frustration, confusion, depression and then back to even deeper sadness. While he's playing, he's so caught up, it's like he's in another world. Unfortunately it's a world that doesn't include me. It makes me wonder how much about him I really do know. Has he only shared surface stuff with me like Danielle did with him? Is that a Corvus thing?

Mr. Wicklow had said Corvus are hard to get to know, difficult to talk to. All this time I thought he was wrong, that he didn't know Ethan like I did. But as I watch this side to Ethan unfold before my eyes, I start to question everything I thought I knew about the boy who stole my heart.

I'm just as mesmerized by the songs they play as everyone else, though my fascination comes with soul-searching realizations as the band ends the current set with the lead singer fading out and Ethan soloing the last few lyrics to a crowd-cheering crescendo.

Everyone jumps to their feet, applauding and cheering while the band takes a twenty minute break. I hop into an empty seat looking for Ethan. He's no longer on the stage, but making his way down the side stairs. Once he reaches the floor, a dark-haired girl flies into his arms. Ethan stumbles back and grips her waist.

Heat and fury wash over me when she pulls back and says, "That was fantastic! I can't wait to hear you sing *You Slay Me*." But it's when I see her profile that my chest feels as if it's collapsing inward. It's Danielle. She knows about his music? And she's heard him play before?

Suddenly the room is too small. There's not enough air and my lungs feel as if they're shrinking like fast leaking balloons. I stumble out of the chair and shove my way through the people crowding around the bar to get a drink before the next set starts.

As soon as I find a break in the crowd, I run for the main door, and slam into a group of three guys entering as I try to exit. The one with curly brown hair grabs my arms and laughs. "Whoa, where's the fire—?" He dips down to see my face better. "How do I know you?" Eyes lighting up, he glances to his friends. "Remember Ethan's girl from the woods?"

Straightening, he yells out, "Hey, Adder, your girl's here!" Then he points to the top of my head, grinning.

Ethan's Adder? I push past the guy and his friends, then burst through the crowd waiting to get in. Rain has started in a light drizzle, but I don't care how wet I get. I need to breathe or I'll collapse before I can make it to my car. Bending over, I put my hands on my knees and take a deep gulping, lungful of air. The temperature has turned colder since I entered the pub, and each inhale I take feels icy and harsh.

"Nara!" Ethan's voice calls over the crowd, jerking me upright.

I take off, then turn down a side alley as the rain starts to come down faster, soaking my thin, loose sweater. The boat neck slips down my shoulder as I run. I jerk the clingy, wet material back up and try to focus on putting one foot in front of the other. I don't want to see or talk to Ethan right now.

"Nara, wait!" Ethan says at the same time he grabs my hand.

I try to tug free, but he pulls me through a side door into some kind of back hall that's stacked with wooden boxes and smells of pine cleaner, old building and paint.

As soon as I'm inside, I yank my hand away and stare down the long hall past the wall lined with crates full of beer bottles. I can't face him. Can't look into his eyes. It'll hurt too much.

"Why are you here?" he asks quietly.

I jerk my eyes to his, my fury on high boil. "Is that all you have to say? I just watched Danielle throw herself at you. Surely you can think of something better to say than that?"

Ethan's gaze narrows and he moves closer, backing me against the wall. Just a few inches separate us. The smell of his aftershave makes my heart thump, but I refuse to look at him. Instead, I stare at his black t-shirt boasting the slogan *Bringing the A to Weylaid.*

Ethan places his hands on the wall on either side of me and lowers his eyes to mine. "First of all, you said it right. Danielle threw herself at me. It was either catch her or we'd both fall. I guess you were too busy leaving to see me pull her off and set her down."

"She knew about you being in this band, Ethan, and so did your guy friends, which is a hell of a lot more about you than I know."

Water drips off Ethan's hair as he slowly shakes his head. "I've never told anyone about Adder. The guys found out on their own, much to my annoyance. And Danielle must've followed me. Tonight's the first time she let me know she was here. When I'm in Adder mode, I usually zone completely out."

The meaning of the slogan on his T-shirt hits me with a wave of renewed sadness; he's been in the band long enough to have his own shirt. "Why didn't you tell me about your music?"

Ethan straightens and shoves a hand through his wet hair. "I only fill in with the band when I need to work through stuff, like us fighting earlier. I didn't tell you about the music because this talent isn't mine,

Nara. It's Adder's."

I tilt my head and frown. "You *are* Adder."

"No, I'm not," he says and then snorts, shaking his head. "Remember when I told you that we have memories from others who've hosted the Corvus before us?" When I nod, he continues, "Just like drawing soothes the Corvus craziness going on in my head, I think Adder's sanctuary was music. And because Adder came before me, his music does help me cope in some ways, but—" Ethan brushes a wet strand of my hair from my cheek "—I didn't want to introduce you to a guy who wasn't me. I wanted you to fall for the *real* me. The one who draws and understands what animals are thinking."

My eyebrows shoot up. "I thought the animal thing was just an intuitive sense. You actually understand them?"

"Yeah, mostly. The way I came to work for CVAS was a little different than I originally told you." He shrugs sheepishly. "I wanted to be as normal as possible."

I rub my wet hands on my jeans to hide the fact that they're shaking. His closeness is making me aware of how much I crave him touching me. "I'd rather you just be *you*, past talents included. Authentic and original is all the rage, you know." When Ethan starts to smile, I press my lips together and shake my head. "Why didn't you tell me about Danielle kissing you?"

His mouth thins and his shoulders tense. "For the same reason you didn't tell me about Drystan kissing you. It didn't mean anything. *Right?*"

"But Drystan didn't kiss me. I made sure it never happen— " I cut myself off, but realization filters in Ethan's eyes anyway.

"He *did* kiss you, didn't he? Just not today. That's what you were talking about when you said you changed your dream." Blackness swirls in his eyes and tension etches in his face. "I should've followed my Corvus' instincts and really hurt the bastard this morning."

Why would Ethan think that Drystan had kissed me today? I don't have time to ponder, because he steps close and cups my jaw, his anger shifting to focused intensity. "You're the only reason this Corvus stuff is bearable. The thought of losing you wrecks me."

"Ethan…" I clasp his hand, trying to regain control of my ability to think, but something dark along the inside of his wrist captures my attention. Pulling his hand back, my pulse races as I inspect the tattoo. The artist had masterfully incorporated TTTWFO, the sun, yin-yang, and a raven into an infinity symbol, making a gorgeous piece of art. I turn his wrist and run my thumb over the curved edge I'd only seen a glimpse of in the hospital. Emotion tightens my chest as I meet his gaze. "You got this while you were gone?"

He nods and traces my lips slowly with his thumb. "You were always with me, Sunshine."

The tattoo must have been under the bracelet they'd cut off at the hospital. "I wish I'd seen it before now."

A wry smile twists his lips. "I drew it and had it inked to keep you close no matter how far apart we were, but a tattoo can't tell you this…" Running his knuckles tenderly along my jaw, he says, "You're my direction. I never feel lost when I'm with you. Each time we're together the need to touch you, to *be* with you on a deeper level makes me shake. It grows stronger every day."

When he slides his fingers into my wet hair, the tension in his hold sends goose bumps down my arms, while the fact that he designed the tattoo himself melts my heart. "It means more than you realize," I say and start to press a kiss to his wrist, but Ethan tilts my face and hovers his mouth close to mine.

"There will never be anyone else for me."

His warm lips pressing intensely against mine sets off a firestorm of emotion. When he murmurs my name in his husky baritone, I open my mouth and welcome the urgent thrust of his tongue.

Ethan clasps my face tight and slants his mouth against mine. His hunger ignites my own and I grip his shoulders, digging my fingers deep. We fall against the wall, Ethan's weight pressing my damp sweater against my back. I gasp at the cold, but Ethan chuckles against my lips and slides his hand under my sweater. Flattening his palm against my upper back, he says, "Better?"

The skin-to-skin sensation creates a pocket of warmth that's so intimate, a heated response begins to rise within me, spiraling to every nerve ending. Ethan must have felt it too because his other hand falls to my rear, pulling me up and against him. He's so strong my feet are dangling off the floor. When I grip his neck tight and wrap my legs around his waist, Ethan groans and leans us back against the wall, kissing me harder, deeper, his fingers digging into my butt. As I cup his jaw and whimper against his mouth, wishing we weren't standing in a pub's back hall, Ethan's hips slowly move under me and all thoughts of where we are completely vanish. I cling to him as our world closes in around us in a shock of electric sensations moving between us, fusing our wants and needs toward an intimate connection we're building together.

"There you—" A bald guy at the end of the hall starts to say while noise from the bar floats through the open door behind him.

When Ethan quickly sets me down and I bury my face in his shoulder, the guy coughs and turns his gaze sideways. "The crowd's gearing up, Adder. We're on in five, but I'll give you seven."

My face flames when a wide grin slides up the drummer's face before he shuts the door, leaving us alone. "I'm so embarrass—"

Ethan clasps my face and presses a kiss to my forehead, whispering in a hoarse voice, "Don't you try to erase what just happened between us."

He's so adamant, I can't help my wide smile. "I would just rather not share it with anyone."

The tension in his shoulders eases and he gently pushes my damp hair away from my face with his fingertips. "I definitely don't like to share."

"Really?" I tilt my head and laugh. "Never would've guessed that about you."

Ethan mock scowls, then his brow settles into a serious look. "Why didn't you call me back earlier? I left several messages and texts, then spent the rest of the day thinking you might never speak to me again."

I know we only have a little bit of time, but I think it's important he knows his training with Danielle is dangerous.

I lightly place my hands on his chest. "There's something I want to tell you, but you have to promise not to freak out."

Ethan's hands freeze halfway down my waist. "For the record, that's a terrible way to calm me."

I shrug. "If you want to hear what I have to say, you have to promise."

Taking a deep breath, he raises his hands. "Not freaking."

"I've spoken to the Order."

"What?" Ethan begins to pace, then faces me. "Why?"

"It was after Danielle's nocturnal visit. I needed another perspective."

"But I told you not to seek them out—"

"Technically, I didn't. One of them found me."

Apparently that was the wrong thing to say. Ethan steps close, his broad shoulders blocking out the light bulb above us, and says in a calm tone, "Tell me where to find this Order person."

I push on his chest. "Don't worry. I was careful. That's why I didn't call or text you. Just in case, I didn't want him to trace me to you. He has no idea you're Corvus. He approached me because of my Internet searches. He thought I was Corvus."

"Approached you—where is he, Nara?"

His tone might sound normal, but his eyes are glittering black and his face is as hard as steel. I shake my head. "If you don't calm down, I won't tell you anything else."

"I'm calm." He juts his hand out between us, palm down. "See, steady."

I twist my lips. "Uh, yeah. Like the eye of a hurricane."

"I can't keep you safe if I don't know where he is, Nara."

I ignore the warning in his voice and finish telling him what he needs to know. "I went to him to learn what I can about the Order's history with the Corvus." When Ethan's brow furrows, I put my finger up. "I needed to figure out how I fit in, but I kept my questions very general. You have to give him credit for admitting that the Corvus and Order's current relationship isn't fully healed, that they'd had some kind of falling out in the past. He said the Order has spent the last three decades trying to rebuild after that happened."

Ethan scowls. "Where did the trust fail?"

"He said the *Master Corvus* killed the leader of the Order and the only knowledge as to what transpired between them died with that man."

"This doesn't make sense. A Corvus can't kill a human. It's ingrained in us not to."

I lift my shoulders. "There's obviously stuff we don't know."

Ethan looks away, his face lined in frustration. "Danielle refuses to discuss it, but I feel an inexplicable pain in my chest just hearing about it."

"I'm sorry I couldn't find out more. He did tell me that each Corvus is assigned a Paladin—a person who also must have some kind of special ability the Corvus can relate to—in order to help keep the Corvus grounded in the human world. When he told me what the Paladin does—helping you accept your Corvus, training with you, being a friend to talk to, whatever the Corvus needs—at first I thought that's what Danielle is. But when he told me he hasn't assigned a Paladin in

Virginia, that's how I knew Danielle had to be Corvus."

Ethan's gaze narrows. "You knew she was Corvus when you asked me what she was?"

I shrug. "I guessed that's what she might be. You just confirmed it."

He folds his arms and grunts, clearly unhappy I'd tested him.

Be glad you passed, Mister. "That night Danielle came to me, she told me that you need to fully embrace your darker side to fight effectively, but that's not what the man from the Order told me. He said that the Corvus will go dark from constantly fighting demons without a Paladin to be there to help the Corvus stay grounded in the human world. He said that a Corvus training another Corvus is putting two dark forces together, which will only accelerate the two Corvus' absorbing the evil they fight that much faster. It's the kind of darkness you can never recover from. Your human body can't take that kind of contamination, Ethan. It will die."

He stares at me, his eyes intense and focused. "What does the darkness do to the Corvus spirit?"

After I explain what happens to the Corvus spirit, I say, "You can't continue to train with Danielle. You need a Paladin."

"If any of what this man from the Order told you is true...where does the *Master* Corvus training a Corvus fit into his scenario?" he asks, raising an eyebrow. "If I can't trust my creator to train me with the intent that I survive, who can I trust?"

Me! I want to scream, but he has a point. If the Master Corvus is where broken Corvus spirit goes to heal, why would she do this to Ethan? "Did Danielle tell you why she's here? Who she's supposed to stop?"

Ethan shakes his head. "We haven't had a chance to talk yet."

"Why don't you at least consider talking to this man? Let him assign you a Paladin."

His lips form a stubborn line. "Even before Danielle told me not to trust the Order, my gut told me not to either. She just validated what I already felt. And if you didn't call me because you didn't want to expose me, then you don't quite trust him either."

I fling my arms wide. "With everything that's happened to us, I don't trust *anyone* blindly."

"But you trust me, right?"

I nod. "Of course, I do. Danielle's a different story. She's very bad for you. She's definitely bad for *us*."

His face sets in harsh lines. "Even though I know why Danielle was here tonight—she's been constantly telling me that if I don't accept all my abilities, I can't fully accept my Corvus either—her idea of celebrating went over the line. I told her to stay away from me for a couple of days."

A couple of days? Permanently is my preference. "I'm scared for you, Ethan. I don't trust her."

"How do you know you're not buying into this Order guy's story because you want to? That woman you talked to was wrong about Furiae existing."

I open my mouth to speak, but don't have an answer; my feelings definitely skew my opinion. It basically comes down to Danielle's word against Mr. Wicklow's.

"What do you want me to do, Nara? She made me what I am and expects me to fully live up to my potential."

I want to tell him to cut ties with her completely, but I would never forgive myself if he didn't learn something from her that could save his life in a battle with a demon. Instead, I speak from my gut. "Question her methods. Challenge her when you feel something isn't right."

"How do you know I haven't done that already?" he snaps.

His sharpness sets me off. "Well, I hope you figure it out before I end up standing over your grave in Oak Lawn Cemetery too." I turn and grab the door handle to walk out into the alley, but Ethan puts his hand on my shoulder.

"Nara, wait." I try to pull away, but his hold tightens. "When did you get this?" His voice is laced with worry as he pushes my hair out of the way, then slides my sweater's wide collar fully over my shoulder.

He's seen my feather. I close my eyes, my stomach tensing. "I discovered it when I woke up Sunday morning after you left."

"Why didn't you tell me?" he asks as he pushes my bra strap aside.

"I didn't know how. I didn't know what it meant." My voice breaks as I finish, "I still don't."

His fingers tremble on my shoulder. "Why is it white?"

I turn and face him. "The feather hasn't changed, but it came from you."

"No, Nara." He grips my shoulders and shakes his head. "I would never do that to you."

I blink away the emotions surging. "You don't want me to be like you?"

His anguished gaze travels over my face. "I don't want this life for you."

I hold back the sob that lodges in my throat. Corvus or not, I like the idea of the feather linking us together. "You did this, Ethan. I remember feeling strange yet connected when you kissed my shoulder in that coach's closet."

Ethan's looking at me, but his gaze is unfocused. Just when that moment between us clicks in his mind, his face pales and regret filters in his eyes. "I'm sorry, Nara. I never meant to—"

"Mark me?" I shrug and act nonchalant.

Ethan shakes his head. "I don't understand how this happened."

Someone knocks three times before excited cheers filter into the hallway as the drummer pokes his head through the doorway once more. "Adder! Show time, bud." Then he lets the door slam behind him.

I pull the door open and look at Ethan over my shoulder as I slide my sweater back up to cover the feather. "Don't worry. I guess that's one connection that never formed between us. I'm not Corvus."

Before he can say anything, I step out into the rain and let the door shut behind me.

Ethan

"We need to hunt. I saw two demons entering Wave nightclub earlier."

I pause from sliding my key in the car door and turn to see Danielle standing behind me in the empty parking deck, dim lights shining down on her. "I told you to stay away from me for a couple of days. I'm not going."

She stiffens. "You don't get a day off. Corvus never do."

The band played an extra long set tonight. I'm tired and frustrated that I didn't get to finish talking to Nara. "I'll take a day off when I damn well please. Go on your own. The *Master* Corvus shouldn't need my help."

Her lips press together. "Stop being an ass. This is for you, not me. This helps you train."

"Not this way." I shove my hands in my jeans' pockets and lean back against my car. "I've told you before, you risk too much by going after them the way you do. What if one gets away?"

She snorts, arrogance in her expression. "That'll never happen."

My shoulders tighten. "I don't understand why we don't follow them, find out where they live, and then take them out in their sleep. That way the demon is caught completely by surprise."

"What's the sport in that?" She huffs, tossing her hair over her shoulder.

"You might think you're invincible because you're Master Corvus, but your body isn't. We should only take risks when we don't have a choice, not because we want to feel superior by going on the offensive. Your arrogance is going to get you killed."

"I shouldn't have to remind you that our job is to send demons back to Under, Ethan. That's our first priority. Battling with demons isn't a once in a while luxury. It's a necessity to stay primed so that when we're *attacked* by them, we are ready and not caught unaware."

"Then we work out with each other." I narrow my gaze. "It'll be a good way to deal with you when you piss me off."

Her nostrils flare and she tilts her head. "Fine. Come spar with me."

"Hell no, I'm ticked even talking to you." I yank my hands free of my pockets and push off my car, taking a step toward her. "Why are you here, Danielle?"

"I'm here to train you."

"I'm asking why the Master Corvus is here on our plane. Is there some major threat?"

She flings her arms wide, annoyance lacing her tone. "There's always a threat."

"No, I mean a global threat. That's usually the only reason the Master Corvus appears in physical form. Is Lucifer coming? Is he already here?"

"Who told you that—?" Cutting herself off, she snorts. "Nara." Shrugging, she continues, "She doesn't know *everything*. Sometimes I like to check up on my Corvus. To see how they're doing and direct them to do their job as best they can."

"By teaching us to inadvertently create more demons?"

Danielle's face flushes, her lips thinning. "We've already discussed this."

I cross my arms. "And I'm asking you again. When I asked you before, you walked away and brushed my question aside with a curt response. I want you to look me in the eye and tell me that we're not creating Furiae."

Danielle's jaw works and something flickers in her eyes. I can't tell if it's hesitation, confirmation, or just irritation that I'm challenging her. "*Are* we?"

She jerks her chin up, her dark gaze glittering. "Even if we are creating them, have you thought about the overall greater good? We've just made it harder for a Lucifer Demon—what did you call it? An Inferi?—to come back to this plane. A Furia is nothing. We can squash one like a bug."

"What?" I fist my hands by my sides. If I don't, I might actually go after her. "There's a possibility?" I say in a cold, low tone. "What about the innocent people who get hurt until we discover that the Furia exists, not to mention exposing our *identities*?"

A bold smile tilts her lips. "We always find them," she says with confidence.

When I start to shake my head, she steps to my side. "We are waging a war, Ethan, and strategy is part of war. It always has been. If you don't think ahead, you die."

Grinding my back teeth to stay calm, I slowly turn to her. "This is between us and Inferni. Period. Furiae shouldn't exist."

She tucks her hands in her jacket pockets and rolls her shoulders. "Lucifer found a loophole and exploited it by taking the lost souls we killed during battles with Inferni as his slaves. If he's building an army of Furiae, which we can easily defeat, then why not use their creation to our advantage?"

"A Furia wouldn't exist at all if we'd looked deeper at the soul inside to see if it had been fully corrupted by the demon. This is something *we* did, Danielle. How can you not see that we're creating the problem?"

"You just don't get the bigger picture." She lets out a condescending laugh. "If creating a Furia means that's one less Inferi on this plane for a lot longer, I'll take the risk. In the game of chess it's all about taking out the pieces that'll cause you the *most* harm."

I step forward and get right in her face. "You're forgetting something very important in your *war-games'* strategy. A human's soul just got turned into a demon, Danielle. By our hand. That's not supposed to happen."

"That soul was already lost. It couldn't turn into a Furia otherwise."

"*That* makes it okay to use a lost soul to send an Inferi to Under for longer? Just to buy you more time?"

Arrogance fills her expression. "Yes, it does. I'm the *Master* Corvus. I know what's best."

Fury flashes through me. "People's souls aren't pawns in some fucking *game*."

"How dare you speak to me like that!" she rails, her eyes flaring.

"Because someone has to." I walk away and pace for a second to try to calm down. I need to talk reason into her.

When Danielle starts to turn away, I stop and say in a calmer tone, "Have you thought about the fact that maybe this *is* Lucifer's plan? He doesn't even have to show his face to win this time. He's finally getting what he wants, God's children. Not only does he have his own personal slaves in the Furiae, he also now has potential knowledge of Corvus' identities."

Danielle faces me, seething. "You are *wrong*. Lucifer always comes back to this plane in physical form. And there will be less Inferni to aid his plan this time around."

I roll my head from one shoulder to the other to remain calm. "*Chess* is about strategically sacrificing important pieces to lull your opponent into mistakenly believing their skills are superior. In their arrogance, they'll make moves that leave them vulnerable." My expression hardens. "Lucifer's *this* close to check-mating you, and you're feeding right into it."

Danielle bristles, then sets her jaw. "This is between Lucifer and me. I'm the only one who can defeat him. I know what I'm doing."

When she turns to walk off, I call after her, "Think about what I've said. I won't be involved in handing souls over to Lucifer. No matter how evil they've been on this plane, they should have a choice to seek redemption. We shouldn't take that away from them."

CHAPTER 23

Nara

As I lie in bed rubbing Houdini's back, I think about everything that happened from the moment I walked into school this morning.

To say it has been a roller coaster of a day would be an understatement, but instead of wallowing, I try to stay focused as I mentally walk through the whole day.

My heart races and my stomach pitches during certain parts, but several times today I felt like I was missing some bigger, obvious piece, and I'm pretty sure it was because I'd been too caught up in my emotions to see it.

I don't know what to do about the Danielle issue. Ethan and I seem to be stuck in this back and forth tug-of-war between our heads and our hearts, duty and loyalty, and logic and gut feelings. It doesn't help that we're *both* stubborn. But one thing I know for certain is that when it comes down to it…we'll always put each other's well-being first.

Is that what Ethan was doing this morning when he went after Drystan? Protecting me? Or was something else behind it?

The questions pinging through my mind are why I'm lying here replaying everything in my head, over and over. That, and the fact that I'm delaying falling into yet another dreamless night of sleep. After experiencing normal dreams for a while, the blank screen from the last couple of nights feels so…purposeless. I'd take having crazy-Danielle dreams over nothingness.

Nothingness!

I smack my forehead as things I hadn't put together earlier click into place. *That's why Ethan was certain Drystan had kissed me.* He has some explaining to do. Punching my pillow with determination, I close my eyes and welcome sleep. Tomorrow can't get here soon enough.

Nara

My eyes pop open at five in the morning. I'm up and showered before Patch arrives, tapping hard on my window. He seems more impatient than usual; it's probably the new layer of snow on the window ledge making his feet cold.

While Houdini and Patch settle into their "ignore the *other* animal in the room" routine, I sit in front of my mirror with my hair dryer and comb. Before turning on the dryer, I fish out a dry eraser pen from my drawer and write a message in bold red letters on my mirror. As I dry my hair, I stare at the message the entire time so Ethan couldn't possibly have missed it.

How long have my dreams been back?

The flutter of black wings draws my attention. Patch has landed on my dad's hat hanging on my mirror. I cut off the dryer and watch in fascination as he flaps his wings and tries to pick it up with his clawed feet.

Miraculously, he actually does lift the fedora, but instead of carrying it to the bed, which is his usual M.O. with new items he discovers, he drops it in my lap, then flutters to my bed. As he walks around on the fluffy comforter making soft guttural noises, I glance in the mirror at my freshly dried hair.

"Are you telling me it's a hat kind of day? Does my hair look that bad?"

Patch stops walking and fluffs his neck feathers, then shakes before turning to groom his wings.

Where are you, Dad? I pick up the hat and run my fingers along the brim, deeply regretting that I didn't respond to my dad's texts when he first tried to contact me in the fall. My gaze drifts to Patch, who's staring at me, all regal and proud. I instantly think about Ethan encouraging me to answer those couple of texts from my dad that came right after I called in the bomb threat to the school. Ethan had told me he'd kill to have someone who shares his abilities that he could talk to. I'd been so afraid of being hurt by my dad all over again that I'd blown my chance to reconnect with him, to make up for lost time and find out more about myself. And now I may never be able to do any of that.

"Why did you have to have it dry-cleaned, Aunt Sage?" I whisper in a sad tone.

Sighing, I set the fedora on my head and turn to pose for Patch. "What do you think? Ethan says I look hot in this hat. I don't think he meant 'steamed,' but that's the Nara he's going to get."

Nara

The first bell rings as I walk into school and kick off the layer of snow from my boots with a determined stomp.

After checking the atrium for Ethan, I head to the locker hall. "Have you seen Ethan?" I ask Lainey and Matt standing by her locker.

"Love the hat," Lainey says, grinning. "No, I haven't seen Ethan. Did you two talk?"

About many things. "Yeah." I frown as I glance over her shoulder toward Ethan's locker. He's not there. "But we've still got stuff to work through."

"I haven't seen her either," Lainey volunteers, drawing my attention.

"Who?"

"Danielle." She lowers her voice as Matt turns to high five one of his teammates.

Where is Ethan? "I'm not looking for her," I say and glance away to scan the crowd in the hall once more.

"That's good. Are you okay, Nara?"

The concern in her voice pulls my gaze back to her. I start to answer when the fedora flies off my head.

"Cool hat!" Drystan says right before he sets it on his head, then pulls the brim down and strikes a pose. "What do you think?"

"The purple streak on your jaw and shadowed moon under your eye destroy the model arrogance you're going for, Dryst," I say in a dry tone as I try to reach for my hat.

"I think it gives me a dangerous look." He grins and backs away, hand raised to block me. "Like I stepped out of one of your American gangster movies."

"Drystan!" This time I grab his blocking arm and lift up onto my toes to retrieve the hat from his head.

As soon as I grip the top of the hat, the second bell rings. I quickly snag it and start to turn away, placing it on my head, when Drystan grabs my hand, his demeanor turning serious. "Stay for a minute, Nara."

Once Lainey and Matt tell us they'll see us later and walk off with some of his teammates, I turn to Drystan. "What's up?"

Drystan looks less confident than he did when he was teasing me with the hat. "Are we okay?"

"Of course. No worries." I touch the brim of my hat and move to my locker. As I spin the combination, I glance up. He still hasn't moved, so I smile. "Just keep your paws off my fedora."

As the last person leaves the hall, Drystan slides his hands in his pockets. I pause pulling books from my backpack and glance his way. "I can tell something's on your mind. I hope you can make it quick. I've already skipped class once this week so I can't stay long."

"Whose hat is that?"

I push my backpack to the back of my locker and swallow a couple of times so my voice doesn't shake. "It's my dad's."

"Is he okay?"

His quiet intensity raises my heart rate. I slowly shut my locker door and face him. "Why?"

He nods to my hat. "When I put it on, I saw a flash of someone a bit taller than me with dark hair."

I grab his arm and squeeze. "Where is he? What else did you see?"

Drystan shakes his head, wonder in his gaze. "He must be psychically strong like you. I wasn't even trying to find him."

"He is." I nod. "My dad has been missing. We've tried to find him, but there were no leads." I shift the hat from my head back to his, then shake his arm. "Tell me what you see!"

Drystan pries my hand from his arm and cups it between both of his. "Calm down, Nara. Why didn't you ask me to help you before now?"

"My aunt had it dry-cleaned. I didn't think you could…" I stammer, then shake my head in fast jerks. "My dad lives in D.C. My parents aren't together, so I didn't have access to any of his other stuff. It's... complicated." I squeeze his hand. "Please, Drystan."

Drystan closes his eyes, then snaps them open. "Just try to calm down. It's messing with my ability to focus on combining your ability with mine." He clasps our fingers together and says in a calm tone, "Close your eyes and breathe, Nara."

"Okay." I close my eyes and take several deep breaths until my palpating heart starts to slow.

"He's in a hotel room," Drystan says, his tone changing to worry. "He looks drugged or something. He's unconscious."

My breathing ramps, but even though I want to open my eyes, I don't. "Which hotel?"

"I don't know. I'm seeing a hotel crest on the door, an R on a plaque with scrollwork on the edges."

"What's the room number? Can you see it?"

"809."

Tears gather in my eyes as I open them and look at Drystan. "Thank you."

He frowns. "I see us standing outside in the snow, looking up at the side of a hotel. The White House is in the distance." His hand tightens on mine. "There are at least two men with Eastern European accents guarding your father with guns. I see more guns in the room with them too. That's probably why I don't see us getting to your dad. God, Nara. What does your father do? We should call the police."

"No, Drystan!" My hand trembles as I clasp his tight. "We can't. My father's business is very security sensitive. He works for the government. I will call someone who can help while I'm on my way to D.C."

His green eyes take on a determined sheen. "You're not going to D.C. by yourself. I'm going too."

When I nod my thanks, he glances at my locker. "You might want to get your backpack. We need to write ourselves excuse notes. I'd rather not see the inside of Mr. Wallum's office twice in one week."

I let Drystan drive my car so I can focus on the two phone calls I need to make.

The first one is to my aunt. I'm not really sure what I'm going to say to her to convince her that my information is solid—the truth is probably the only way she'll believe anything I tell her, so I concentrate on my goal of saving my dad and hope the right words will come to me so that I don't freak my aunt out.

Just as I start to dial her number, my phone rings. I'm surprised and relieved that it's Ethan. He was going to be my second call, but if he's seeing my dreams like I suspect, he knows everything that's happened.

"I'm so worried for him, Ethan."

"Do *not* call your aunt."

"Why?"

"Whoever she calls for help doesn't send a government security team for him like she requests. Instead, the men who have your dad move him to another hotel. For now, the police are the best option."

The scenario Ethan has seen sends a shiver of worry through me. The only contact my aunt has is my dad's secretary. Is it possible she's involved? "But how am I going to convince the police to check out the hotel?"

"You'll call them once you get here. After I get your dad safely out."

"Are you already there?"

"I've been here for an hour and have scouted the hotel room he's being held in. Unfortunately the guys who have your dad aren't demons or the police wouldn't be necessary."

For the first time, I wish Ethan's sword worked on evil people too. "Thank you for helping," I say, my voice trembling.

"We're a team, remember? I'll be waiting for you in room 1201 in the Stars Hotel on fourteenth street Northwest."

"The Stars? But the hotel my dad is in starts with an R."

"We'll talk about all that when you get here. Oh, and Nara?"

"Yeah?"

"I got your message, but this is one dream I'm really glad you didn't see. Since Fate can't see me, there's no way he'll see me coming and try to stop me from helping your dad."

I thank him again and finally let out the sob I've been holding back once I hang up my phone.

"Ethan's already in D.C.?" Drystan glances away from the road, confusion written on his face. "How could he possibly know what you just learned from me?"

I open my mouth, but I don't know how to begin to explain.

"Wait...did you dream all this already and call him this morning? If you did that, then why go through all that trouble to pretend like what I told you about your dad was all brand new?"

Drystan looks so hurt and offended, I can't let him believe that scenario, so I get as close to the truth as I can without mentioning the Corvus aspects. "No, Drystan. Ethan and I have this unusual connection. Whenever he touches me, my dreams disappear and he sees them instead."

He blinks at me a couple of times. "I knew there was darkness in him! Is he like a dream stealer or something?"

I shake my head and laugh. "No. We just sync in a unique way."

Nara

"Why are we meeting here?" I ask Ethan as Drystan and I close the door behind us. Room 1201 is on the top floor and any other time I'd enjoy the nice view, but right now my nerves are too tied up.

Ethan strolls over to the window and points.

I follow his direction and see another hotel across the way. The Reardon.

"That's where your dad is. We need a place to wait, and this is the closest one that gives me a view of the hotel."

My eyes go wide. "Wait? My dad's over there. Why are we waiting?"

"He's waiting until it's dark," Drystan says, drawing my attention his way. "That's what I would do."

He's not looking at me. Instead he's staring at the Reardon, his hands in his pockets.

"But—" I look at Ethan. "Is that right?"

Ethan nods. "It's the best way to sneak your dad out without being seen. It's not easy to haul an unconscious man around in the daylight without attracting attention." His lips twist in a wry smile. "Not that it's easy at night. There are just more excuses we can use if someone looks twice at us like—"

"He's drunk and needs to sleep it off, or he got in a fight over a stupid game and we're carrying him home," Drystan supplies, voice full of sarcasm.

I cut my gaze back to Drystan, but he's staring at the heavy clouds that are ready to drop snow any minute, lost in memories. My heart aches that he could so easily come up with those excuses due to his past experience. "Drystan..." I touch his arm.

He glances down at me, then rubs the back of his neck and shifts a shuttered look Ethan's way. "Those are just a couple of suggestions we could use, and yeah, they'd work far better at night."

Ethan holds his gaze for a moment, then nods. "It's good to have a back-up plan, but hopefully we won't have to use it."

"We won't?" Relief washes through me that he has a better plan than trying to sneak my dad through a crowded hotel lobby. Right now my biggest concern is how the three of us are going to distract his kidnappers long enough to get my dad out of the room.

Ethan quickly shakes his head. "No. You and Drystan will stay downstairs while I go get your dad."

'The 'ell I will," Drystan says at the same time I say, "No, Ethan. You're not doing this alone." I fan my hand between the three of us. "Together we'll come up with a plan that keeps everyone as safe as possible. Do you know if the room next to 809 is empty? And is it an adjoining room?"

Ethan's mouth sets in a stubborn line. "You being anywhere near these guys isn't an option. They're professionals and part of a larger terrorist cell. They plan to take out some government buildings on Friday. While the city's emergency people are responding to those attacks, they'll hit their main target: the White House. They won't let anything or anyone stop them."

My trembling hand flies to my mouth. "Is—is that why they have my dad?"

Ethan slowly nods. "It makes sense. With him out of commission, they've considerably increased their odds of pulling off their elaborate plan."

"How do you *know* all this?" Drystan demands, his gaze suspicious. "It's Wednesday. If this is going to happen on Friday, Nara's dreams wouldn't have told you that yet."

Ethan shifts his attention to Drystan briefly, his gaze hard. "I have my own ways to get information. Let's just leave it at that."

Looking at me, Ethan continues as if Drystan hasn't interrupted him. "You and Drystan will wait on the back side of the hotel. As soon as I get your dad out of there, I'll bring him to you, then you'll drive straight to the hospital and check your dad in under a fake name. Once he's safe, call the police."

I tense my shoulders, worry for Ethan and my dad making my voice wobbly. "We're not leaving you."

Ethan cups the back of my neck, his warm fingers massaging the stiff muscles. "I'll be right behind you."

I grip his jacket and my eyes water. "I won't leave you."

"Yes, you will." He pulls me toward him, then presses a tender kiss to my forehead. His voice turns harder. "I'm depending on you to get them out of there. Got it?" he demands.

At the same time I realize his last comment was directed to Drystan, my friend's Welsh accent floats behind me, resolute, determined. "I'll get them there. Nara's my priority."

Ethan's fingers flex, cupping tighter around my neck. "I don't doubt that for a second."

The tension between Ethan and Drystan is so thick my stomach knots. Taking a deep breath, I step away from Ethan and sigh. "If we're going to be stuck here until after dark, I've got to call my mom, and then ask Lainey to cover for me, since her house is where I'll supposedly be."

"What are you going to tell Lainey?" Drystan asks.

I shrug. "The truth. That I might have a possible chance to see my dad, but I don't want to tell my mom about it yet." Nodding to him, I ask, "Do you need to call anyone?"

He starts to shake his head, then grimaces. "I forgot. I have a thing with my uncle at nine, but I'll just cancel."

I wave my hand. "No, you don't have to cancel. You can take my car back to Virginia. I'll ride with Ethan."

Drystan nods. "Once I'm back, I'll leave your car at Lainey's." Rubbing his hands together, he glances between us. "Who wants food? Anticipation always makes me hungry."

Nara

Just like Drystan foresaw, he and I are standing in the back parking lot of the hotel we're staying in.

Snow falls around us as we both stare at the Reardon hotel across the street. "I *hate* just waiting here," I whisper in the darkness and zip my leather coat up to my throat to stay warm.

"Ethan's right," Drystan says without looking away from the hotel.

"Right about what?"

He turns to me, shaking the snow off his hair. "To protect you from these people. Though, I'd still like to know how he's figured out their plan. Those guys had Eastern European accents. Even if Ethan's been able to listen in somehow, I seriously doubt they're speaking English the entire time. How does he know their language? Or is that another talent of his you didn't mention?"

I shift from foot to foot, stomping the snow beneath my boots to try to calm my nerves. Drystan's question does make me wonder, but then Ethan plays guitar without taking a single lesson. The Corvus in him will probably always continue to surprise me. "Ethan's very good at intuiting. I'm sure he's putting two and two together."

As soon as I finish speaking, Ethan rounds the corner of the building carrying my dad. Why is Ethan shirtless? Did he shirt get torn to shreds? I scan his body for wounds as I run to them. Relieved that I don't see any blood on Ethan, I try not to stare too closely at my dad's thinner body and ashen color. Instead I wrap a towel I'd pulled from my trunk around him and babble, "Oh God, Ethan. Is he okay?"

"His pulse is strong. He'll be fine," is all he says as he brushes past me.

Drystan's already holding the back door open. Once Ethan carefully sets my dad inside, he straightens and stares back toward the Reardon hotel.

Drystan shuts the door, then eyes Ethan's bare chest and says in a dry tone, "Might want to put your shirt back on. Walking around half naked in the snow will definitely draw attention."

Ethan doesn't acknowledge his comment as he rolls his right shoulder. "I have to get back."

When he walks away at a brisk pace, I'm so stunned it takes me a second to run after him. Once I reach his side, I grab his arm. "Where are you going?"

"Damn, that had to hurt like 'ell," Drystan says, eyeing the sword on Ethan's back.

Ethan's gaze is completely black. He's ramping for battle mode. *Crap, what if the sword starts forming right on his back?* I use my hold to angle Ethan's shoulder away from Drystan's view, then lay my palm on Ethan's jaw and turn his face in my direction. "Ethan, come with us. Please."

My touch seems to pull his focus back to the parking lot. Glancing down at me, Ethan cups his hand over mine. "Get your father to the hospital so they can flush his system of whatever sedation they were using."

"I will." Tears spill over my cheeks. I know I need to get my dad out of here, but I don't want to let Ethan go. I'm so worried he'll get hurt... or worse. I glance back to my car, thankful Drystan is inside already warming it up. "Do you have to go?"

Ethan pulls my hand from his face, his expression hardening once more. "I need to get back before they discover your dad is gone and try to leave. As soon as you get your dad checked in, find a payphone and call the police. Tell them the room number and everything I've told you about their plans. I'll make sure the police will find them. Don't mention your dad. Since we don't know who's involved, it's best to keep your dad's identity out of this so they can't come after him again while he's still out of it. When he's ready, he can bring in the big guns to investigate."

"You're learning more, accepting your Corvus' knowledge, aren't you?" I ask in a low tone. "That's how you understand their language."

When a confident smile crooks his lips, I sniff back my tears, and the worry squeezing my chest loosens a little.

Ethan lifts my hand and presses a kiss to my palm, his gaze never leaving mine. "I'll be fine, Nara. Now go help your dad."

Before he walks away, I pull free and grip his face with both hands. Staring into his deep blue eyes, I speak in a stern voice. "Protect him this time, or you'll have *me* to answer to."

Ethan folds his fingers around my wrists, confusion flickering in his eyes. "Are you...talking to my Corvus?"

Releasing him, I shrug. "I talk to him all the time. You're just usually asleep when I do."

As I walk away, I feel the heat of Ethan's surprised gaze following me, so I call over my shoulder, "Stop looking at me and go save the city."

CHAPTER 24

Nara

"Please hurry!" I say to the 911 operator, then quickly hang up the phone, my heart thumping.

Drystan nods to the handset I'd set back in its cradle. "Be sure to wipe your prints off it. They really didn't want to let you off the line, did they?"

I grimace. "Considering I just told them about a threat to our nation's capital, I understand them wanting to know who I am. I'm really glad Ethan suggested this plan."

Drystan pushes my dad's hat further down on my head, then tucks the scarf I'd given him tighter around his face before glancing in the opposite direction we'd come to find this phone. "Let's go this way, then double back around another building to get to your car. I don't trust that there aren't cameras near that convenience store."

I scan the empty street, thankful for the snow. No one's around. Everyone has rushed home to beat the six inches of snow that's coming.

We had to drive seven miles before we finally found a payphone. Tucking my hands in my jacket, I hunch my shoulders and say, "You lead. I'll follow."

As soon as we walk into the emergency room and brush the snow off our coats and hair, Drystan heads off to find a vending machine while I go straight to the main reception area and approach the receptionist. "Has the doctor given any information about Mr. Col—lier yet? Do you know what room he's in?"

She glances up through her thick curtain of black bangs, then shifts her gaze back to the computer screen to tap on her keyboard. "Let's see. Yes, your father has been moved to a room. I'll let the doctor know you're here and she'll take you back to see him."

"Is he awake?" I ask, hope surging.

"No, he's still out, but his vitals are good. The doctor will discuss all that with you once she comes to get you after her rounds are done."

When I nod and move to turn away, she taps her pen on the clipboard on her desk. "Did you get in touch with your mother? We need to know what to fill out on the admission form for insurance."

I shake my head. "Not yet, but as soon as I do, we'll get you the information you need."

Her question reminds me that I need to call my aunt. Pulling out my phone, I walk out of the reception area and into the heated glassed-in area between the front door and the main lobby. I'm so thankful my aunt picks up quickly.

"Hi, Aunt Sage," I say, trying to sound normal and calm. The last thing she needs is to hear me freaking out over worry for my dad or Ethan.

"Something's wrong, isn't it, Inara? I know it. Are you all right?"

I press the phone tighter to the side of my face. "I'm fine, Aunt Sage. Really. I'm actually not calling about me. I'm calling about Dad."

"What do you know about your dad? Did you see something? Why are you just now waiting to tell me?"

"Take a breath, Aunt Sage," I say in an even tone, then sigh. "There is no easy way to explain this, so I'm just going to do the best that I can. Can you do me a favor and not say anything until I'm done?"

My aunt inhales, then exhales slowly a couple of times, bangle bracelets jingling in the background. I can just picture her shaking her hands out and then pressing on her temples. "Okay, I'm ready. Talk away."

Sitting down on the wooden bench along a side wall between the outside door and the main lobby entrance, I tell her about Ethan seeing my dream, about Drystan's part in helping me find my dad, and what happened when I called her and she tried to call the secretary for help.

Gasping, she begins in a hard tone, "That woman might be involved—?"

"You're waiting 'til I finish, remember?"

"Yes, yes. Go ahead."

"But in answer to your question, her involvement or not wasn't known in my dream, although that's not why I'm calling. I'm already here in D.C. With Ethan and Drystan's help, the three of us managed to sneak Dad out of that hotel room and get him to the hospital. He's safe and under a doctor's care here at Memorial. Just in case the men who took Dad try to find him, I've checked him in under the name Jason Collier—I told the hospital Dad's ID wasn't on him when he got home. And yes, I've already called the police on his kidnappers."

"My God, Nara! What were you thinking doing this by yourself? Anything could've happened to you—any one of you could've been killed."

"Please calm down, Aunt Sage. I did it this way because you know better than anyone that the less variables introduced when changing someone's fate, the better."

"Do you—?" She starts to speak, but has to take another couple of breaths before she can try again. "Do you have any idea why those men took your dad? What they wanted?"

"I do, but I don't want to discuss it over the phone. I'll tell you all about it when you get here. I'm assuming you're already packing a bag? I don't plan on calling mom yet. Not until we hear from the doctor about Dad's condition."

A zipping sound comes across the line. "Yes, I'm packing while trying very hard not to yell at you even more, Inara. Where does your mom think you are?"

"I told her I'm at Lainey's and we're having a sleep over to enjoy the snow."

"Well, I guess that just leaves *one* of us in a panic. I'm thankful my brother's okay, but you putting yourself in harm's way isn't acceptable. Not at all. You're—" She sighs heavily. "Just don't move a muscle. I'll be there as soon as I can."

"I'm not going anywhere. Drive safe. The roads will get worse the closer you get to D.C."

Drystan's in the main lobby area, and after I finish my phone call with my aunt, I step through the sliding glass doors and join him.

I smile as Drystan holds out a steaming cup of coffee. "Thought you might need this."

"Thanks, Dryst."

He eyes my shaking hand as I take the cup from him. "Your dad's going to be okay, Nara. I know it."

"So you're a psychic now?" I say before I inhale the slightly burnt smell of vending machine coffee.

Drystan stiffens, his fingers bending his cup inward. "Why not? All kinds of people are popping up with abilities I didn't know about. Ironic considering everyone *else* seems to know about mine."

I wince, then gulp back a sip of coffee, letting its bitter warmth slide down my throat. "I kept your secret. Ethan only knows what you can do because he *saw* it in my dream last night."

Drystan stares at me for a long second, then nods, his gaze turning reflective. "The symbol...on the sword on Ethan's back? It looks just like that raven yin-yang necklace you wear."

"Wore," I correct him before taking several sips of coffee. Swallowing the bitter liquid along with the memory, I turn and walk down the hall that leads to the emergency room entrance.

Drystan dumps his cup in the trash by the door, then quickly falls into step beside me and gives me a sidelong glance. "I thought you couldn't take it off."

I shrug and swallow down the last of my coffee. Crushing the paper cup, I drop it into a nearby trashcan and keep walking. "It didn't belong to me."

His brow furrows. "Who'd it belong to?"

"Danielle," I say, barely keeping the snarl out of my tone.

As I start to reach for the door, Drystan clasps my hand and turns me toward him. Stepping closer, he asks, "Does that mean what I think it means?"

I blink up at Drystan. I can't take a step back or I'll run into the door. "What does *what* mean?"

"You never did answer my question the other day." His green gaze searches mine. "Are you and Ethan together or not?"

Just when I open my mouth to speak, Ethan's deep voice sounds right behind Drystan. "We're together 'til, right Nara?"

When Drystan steps back and glares at Ethan, my gaze locks with Ethan's intense one. I step around Drystan and into Ethan's personal space to see his eyes better. Black swirls in the deep blue, making my heart thump. "I'm glad you're okay. Would've been nice if you had texted to let me know that."

"We always do better in person." Ethan tucks a loose strand of hair behind my ear. "I waited until the police and other elite team members arrived before I left. How's your dad?"

I lift my chin toward the door. "The doctor is supposed to come talk to me soon."

Ethan, Drystan, and I have only been seated in the emergency waiting room for a few minutes when the doctor comes through the swinging door behind the reception desk and calls out, "Miss Collier?"

I quickly jump up and approach. "I'm Nara Collier. Is my dad going to be okay?"

The petite, curly-haired blonde puts out her hand. "Hello, Nara. I'm Dr. Krell." As I shake her hand, she says, "Your father will be fine. Though you might want to encourage him to join a gambler support group if he can't stay away from gambling. He might think those underground establishments are exciting and fun, but hopefully the experience of being drugged to collect the money he lost will get him to kick the habit."

Great cover, Dad. All I could think to tell them was that my father had been out all night. And when he'd finally come home, he'd been incoherent right before he passed out. Dipping my head in acknowledgment, I say, "Can I see him now?"

The doctor smiles and gestures for us to follow. I start to walk forward, when a jangling sound draws my attention.

Holding my keys in his hand, Drystan smiles. "I'm glad your father is going to be okay, Nara. I think I'm going to head out now though. With this weather, it'll take a lot longer to get back."

Nodding my understanding, I walk up to Drystan and push up on my toes to give him an appreciative hug.

As he folds his arms around me, I whisper in his ear, "Thank you for finding my dad, Dryst. I couldn't have done it without you." Pulling back, I add, "Hopefully the drive back won't be too bad, but at least we have school off tomorrow. Drive safe and thank you for everything."

When Drystan nods and releases me, the cocky grin that hides his true emotions is back. Flicking his gaze to Ethan, he says, "I'm always here for you, Nara. You know that. See you at school."

Ethan doesn't say anything to me as we follow the doctor through the door and into the elevator. Instead he reaches for my hand and pulls me to his side once the elevator doors slide open on the third floor.

"Your father's kind of woozy right now," the doctor says over her shoulder as we walk past the nurse's station and down another hall. Before we walk into my father's room, she says in a low voice, "He'll be in and out for the next hour or so, but you can go on in and talk to him. He was very agitated when I told him you brought him in, insisting that he see you right away. I finally got him to calm down when I let him know you were fine and right here in the waiting room."

I nod, and she turns and walks into the room. "Good evening, Mr. Collier," she says in a friendly voice.

My stomach is a tight knot and my feet don't want to move on their own. I'm so nervous to see my dad in person after so much time has passed. Ethan rests his hand along my waist and then pushes me into the room, murmuring in my ear, "Time doesn't strip away love, Nara. He's family. That's all that matters."

"Come closer and let me look at you," Dad says in a shaky voice.

Emotions clog my throat, but I manage to put one foot in front of the other until I'm standing beside his bed. Still, I can't bring myself to touch him. I'm afraid if I do, he'll disappear again.

Dad waits until the doctor leaves the room before he says, "Did you get my videos?"

I nod and tears track down my cheeks. I have to bite my lip to keep from bawling like the scared five-year-old I feel like right now. It's as if time hasn't healed the part of my heart that broke that day he left.

"Do you…understand now? I never wanted to hurt you, Nari."

This time I don't hold back. Hearing my childhood nickname washes away my fears. I step close to my dad and fall into his open arms, letting all the wasted time pour out of me in a new round of tears.

His big hand cups the back of my head as he holds me close, kissing my hair. "I've missed you so much. I thought of you every morning when I woke up and every night before I fell asleep, wondering how your day went."

I let out a watery laugh and rub my nose against his hospital gown. He feels so thin. He's probably lost ten pounds during this ordeal. "You must have had willpower of steel not to peek every once in a while. It would've been so easy with your ability." I glance up at him and smile. "I know I would have."

My dad's laugh comes out short and forced, as if he doesn't do it often enough. "I wasn't taking a chance on cheating. I had to stay away. It seemed to be the only way to keep you and your mom safe. It was definitely the only way the accidents stopped."

I sit down beside him and clutch his shoulder. "That's one of the reasons I was so frustrated with your video. There were things I needed to tell you and you just disappeared."

Tired lines form around his mouth and regret reflects in his eyes. "For once I didn't see it coming, Nari."

I think about all my crazy dream experiences lately. "Have you always seen everything? You've never been surprised?"

My dad nods. "With very few exceptions, yes. I've always seen ahead. There were a few though. Once, a stranger walked right up to me at the airport and told me to pay attention, that something was about to happen. The man wasn't in my dream, so of course I was instantly intrigued.

"An hour later, I sat beside a man in his early twenties on the plane. We talked about his weekend trip with his buddies, and I asked if he had a family. He told me about his troubled younger brother, and he said he wished he was responsible enough to take care of him, because his parents sucked at it."

Rubbing his hand across his thigh, my dad holds my gaze. "In my dream, he didn't talk about a brother. He just flipped through a magazine. The different scenario from my dream was so unexpected that the stranger's odd comment wouldn't leave my head. The whole time the guy on the plane talked about his brother, my chest kept getting tighter and tighter. I finally turned to him and told him to go get his brother. Actually, I insisted on it rather vehemently." My father snorts, then palms my cheek with his warm hand. "He must've thought I was crazy, but I knew all about loss. I didn't want him to have to experience it."

I stare at him with wide eyes. "Did the guy go get his brother?"

He lowers his hand back to his lap and nods. "I think he did. I saw him head for the ticket counter instead of the terminal exit."

My dad's story is too close to Samson's experience for it to be a coincidence. But there's one way to know for sure. "What did the stranger who told you to pay attention look like?"

Tilting his head, he stares at the wall behind me. "He was tall and blond. Well dressed. I remember his eyes were an unusual color. Kind of golden."

It's surreal enough that my father helped save Ethan, but the fact that the blond man was responsible for pointing him in that direction is even more puzzling. My dad makes the fourth person he's interacted with who ties back to either me or Ethan. Who *is* he? He obviously wants me to help Ethan, but if he won't tell me how I'm connected with Corvus, then what is his purpose?

"Nari?" My dad waves his hand in front of me, yanking me out of my musings. "Are you okay?"

I inhale deeply and nod. "Yeah, I was just trying to think if anything like that has happened to me."

His eyebrows raise. "Has it?"

"Nothing like that. You mentioned other things that happened you hadn't expected. Do you remember them?"

Pushing his hand through his hair, my dad exhales deeply. "There was an inexplicable building implosion five years ago. Then a subway collapse last year, and just recently a massive sink hole that swallowed an entire amusement park, killing hundreds."

His comments remind me that I wanted to show him those videos. I quickly grab my phone. "Watch these." I play the two videos I'd saved: One of the plane crash from when I was little, and the recent train wreck. Once both videos finish, I ask, "What did you see?"

Sadness fills his gaze. "I'd forgotten about that plane crash. Probably because no one was hurt. Did the train wreck just happen?"

When I nod, his shoulders sag. "What I see in those videos is my failure."

"You didn't see anything else? Like what caused these accidents?"

He slowly shakes his head. "Do you see something more?"

I grip his hand. "Yes, I do. It's hard to explain. It's like some kind of atmospheric rupture. I don't think these events are ones you could've predicted."

My dad blinks. "How can you see this? And why do you think I couldn't have seen them?"

"Because I only saw the cause while watching the videos. Oh, and once in real time, but never in my dreams. As for how I can see them, I have no idea. I thought I inherited the ability from you, but apparently I didn't."

"What do you think they are?"

I shake my head and protect the Corvus secret. "I have no idea." When he stares at me, I shrug. "So tell me why you didn't see your kidnapping coming?"

He runs a hand down his face. "A fire alarm went off in my apartment building in the middle of the night, so I didn't see my entire day. The next day, I remember leaving the coffee house and then everything just went blank."

"I believe someone in your office set you up."

His dark eyebrows elevate. "What?"

"Either your secretary or your boss is involved, or somehow connected with the men who kidnapped you, Dad. My dreams showed a connection. It's why I had you admitted in this hospital under a different name…and also why the police were called to take care of the men who took you. In my dream, when we tried to contact the people at the agency you work for to send help, suddenly you were moved to a different hotel."

My dad pushes the heels of his hands against his eyes, then shakes his head and blinks to keep his eyes open. "How did you get me out?"

"Ethan rescued you—" Cutting myself off, I walk to the door and pull it open. Ethan's just outside, leaning against the wall. I smile and wave him in. "Come on. I want to introduce you."

Clasping Ethan's hand, I tug him inside and start to speak, but my dad's eyes are closed. Heart racing, I step close to the bed and watch his chest, then exhale a tense breath when I see he's breathing fine. I turn toward Ethan. "Guess this is one of his 'out' phases the doctor mentioned would happen."

Ethan grabs the two chairs in the room and sets them side by side so we can talk quietly while my dad naps. As soon as he settles into the seat beside me, I reach for his hand. "I'd like your permission to tell my dad about your ability. Would you be okay with that?"

His mouth presses together for a couple of seconds before he speaks. "No one is supposed to know about Corvus."

I quickly shake my head. "I won't mention Corvus stuff. I just want to tell him about your ability and your dreams. He doesn't have to know how you do what you do or where your ability comes from. I seriously doubt he'll question it considering we don't know how ours works. It just does."

Ethan laces our fingers together. "Why do you want to tell him?"

I nod toward my dad. "I want him to know that he made the right decision. That something would've happened to us if he'd stayed." Swinging my gaze back to Ethan, I tighten my grip on his hand. "I want to tell him that Fate is a real entity and that we can help him face Fate."

Ethan's jaw muscle jumps. "I don't want you to have anything to do with Fate, Nara. Not ever again. I almost lost you the last time."

By the slant of his mouth, I can tell he's going to be stubborn about this. When I stand, he doesn't release my hand, so I turn and slide into his lap. "I need to do this for my dad, Ethan. To help give him the same peace that you gave me. I'm willing to chance facing Fate again if I can give him that."

Ethan wraps his arms around my waist and stares into my eyes. "*I'm* not willing to risk you. That fact has never changed and it never will."

I touch his jaw. "Then come with me to talk to Fate."

He shakes his head. "I've never been able to see your conversations with Fate. For that matter, are you even sure you'll be able to see your father talk to him?"

"Hopefully I can help my father talk to Fate. I can't imagine Fate passing up a chance to have us both there at the same time. And I think you can be there to help somehow. This last time I heard your voice calling to me right before your Corvus saved me."

"You're ignoring the whole point that you *had* to be pulled out the last time."

I smooth the scowl lines on Ethan's face with my fingers. "Are you really going to let your Corvus one-up you like that?"

The lines on his forehead only deepen. "You have no idea if this will work."

I lay my head on his shoulder and say, "You're right, but I have to try."

Ethan touches my chin and tilts my head so he can meet my gaze. "I'll help, but under one condition."

I grip his jacket and sit up, relief flowing through me. "Name it."

He runs his thumb along my cheek. "That you and I go someplace where we won't be interrupted and have an honest talk about us."

So much emotion swirls in his gaze I can't begin to decipher what he's thinking, but I quickly nod. "Of course. Whatever you want."

Ethan exhales a deep breath, then starts to nod, but jerks his gaze to my dad. "Did you plan on helping him try to see Fate here?" When I nod, his eyebrows shoot up. "You don't have your crystal, remember?"

I can tell by the look on his face that he's relieved.

I smirk. "Then it's a good thing I asked my aunt to bring a necklace from her Inara Designs Collection, isn't it?"

"Nara," Ethan begins just as someone knocks lightly.

My Aunt Sage's curly red head appears from around the door.

"You made it," I say in an excited whisper. I slide off of Ethan's lap and then help my aunt take off her coat.

I don't even get a chance to hang her coat up before Aunt Sage quickly pulls me into a tight hug and speaks into my ear. "You and I are going to have a talk about all of this later, Inara. You scared me to death!"

"I'm awake. You don't have to whisper," my dad says from the bed.

"Oh, Jonathan…" My aunt quickly moves to the bed and hugs her brother. Tears stream down her face as she leans back and pats his cheek. "I was so scared for you. I'm still not sure what to do or who to contact at your office about all this."

My dad sets his lips in a thin line. "I've been with my team for a long time. It's so hard to believe they would betray me like this, but worse is that they would turn their back on their own country. There's one person I can call to speed things along. I'm sure the Nationsafe Security team is already investigating the men the police arrested at that hotel. Can I use your phone?"

We wait while my dad dials a friend who works for the CIA and gives him the information for his boss, his secretary, and two other higher-ups in the Department of Defense who knew about the secret division he worked for.

"I'd like you to dig deeper into all four of those names, much deeper than traditional background checks. There must be something we missed. One of them is responsible for my kidnapping. Yes, I'm receiving medical treatment, but am still having moments of grogginess. No, I'd rather not disclose where I am right now. Once you start investigating, you'll find their connection to the terrorists that were apprehended tonight at the Reardon. That's where they held me hostage. No, I'm not sure what happened. I was heavily drugged. I just woke up in an alley. I'm going to turn this phone off. In a few days, once my head is fully clear, I'll come in for a full statement."

He shuts my aunt's phone completely off, then hands it to her with a sigh. "I guarantee you they're already tracing it. I've probably got less than twenty-four hours before the Nationsafe team descends on this hospital."

Turning to me, he says in a stern tone, "I don't want you here when they arrive."

He's sending *me* away this time? My heart sinks. "Why?"

His expression softens and he lifts his hand, gesturing me to his side. As soon as I move closer, he takes my hand in his. "They got their hooks into me a long time ago. I don't want them reeling you in too."

Don't worry, Dad. I promised Fate that'll never happen. Nodding my understanding, I look at Ethan. "Then we don't have a lot of time."

"A lot of time for what?" Dad and Aunt Sage say at the same time.

Gesturing to Ethan to come stand beside me, I say, "Dad, this is my boyfriend, Ethan Harris."

When Ethan reaches out to shake my dad's hand, my father holds on to Ethan's hand for a second too long. "Why does your name sound familiar?"

Ethan shrugs and pulls his hand free. "I don't know. We've never met before."

My dad looks into Ethan's eyes for another second or two, then narrows his gaze slightly. "I want to thank you for helping rescue me, but my fatherly side isn't pleased my little girl was involved in this at all."

"You and me both," Aunt Sage murmurs from the chair next to the bed.

"Would you two stop judging!"

"Nara didn't go near the terrorists," Ethan says to my dad.

"Ethan is the only reason—" Ethan slides his fingers between mine, cutting me off. I want so badly to tell my father everything, but Ethan shakes his head, so I temper my response. "I have a mind of my own, and nothing you can say will ever stop me from doing what I feel is right."

Just as I finish speaking, the doctor knocks and walks in. "I wanted to let you know that visiting hours end in fifteen minutes." Looking at my dad, she continues, "Once your family leaves, I'll check back in with you."

My father nods to the doctor, then jerks his gaze to me as soon as she shuts the door. "I'm your father. I'll always want to protect you. That's my job."

Stepping close, I touch his shoulder. "Sometimes, it's the kid's job to protect the parent. I smile, then tilt my head. "When you feel the drug grogginess coming on, does it feel different from just being tired?"

He nods. "Yes, it's a heaviness I can't control. It just comes over me."

"Then we'll have to wait until you actually need to sleep. Your dreams won't be right until the drugs are completely gone."

His hand clamps around mine. "Why are we waiting for me to see my dreams?"

My gaze shifts from my dad to my aunt and then back. "So you can meet Fate."

CHAPTER 25

Nara

"**A**bsolutely not!"

My dad's adamant refusal to let us help him face Fate surprises me.

Of course, the whole time I was describing that Fate was real, and how the vengeful entity went after me for changing others' fate, I never look at my aunt. Hearing her gasps in the background are hard enough. I know when she finally gets me alone, she's going to rip into me for not telling her the whole truth—how Ethan's dreams and the crystal have allowed me to see Fate in the past.

I tap the toe of my boot on the floor in frustration. "Why won't you let us do this for you? If it weren't for Ethan, I never would've discovered that Fate was real and stalking me. I never would've been able to make him back off. Ethan can help you, Dad. Let him."

My dad's attention snaps to Ethan. "Can you do this without Nara?"

Ethan lifts his shoulders, then lets them fall. "I've never been able to see Fate. Only Nara can see him."

"I'm sure Fate just *loved* being discovered too." My dad's sarcasm is heavy as he fists his hands on the bed.

"He resents you so much, Dad. All those lives you've saved in the past, all those fates changed. I want to be a part of your life, but he's not going to stop threatening our family unless you make him stop like I did. With Ethan's help, I faced Fate not long ago and made him back down from my daily life. Please, can you do this for me?"

My dad looks directly at Ethan. "I can tell by your expression you aren't happy. Is Nara at risk when she's interacting with Fate in your dream world?"

Ethan nods. "Yes, she is. Fate wants her out of his way."

"Ethan!" I round on him, angry that he said too much.

He turns a hard expression my way. "I'm not going to lie, Nara. You know I don't like this idea any more than your dad does."

"That's it. End of discussion." My father folds his arms, then looks at his sister. "Sage, I don't want you and Nara driving back so late in this weather. Why don't you two check into a hotel tonight, then you can both head back to Blue Ridge tomorrow morning."

"So that's it?" I throw my hands wide, my body tense. "You're going to walk back out of my life again just like that?"

Sadness creeps into my dad's expression. "It's not what I want, but just because Fate has a name hasn't changed reality. This is how he punishes me."

"But all you have to do is face him down."

"Your life isn't worth risking, Nari. Fate is just waiting for one more chance to finally take you from me. Otherwise, all that I've sacrificed for you and your mother has been for nothing. How can you not understand that?"

Because my heart screams louder than my head, I want to yell at him. Instead, I square my shoulders and say, "Goodbye, Dad." Then I grab my coat and storm out of the room.

I refuse to look at Ethan as I walk behind my aunt down the hall and into the elevator. Now that she knows the truth, there's no way she'll give me that crystal I asked her to bring. My chest hurts and it's hard to breathe. It feels as if everyone is against me.

As we reach the parking lot, Ethan says, "Ms. Collins, Nara didn't get to eat dinner. I'd like to take her to get some pizza if that's okay."

My aunt glances my way, her lips twisting. I can tell she feels bad that I'm upset with my father and with Ethan. "It's up to you, Nara."

The last thing I want to do is sit in the hotel room with my aunt and listen to her lecture me about trying to save my dad and about how I shouldn't leave things out when asking for her help. That's one painful conversation I'd rather avoid as long as possible, even if it means having a silent dinner with Ethan.

I nod. "I didn't eat, so yeah, pizza sounds good."

"Do you want us to bring you anything?" Ethan asks my aunt.

"I've already eaten, thank you." Glancing up and down the street, she says, "It looks like they've cleared the roads, but be back before midnight in case they get icy. I'm staying in the Hamilton Inn a couple miles from here on Sycamore Street. I'll make sure they have a key for you at the front desk." Looking at Ethan, she asks, "Where are you staying?"

He shrugs. "I planned to head back tonight."

My aunt shakes her head. "That's not a good idea. The snow is moving toward Virginia. You can stay in our room. I'm sure we can get them to bring in a cot. If your brother has an issue with it, I'll talk to him."

Ethan smiles. "Thanks, Ms. Collins. Samson's out of town for a few days for work, so it's not a big deal."

Ethan's car is cold. I rub my hands back and forth, trying to get warm as we head away from the hospital. I'm so frustrated with Ethan I don't even know where to begin, so I just keep my mouth shut and stare out the window. He navigates through so many streets that I'm lost after the first five minutes.

"I think I might know why you lost your dreams."

Ethan's comment jerks me out of my sullen state. "Why?"

He glances away from the road. "Didn't you say that you stopped having your dreams the Saturday night after I left?" When I nod, he sets his mouth in a firm line. "You got them back a few days ago. What changed?"

I squint, trying to remember and then it hits me. "The raven necklace?"

"It must've blocked your dreams somehow." His jaw works as he stares out the windshield. "It's ironic that the one thing that protected you also blocked you from me."

"How did it protect me? Do you know now?"

He nods and turns right down a familiar road. "As long as you're wearing it, a demon can't possess you."

"That's what that Harper demon was talking about when she said I was blocked." I twist my lips. "And here I thought it was my stubbornness that kept her from possessing me."

"You've got a will of steel." Ethan snorts. "But I didn't want to take a chance that you couldn't naturally block them."

"You're calling *me* stubborn? I'll bet if I looked up the word in the dictionary, *your* name would be the second definition, right after Corvus."

Ethan's lips quirk. "Guess we both come by this trait honestly."

"So far, bull-headedness has kept us breathing," I admit, then sigh. "Speaking of being honest, why didn't you tell me you had my dreams?"

He rolls his head from one shoulder to the next. "Because Fate is determined to kill you. I care too much to let you put yourself in danger to save someone else."

I open my mouth to argue with him, but we've come full circle and are right back where we started. Only this time it's about my dad.

Ethan takes a left into a parking lot, the scraped snow crunching under his tires. I look up at the Stars Hotel sign, then back to him. "The hotel restaurant serves pizza?"

He shrugs. "Probably, but I brought you here to talk."

I fold my arms. "That was when you promised to help me with my dad."

Ethan murmurs, "Stubborn," as he reaches over to open the glove compartment. Pulling something out, he dangles my crystal necklace in front of me. "I didn't trust you not to search my room for it."

My gaze jerks to his. "You're going to help me? But you told my dad—"

"I don't know if it will work." He captures the crystal in his palm and turns to face me. "But I'm willing to attempt it *without* you."

Hope dies in my chest. "But we know the formula that works. What if my dad can't figure out how to see Fate? I don't even have to try now. Fate just zaps me into his world."

Ethan slides his finger down my cheek. "I'll try to help your dad, but I'm not putting you in jeopardy again. You didn't feel the panic I felt. I was terrified I'd never be able to wake you." His jaw sets and he slowly shakes his head, curling his hand around the crystal. "Never again, Nara."

At least he's willing to try. That's something. "I discovered something while I was talking alone with my dad. I know why your name sounded familiar to him."

His eyes widen. "You do?"

I nod. "My father was the man on the plane beside Samson."

Ethan expels a disbelieving laugh, then rubs his eyes with his thumb and forefinger. "What are the chances?"

I raise my eyebrows. "Guess who walked up to my dad at the airport and told him something would happen and he needed to pay attention?"

"The blond man?" Ethan's brow creases. "Who *is* he?"

"I have no idea, but whoever he is, you and I have both been on his radar for a while." While we stare at each other in silence, the sight of our breath forming in the car makes me realize just how cold it is. I nod toward the hotel. "Let's go inside where it's warm."

As soon as we walk into the room, Ethan tosses the keycard on the small desk by the door. "I think we should wait at least an hour to make sure your father is good and asleep before heading back to the hospital."

"I agree. Hopefully that'll leave us enough time before we have to get back to the Inn."

Ethan shrugs out of his jacket. "After dealing with those guys who had your dad, I need to take a shower." He nods toward the coffee table. "There's a room service menu if you're hungry. We can talk while you eat."

Pulling off his shirt, Ethan starts to walk out of the room, but turns back to me. "Danielle admitted that Furiae are a possibility."

"She did?" I clench my jaw. "How can she willingly do that?"

He crushes the T-shirt in his hand and brushes his other hand through his hair. "She believes creating a Furia is worth the risk if doing so sends an Inferi to Under for longer."

"But she's creating *demons*, Ethan."

He sighs. "I told her I won't be a part of it."

"So you walked away from the Master Corvus." I smile, relief flowing through me.

He shakes his head, his expression determined. "I'm still Corvus, Nara. I have a duty to fulfill. In the future before I turn my sword, I'll look deep enough to know if the Inferi has fully corrupted the person."

"Does that mean you'll at least consider talking to the Order?" When Ethan stiffens, I say, "Danielle lied to you about Furiae before. At least this man was honest with me." When Ethan starts to turn away, I can't stand that he's unwilling to consider talking to the man. "He lives in my neighborhood."

He turns back, his expression unreadable as he stares at me for several seconds. *What is he thinking?* Just when I start to fidget under his forceful gaze, Ethan walks into the bathroom and shuts the door. Great. Probably not good thoughts. What else does he want to talk about? I wonder as I kick off my snowy boots and set them by the door.

We'd definitely left the conversation hanging in that back hall last night. So much has happened since then we haven't had a chance to really talk. That's probably it. He wants to finish that talk. But which part does he want to talk about? Danielle? Corvus? The feather on my back? The Order?

Seeking a distraction, I consider the menu, but food is the last thing on my mind. I begin to pace in front of the huge glass window, then quickly strip off my jacket and toss it on the couch. The room felt warm when I walked in, but now it feels like a hundred degrees. As I drop my sweater on top of my jacket, I'm thankful I'd layered it over a tank top.

Knots form on top of other knots in my stomach as I wait. When my gaze strays past the window, the bright glow outside draws my attention. I stop pacing and turn off the light to stare at the city covered in a blanket of white. Even several stories below it still shines brilliantly in the night. Smiling, I exhale and soak in its calm, tranquil beauty, letting it soothe my nerves. Light flakes of snow start to fall and I get so caught up in watching them that I let out a small gasp when Ethan touches my shoulder.

As soon as I realize his thumb is brushing the feather on my skin, I stiffen and start to turn, but his question makes me pause.

"*Are* we together?" His fingers splay over the feather, pressing lightly against my skin. "You said you stopped Drystan from kissing you in your dream, but yesterday, when he asked…did you want to kiss him then?

He sounds so tortured. *How can he ask me that?* "Ethan—"

"I saw the way he hugged you before he left, like he never wanted to let you go." Ethan swallows. "Does he make you feel the way I do when he touches you?"

I start to shake my head, but inhale deeply instead when he presses an intimate kiss to the feather, his warm lips sending tingles all the way down my back.

"You are *mine*," he says right before he nips at the skin on top of my shoulder. As the tiny hairs on my arms rise up and my stomach tumbles in response to his primal branding, another kiss quickly follows, this one lingering and tender, caressing the same spot with moist heat. "I might not know why you have this feather, but I *did* claim you that night, Nara. With all my heart I wanted that. You're the light to my dark." Straightening, he brushes his lips against my temple and chuckles lightly. "I'll always try to keep you out of the darkness, yet it seems you'll be the one shining your brilliance on me, lighting my path no matter what."

"Why didn't you say this last night?" I ask in a shaky voice.

Chill bumps race along my arms as he slides my tank top and bra straps down at the same time, exposing my entire tattoo. "Your stubbornness tears the insanely protective parts of me in two." He trails his fingers over the top of the feather, curving his finger around the soft vane. "You have no concept of how incredibly sexy you are," he continues in a hoarse rasp, sliding his finger right down the middle of the feather. "This intense jealousy makes me want to commit murder half the time, but because of who you are..." He traces the pointed tip of the feather ever so slowly. "You make me want to be worthy."

Folding his strong hands on my shoulders, Ethan's warm chest cocoons my back as he bends close, his deep voice washing over me. "What I feel for you goes way beyond any kind of Corvus connection. It's soulful, Nara."

My legs tremble as he turns me around and cups my face. "You are my existence, my sustenance, my every breath. I don't know how else to tell you how much I love you."

I inhale to calm my rushing pulse, then clasp his wrist and kiss the tattoo there. "I love you too. I never stopped, you know."

Ethan snorts and lightly kisses my nose. "Could've fooled me."

I flatten my palms against his chest and curl my fingers over the smooth, hard surface. I smile and tease, "I mean, who would pass this up?" Sliding my hand down and around his waist, I step close and trail my fingers up and then down his thick back muscles. "Or this?"

He inhales deeply, but doesn't move as I step back to run the tips of my fingers around the waistband of his jeans. I glance up at him and smile. "And definitely not these." I bite my bottom lip as I leisurely trace every single deep indention between his well-defined abs with my thumbs.

By the time I reach the hip muscles that dip into the top of his jeans, Ethan's expression has lost every bit of lightheartedness. His nostrils flare and his hands flex on my shoulders, slight pressure pushing against my skin. Heat sparks in his eyes, his body poised, a taut bow ready to snap.

When his hand shakes as he touches my bottom lip, pulling it free of my teeth, the teasing melts from my gaze and I slide my hand up his chest, cupping my palm over his thumping heart. "This is what matters to me, Ethan. I love your heart. It's fully worthy. I'm in awe that no matter how dark things seem, you always find a way to the light. I just want to be together. The rest will work itself out."

His hand falls over mine at the same time he steps close and captures my mouth in a crushing, passionate kiss.

I slide my hand free and wrap my arms around his neck. Straining close, I kiss him with every emotion that has built for him during all we've been through.

Ethan groans against my mouth, his tongue tangling with mine as he wraps his arms tight around me, crushing my ribs with this strength. I press against him, pushing higher on my toes, wanting more.

Cool air touches my belly as he starts to pull my tank up, but then suddenly we break apart. Ethan has stepped back. I'm confused as we stare at each other in the darkness. Then I notice his chest rising and falling in rapid succession and his hands clenching and unclenching by his sides.

He's waiting for me to move forward.

Reaching for the hem of my shirt, I start to pull it over my head. I don't get very far before I'm being scooped up in his arms and he's kissing the curve of my breast above my bra.

I giggle that he's taking advantage of the fact I'm struggling to get my shirt off. "Patient much?" I mumble before I finally free myself.

"I'm definitely out of that," he says in a dry tone.

I don't know how he manages it, but Ethan holds me with one arm, while he rips the cover completely off the bed. Then we fall together on top of the white sheet.

Sighing happily, I wrap my arms around his neck. Ethan slides his thigh between mine and buries his face in my throat, lightly nipping my shoulder.

"Why are you still wearing pants?" I whisper in his ear.

He runs his nose along my chest, his hand moving to my bra clasp. "Because we only have a little bit of time before we have to leave."

Just as he unsnaps my bra, my arms cinch tight around his neck. "What? I'm not taking off my pants if you aren't."

He lifts his head and cool air teases my exposed breasts as a dark, sensual smile tilts his lips. "That's because I'm going to take them off for you," he says right before he dips his head and heat consumes my breast with the aggressive pull of his kiss.

Fierce pleasure jolts from my chest down to my belly. I dig my toes into the mattress and curve into him, whimpering through the sensations shooting to every nerve ending.

Reaching between us, I try to find his jean button, but Ethan chuckles and captures my wrist. Before I can use my other hand, he pulls both my arms above my head. Holding my wrists captive in one hand, he runs the fingers of his other hand down my chest and along my ribs, caressing my skin before trailing his warm mouth to my other breast and applying the same torturous pleasure.

"Ethan," I pant and move under him.

"You're so sweet." His voice is rough and deep as his palm moves slowly down my stomach. "I can't wait to taste every part of you."

When his thumb slides under the waistband of my jeans and then the top of my underwear, curving around my hip, a round of fireworks sets off in my belly and heat shoots up to my cheeks. I'm ready for more, but I don't want to be the only one exposed.

"Your pants for mine, Ethan. It's the only way these jeans are coming off."

His fingers pause on the button of my jeans and he looks up at me, his gaze swirling in blue-black intensity. "I need to keep them on, Nara. I wasn't expecting us to…I don't have any protection with me."

"I'm on the pill."

His eyes light up. "You are?"

When I nod, his brow furrows. "Did you bring them with you?"

I sigh. "No. I came straight from school. I didn't expect to be spending the night away." When he drops his head to my chest, I ask, "You're wearing underwear, right?"

His head pops back up. "Yes."

I smile. "Your jeans for mine."

Ethan's jaw muscle flexes a couple of times. Just when I think he's about to refuse, he releases my hands and sits up to unbutton his jeans.

My heart thumps at a crazy rate as I sit up and shrug out of my bra. I start to unbutton my pants when Ethan's hand closes around mine. "Let me do it."

He's sitting beside me in his black fitted underwear, his ripped body begging to be touched, so I move my hand and lean back, intending to admire every delicious dip and hollow that sculpts his mouthwatering shoulders, chest and thighs.

But Ethan doesn't just unbutton my jeans. He presses his mouth against mine and kisses me deeply as he tugs the button free and slides my zipper down.

By the time he's tugged my jeans open, I'm shaking so much my arms can't support my weight. I fall back against the bed and lift up so he can slide the material past my hips and down my legs.

As my jeans drop to the floor, I lift a trembling hand and run it along his bicep, mesmerized by the strength. "Are you ever going to tell me how you got my dad out of that hotel room right under those men's noses?"

"One day." Ethan flashes a confident smile, then curves a hand over my hip and down to my rear. Clasping the cheek, his gaze traces my body before his hand moves to the back of my thigh, flexing against the muscle. "You are so beautiful," he says quietly, his tone reverent and full of longing.

Before I can say anything, he kisses my bellybutton. When his tongue dips inside and his hand tightens around my thigh, I arch and dig my fingers into his scalp, panting, "You're teasing me on purpose."

He sits up on his elbow and a dangerous smile curves his lips as he captures the hand I threaded in his hair. "I'm savoring. Huge difference."

"Still feels like tort—" The sensation of Ethan's thumb sliding my underwear down one hip cuts me off.

When he leans over to kiss my birthmark, then just keeps his mouth pressed against the crease of my leg, the tender and lingering kiss pushes new emotions to my throat. How does he manage to burrow even deeper into my heart? I hold my breath and trail my fingers down his back, tracing the top of the sword before resting my hand against his skin.

Ethan's back muscles flex under my hand and a burst of heat gusts from his mouth, spreading along my thigh. The carnal sensation sends warmth flooding through my veins. I moan and grip his shoulder, pressing my palm flat.

Ethan's hips jerk against me and his fingers grip the inside of my thigh next to him, pulling me tight against his hardness. He quickly lifts his gaze to mine, his face rigid. Shoulders tensing, he shakes his head and says in a raw voice, "I can't. Nara. Stop."

"What?" I lift my hand, unsure what I've done wrong.

Ethan exhales and his tense shoulders relax, but he doesn't release me. "I'm sorry. I couldn't concentrate while you were touching me. It's just too intense."

"You don't want me to touch you?" I try to sit up but Ethan doesn't move. He's blocking me in.

"I'm on the edge." He lets out a strained laugh. "When you touched me like that, it feels like you're *touching* me. I definitely want that. Just not yet."

My eyebrows shoot up. "But all I did was touch your back."

He lifts my hand and kisses my fingers. "Apparently you've got the magic touch. Let me focus on you right now."

I shake my head. "Somehow that doesn't seem fair."

"Trust me, this is just as good for me." His grin could melt my pants off if they weren't already on the floor. With a soft laugh, he runs his thumb along my fingers, pushing them out of the way so he can nuzzle my palm. As soon as his nose touches my scar, I close my eyes and move closer to him.

When Ethan suddenly slides his thumb from one side of my scar to the other and an involuntary groan rushes past my lips, I tense and my eyes fly open.

Ethan's watching my face intently. "What do you feel when I do this?"

Before he can touch my scar, I clamp my fingers closed. If he does it again, I have no idea what kinds of embarrassing sounds might erupt before I can stop them.

I try to pull my hand away, but Ethan doesn't release it. "Why didn't you tell me that pressure on this scar turns you on?"

Face flaming, I try to roll away, but Ethan slides his leg between mine, locking me in place. "Why, Nara?"

"Because I'm already turned on by you. It's just another way to make me feel—" His thumb wiggles past my folded fingers and he pushes on my scar again. "...*aahhhh.*"

"Even more turned on?" Ethan supplies, his dark eyes glittering with wicked triumph.

I attempt to tug my hand away, but he shakes his head, smiling as he trails his other hand down my neck, over the swell of my breast, then along my belly. "I've finally found a way to make you feel as intensely about me as I do about you. And I'm taking full advantage of it."

"But you don't need that," I say as he pulls my hand to his mouth and presses his lips to my scar. I gasp and arch off the bed, my body trembling all over.

"Amazing," he murmurs against my hand before he turns and plants a kiss on my belly, and then another kiss, moving lower.

The feel of his hand moving up the inside of my thigh rockets my heart rate into the stratosphere. I thread my fingers through his thick hair and welcome the press of his hard body against mine, my stomach flexing in anticipation.

Time seems to stand still as Ethan doesn't leave a single bit of my skin untouched. My pulse races and my love for him rises and swells. His hands caress and slide over me so intimately and tenderly my chest aches. I press harder against him, because I just can't get close enough.

Ethan nips my skin, branding and teasing me with hot kisses. His touch grows bolder and his words and movements amp in intensity, sweeping me along with him on the wave of building passion. I'm a quivering mess by the time he finally connects where I desperately want him. The warm press of his hands along my thighs and the heat and intimacy of his mouth moving over me take me higher than I ever imagined possible.

Crying out, I cling to him. Marveling in the flood of buzzing sensations flowing through me, I absorb every bit of pleasure he selflessly gives.

As I come down from my high, Ethan moves over me and murmurs in my ear, "I'm forever addicted to you, Inara Collins."

He truly owns my heart.

I wrap my arms around his broad shoulders and pull his full weight on me. Pressing my face to his neck, I shake my head with a regretful sigh, then meet his gaze. "I wish we didn't have to leave so I could make that a *true* statement."

Heat flares in his gaze and he grunts his frustration. "I'll need an entire night to do everything I want with you." Clasping my waist, he flashes a smile of pure sin and presses his hardness against me. With nothing but a pair of cotton underwear between us, I feel everything he wants, and I can't help but squirm under him. I desperately want that too. When I start to wrap my legs around his waist, he clamps a hand on my hip to hold me still, then sets his forehead on mine and exhales a harsh breath. "It can't get here soon enough."

I cup his jaw and kiss his forehead, then whisper against his ear, "I can't *wait*."

Ethan drops his head to my neck and groans deeply, then rolls over, pulling me with him. "You're killing me, Sunshine."

CHAPTER 26

Nara

"Don't even think about touching me," Ethan says in a low voice outside my dad's hospital room.

Even though the nurses aren't at their station right now, I glance at the crystal necklace in his hand and whisper, "My dad will be the one wearing it."

"I can't control what you do while I'm asleep." His gaze narrows. "And don't touch your dad either."

I shake my head. "You really don't trust me, do you?"

His only answer is a cocked eyebrow.

I raise my right hand. "I solemnly promise not to touch you *ever* again."

When he scowls, I sigh. "Fine. I promise not to touch you or my dad while you're asleep."

Nodding his approval, he pulls me into my dad's dark room.

While I wrap the necklace around my dad's wrist and gently lay the crystal in his hand, Ethan quietly moves a chair close to the bed. Setting it down, he gestures for me to get the other chair, then settles in the one next to the bed.

As soon as I sit down, Ethan grasps my hand and brings my fingers to his lips. Pressing a soft kiss to my knuckles, he glances at my pockets with a stern look.

I sigh and tuck my hands inside my pockets as Ethan lightly touches my dad's arm.

Ethan quickly lifts his hand when my dad stirs and rolls onto his side facing us. We glance at each other, both frozen, waiting. My gaze strays to my dad's hand to show Ethan he's gripping the crystal. Ethan dips his head in a curt nod, then sets his elbows on the bed and his hand on my dad's arm.

I exhale, relieved my dad's eyes don't fly open. While Ethan slowly folds his arms on the bed, then lays his head on his forearms facing me, I want so badly to touch him. Just to tell him thank you for helping, but I know he'll misinterpret my action, so I curl my fingers inside my coat pockets and smile instead.

Ethan's lips quirk, then his face relaxes as he closes his eyes.

It seems like I wait forever before I allow myself to glance at the clock on the wall. An hour has passed. It's almost eleven. Both Ethan and my father are so still. I've never watched anyone sleep before and it's far more nerve-wracking than I thought it would be.

Shouldn't they be shifting some? Or making noises in their sleep? Shouldn't I hear them breathing?

The last thought brings me to my feet. Ethan's breathing is strong and even. I lean over my father and strain in the darkness to watch for the rise and fall of his chest for proof that he's not struggling in any way. Finally I make out his shoulder lifting.

Blowing out a quiet breath, I start to sit back down in my seat when warm breath tickles my neck. My gaze jerks to Ethan, and I swallow a gasp.

He's sitting up, and his glittering black eyes follow me back to my seat with brutal intensity.

"I didn't touch any—"

Ethan's hand whips around my wrist in a crushing grip and a ruthless, dark smile curves his lips, his voice low and commanding. "You're needed."

Nara

As light bleeds into the hotel room, Ethan moves with lightning speed, ripping the machine gun from the dark-haired man's hands, then slamming the butt against the man's jaw in one smooth, swift movement. The second the guy crumples to the ground, something whizzes past Ethan's shoulder.

My stomach drops as a bullet hole appears in the wall beside him. "Look out!"

Ethan pivots and glares at the other dark-haired man behind him holding a handgun. The man's eyes slit hatefully as he trains the gun's silencer on the center of Ethan's bare chest. Jerking his chin to the right, he motions through the doorway to an empty bed, speaking hurriedly in a language I don't understand.

Ethan's lips crook in bored amusement. He says something to the guy in the same language, then glances at the gun as if challenging him.

The kidnapper's face turns bright red and he pulls the trigger. Ethan jolts to the right, avoiding the bullet. Another hole appears in the hotel room wall. Ethan faces the man once more, his eyebrow raised.

Veins bulge in the man's forehead. Cursing Ethan, he charges him, pumping the trigger several times in rapid succession.

Ethan dodges so fast the bullets seem to move right through him. With one aggressive step forward, he meets the man head-on, hammering his fist into the guy's face so hard the man slams against the far wall, unconscious before he hits the ground.

Once both men are down, Ethan uses telephone and cable cords to bind their arms and legs behind them.

Just as Ethan finishes tying up the last man, a vile smell reaches my nose. I stiffen and turn, following Ethan's line of sight as a skin-crawling sensation slides up my spine, lifting the hair on my scalp.

A man with thinning light brown hair stands in the hotel room's doorway. One arm is the size of a child's and his shriveled, deformed fingers grip a gun. His other arm hangs to his thigh with an oversized meat cleaver for a hand. He could've stepped right out of a horror movie. But it's his face that makes my stomach nauseous. It's misshapen and twisted as if someone took a hammer to it and the bones and features reformed in all the wrong places.

He steps inside and shuts the door, a look of evil delight spreading across his gnarled, sunken face. His appearance is frightening enough, but the malevolence that pushes into the room with him rips a scream from my throat. I stumble back, my legs barely holding me up.

Ethan runs his hand through his hair and shakes his head, snorting. "I should've known one of you would be behind this." As he curls his left hand in a "come and get me motion", his raven sword slowly extends behind his right hand. Gripping the hilt, he steps forward, an arrogant smirk forming on his lips. Ethan slides a booted toe across the carpet, drawing a line between them. "Try and cross it."

The creature throws his gun to the side like a water pistol, then charges at full speed toward Ethan. As the floor rumbles under heavy footfalls that sound much bigger than the creature itself, I hear my name.

"Nari," my dad calls from the bedroom doorway. He's standing there, watching the interaction between Ethan and the monster in wide-eyed disbelief.

I skirt the room and rush into his open arms. Shivering, I'm happy to have found him, but I'm also worried for Ethan. He'd told me there weren't any demons holding my father hostage. Is this man just an invention in one of Ethan's crazy dreams?

Ethan feigns right, then slices his sword down the creature's left side, cutting off his shriveled arm.

Instead of blood gushing, the putrid smell of death fills the room, along with the man's piercing roar of fury. The sound is so similar to Ethan's fight with Drake, I know this is a demon.

Ethan plows a fist into the guy's face, knocking him over the coffee table and onto the couch. The second Ethan bounds over the table, the creature swings his foot, hooking Ethan in the chest. I wince when Ethan's side hits the bar, then exhale in relief once he pushes off and grips his sword tight, anger burning in his gaze.

"Where are we?" my dad asks, his voice hoarse, barely above a whisper.

As Ethan and the demon circle each other, looking for weaknesses, I turn to my dad. "We're in Ethan's dreams."

Anger flits through my dad's features. "But I told you—"

Ethan slamming against the doorjamb next to us cuts our conversation off. We both jerk back and keep our attention focused on Ethan and the demon.

A deep guttural laugh erupts from the creature's mouth located where his jaw would normally be. Inhaling through his smashed nose, he widens his beady eyes and advances on Ethan, stomping as he closes the distance between them.

Ethan shakes the grogginess from his head and swipes the trickle of blood from his mouth. Raising his sword, he braces his stance. "Come on, asswipe. I'm ready to end you."

Once the creature takes one more step, Ethan arcs his sword and shoves it right through his chest. Tension eases out of me as a poof of yellow smoke expels from the man's body. Then I tense all over again when Ethan stares at him for a couple of seconds, then twists his sword. The man explodes into a fine cloud of powder that disappears before it hits the ground.

Satisfaction reflects in Ethan's face as he draws the tip of his sword across the carpet. "That was one step too many."

Just as the blade starts to disappear and the sword's ink begins to snake up and around Ethan's arm, crackling electricity fills the air.

When the room spins, I grab onto my dad's hand and speak as fast as I can. "You're about to meet Fate. All you have to do is tell him to back off. That you have free will and your fate is your own."

Fate's pleased laughter echoes in the darkness around us like creepy, three-dimensional surround sound. "What good deed have I done to deserve this Collins duo windfall? Two birds with one stone."

My dad tenses beside me, which only fuels my anger at Fate. I raise my chin. "Stop skulking in the dark," I snap. "Turn on the lights so we can talk. Don't you want to see our faces?"

"Inara!" my dad hisses, wrapping a protective arm around my shoulder.

"I can see you just fine," Fate says, "but I would like to see your father's face when he meets me."

As soon as Fate lights up the blank space, he's twice the size of the smoky figure he's always presented to me. Hovering in front of us like a swirling, human-shaped storm cloud, his sunken eye sockets appear even larger and eerier than usual. He crosses his gaseous arms and slants his gaping mouth in disapproval as his frigid presence expands, making our breaths plume in front of us.

"So we finally meet, Jonathan. Aren't you at least going to acknowledge me?"

Clearing his throat, my dad tries to push me behind him, but I don't trust Fate's mild mannered disposition. I refuse to budge. "Listen, Fate—"

"How dare you fuck with my world like your own personal strategy game!" Fate roars at my dad, expanding his dark cloud so big and fast, he's curled over us like a California Mavericks wave about to crash down. "I want to draw this out for a your blasphemous acts. I *want* you to feel pain…"

"Say it, Dad!" I call out over Fate's freight train of fury.

My dad starts to speak, but Fate knocks me back and quickly swirls around my dad, a massive python squeezing. As my father gasps and wheezes for air, Fate's head appears next to my father's face, a gloating smile cutting into the smoke. "Even though I've dreamed of making you suffer..." He pauses, swiveling his head to look at me. "She's an even bigger problem."

"Dad!" My heart in my throat, I try to run through Fate to free my father, but this time I bounce right off him, falling back on my ass.

Fate laughs and cinches tighter. As my father's face changes from bright red to purple, I quickly stand up and scream, "What do you want?"

"You know what I want," Fate sneers my way. "Give me your ability. Or poor little Nari will never be reunited with her father. He'll finally be out of your life permanently."

Tears stream down my face and I clench my hands by my sides. My father's teeth have started to chatter. Fate will either squeeze out his air or freeze him to death. "How do I know you won't kill us anyway?"

Fate laughs and flicks a long snaking tail toward me, snapping the whip-like tip against my ankle. "You don't. But then, what's the fun of taking your ability if I'm just going to kill you?"

He has a point. Jumping back to avoid another stinging whip, I gulp down a sob and start to speak, but my father croaks, "I'll give up my ability. All of it."

"You will?" Fate eases his tight grip enough for my father to take a deep breath.

"No, Dad." I take a step forward, reaching my hand out. "Don't agree."

When my dad nods, my heart lurches and my stomach bottoms out.

"Well isn't this a wonderful surprise." Smiling, Fate says, "See how easy that was, Nara? His powers are mine now." A vaporous arm unwinds from the icy cold coil around my father and Fate snaps, smoke puffing off his fingers right in front of me. "Poof. Just like that." His smoky brow pulls down and his voice hardens. "Now your turn."

"You have mine," my dad says. "You don't need hers—"

My father's head snaps sideways from Fate's backhanded slap. "Shut up. This is between Nara and me. You're no longer of conse-quence." Fate turns to me. "If you want him to live, you'll have to give up your ability."

"That wasn't the deal." My father struggles to free himself even as his breathing turns shallow.

Fate *tsks*. "I never made a deal. This is about survival."

My heart splinters and tears. Fate's making me choose between my father's life or my ability to provide peace for Ethan in his dark dream world. Ethan needs light now more than ever. How can Fate do that to me? Rage fills my chest; I'm being torn from the inside out. A gust of strong wind suddenly tunnels through the empty void around us, whipping my hair, pulling at my clothes.

As Fate's vaporous form begins to disperse into the air, he yanks my father tight with the solid part he has left and rumbles his fury at me. "How are you doing this?"

Whatever I'm doing, it's working. Fate is losing his strength. I keep my rage high and focus all the air in the room on Fate.

When Fate fully scatters into pure mist, a howl fills the space before his dark cloud encloses me and stinging icy needles hammer my skin with merciless ferocity. With the strong wind cycloning around him, that seems to be all he can accomplish. I cover my eyes and face with my arms and bite my lip to keep quiet.

The pain is excruciating, like my skin is being flayed, but I hold it inside and concentrate until the sound of my father's gasps bleeds through. When I spread my fingers slightly and peek through the stinging mist, I see my dad writhing on the ground, holding his throat.

I let go of my anger when I realize what's happening; I'm sucking all our air out to create the wind.

Once the gale stops, Fate re-forms into a humanoid shape right next to me. Folding his arms, his laughter echoes from all angles in the void. He slowly rubs a pretend jaw as he looks at me, his eye sockets half-closed in contemplation. "Who would you rather kill your father—you or me? Personally, I vote for you, but I have a feeling you're going to push me to do it."

Just when he starts to move toward my dad, Ethan appears between my father and Fate. "You got what you wanted. Leave them alone."

While I rush around them both and squat beside my dad to make sure he's okay, Fate sneers at Ethan. "What are you doing here? You can't interfere." Fate's tone elevates as his body begins to vibrate back and forth in agitation.

Ethan's commanding voice booms in the open space. "I told you to back off." His bicep muscles flex against his black T-shirt as his hands curl into fists by his sides. When Fate just snorts at him, Ethan relaxes his fingers and his sword instantly appears in his right hand. "I won't tell you again."

Fate tries to zoom around him to get to me, but Ethan blurs between us, matching Fate's supernatural speed with his own. Pointing his sword toward me, Ethan says in a forceful tone, "She is *mine*."

Fate roars and starts to blink in and out. "I want—"

The second he blinks back in, Ethan's hand lashes out. He grips Fate's throat, holding him still. Pulling Fate's face down to his, he says in a fierce tone, "I know exactly what you want. It's not yours to take."

Fate tries to morph, but Ethan's hold seems to have locked him in his current form. "Defy me and I will destroy you, Fate."

Darkness rolls off Ethan in pulses of power and vengeance. The impact rushes against my skin in intense waves, making goose bumps form.

When Fate looks at me and chokes out, "He doesn't know," the defined realization and true alarm forming across his amorphous face tenses everything inside me. Something feels wrong. I jerk to my feet and hurry to Ethan's side.

I'm not sure if he can kill Fate, but I'm not taking the chance. Touching Ethan's tense arm, I push his sword's point away from Fate's neck. "You can't destroy him, Ethan. Everyone has a fate."

When he looks down at me with pitch black eyes, and I hear, *I don't*, in my head, a deep abiding sense of loss and loneliness flows through me, squeezing my heart. I swallow and clasp his arm fully. "But you have a destiny. As much as Fate ticks me off, I still need him. We all do. Just like you need me."

One corner of Ethan's mouth crooks and he mutters, "Lightweight," before shifting a calculating gaze back to Fate. "You don't have the authority to take what you did."

I gape, then look at Fate. "He doesn't?"

"They *shouldn't* be able to see me." Fate gathers his composure, then glares at him defiantly. "If they offer it to me, I can take it."

Ethan shifts his attention to my father, who's sitting up watching us with wide, disbelieving eyes. "Do you willingly give your ability to Fate?"

When my father nods, I drop to my knees beside him. "Why? You don't have to, Dad."

Ethan holds my father's gaze for a second, then dips his head in a curt nod. "Good choice."

Nara

We all jerk awake at once and my father instantly pulls his arm from Ethan's hold, scowling at him in the dark room. "How dare you risk my daughter's life like that."

Ethan looks at me and then at my dad, confused. "I didn't, Mr. Collins. I told Nara she couldn't be included. That was the only way I agreed to help. Did you see Fate?"

When my father blinks at Ethan like he's gone mad, I realize who had purposefully pulled me into Ethan's dream world, and who'd just threatened Fate: his Corvus. I quickly stand and pick up my crystal necklace where it had fallen onto the bed.

"It's not Ethan's fault, Dad. He insisted that I stay out of it, but I fell asleep too. I must've touched you when I rested my head on the bed. It was an accident."

My father points to Ethan. "He was in complete control over his actions, Inara. He's dangerous and reckless. Can you imagine the chaos in our world if he had destroyed Fate? Especially now that I've given up my ability—"

"I wasn't there." Ethan stands, his hands fisted by his sides.

"The hell you weren't," my dad snaps in a low voice. "You threatened Fate with that damned sword of yours. If it weren't for Inara talking you down, who knows what might've happened."

Ethan's gaze swings to me, but I look at my dad and attempt to smooth things over. "It was just a dream, Dad. Well, the way your mind interpreted everything that happened."

"The intent behind it wasn't," Ethan says in a flat tone, shifting his gaze to my dad. "If you saw me go ballistic on Fate, it's because he threatened Nara. The reason I offered to help you face him was never about you."

"It wasn't?" My attention darts to Ethan, but his stays focused on my dad.

"It was to protect Nara. She had mostly figured out a way to keep Fate at bay, but with you back in her life, Fate would come after her again. And this time, he'd use you against each other. *That's* why I offered. I wanted Nara safe. Giving up your ability was the absolute best thing you could do for her."

"At least *that* we agree on." My dad grunts his annoyance, crossing his arms.

Ethan nods. "You really don't have your ability anymore?"

My dad shrugs and rubs a hand across his jaw. "I won't know until I go back to sleep. Speaking of which…" He glances at the clock, then at me. "It's almost midnight. Shouldn't you be with your aunt?"

I raise my hands and let them drop to my side. "I wanted you back in my life, Dad. Enough that I was willing to go up against Fate to make sure of it."

"Fate went after you, Nari, and there wasn't a damn thing I could do about it."

"I have this ability for a reason. I might as well use it to help you." When all I get is a strong parental stare from my father, I sigh and zip my jacket closed. "Aunt Sage said I needed to be back by midnight and I will be."

As Ethan and I turn to leave, my father says in a quiet voice, "Thank you for helping me."

I turn back to him. "You're welcome, Dad. I've really missed you. I'm sorry."

He shakes his head, a bemused smile forming. "I'm free, Nari. Before, I couldn't walk away. My conscience wouldn't let me. Now I don't have a choice. I won't be able to do this job anymore."

I nod even though it makes me a little sad. I liked having something unique in common with him. "Good night, Dad. Good luck with all the security people tomorrow."

As I walk out the door, he says in a low tone, "Night, sweetheart. See you soon."

Just as Ethan and I enter the stairwell, my dad's last comment hits me. "Oh, no. What if my dad just shows up at our house and Mr. Dixon is there?"

I start to turn back around, but Ethan grabs my hand. "Your dad can't expect that your mother didn't have a life all these years while he was gone. Let your parents work out their issues on their own."

"But I'll have to explain to my mom about my ability so she'll believe my dad and understand why he left."

Ethan lifts our clasped hands to his mouth and kisses my knuckles.

"Show your mom the videos he left you first. Then talk to her."

Nodding my agreement, I let him lead me down the stairs.

We ride to the Inn in silence. I worry my lip the whole way, wondering when he'll ask about "his" appearance during the confrontation with Fate.

Once we reach the parking lot, Ethan cuts the engine and turns to look at me. "Were you going to tell me?"

"Tell you what?"

"About the Corvus putting you in danger tonight."

He *can't* know what his Corvus did. He won't understand. "Ethan, I told you. I fell asleep."

"That's a lie." Ethan slams the flat of his fist against his chest, his nostrils flaring. "I fucking want to kill the bastard!"

"Calm down." I spread my hands wide. "Okay, so he pulled me in, but I think it's because he knew what you wanted and acted. It wasn't working, Ethan. My father hadn't seen Fate and most likely wouldn't have without my help."

"Fate could've killed you and your father." Ethan stares out the windshield and sets his jaw. "And I wouldn't have been able to stop it."

I reach for his hand and grip it between mine. "Your Corvus is powerful, Ethan. He would never have pulled me in if he didn't think he could keep me safe." I snort, thinking about the way he'd held Fate by the throat. "He's arrogant for a reason. He truly scared Fate."

"Do you think he would've actually killed Fate?" Ethan asks, conflicting emotions pulsing in his deep blue eyes.

"I think he'd do anything to protect me. Just like you would." I thread my fingers through his. "I believe your emotions are intertwined with his. He feels what you do just as strongly."

Ethan grips my hand, his expression turning hard. "I don't like him feeling any emotions toward you."

I shake my head. "Your Corvus is protective vengeance, sadness, and loneliness all rolled into one. He's spirit, who happens to feel a connection to me through you. You're not allowed to be jealous of something powerful enough to keep us both safe."

Ethan cups my neck and pulls me close. "He can have out there." He glances past the windshield, then back to me. "But he can't have you."

"I'm *only* yours." I kiss his jaw, then look at the clock on his dash. "It's midnight. We need to get inside."

As we walk under the Inn's awning, I slide my arm around his waist and look up at him. "Thank you."

He hooks his arm around my shoulders, glancing down at me. "For what?"

"For rescuing my father and helping him face Fate. Oh, and for being a buffer tonight so my aunt can't lecture me as soon as I walk in the room."

"Well, when you put it that way, I *am* pretty awesome. Maybe you don't deserve me."

When I poke him in the ribs as we enter the building, Ethan pulls me close and presses a tender kiss to my lips, murmuring, "You're so worth it."

CHAPTER 27

Nara

On the way back to Blue Ridge early in the morning, Ethan yawns several times.

"Was the cot that uncomfortable?" I ask, wincing. "Do you want me to drive?"

He shakes his head and clasps my hand. "Sleeping in the same room with you and not being able to touch you was very distracting. Made falling asleep impossible."

My stomach flutters and I bite my lip. "So you just stared at the ceiling all night long?"

He pulls my fingers to his mouth, the heat of his breath warming me all over. "Why would I do that when I could watch you instead?"

Heat shoots up my cheeks. "Don't tell me if I snore. I don't want to know."

He gives a secret smile and kisses my knuckles. "You make the cutest little sounds in your sleep."

As my face flames, I glance down and notice my voicemail light blinking on my phone. When I see it's from my mom, I look at Ethan. "My mom left a voicemail last night. That's not good. She always texts."

Does she know I wasn't at Lainey's? My stomach tensing, I click the voicemail button and listen.

"Hey sweetie, I hope your project is going well. I just wanted you to know I changed the code on the garage. Someone tried to break into the house last night while I was out to dinner with David. I'm really glad you stayed at Lainey's! We have some damage to the doorjamb, but thankfully they didn't get too far." Sighing, she continues, "My guess is Houdini scared them off. David stayed over, and he'll be here with me today while the alarm people are installing a security system. See you when you get home and I'll give you the alarm code then."

Hanging up, I quickly dial our house. "Hey, Mom. I just got your message. Are you sure you're okay?"

"Yes, I'm fine—please put the keypad to the right of the garage door in the kitchen—sorry, Inara, they're getting ready to install the panel. When will you be home?"

I glance at the clock. "In a half hour."

"Sounds good. I'm glad you have a day off from school today. I need you to run some errands for me since I'm stuck here right now."

"Okay, Mom. See you soon."

As soon as I tuck my phone away, Ethan glances away from the road. "What happened?"

"Someone tried to break into our house while she was out to dinner last night. Mom's there with the security system people now. I hope it wasn't Harper."

Ethan's brow furrows as he threads his fingers with mine. "After I drop you off at Lainey's, I'll get a quick shower and stop by. I'll be able to tell if a demon was there."

Exhaling an unsteady breath, I squeeze his hand.

Nara

Before I hop in the shower at home, I check my text messages. My aunt has sent one.

Aunt Sage: Jonathan's interviews with the security team are done. He wasn't kidding about their promptness. His secretary was the one who set him up. Her husband was $300K in debt for gambling. She sold your father out to pay off an angry loan shark. The doctor wants him to stay one more day and will release him tomorrow. He insists he's fine, so I'll be home late tonight. Got to get ready for the Blue Ridge Artisan show this weekend.

Apparently my dad didn't mention Ethan and my late night visit to his sister. I wonder if his ability really is gone. I quickly type a text back.

Me: *I'm glad he's doing well and that they caught the people responsible. Thank you for all your help.*

Aunt Sage: *Ha, don't think you're not going to hear it from me.*

Me: *I know and I'm sorry.*

Aunt Sage: *All has ended well, but that might not be the case the next time. I always want you to tell me the truth, even if you know I'll be upset. It hurt me more to learn you'd kept things from me.*

Me: *I didn't mean to hurt you. I'm truly sorry.*

Aunt Sage: *I guess that means you're growing up, since you don't always depend on others to help you now.*

Me: *No matter how old I get, I'll always need you.*

Aunt Sage: *Awww. Love you, sweetie.*

Me: *Love you too. I hope you get tons of business from the show.*

Aunt Sage: *I'm debuting the Inara Designs Collection. Actually, that's how you can make it up to me. I need help putting sets together, labeling and such. Can you come over Friday night? I'll make dinner and we'll get all the stuff ready. Come around six.*

Me: *I'll be happy to help. See you then.*

After I hit send, I jump in the shower. I'd just finished blow-drying my hair when the doorbell rings.

"I'll get it," I call as I run down the stairs.

I make it to the bottom step to see Mr. Dixon holding the door open and Houdini throwing himself excitedly at Ethan.

"Down, boy." Ethan laughs and pats Houdini's head. He steps inside and nods to Mr. Dixon, then shifts his gaze to my mom standing in the kitchen and talking to the tech guys about how to operate the keypad.

"We're getting a security system installed." I pretend Ethan doesn't already know what's going on as I walk up to him. "Someone tried to break in last night, but Houdini saved the day."

He rests his hand on Houdini's head and glances down at him. "I told you he's a great watch dog."

"I doubt whoever was trying to get in wanted to tangle with Houdini." Mr. Dixon shuts the door and gestures to the back of it. "He really wanted to tear them to bits."

Deep claw marks gouge the door from the middle all the way down.

"That's some fierce defending." Ethan scrubs the dog's ear and glances away to hide his satisfied smirk.

My heart sinks. "Was it a demon?" I whisper once Mr. Dixon joins Mom in the kitchen.

Ethan snorts as if trying to get a nasty smell out of his nose, his expression hard. "Yes."

Nara

"Coach said to be there at five." Lainey glances at me after she backs her car out of my driveway and puts it in gear. "Matt said Drystan's not coming tonight. He had other plans he couldn't get out of." Tucking a piece of hair from her ponytail behind her ear, she says, "Tell me all about your dad."

She'd insisted on driving me to practice, since running errands for my mom took up the rest of my day. Thinking about my dad makes me smile and my stomach tense. I wish I knew for sure if I'd see him again. "It was so great seeing him after all these years. Thank you for covering for me."

Lainey's ponytail swings as she raises her eyebrows. "Why don't you want your mom to know you were seeing him?"

"My parents had a rough separation. I have to break it to my mom gently. Not slam her with the news I snuck up to D.C. to see my dad for an evening. She'd feel so betrayed."

"Wait…separation? Your parents are still married?"

I'd always let Lainey assume my parents were divorced. It's the conclusion most people came to since he wasn't part of our lives.

When I nod, Lainey snickers. "I wonder if Mr. Dixon knows he's an unwitting participant in adultery?"

"Don't you dare tell anyone," I say, then snort. "Seriously though, it's not like that. My parents have been apart since I was five. They're divorced in every sense of the word *except* the paperwork."

"Then why didn't they just make it legal?"

I shake my head. "It's complicated. And now that I've decided to hopefully see more of my dad, I'm going to have to figure out a way to let my mom know without hurting her."

"And parents say teens are all drama." Lainey rolls her eyes, then pulls into the gym's parking lot. Nodding toward my soccer bag, she says, "Go on inside so Coach knows we're here. I just remembered I need to ask my dad if I can go to the Coldplay concert with Matt. Tickets go on sale tonight. I'll be inside in a couple minutes."

Grabbing my bag, I'm thankful the snow has already melted in the parking lot. I head into the gym's bathroom to change clothes. Once I'm dressed, I start to walk out of the bathroom when Lainey bursts through the door. Crying in hysterical gulps, her ponytail askew, she holds her hand to the left side of her face and babbles incoherently.

"Lainey, I can't understand you. What's wrong?" When I pull her hand away and see a bright red handprint across her cheek, I quickly wrap my arms around her and hug her tight. "Who did this to you?"

Pushing back a little, Lainey takes a breath, then points toward the main door. "Har—Harper attacked me while I was trying to lock my car."

"What?" I grab my phone, intending to dial Ethan's number, but I have a text from him that he must've sent while we were talking.

Ethan: Tried to call. Turn your ringer on! Harper's around. Get inside the gym with Lainey and stay there. On my way.

"It's too late to call for help," Lainey says, drawing my attention as I start to type a message to Ethan. "Harper's gone. Danielle knocked the crap out of her and she took off."

"She did?"

When Lainey nods, I say, "Wait here."

She grabs my arm before I can walk out. "You're not going out there, are you?"

I shake my head. "I just want to talk to Danielle."

"Don't go. Harper was after *you*. She said she was going to hold me hostage until you gave her what she wants. She was dragging me away when Danielle jumped in between us and whacked her hard."

"I'm so sorry, Lainey," I say, my voice trembling slightly.

Lainey frowns and releases my arm. "It's not your fault she's a nut job. And you weren't kidding about her strung-out strength. She pulled me around like a rag doll, and damn my face hurts like a mofo." She finishes, flexing her jaw. "Glancing up at me, she asks, "What does she want from you?"

"I have no idea. The girl has fixated her cray-cray sights on me for some reason." I shrug, then tilt my head. "What was Danielle doing here?"

"She mentioned coming to watch us play the other day." Turning to face the mirror, Lainey pulls her rubber band out. Her hands shake slightly as she grabs up her loose hair to fix her ponytail. "I know you don't see eye to eye with her, Nara, but I'm really glad she came tonight."

"I'm glad she came too." I might not like Danielle, but I'm so relieved Lainey's safe. "Did Harper say anything else to you?"

"No, nothing else."

While Lainey pats a wet paper towel on her cheek, I send a couple of quick texts. I sent Matt a message, asking him to come watch the scrimmage and follow us home. I'd also sent Ethan one filling him in and asking him to touch base with Danielle. Meeting Lainey's gaze in the mirror, I squeeze her shoulder. "Are you okay to scrimmage? Or do you want to wait for Matt and then go home?"

Tossing the paper towel, she steps back and shakes out her hands as if trying to knock off water. "I'll play. It'll be a good way to work off this freaked out adrenaline."

Ethan and Matt sit on the bleachers and watch our scrimmage. Once it's over and Lainey and I meet them at the gym's entrance, I'm glad to see the red mark has disappeared from her face.

Matt quickly pulls Lainey into a tight hug, mumbling, "They need to arrest that bat-shit crazy chick."

"I'm okay. I'll tell my dad when I get home. It's time to press charges…well, if they can find her." Lainey says against his shirt and then pulls back to look around. "Where's Danielle?"

Ethan shrugs. "I didn't see her when I got here."

"I didn't see her either," Matt says.

"How weird that she didn't come in." Lainey wraps her arm around Matt's waist. "I wanted to thank her for saving me. Guess I'll tell her tomorrow at school."

I glance at Ethan. I know we're thinking the same thing. She probably went chasing after Harper. "Lainey, I'm going to ride home with Ethan, okay?"

She nods and smiles at him. "Thanks for coming, Ethan. It's nice to know people have my back."

"I'm glad you're okay, Lainey." Ethan hooks his arm around my neck and presses a kiss to my sweaty temple. "And I'm sure Matt will agree it was our pleasure. We love watching you girls run."

As Matt reaches over and high fives Ethan, I arch an eyebrow at Ethan until his gaze drops to mine. The look that passes between us makes my legs tingle. Smiling, I grip the back of his jacket and move closer to him as we walk outside.

"Did you dream about Harper?" I ask once we're alone in his car.

He nods. "Yeah, I was so tired I took a nap and dreamed Harper got ahold of Lainey and made her call you and lure you outside the gym. I woke up and tried to call, then sent a text."

"Danielle showed up and nixed that plan. Did you get in touch with her?"

"She took her time responding to my text asking about Harper." He shakes his head as he starts the engine. "Unfortunately, she never caught up with her."

My shoulders slump. "Harper got away?"

Ethan touches my cheek. "As soon as I drop you off, Danielle and I are going looking for her."

Nara

Of course, the minute I get home, Houdini has to go out. I swear this dog has a sixth sense when it comes to holding it just for me.

Sighing, I zip my sweat jacket closed and hook his leash on. I'm thankful the snow on the sidewalks is gone as I walk him in the dark down the street. At first, I look over my shoulder every couple of seconds and jump at every little sound, but when I see how calm Houdini is, I take my cue from him and force myself to settle down.

Up ahead a car pulls into Mr. Wicklow's driveway. I pause as the headlights dim and the engine shuts off. I hear two sets of deep voices, but I can't make out anything in the dark. That's one downside of our neighborhood. The streetlights are only at the entrance. Unless people turn on their porch lights, it's really dark at night.

As Mr. Wicklow and his guest walk up the sidewalk, his porch light comes on, bathing their heads in a soft yellow glow. I blink and shake my head, staring at Drystan talking and laughing with Mr. Wicklow. Their voices fade as they walk inside and I stand there unmoving as pieces start falling into place.

Mr. Wicklow works at the University. Drystan said his uncle was a guest visiting the university at the request of the history department. And even though Drystan's from Wales, he'd told me his uncle lives in England. I feel so dumb for not putting it together before now, but Drystan had never called his uncle by name. And his uncle never mentioned he had a nephew here in Virginia.

My gaze narrows as lights come on in Mr. Wicklow's house. Distrust tightens my chest. Why didn't Drystan tell me about his uncle? What is he hiding? Why did he pretend not to know the significance of the raven necklace he'd seen me wearing? With his uncle running the Order, he has to know why the necklace is important even if I don't.

I turn back toward my house, walking in brisk steps, pulling Houdini along.

Just as I step inside, my stomach pitches and the leash drops from my hand when another thought crosses my mind.

Oh God, does Drystan think I'm Corvus? Is that why he insisted that I learn to defend myself? And why he pursued our friendship? Was being an exchange student just a cover to get closer to me?

Drystan fits the criteria for a Paladin. He has a special ability and with his parkour skills, he knows some unique defense techniques. Did his uncle assign him as my Paladin without my knowledge? Is that how the Order works? Through subterfuge? Anger flashes that he and his uncle deceived me so thoroughly, leaving a bitter taste in my mouth.

"Nara?" Mom calling in a raised voice draws me out of my worried musings. "Are you okay?" She's looking at me with concern. Half the spaghetti noodles are still in the pot as she hangs it over the strainer in the sink.

"Um, yeah. Just thinking about a test I have coming up. What did you say?"

"I asked if you're hungry. Dinner's almost ready."

My stomach rumbles as the smell of simmering meat sauce hits my nose. "I'm starving. Let me get a shower and I'll be right down."

Mom nods. "I want to go over the security system with you. I have to leave very early Saturday morning and won't be back until Monday around five."

"You're going out of town for work?"

She nods again and raises her hand. "But don't worry. I'm going to call Sage and have her come stay with you while I'm gone."

I shake my head as I pat the top of Houdini's. "Between the security system and this big guy here, no one's going to mess with me."

Mom presses her lips together. "I'd feel better if your aunt stayed with you or you stayed with her."

"Aunt Sage has a booth at the Artisan show this weekend. It's one of the biggest draws for her business. I'm helping her put stuff together Friday night for it. Don't worry. Houdini will take good care of me."

Mom finally nods, then says, "I won't be gone long. I'll be back just in time to celebrate Christmas on Tuesday."

"We're celebrating on Christmas day?" I gesture toward the living room. "But we don't even have a tree yet."

Mom laughs. "David is going to bring a tree Monday night and we're going to decorate it together."

My stomach drops. We're celebrating Christmas with David? I want so badly to tell my mom about Dad, but the words stick in my throat.

Mom smiles and pats my cheek. "I see I've shocked you speechless. I know, we haven't celebrated Christmas *on* Christmas since you were little. It'll be a nice change of pace, I think. Go on and get your shower, and then we'll go over the password and phone number for the monitoring service. I want to do it now while it's fresh in my mind."

As soon as I get upstairs, I receive a text from a number I don't recognize.

Unknown: This is my new cell phone. Text whenever you like. I've got several loose ends to tie up here. Probably be a week before I'll get down to see you, but I'm coming, Nari. And in case you're wondering, my dreams are definitely gone. It's strange to have dreams that make no sense whatsoever.

A week? But Christmas will happen before then. I think about Ethan's advice and let the panic in my chest go. My parents are adults. They'll figure things out. At least I hope they do.

Me: Got you in my contacts now. Looking forward to seeing you. I want to show Mom the videos you made. Text me the day before you plan to get here. I'm not going to mention Ethan. I'll tell her that after you recovered from the kidnapping, your dreams just stopped.

Dad: The videos might help her understand. Agree it's best to leave Ethan and Fate out of this. Will let you know when I'll be heading down.

Me: I'll be happy to have you back in my life.

Dad: You and me both, kiddo.

At least I have a few days reprieve before the Christmas "event" happens. I have no idea how my mom will react to my Dad's videos or what she'll say. Having David in her life complicates things, but she deserves to know the truth about why my dad left and that he never stopped loving her.

After dinner, I have to endure Mom going over the security system three times before she sighs and announces, "Okay, I can fly out tomorrow morning without worrying about you."

She's so tense I raise my right hand and say, "I solemnly promise not to set it off by accident and bring the police, ambulance, and fire trucks to the house while you're gone."

Mom cups my face and shakes her head. "You know I want to keep you safe."

I think about my dad and smile. It's nice to have both my parents' concern again. "I know, Mom. Don't worry. I'll be fine."

I didn't get a text from Ethan until almost midnight.

Ethan: We haven't found Harper. None of the people in the places she supposedly hangs out have seen her. We'll try again tomorrow evening.

Me: Mom's got the house locked up like Fort Knox. I'll be fine. By the way, she's going out of town Saturday morning and won't be back until Monday night.

Ethan: Hmm, I think someone should stay with you and keep you safe while she's gone.

I snicker and type back.

Me: I have Houdini.

Ethan: He doesn't know how to make you purr. Night, Sunshine.

Me: Night

Stomach fluttering, I roll over and sigh happily, looking forward to Saturday night already.

CHAPTER 28

Nara

"What have I done to upset you?" Drystan speaks right in my ear, making me jump. I gulp back a yelp of surprise, my fingers skipping across the computer keyboard.

When the teacher sitting in the corner of the school library whispers a loud, "Shhhhh!" and then glares at us, I quickly toggle away from the screen where I've been researching other past natural disasters and cross-referencing them with any videos I can find that tie to inexplicable accidents. Inferni breaking through don't always leave a path of destruction to follow, but having a larger sample size would help prove that natural disasters are definitely a precursor to the thinning veil and potential Inferni breakthroughs.

"What are you doing in here?" I say in a low voice.

"Getting answers." Drystan sits down at the computer terminal right next to mine, then pulls his chair close. "This morning, I asked how your dad was and got a one word response. When I asked how the scrimmage went last night, you just shrugged. Then Dark Boy shows up and I'm completely ignored."

Not completely. When the class bell rang, Ethan made sure to kiss my forehead and say one thing to me before he headed off to class. "I still don't trust him." As Ethan walked away without another word, I wanted to shake him for leaving me hanging. He knew this conversation with Drystan would happen, and his comment gave no indication how it would turn out.

Scooting my chair away from Drystan's, I click the mouse to open a new browser window. "I just had this research project on my mind." I cut a meaningful gaze his way, then shift my focus back to the computer screen. "And I really need to get back to it if you don't mind."

His hand lands on mine over the mouse. "But I do mind." Squeezing my fingers, he dips his head, his green gaze seeking mine. "Talk to me, Nara. Tell me what I've done wrong."

I yank my hand from under his. "Aren't you supposed to be in class right now?"

"It's my lunch period." He leans back in his seat and crosses his ankles in a casual pose. "I'll sit here the whole hour if I have to."

"Whatever." I start to get up, but Drystan bolts upright in his seat and grips my wrist.

"How can I defend myself when I don't know what I've done?" When my gaze meets Drystan's, his fingers loosen on my wrist. "I'm sorry for whatever I did. Now tell me what that was, so I can fix it."

Sincerity shines in his eyes. I sit down, my shoulders stiff. "Why didn't you tell me about your uncle?"

"My uncle?"

"Yes, your uncle, Mr. Wicklow."

Realization dawns. "Oh, you mean that he lives down the street from you?" Drystan releases me and shrugs. "I had no idea where he lived until we drove up to his house last night. I even mentioned when we turned into your neighborhood that a friend lives on his same street." He tilts his head. "You know my uncle? When did you meet him? I wonder why he didn't mention that he'd met you?"

I ignore his questions and ask my own.

"Are you saying that every time you've met your uncle it has been somewhere else until last night?"

Drystan nods. "Yeah, it's usually at the university. One was a faculty/family event, another was a charity thing he helped host. Last night was a dinner."

I spin my hand in a circle. "Any meetings with other groups?"

He lifts his eyebrows and shrugs. "Nope. That's it."

I lean closer, my spine rigid. "Your uncle's not part of a special group? Did he ask you to join?"

"What kind of group? Like a faculty thing?" He shakes his head, his eyebrows pulling together. "All my uncle talks about when we're together is how excited he is that I'm coming to live in England when the semester is over."

Drystan has no idea what I'm talking about. He really doesn't know about the Order. Now that I think about it, he didn't look twice at Ethan's sword tattoo when he saw it—well beyond normal curiosity—but certainly not like he would have if he knew about Corvus. I glance away, completely confused as to why his uncle hadn't told him about the secret organization he leads. Drystan fits the profile of a Paladin like he was born to it. The way he's been with me…he really must have it in his blood and he just doesn't know it yet.

Drystan touches my arm. "Am I missing something? What group are you talking about?"

I shake my head and smile. "Nothing. It was just a misunderstanding. I'm sorry I was quiet this morning. We're good, Drystan."

He looks at me sideways, like he doesn't quite believe me. "How did you meet my uncle?"

"He borrowed our leaf blower and we chatted for a bit, but he never mentioned he had a nephew living here in Blue Ridge."

Drystan's eyes light up. "You saw me at his house last night, didn't you?"

I nod. "While I was out walking Houdini. Seeing you there made me wonder why you hadn't mentioned it."

Drystan spreads his hands wide and grins. "Mystery solved."

Um, yeah, clear as mud. What kind of plans does Mr. Wicklow have for his nephew? Drystan only met his uncle for the first time a few weeks ago. He'd been nervous about their meeting, telling me he wanted his uncle's interest in getting to know him to be about him and not about what he can do.

Mr. Wicklow may not plan to involve Drystan in the Order, but if he does, I hope Drystan joins with his eyes wide open. Pasting on a smile, I say, "Remember how you earned my trust?"

He snorts. "Yeah, worked like 'ell for it."

"Yours should be just as hard to earn."

He eyes me for a second, then grins. "Go on, say I'm worth it."

"My dad thanks you." When he scowls, I smirk and pat the top of his head. "You're definitely worth the effort."

Nara

A text comes through on my phone right when I get home from helping my aunt get ready for her show.

After I set the security alarm for the night—using Mom's note she'd taped to the panel before going to bed early. *I have a six a.m. flight. Here are the alarm instructions in case you forget*—I read the message.

Drystan: I want to talk to you about my uncle. You seem to know something. You know I have trust issues. Come get me and we can get some takeaway.

Me: I'm not eating fast food at eleven. Anyway, I'm exhausted. Going to bed.

*Drystan: After all I've done for you? *pouts**

He's playing the guilt card? I frown.

Me: I really am tired.

Drystan: What do you know that you're not telling me? It's going to bother me all night.

I bite my lip. Should I tell Drystan about the Order? Is it my place? What if his uncle never plans to bring him into his secret world? But then, what if he does? Will he be honest and upfront about the current status of the Corvus/Paladin relationship? Drystan deserves to know the truth before deciding to join. It seems to me that being a Paladin is a life choice and not something taken lightly.

Me: Let's talk tomorrow.

Drystan: We can go to the gym and work out. It's a by weekend for basketball, so we'll have it to ourselves.

Me: Okay. I'll pick you up in the morning around nine.

As I set my phone down, I'm still not sure what I'll say to Drystan. Maybe I'll just talk in generalities and not say anything specific about Corvus. I could tell him his uncle runs a group that tries to protect society. Would that be unfair to him if his uncle does plan on recruiting him? Ugh. I just don't know what to do.

I start to text Ethan to get his opinion, then remember he's out with Danielle and will probably stay out until the wee hours. I hope they find Harper tonight. Knowing this demon isn't going to stop until it gets Freddie's book is setting me on edge.

Nara

Nine a.m. comes way too soon.

After responding to a text from my mom letting me know she's arrived at her destination, I climb in my car and yawn three times while driving to Matt's to pick up Drystan. I'm tempted to stop by Mocha Java and get a large latte, but then I remember what happened to the last one I brought to a workout with Drystan.

Grimacing at the memory, I pull into the driveway. I don't even have a chance to get out of my car before Drystan comes bounding out of Matt's house.

Wearing fitted black athletic pants and a matching jacket with a red stripe across his chest, he's smiling and wide-eyed. I want to growl at the pep in his step as he quickly slides into my passenger seat with the grace of a gazelle.

My movements resemble an elephant's, lumbering and slow. I really need to wake up or he's going to smear me all over that gym.

As soon as I drive off, he turns on my radio, flips to a rock station and blares it full blast.

I wince and turn it off. "If I can't have a latte before workouts, then you can't blast music like that in my ear before caffeine has a chance to wake me up."

Drystan glares at me for a second, then laughs. "You're so not a morning person."

"And you're scowling at me one second and amused the next. What's wrong with you?"

"I didn't sleep well." He slants an annoyed gaze in my direction. "Told you it would bother me all night."

"I'm here, aren't I?"

Drystan grins and rubs his hands together. "That you are. Let's get some training *and* talking done."

The gym lights aren't even on when we get there. While Drystan goes to find the main switch, I stand inside the freezing gym, glad that I wore a sweat jacket that covers at least part of my butt. My yoga pants might be perfect for ease of movement, but not so great for warmth.

Finally the lights pop on, their buzzing adding a warming comfort to the cold space. Most of Drystan's parkour equipment is up, but a couple extra mats and one wall have been removed to accommodate the fully extended bleachers.

Drystan runs back in the room and instantly steps onto a mat, his hands up in ready stance. He's taken off his jacket and a leather necklace with a small vial full of something gray hangs around his neck. "Better remove your jewelry, Dryst," I mock and quickly move into position in front of him. If he wants to workout first, then talk about his uncle later, I'm fine with the delay. I'm still undecided as to what I'll say to him.

"I don't plan to hang myself." He smirks, then swipes at me with a face tap. "Wake up, Buttercup," he says, bouncing on his toes.

His fingers smacking my cheek are so unexpected, my head snaps sideways. I turn a narrowed gaze back to him and lift my fists to block. "That wasn't necessary. I'm awake enough."

"Tell me what I want to know." He moves quickly, the flat of his palm blowing past my arms as if they aren't even there. I stumble back and gasp at the pain exploding across my chest.

Drystan has never hit me like this. I'm so stunned, I shake my head and grit my teeth. He's really giving me a hard time for making him wait. I swing my leg, my foot hitting his thigh. When he grunts, I say, "Ask your uncle why he's so interested in having you with him in England."

"He hasn't told me shite. You know exactly what he's holding back, don't you?" His green eyes darken as he pivots, then swings back, arcing his foot. He's so fast, he catches the back of my knee before I can twist away. When my knee buckles and I fall to the mat, he grunts his annoyance. "Quit delaying. What's the deal with my uncle? And how do you know?"

I'm pissed that he's being so rough and taking his frustration out on me. I jump up and glare at him, rubbing the back of my leg. "This has nothing to do with me. You know what, I'm done helping you avoid asking your uncle tough questions. If you don't trust his motives, then ask him yourself, Drystan. Follow your own instincts. Mine have never steered me wrong."

His face reddens and before I can move, he takes two fast steps toward me. Getting right in my face, he lets out a low laugh. "And what are *your* instincts telling you right now?"

He looks half-angry and half-amused. My stomach tenses, my instincts battling with my heart. I start to take a step back and he smiles, then moves with lightning speed, shoving my shoulders hard.

As I stumble backward, Drystan looks down and shakes his head.

Fear shooting through me, I try to regain my footing, but my heel catches on a place where two mats meet. Just as I start to fall, Drystan jerks his gaze back to me, his expression tense with anxiety. "Run, Nara!"

Drystan laughs suddenly, his voice switching to a maniacal one that sends trickles of icy fear down my spine. "Yes, Nara. Run! It's more fun this way." He leaps the distance across the mat between us, the look on his face quickly shifting to gleeful excitement.

Fear knocks my heart against my chest, but I manage to roll and get to my feet before he lands, barely avoiding his grasping hand. Oh God, a demon has Drystan! He must've fought like hell past the demon's possession to warn me.

Screaming, I run around one of the parkour walls, trying to put a barricade between us, since he's blocking my way to the gym doors. As I squat down, thoughts race through my head. *Can I make it to the door before he reaches me? Is he going to torture me first or kill me the second he gets his hands on me? Where are you, Ethan? You have to have seen this last night.*

"Oh, Nara," the demon says in a sing-song voice. "Come out and play. There's so much I need you to tell me. Like…"

The wall I'm hiding behind suddenly vaults across the room, flying into the bleachers like a paper airplane before sliding onto the floor below.

Drystan looms over me, his head tilted to the side. "Why is the uncle so important to you? What's so special about that man? And where is that damned raven book? I'm tired of asking."

Even worse, it's Harper's demon. I jump up to run, but he grabs my hood and yanks me back against him. "But, we'll get to those questions later." His voice drops as he quickly unzips my jacket. "This boy wants you so bad, little Nara. I might as well enjoy what he was too weak to take."

I struggle against him, trying to pull away. My shirt rips right before his hand clamps brutally hard on my breast. Terror ramps in my belly and I stomp on his toe, then elbow him hard in the gut. He chuckles in my ear and gouges his thumb roughly along the curve of my breast above my bra, while his other hand slides down my stomach. "That tickles. Come on get rougher with me. Makes things interesting."

I scream and claw at his hands. But nothing I do can pull them away. Just as his fingers start to brush past the elastic waistband of my pants, a female voice shouts, "What the hell are you doing?"

Danielle. I gulp back my terrified disgust as I realize his arms aren't locked around me. If I move fast enough while he's glancing back at her...

Twisting sideways out of his grip, I quickly pull my arms free of the jacket's sleeves and take off running for the gym door. Danielle's standing inside the door, two swords in her hands and a fierce look stamped on her face. Her swords are half the length of Ethan's, but with two, I'm sure just as effective at dispatching demons. I skid to a stop in front of her as Drystan walks toward us. His eyes glitter with excitement, like he's looking forward to battling her.

Tears streaming, I sob, "Harper's demon is in Drystan."

Tension edges through me as Drystan moves closer. Danielle's glaring at him, so I step behind her to give her room to fight.

Drystan stops a few feet away, then grins and raises his hands. "What? Can't I have a little fun?"

"I don't have time for your bullshit games," Danielle says in a cold voice as she turns and grips my arm, yanking me between them. "You're here for one reason." Flipping her sword around in her hand with a swift, expert movement, she holds the handle out to him. "Finish her now."

Ethan

I jerk awake with a tight feeling in my chest.

Nara.

Something is wrong. A hard tapping on my bedroom window, followed by other things hitting the glass, pull me out of my bed. I yank the curtain back and the raven Nara calls Patch is standing on the ledge hammering his beak on my window like a wood pecker, while a hoard of ravens fly and crash into my window too.

Patch's frantic tapping only amps my own worry. I sense his anxiety. "You know something's wrong too, don't you?" I quickly drag on my jeans and a T-shirt, and then grab my phone and keys.

Nara doesn't pick up as I call her cell for the fifth time. As I pull into her driveway, I hear the radio announcer's voice for the first time. It's a news bit they run every morning. Except this time the name catches my attention.

A teen girl has been recovered from a river not far from downtown

Blue Ridge. She's been identified as Harper Dabney. A student at Blue Ridge High. Foul play has not been ruled out. The investigation is ongoing.

I grab my phone and dial Danielle's number as I run to Nara's door and ring the bell.

I wait a full minute, but all I hear is Houdini barking by the front door, then whining when I call through the door and tell him to settle.

I glance at my phone, surprised Danielle didn't pick up. She always does when I call, because I rarely do. Danielle had been acting kind of weird the last couple of nights we went looking for Harper. She seemed edgy, yet oddly excited. Did she find Harper without me? What happened?

I stand on Nara's porch, tension ebbing through me. I have no clue how to find her. As I turn, my gaze locks on the houses down the street, and the conversation Nara had with Drystan yesterday in the library hits me. I didn't see her *whole* day yesterday in my dream. I only saw up to the point that she got home from her aunt's house. Why didn't I see it?

Setting my jaw, I turn toward my car and Patch is standing on the roof staring at me. As I approach my car, he bobs his head and doesn't take flight until I open my door.

I head straight down the street to Drystan's uncle's house.

I ring the bell and wait impatiently for the man to answer.

An older man with gray hair and a goatee opens the door, a curious expression on his face. "Can I help you?"

A renewed layer of anger rockets through me. I grab him by his stodgy cardigan and set him against the doorjamb. "Where's Drystan?"

He starts to shake his head, but I just tighten my hold. "I know who you are. I know about the Order. Don't try to bullshit me. I don't have the patience for it. Something's happened to Nara, and my gut tells me he's somehow involved."

"It's hard to speak with a doorjamb digging in my back," he rasps.

I release him, but I don't step back. "Talk."

Straightening his sweater, he eyes me. "*You're* the Corvus. Nara's friend. I'm Mr. Wicklow."

"I'm not here for introductions," I say, staring him down.

He clears his throat. "I really hope you're wrong and Nara's not in trouble. She's a truly amazing girl. With her passion for Corvus, she doesn't need a special gift to qualify. She'd be a valuable asset to the

Order as a Paladin."

"She'll never be anyone's Paladin," I say on a near growl. "Tell me where to find Drystan."

The old man sighs. "Maybe you should consider the Corvus you've been training with. I suspect she would definitely see Nara as a threat."

I frown, not liking his line of thought. "Danielle? She would never hurt—" Harper's name being announced on the radio flashes through my mind.

"Corvus can be very territorial." Mr. Wicklow jumps in, a grim look creasing his goatee around his mouth. "Though it's usually over actual territory, not people. Corvus don't like other Corvus hunting demons on their turf. But if Danielle has attached to you and thinks of you as hers, then she would definitely see Nara as a threat."

"Why are you so sure Drystan's not involved?"

The man shrugs. "Drystan really likes Nara. He lit up when he talked about her recently. He's no threat to her. Of that, I'm sure."

The possibility that Danielle might be behind Nara's disappearance makes me even edgier. Drystan I can handle, but can I take down the Master Corvus? One thing I know for sure, I'll die trying to protect Nara.

My gaze narrows on the man. "Since you're the authority on all things Corvus, how can I find another Corvus?"

Mr. Wicklow looks left and then right to the neighbors' houses on either side of him, then waves me forward. "Come inside. What is your name?"

"Ethan." I step in the foyer, but don't shut the door, my stance tense.

He gives a resigned sigh. "Nara said she would keep the raven medallion somewhere safe. Can you get to it? Depending on how new a Corvus Danielle is, we might be able to get a location on her."

I eye him with suspicion. "The medallion is a Corvus locator?"

He nods. "I thought the only one was at the Order's sanctuary, but that one stopped working thirty years ago. When I saw the one Nara wears glowing while she was looking at the globe in my office, I was so excited. It starts glowing after a new Corvus is formed. Over time the glow dims. As soon as we see the glow, we hold the medallion over a map and it would be drawn almost like a magnetic force to the area where a Corvus exists. That was the medallion's purpose, to alert us so we can find the fledgling Corvus and assign him or her a Paladin."

"I thought the medallion was meant to protect a person from being possessed by a demon."

He nods. "The Corvus raven symbol itself protects against possession. It doesn't have to be that particular medallion." He takes off his watch and shows me the back, where the symbol is etched on the silver. "Each member gets a unique item with the symbol when they're inducted into the Order. Silver with the symbol seems to be the strongest deterrent." Sliding his watch back on his wrist, he asks, "Can you get to the medallion?"

I swallow the knot of guilt in my throat. "I destroyed it."

Mr. Wicklow's face flushes and his eyes bulge. "You what? Didn't Nara tell you to keep it safe?"

I hear Patch's call behind me, but I ignore him and grit my back teeth. "It's gone."

"That's so disappointing. It could've made finding new Corvus much more accurate and efficient, like it was three decades ago."

While the old man's shoulders slump, I glance back to see Patch standing in the middle of the man's yard. He's surrounded by so many ravens I can't see the grass, yet he's the only one making any sounds. I can tell he wants something.

"I've never seen so many at once. This is more than I saw the day I first spoke to Nara about Corvus. Except for the one, they're strangely quiet. It's like they're waiting."

As soon as Mr. Wicklow speaks, I realize what I need to do.

I hold Patch's black gaze, wishing with all my heart to see Nara. *Help me find her.*

Patch lets out a loud *raaaack*, then all the other ravens start chattering. Even the birds in the trees begin to join in the cacophony. They're so loud, Mr. Wicklow covers his ears and shouts over the noise, "Amazing."

When Patch suddenly takes off and all the birds in the yard quickly follow, I step through the door and rush toward my car to the sound of Mr. Wicklow calling out. "I hope you find her."

The birds circle once while I back out of the driveway. When they take off, I follow the cloud of black wings, my heart lodged in my throat.

Please let Nara be okay.

CHAPTER 29

Nara

Drystan eyes Danielle with caution. "Is it going to burn my hand?"

"Possibly." She shrugs and holds the sword out, the black and silver raven symbol standing out near the hilt, just like on Ethan's sword. "But it's far better than the alternative I offered you, so take it."

Drystan hisses as he takes the sword in his right hand. His skin bubbles and sizzles and the smell of burning flesh makes me want to hurl. After a few seconds, he grunts past the pain, then swishes the sword around in a circle as if measuring its weight.

I glare at Danielle, but my voice shakes. "A Corvus sword won't kill me."

Grabbing my hand, she looks at the scar on my palm. "Ethan told me about his sword cutting you. I'm not sure why, since you're neither possessed by a demon, nor Corvus, but if it can hurt you, it can kill you." A pleased smile curls her lips as she drops my hand. "And the great thing about this scenario is that Drystan kills the girl he has a crush on and my sword will wipe you out completely, leaving no evidence behind. A perfect end to you." Patting the top of my head, she smirks. "Don't worry about Ethan. I'll be there for him during his grief."

She glances at Drystan, her tone all business. "Take care of her now."

He shakes his head, his mouth set in a firm line. "Not until I find out where she's keeping the book."

Danielle rolls her eyes. "Why is it so important to you?"

"You really don't know?" His eyebrow lifts with cocky arrogance. "It's rumored to hold the key to destroying the Master Corvus—something Lucifer will greatly reward me for when I present it to him."

When Danielle laughs, I look at her in disbelief. "You think that's funny?"

Danielle puts her finger on her pursed lips, her dark eyes dancing with secrets. "The Master Corvus doesn't exist. It's just a fairy tale meant to throw demons off. We're everywhere. We're many, with power and strength."

I gape, my stomach dropping. "You lied to Ethan?"

She snorts. "Of course I lied to him, but I *am* special. Sadly my adoptive father couldn't accept my superiority over his Corvus. He blocked my ideas on hunting one time too many. I wasn't going to let Ethan do that to me too."

As the meaning of her comment sinks in, I say in a low voice, "The fire that killed William wasn't an accident, was it?"

Danielle's gaze narrows, then she shrugs. "How do you think I figured out how to block Corvus from seeing demons? While the fire raged at our home, burning evidence of his death, demons I'd been chasing the night before attacked." She lifts her sword toward the vial around Drystan's neck. "With all the Corvus ash floating through the air, I couldn't see the demons' faces in the human bodies they inhabited. In his death, William's ashes showed me how to hide a demon in plain sight." She shrugs unapologetically. "He just didn't get the bigger picture of the battle we wage with demons. I'd totally evolved beyond him."

Her accidental discovery is so incredibly dangerous to Corvus. Why can't she see that sharing this information with a demon could have devastating consequences? "You've gone dark, Danielle. You need help."

Her gaze slits on me. "You influence Ethan too much. His love for you is unnatural. Because he left D.C. before he accepted his Corvus, he didn't know demons had apparently followed him. His mangled car in the shop reeked of their trace. I had to take care of them myself since his memory had been wiped." She puts her face close to mine, gritting out, "Ethan putting you first goes against everything Corvus stand for. Hunting demons is our *purpose*, the only thing we should be looking out for. Nothing else matters."

Straightening, she tosses her hair over her shoulder and looks at Drystan. "Get this done now so we can move on."

He eyes her with a wary gaze. "You'll still hold up your end of the bargain?"

She dips her head in a curt nod. "This one time I'll make an exception. You'll live. Now take care of her."

I know there's no way I can outrun both of them, so I turn to Drystan. "Before you kill me, can I have one request?"

His lips quirk. He has all the power and he knows it. "If you tell me where the book is." He glances at Danielle. "It might be worthless according to you, but I still want it."

I lift my chin high, my pulse bulleting through my veins. "It's buried in my yard by the tall tree outside my window."

When the demon nods, I know he realizes I want to say my peace with Danielle and he won't interfere. I turn to face her. "You never deserved the honor of being Corvus." As she opens her mouth to reply, I aim my right fist for her face. When she easily blocks my punch, I sling my stronger left hook and clock her in the jaw.

Swallowing my howl of pain from my throbbing knuckles, I take advantage of her stumbling back against the door and bolt away.

The demon lets out a belly laugh. "He taught her that move."

"Shut up." Danielle grunts as two sets of feet hammer the wood floor in fast pursuit. "Get her, you sack of shit. It's your fault she's not already dead."

I run around the side of the bleachers and head for the door that leads into the school, praying it's not locked. My arms jolt hard when I run into it. Pulse racing, I shove with all my might, but it refuses to budge.

Excruciating pain suddenly splinters through the back of my head. Danielle has a handful of my hair and she yanks, hissing in my ear, "You little bitch! I want to kill you myself but my Corvus won't let me." When she twists her fingers tight in my hair, I yowl and try to pull her hand off, but she just uses her hold to turn me around and shove me into Drystan.

He laughs and hooks his arm around my throat as he moves behind me. Slicing Danielle's sword through the air near my body twice, he says, "Aren't you going to beg for your life?"

I grit my teeth. "You'll enjoy that too much."

When he chuckles, Danielle moves behind his right shoulder and says in a low, spiteful voice, "Make it hurt before you twist the sword and disintegrate her completely."

Resting the sword's point against my stomach, he says near my ear, "Are you ready to die now?"

"Just stab her!" Danielle snaps, her voice close, as if she wants to watch my agony.

My breath gushes in frantic pants, but I manage to get out, "Ethan will kill you both."

"Danielle's right," the demon says. "He'll never know what happened to you." He lifts the sword and I tense my stomach as he swipes it in a fast downward arc right past me and into Danielle's gut.

While Danielle gasps in shock, followed by a groan of pain rushing past her lips, the demon glances over his shoulder and pushes the sword all the way through her, letting out a pleased laugh. "Did you really think you could trust a demon?"

Gripping the back of my neck in a vise hold, he flips his other hand around on the sword's handle and turns to face her. "How does it feel to be skewered, Corvus? We might not remember our lives after being sent to Under, but we never forget the pain."

Oh God, this is an Inferi, not a Furia, I realize as Danielle hisses, "Fuck...you!" hatred lacing her voice. Blood seeps over her hands and down her clothes, dripping onto the toes of her boots.

"You're the one who just got screwed." As she falls to her knees, he leans over and muses out loud, "I wonder what happens when a dark Corvus is killed with its own sword? Will you go to Under?"

"No, Drystan," I beg from my bent position, since he dragged me to his level when he bent to talk to her. "Please don't let him do this." Tears drip off my face as I fruitlessly try to uncurl his tight hold from my neck.

Drystan glances at me, but an eerie blankness reflects in his green eyes. Smiling, he returns his gaze to Danielle and twists the sword. "Buh-bye."

When Danielle explodes, I wince. Up close, I realize her obliteration doesn't create ashes like I thought I'd seen when Ethan killed Drake. It's a haze of fine mist. Most of the cloud had burst into the air, but some of the moist droplets had splattered on my nose and lips. As I shudder and quickly swipe my sleeve across my face, the fog hanging over us completely dissipates.

The Inferi straightens and pulls me upright. He sulks at his empty hand. The sword had disintegrated right along with Danielle. "Well damn, I wanted to keep that."

When his eyes shift to me, a sour taste fills my mouth. A cold smile tilts his lips and he rubs his thumb with bruising hardness along my neck, his eyes lighting with lust. "But I still have you. Might as well let the boy enjoy himself before I kill you."

The second the demon starts to pull me toward him, I reach up and grab a fistful of his hair and twist. Slamming the side of his head against one of the metal bars supporting the bleachers, I quickly release him and jump back.

The Inferi holds his head and lets out an ear-splitting howl. He whirls on me, but sways from side to side, slightly unsteady on his feet.

While he's still groggy, I rip the leather strap holding the vial of ashes from around his neck, then duck his wildly swinging backhand to hop onto the bottom bleacher. Running up the stairs, I intended to stomp on the vial, then head straight across the bleachers and jump off the other side, but the demon lands on a stair below me, blocking my exit.

"Give that back," he snarls, his hands curled into tight fists.

He recovered faster than I expected. I bolt higher up the stairs, the vial swinging between my clasped fingers as I try to think of a way to destroy it. It can fall through the stairs if I try to stomp on it while running. Glancing up, I realize there's only one way to break it. My lungs heave as I head for the top of the bleachers.

The wooden stairs shudder under my feet with his heavy footfalls in fast pursuit, but I don't take my eyes off my goal. As soon as I reach the top stair, I turn and run across it. Swinging my hand away from my body, I slam the vial as hard as I can against the cinderblock wall.

The glass shatters and the demon lets out a horrific roar, then hops the last three stairs, landing on the top. My heart slams against my chest as the bleacher stair vibrates under his thundering feet. I'm running out of room, and we're easily twenty feet up with nothing below to break my fall. I'm not even sure if there's enough room for me to "roll" out of a jump this high like Drystan had taught me to do.

I stop when I have two feet left on the bleacher stair and turn to face the Inferi behind me.

He's five feet away, leaning against the wall, a smile of pure malice on his face. "Looks like you've run out of options." Pushing off the wall, his gaze narrows. "I'm going to make you suffer for destroying that vial."

He takes a step toward me, and something slams into the wall in front of him.

A Corvus sword is embedded halfway, the raven symbol between us. "Take one step closer to her, and I promise your trip to Under will feel like an amusement park ride before I'm done with you."

The demon stops short and turns a hateful gaze on Ethan standing at the bottom of the bleachers, his face a ruthless mask.

Shoulders tense, Ethan's poised like a panther ready to pounce, his solid black eyes locked on the Inferi with predatory anticipation.

Rolling his head from one shoulder to the other, the demon cracks his knuckles and smiles at Ethan. "Come and get me."

Ethan shoots up the bleachers so fast I don't even see his feet move, but when the Inferi quickly turns and pulls Ethan's sword from the wall with a hard yank—I decide I can't let Ethan die like Danielle did.

As the demon turns toward Ethan, I lean against the wall for leverage and kick my foot out, jamming my shoe hard against his hand.

The sword clatters to the stair below, and I quickly squat, barely avoiding the Inferi's fist swinging for my head. Cinderblock dust explodes over me as I slide down the next stair and push the sword through the opening.

Ethan grabs Drystan by the throat and squeezes hard. The Inferi sneers and chokes out, "Me or her. Choose!" Before I can dodge out of his way, he jams his foot on my shoulder, sending me tumbling over the edge of the bleachers.

So many regrets flash through my head as I hurl toward the wood floor below; all my thoughts happen in an instant, yet seem to go on forever.

I'll miss not learning and sharing new things with my father. I won't get to watch my parents grow close again. I failed to help the Corvus, and probably made things worse. Being unable to tell Ethan about Danielle's death. I hope Ethan eliminates this demon. He knows too much. And Ethan and me, that's my biggest regret. So much wasted time...

"Open your eyes, Nara. I've got you," Ethan breathes against my temple, then presses a kiss there. He's holding me tight against his chest, his arms cradling me close.

I blink and stare up into his eyes, then quickly glance around the gym. "Where's the demon? Ethan, you have to go after him."

Ethan sets my feet on the floor, then pushes my hair out of my face. When his gaze drops to my torn shirt, his jaw muscle jumps. His fingers tremble slightly as he lifts the material and sets it right against my chest. "There's never a choice when it comes to you."

I grip his waist. "You have to go after Drystan and send that Inferi to Under. He killed Danielle with her own sword. He needs to forget everything he's learned. Its dangerous for him to have that kind of information against Corvus."

Worry crosses his face and Ethan cups my jaw, his expression focused. "I'm not leaving you."

I shake my head and sigh. "How did you find me?"

His lips set in a hard line. "I knew something wasn't right when I woke up and my dreams from the night before were completely blank. *Your* dreams. Patch and his cronies led me here."

"Patch?" A brief smile of appreciation curves my lips. "He's always watching over me. I'm pretty sure my dreams were blank because I was with Drystan, who had a vial of Corvus ashes around his neck."

Ethan's fingers flex on me. "Corvus ashes?"

"Danielle gave them to him. She made a deal with Harper's demon to kill me and she'd spare him. That's what I'm talking about. This Inferi knows too much that can hurt Corvus. We need to find him and free Drystan."

Ethan's hands fall to his sides, his fists clenching tight. "Wicklow was right. He said that Corvus are very territorial and Danielle might've attached to me. It definitely sounds like she lost it. I can't believe she plotted to kill you." Deadly fury fills his gaze. "It's a good thing she's gone. It wouldn't have been pretty if I'd gotten ahold of her."

Despite the retribution in his tone, I notice the sadness and disillusionment lurking in his eyes. I touch his arm, glad he didn't have to make the choice. "You went to see Mr. Wicklow?"

He nods. "I needed answers."

My fingers curl around his skin. "We should call him. He needs to know what's happened to his nephew, and he might be able to tell us where Drystan would go."

Ethan's expression turns resolute. Walking over to get my jacket, he holds it out for me. Once I slide my arms in the sleeves, he zips it up past the tear in my shirt. "I'll get my sword, then you can call Wicklow. Once we get back to your house, you can fill me in on what this Inferi knows. I have stuff to tell you too."

"Hello?"

"Mr. Wicklow? It's Nara Collins." I put my phone on speaker and glance at Ethan's Mustang driving ahead of me on the way back to my neighborhood.

"Oh, Nara. I'm so relieved you're okay. Ethan was here not that long ago. He's definitely a Corvus, that one. He was under the impression something had happened to you—"

"Sorry to cut you off, but this is urgent. A demon has possessed Drystan and had attacked me. When Ethan arrived, he got away, and now Ethan's trying to find him. Do you have any idea where Drystan might go?"

Mr. Wicklow mumbles, "Now his disorientation makes sense."

I hear a car start in the background. "What do you mean?"

"I'm on my way to pick up Drystan. He called and sounded confused enough that he was unable to tell me where he is or how he got there. Based on his description I think he's near the train station not far from the downtown mall. I thought he'd been on an all-night bender with school buddies."

"We'll meet you there."

"There's no need. The demon is already gone."

My brows pull together. "How do you know?"

"That's where Drystan's disorientation is coming from. When the demon leaves a body, the person has no memory of the possession or what happened during it. They just know they've lost a period of time." He heaves a regretful sigh. "This is all my fault."

Ethan pulls into the far side of my driveway and I push the garage door button, then drive past him into my garage. "Why is it your fault?"

"Once I learned of your existence, I had your background checked. One similar interest you and Drystan had was soccer, so I brought him to Blue Ridge in the hopes he would bond with you on his own."

"You planned this all along?" I say, unable to keep the anger from my tone.

"I had good intentions. It doesn't surprise me that my nephew gravitated to you. You are special in your own way. Once your friendship had fully developed, I planned to tell him all about the Order and ask him to be your Paladin."

"But I'm not Corvus," I whisper, more to myself than to him.

"Precisely. If you had been Corvus, as a new Order inductee,

Drystan would've received his gift with the raven symbol that protects him from demon possession. I did try to give him a family heirloom, a watch that had the symbol hidden in the etching on the back of it, but Drystan refused to wear it. So I thought I'd wait until we got back to England to tell him about the Order and ask him to join our ranks as a Paladin for a future Corvus. Then he could fully appreciate the watch's importance."

"How could you do this to Drystan?" My voice rises. I can't help it. "Why didn't you tell him up front?"

"I was trying to make it as natural a transition as possible for you both. Most Corvus are very resistant to their Paladins even though they know they're a necessity to keep their lives balanced. This time, I'd hoped to let mutual respect and friendship happen on its own without Corvus/Order ties, yet it seems I've made a mess of things."

He couldn't have anticipated Danielle. We all underestimated her. "Even if you had the best intentions, we didn't deserve to be lied to, Mr. Wicklow."

"I'm sorry I put you and my nephew at risk, Nara. That was never my intent. I'm very glad to hear you're okay. I just hope Drystan can forgive me."

"I don't know if he will, but if you want Drystan to forgive you, you'll have to tell him everything. Don't hold back."

Ethan's standing outside my window. The expectant look on his face tells me he hasn't already seen any of this conversation I'm having with Mr. Wicklow. Ethan had said my dreams last night were entirely blank. I suppose that makes sense considering anything Corvus related—from conversations to interactions—had never shown up in my dreams in the past. So far, my entire morning has been nothing *but* Corvus stuff.

I nod to Ethan then ask Mr. Wicklow one last question. "What about Ethan? Are you going to assign him a Paladin?"

Mr. Wicklow lets out a low chuckle. "He doesn't need one. He has you. I told him I want you to join the Order. To become a Paladin. But he told me quite forcefully that you'd never be anyone's Paladin."

I jerk a questioning gaze to Ethan. Did he say that because he doesn't think I'm cut out to be a Paladin? Or did he say it, because he doesn't want me to have anything to do with the Order?

"Um, I'll get back to you on the whole Paladin thing. Please let me know if Drystan's truly okay."

"I will. Take care, Nara."

As soon as I open my car door and step out, Ethan scoops me up in his arms.

I quickly wrap my arms around his neck. "Where are we going?"

"To take a nap."

I turn in his arms and unlock the kitchen door with my key. "But don't you want to hear what Mr. Wicklow said?"

"I heard your half of the conversation. I'm back to trusting my first instincts about the Order."

"Ethan."

"We'll talk, but for now I just want to hold you, Sunshine."

Sighing, I rest my head against his shoulder and let him carry me upstairs.

CHAPTER 30

Nara

Houdini's wet nose touching mine wakes me from a deep sleep. It's dark outside, and as I pet my dog's head, my gaze is drawn to the clock on my nightstand where Ethan had left me a note. Flipping on my light, I pick up the paper.

Had to run a couple of errands. Houdini's on guard duty. He won't leave your side. Be back soon.

After we shared everything we learned from Danielle and Mr. Wicklow this morning, Ethan had pulled me close, pressing my back against his chest. He voiced how he couldn't believe Danielle had lied about being the Master Corvus.

That part seemed to bother him the most. Danielle's death hit him hard, but more in a physical sense than an emotional one. He told me he'd fallen back against his car when Danielle got stabbed with her sword, and it took him a few minutes to stand up straight. At the time, he didn't know that what he felt was Danielle's wound, but once I told him when and how it happened, the timing of it lined up.

We grew quiet, and I was surprised he didn't try to kiss me, but his fingers running through my hair had felt so good, I drifted off to sleep.

Setting the note back on my nightstand, I wonder how much time I have before Ethan gets back. I really want to shower before then. Jumping up, I grab a new set of clothes, then step into the bathroom.

Fifteen minutes later, as I start to walk out of my bathroom while tugging an emerald green sweater on, I almost trip over Houdini. "You really are taking this job seriously, aren't you?" I say as I step over him and pull the sweater's hem down over my dark fitted jeans.

He looks up at me with big brown eyes and whimpers. I glance at the clock on my nightstand. It's already six. "Ah, no wonder you're whining. You want to eat?"

The second I say "eat", he bolts out of my room, his heavy paws thumping down the stairs. Laughing, I grab my phone and follow him. After he wolfs down two cups of kibble in thirty seconds and then lets out a loud belch, I snicker and pick up his leash. "Come on. You'll be asking five minutes after we get back upstairs otherwise."

While Houdini drags me to the side of our house, I glance at my phone and see I've missed a call. Pushing the voicemail button, I listen to the message.

"Hello, Nara. I just wanted to let you know that Drystan is fine. He's upset about what happened though and has decided he's going to cut his semester short and finish up this school year in England. I'll be flying out with him on Monday. Now that he knows everything about the Order, it'll be up to him to decide if he wants to join.

"Be sure to let me know what you decide about being a Paladin. The Order could use someone like you; you have this remarkable empathy and I think any Corvus would be lucky to have you. And yes, a few Paladins have been assigned another Corvus if they can handle the double duty. So definitely think about it."

My heart is heavy as I tuck my phone in my back pocket. I hate to think Drystan would leave without saying goodbye, but then I'm not sure I'm ready to see him right now anyway. Even though I know a demon was doing those things to me, all I can picture is Drystan's face and the feel of his hands touching me with rough, punishing intent. I shudder at the memory as cool wind whips around me, blowing my slightly damp hair. Tugging on the leash, I lead Houdini back toward the front of my house and freeze.

Drystan's standing on my front porch, hands tucked in his leather jacket as the porch light shines down on his tousled hair.

Panic rises as he walks down the porch steps. It takes everything in me not to turn and run in the other direction, but Houdini sitting on his haunches and staring up at Drystan with open curiosity lets me know this is just my friend.

"I wanted to say goodbye," he says, his tone subdued, guarded.

Words stick in my throat. I don't know how to voice what I'm thinking. How to tell him it's okay and that I don't blame him for attacking me. It's not like he remembers any of it anyway. My head knows this, but my heart is having a hard time reconciling it.

Pain, regret, and sadness scroll across Drystan's features before he masks them behind a stoic expression. "Okay, well then. Just couldn't leave without saying farewell."

As he starts to turn away, I finally find neutral ground. "I'm glad your uncle told you everything. I hope you'll be happy in England."

His mouth presses in a thin, angry line. "I knew I was right to distrust his motives. I'm sorry you were dragged into it as well. But man, Corvus? That blew my mind. You really are good at keeping secrets."

I shrug and give an apologetic half smile that I couldn't share that part of my life before now. "You and I have every reason to be mad at your uncle, but then we never would've met, and that would've been a shame."

A bit of light sparks in his eyes. "Do you really mean that?"

I nod. "Of course. I know you didn't have control over what that demon did."

"I would never hurt you," he says as he steps into my personal space.

My lungs seize and I quickly take a step back, then regret it when I see the hurt in Drystan's eyes. Taking a deep breath, I force all my anxiety away and step forward, hugging him instead. "I know."

Drystan stiffens for a split second, then his arms wrap around me in a tight embrace. "God, I'm so sorry, Nara. You'll never know how much," he murmurs in my hair.

The trembling in his voice, the anguish in his eyes, his utter shock when I hug him; it hits me hard. Drystan remembers everything that happened. Tears blur my vision. Why didn't he tell his uncle?

Swallowing a sob, I hug him tighter. While my face is pressed against his leather coat, the smell helps me separate my emotions and cling to the good times we've had together. "It's not your fault, Drystan. I don't blame you."

He rubs his thumb on the back of my shoulder, his voice tortured. "The fear on your face when I moved close to you…it's tearing me up. How can you hug me when you're terrified?"

I sniff back my tears, but a couple fall anyway as I force myself to meet his gaze. "Because you're my friend."

He lets his head fall back and stares up into the night sky for a second, then returns his gaze to mine. Brushing away my tears with his knuckles, he says, "I can't bear the thought of leaving with that image burned in my mind. Will you let me kiss you, Nara? Please give me a chance to erase the bad memories before I leave."

Drystan's right hand is bandaged and my heart squeezes when I remember the smell of his flesh burning as he held Danielle's sword. The idea of overlaying the nightmare imagery with a pleasant one to remember him by warms my heart. I don't want to have terrifying memories of Drystan floating around in my head forever. I nod and give him a trembling smile.

Tension eases out of Drystan's shoulders, and he cups my face in a gentle hold. As his mouth moves close to mine, I turn my cheek slightly.

Drystan pauses, a corner of his lips quirking up. "You really do love him, don't you?"

I smile. "Very much."

"It's kind of hard to compete with a Corvus," he says, exhaling a resigned sigh.

When I raise an eyebrow, he leans close and presses a tender kiss to my cheek. His fingers lingering on my jaw, he returns his gaze to mine. "You are truly the most amazing person I've ever met. My life is fuller for having spent time with you." The light dims in his eyes. "I'm sorry you can't say the same about me."

I reach for his uninjured hand and lower our clasped hands between us, relieved to feel the apprehension of being around him slowly slipping away. "That's not true. You taught me how to stick up for myself. Literally." Smiling, I release his hand and poke his chest. "Which means, I now know how to kick your ass. And don't think for one minute that I won't do so if you don't keep in touch with me. Just because you'll be living across the pond doesn't mean you can't let me know how life's treating you. Deal?"

He offers a brief smile, a glimmer of the old Drystan shining through. "Deal." Stepping back, he says, "My uncle's taking me over to Matt's so I can get my stuff and say goodbye to him as well. Take care of yourself, and ring me if you ever need to talk. I'll text you my new contact information once I'm settled."

As Drystan disappears in the dark, heading toward his uncle's house, I realize I forgot to ask him if he planned to become a Paladin.

Though he seems upset with his uncle right now, I assume he will tell me what he decides to do when he's ready.

Ethan

I'm nervous when I knock on Nara's door at seven. My errands took longer than I wanted. I hate being away from her longer than necessary.

She pulls open her front door and smiles, her gaze dropping to my black button down shirt and dark jeans. "You look nice." Reaching for my hand, she tugs me inside and tilts her head, her blonde hair flowing over her shoulder.

I wrap my arms around her waist and step close. Any chance I get to hold her, I'll take it. Everything about Nara ramps my pulse. If she wants to slow things down between us because of what happened today, I'm fine with that. I've never been more scared than when Nara went tumbling over the edge of those bleachers.

I still don't know how I went from standing on the bleachers to catching her before she landed. That feat should've been impossible, but I'm just glad I made it in time. If anything happened to her, nothing else would matter to me.

Nothing.

I brush some blonde strands away from her temple and take in her smiling face. She's so awe-inspiring, always finding a way to bounce back. Even though she seems okay, I just want her to feel safe in my arms. I'll let her take the lead with us. She'll tell me when she's ready to move forward.

As I start to drop a kiss on her nose, she presses a palm against my chest. "Drystan stopped by for a few minutes."

My entire body tenses and my fingers flex on her hips. For a second, my vision actually blurs, but for her sake I swallow my where-is-he-so-I-can-beat-the-shit-out-of-him reaction and answer in a calm tone. "Are you okay?"

"I'm fine. I know the demon made him do all those things. That's not who Drystan is. I just wanted you to know he feels terrible about what happened and couldn't leave until he apologized."

"He's leaving?" I don't bother hiding my smile.

She taps my shoulder and huffs. "You don't have to look so happy. Yes, he's leaving. I think he feels the need to get away and start his new life in England now."

"The further away the better," I mutter.

"Ethan!"

I shrug. "I didn't trust him when I first met him, nor when I re-met him, and I still don't."

"And how much of your dislike of him is driven by your feelings for me?"

My lips twitch as she throws my own words back at me—I'd said something similar to her about Danielle. "Every bit of it. I'm not afraid to admit that."

She sighs and shakes her head. "At least you're honest."

I laugh and cross my arms at the base of her spine, pulling her even closer so I can bask in her sweet smell and soft curves. "That's one thing I'll always be with you from now on."

Wrapping her arms around my neck, she lifts up onto her toes and presses a quick kiss to my lips, whispering, "You'd better."

As she lowers her feet back to the floor, she says, "You don't have to dress up for me, you know."

I shake my head and reach over to take her jacket off the coat rack next to the door. "That's because we're going out."

"I thought we were staying in."

When her bottom lip pushes out slightly, it takes major willpower not to pull her against me and suck that sweet bit of flesh between my lips and nip it for good measure. Damn, I ache for her. Too bad we have to be somewhere in a half hour. I swallow back my internal groan of disappointment and hold her coat out for her. "Come on. I have something to share with you."

Nara smiles when I lead her into McCormicks twenty minutes later. "So you're finally going to share your music with me?"

"Something like that," I say, making her laugh and shake her head.

As we move through the crowd and people start calling out, "Adder's here!"

"Hey, Adder, so glad you're here tonight."

I casually nod, but continue forward, bobbing and weaving through the crush of people until we make it to a table in the front where Lainey and Matt are sitting.

Beaming with excitement, Nara hugs Lainey, then leans back and grips her friend's shoulders. "You were in on this surprise?"

Her eyes sparkling, Lainey shakes her head. "I don't know. If we're the surprise, then yeah, I guess. Ethan called and told us he had reserved a table up front for all of us, so here we are."

Nara grins at her friend, then gives me a sly sideways glance. "Oh, you're in for a great show, Lainey. I promise."

I chuckle that Nara's excited to surprise her friend as I lean over and shake Matt's outstretched hand. "Thanks for coming."

Once Lainey, Matt, and Nara take a seat, I kiss the top of Nara's head and say to the table, "I'll be back."

Nara snickers. "Don't be gone too long."

I smile and then stroll away, but as I push through a door that leads to the back, my stomach tenses. I pull out a piece of paper that I'd found laying on top of my broken ribbon bracelet in the memories box under Nara's bed.

It might've been wrong to swipe it, but when I stumbled across it that day, I couldn't let her words go. The paper is worn; I've read her sad poem/song so many times, but I read it again once more to give me the courage to get up there and share like she always has so unselfishly with me.

> Together 'til is all I can offer you.
> Maybe one day we'll be okay.
> Not now. My heart is broken. My soul is torn.
> This isn't how destiny is born.
> We're shattered, splintered, no longer one, but two.
> Where did we go wrong? Am I paying my dues?
> Will you still be there when you remember?
> Will you, when your mind is free?
> It feels like a sin to hold all the pain in.
> But I do. To be together 'til, together 'til, together 'til.
> Even though my heart is breaking, I'm together 'til with you.

Ivan pops his bald head around the edge of the door. His eyebrow piercing is raised high, a wide grin on his face. "You ready, Adder?

We're going to rock the shit out of this crowd tonight."

I glance up and nod. "I'm coming."

Nara

"It would've been nice if Drystan had stayed the whole semester," Lainey says, drawing my attention away from the band members moving mics and equipment around on the dark stage. "I know his uncle was done with his university guest role, but I just wish Drystan hadn't decided to head back with him right now. He'll be missed."

I nod, my heart twisting a little. "I'll miss him too, but he promised he'll keep in touch."

"He'd better," Matt grumbles.

The stage lights flare to life, cutting off our conversation.

Lainey glances at the band as the music starts up. I lift my phone and snap a shot of her bugged eyes and gaping mouth when her gaze lands on Ethan playing the electric guitar.

His sleeves are rolled up and he's bent over the instrument, making the strings sing with amazing skill to the fast beat of the song. The first time I saw him he was playing bass, but tonight he's playing lead guitar, which makes my heart soar.

Lainey jerks her wide brown-eyed gaze to me and grips my arm. "You've been holding out on me!"

I laugh and shake my head, shouting over the music, "I just found out recently myself." Waving my hand toward the stage, I shrug. "Surprise."

Matt's staring up at Ethan and shaking his head. "Weylaid, huh? He has amazing talent. Damn, I'm so gonna come back and watch them play again."

"He's not an official member of the band, but they let him jump in often enough that fans know who he is."

Lainey lifts her hands toward the stage, a duh look on her face. "Why wouldn't they want him? He's got skills."

"He's just kept to himself for so long." When Ethan breaks into a crazy fast solo where I can't keep up with his fingers on the strings, I whistle and clap along with all the fans. "Maybe now he'll join if they ask or at least play more often."

Matt's tapping the table to the rhythm of the rock song. "He'd be crazy not to."

We watch the band play several more songs, and then just before their set is almost over, one of the guys hands Ethan an acoustic guitar.

The crowd quiets as he moves his stool toward the center of the stage. The lights dim until only one light is shining on his dark head.

"I don't usually sing solos…" he says into the mic, his deep voice resonating through the whole place.

Several catcalls ensue.

"We wish you would!"

"Love the depth, Adder."

"Give it to me, baby! I'm yours."

"Adder?" Lainey mouths as she glares over her shoulder in the direction of the last comment.

"Stage name," I say with a smile, happy he seems content.

Ethan chuckles and shakes his head, strumming the guitar slowly, preparing to play. "But tonight is special."

I grin at him, even though I know he can't see past the bright light. I hope he knows how thrilled I am to see him embracing the talent Adder has given him.

"The song is very personal, so I hope you'll humor me. It's called…"

The excited crowd starts to scream and cheer, drowning out the title of the song.

Ethan begins to play a soulful tune that sends chill bumps along my arms, but when he starts to sing in his low, sexy voice, I gasp and raise trembling hands to my mouth.

> *Together 'til the wheels fall off is how we've always rolled.*
> *Now we're just together 'til. That's what I've been told.*
> *Together 'til's a temporary existence, my harsh penitence.*
> *It will never be enough. Not for me.*
> *It wears me down, slows my heart, brings me to my knees.*
> *Tell me there's more than together 'til.*
>
> *I don't want to wait for one day. It's getting hard to breathe.*
> *My music is flat, my art rudimentary.*
> *Baby, my heart needs yours freed.*

Take away the tethers of together 'til.

Let's hit the road and journey. Go 'til we run on fumes.
Our past doesn't matter, what does is being in tune.
I'll fight every evil known to man, and more still
Just so we can go beyond together 'til.

'Cause that's exactly how destiny is born. We'll get to
our destination.
But let's detour, meander, take a leisurely drive.
Paths taken with you make me feel alive.
Move us past together 'til.

We're not shattered. My dark and your light make the
perfect whole.
We're better together. That's one thing I know.
We've always been right, 'cause what we have is rare.
But I wanted to be worthy, have something to share.

What good am I without an identity?
While I was discovering me, memories kept me going.
Your soft lips and sighs, my only company.
You never left my heart. Not once while we were apart.

Kick me, hit me, scream and shout. I'll take all your
pain.
That's it, let it all out.
I just want to touch you and hold you again.
For far, far longer than together 'til.

Together 'til will never be enough, not for me, not ever
enough.
It can't fill the hole in my heart.
The spin of wheels eating up the road, paving a path
forward...
That's where we'll start.

When dawn finally breaks
Will you fulfill my every wish?

Leave me breathless, leave me shaking.
I want your forever kiss.

I need more than together 'til.
I need my wheels.
Baby, no more standing still.
I've waited forever and ever,
Forever for my wheels.
I promise when I get them back,
They'll forever be attached...
To together 'til.

Together 'til and more. Mmm, hmmm.
Together 'til with wheels.
Together 'til the end of time.
Together 'til always be mine.
Together 'til...

Ethan suddenly flattens his hand on the strings and peers through the darkness directly at me. "What do you say, Sunshine? Can I have my wheels back?"

The room is deathly quiet. I'm so shocked that he wrote a song in answer to mine it takes me a second to swallow the lump in my throat. Cupping my hands over my mouth, I call out toward the stage, loud enough so the entire bar can hear, "Together 'Til the Wheels Fall Off. All the way, baby!"

Everyone's suddenly on their feet. The whistling, clapping, and screaming is so loud my ears ring. Lainey squeals and pulls me to my feet. Hooking her arm around my shoulders and Matt's waist, she jumps up and down, whooping with the rest. "That was freaking amazing. Listen to this crowd!"

But my attention is focused on Ethan, who's moved to the edge of the stage.

When he puts his hand out, I step forward to take it.

He lifts me up with little effort and quickly pulls me into his arms. "It feels good to have my wheels. I've missed them."

When he presses his mouth to mine, the crowd goes absolutely nuts, their applause and foot stomps shaking the stage beneath our feet.

I kiss him back and squeeze his neck, smiling against his mouth. "I love you too."

CHAPTER 31

Nara

Ethan pulls into my driveway and cuts the engine. I unbuckle my seatbelt and reach for his hand, lacing my fingers with his. As he glances my way, I smile. "Thank you for the beautiful song. I never did hear what you called it. The crowd was too loud."

Ethan traces his thumb over mine in a slow, rhythmic caress. "The name is Together 'Til and thank you for writing yours. As much as it tore me up to read it, I had to answer you in my own way."

My heart races as he moves his hand to my neck and bends close to whisper in my ear, "By the way, that was all me speaking to you. Adder had nothing to do with that song."

I smile and press my cheek to his, enjoying the roughness of his stubble scraping against my skin. "He's probably a bit offended you went solo."

Ethan turns my chin with his thumb and murmurs, "I don't give a damn," right before his warm mouth presses against mine.

When his fingers thread into my hair, and he cups the back of my head, tilting it so he can deepen our kiss, I move closer and welcome the intimate slide of his tongue against mine.

My heart races as Ethan uses his hold to tug me across the seat, and before I know it, he's shifted his seat back and I'm straddling his lap and kissing him as if we haven't kissed in months.

His warm hands slide under my sweater and massage my back

before trailing down to my hips. As the passion between us rises, his hands move to my rear. Clamping a firm hold on my butt, he tugs me closer while he shifts his hips higher.

I thread my fingers in his thick hair and moan against his mouth, enjoying the pleasurable sensations between us. The sexual tension is so thick, the air in the car feels warm despite the frigid weather outside.

Lights flash in the window as a car passes, and Ethan grips my waist and quickly sets me back into the seat.

I gape at him, confused. "What was that for—"

"Our first time will *not* be in a car," he says, his tone adamant and his breathing labored.

"Well then." Before he can say another word, I hop out and walk around the front of his car.

His hand slashes across his glass, brushing away the fog we'd created. He's frowning as if he thinks I've just ditched him. I smile and I crook my finger.

Once we're inside, I tug Ethan up the stairs. He follows, a sexy smile on his lips. As soon as we reach the hallway, I grab his shirt and pull him close to continue the kiss we'd started in the car.

His mouth captures mine, his palms cupping my hips in a tight grip.

Cool air hits my back as he starts to slide my sweater up my body. Breaking our kiss, his deep blue gaze—full of heat and want—captures mine. "Are you sure, Nara? I have protection this time, but after what almost happened to you earlier, I'm willing to wait—"

I press my finger against his lips and shake my head. "There is no way you're going to sing a song like that to me and not expect me to jump your bones the first chance I get."

When his gaze flares and his lips curve in a dark smile behind my finger, I trace the tip of my finger down his chin, past his Adam's apple and along his chest until I reach the first button on his shirt. "I love you, Ethan Harris." I unbutton the first two buttons on his shirt. "More every day."

Unbuttoning the next two buttons, I smile at his suddenly still body and reach inside his shirt to press my hand to his warm chest. His heart thumps hard against my palm. "You're everything I want. Never doubt it."

Ethan's thumbs slip inside the waistband of my jeans at the base of my spine, his fingers digging into my jeans' pockets. "I love you, Sunshine." His gaze holds mine as he slowly pulls my sweater over my head.

Light from the downstairs shines up the stairwell, giving off a dim glow in the hall. As soon as my sweater hits the carpet, Ethan reaches for me, but I put my hands against his chest and shake my head.

When he gives me a frustrated look, I smile and slide my hands down his shirt where the next button starts. "This is how you know I'm done waiting."

The last two buttons ping off the walls as I pull his shirt apart with a giggle, then quickly tug it off his arms, dropping it to the floor.

Ethan's expression is so intense, I instantly sober. "Don't worry. I'll sew them back on—"

I'm lifted and pressed against the wall so fast, I'm gasping with excitement as my arms settle around his broad shoulders.

His fingers flex against my butt as he presses warm kisses along my throat and down the curve of my breast above my bra. "No more holding back?" he asks, his voice a harsh rasp.

I clasp his jaw and lift his eyes to mine. "You've got your wheels back. Now show me what you can do with them."

I let out a pant of surprise when he dips his head and runs his tongue along the inside curve of my breast, then nips the plump skin over the edge of my bra gently. "You taste like heaven," he murmurs against my breast. His breath warms the skin he just wet, sending tingles jolting along every nerve ending.

Threading my fingers in his hair, I kiss the top of his head. "Don't torture me too long tonight. I think I might combust in your arms if you do."

Ethan's seductive chuckle sends a fissure of delight splintering straight to my belly. "I'm going to find every single spot that revs you up before the night's over." When he presses close, and whispers, "That's a promise, Sunshine," the sensation of his hard chest and abs rubbing against me feels so good, I arch closer.

He feels so strong and warm, a shudder sends chill bumps racing across my skin. I can't believe how deeply he affects me. It seems to only grow stronger. Ethan kisses my jaw and presses his hardness against me, then slowly rocks his hips. The amped desire unfurling in my belly and lower captures my entire body.

I bite my lip and match his movements, wanting to intensify our seductive, pulsing intimacy. As our hips move together in a sensual give and take, I slide my hand down his back and dig my fingers into his muscles.

Ethan suddenly arches, then expels a groaning hiss. Setting me down, he presses his forehead to mine and flattens his palms against the wall, taking deep breaths.

He sounds as if he's in pain. I rest my fingers on his shoulder and try to keep the worry out of my voice. "Are you okay?"

Ethan folds his fingers on the back of my neck and traces his thumb along my jaw. Nodding, he lets out a low laugh, then lifts his gaze to mine. "When we connect this first time, you can't touch my back."

My heart sinks a little. "Why?"

Lifting my hand from his shoulder, he presses a kiss to my scar. When my knees turn to jelly and a desperate, mewling moan escapes, he smiles. "Imagine what you just felt but intensified by twenty. That's what happens to me when your fingers brush the tattoo on my back while we're getting close like this."

My eyes widen. "Really?" I instantly try to slide my fingers down the curve of his shoulder to test his theory, but he captures my hand.

"Trust me. I'm not joking." A corner of his mouth lifts. "I'm on the edge with you as it is. I don't need the extra stimulation."

When I purposefully push out my bottom lip, he clasps my waist and dips his head to capture my lip between his teeth. I feel the rumbling growl in his chest as he slowly pulls away, letting my lip slide sensually between his. My heart's banging so hard, I can't even form words.

His eyebrows lift and he smiles. "I'm all for road testing our uniqueness later, but for right now…" He runs his finger down the side of my face, then hooks it under my chin. "I just want to feel you wrapped around me, where the only magic between us is our own skin making as much connection as possible."

He just melted my heart and stole my soul. Nodding my agreement, I start to tug him toward my room, but he holds a hand up. "There's something I want to show you first."

Before I can say a word, he walks down the hall and closes my bedroom door. I stare in confusion as he approaches and quickly lifts me into his arms, cradling me against his chest. As he carries me toward my bedroom, I hook my arm around his neck and tease, "It's going to be hard to get to my bed with the door shut."

"Close your eyes," he says softly.

When I frown doubtfully, he smiles. "Trust me, Sunshine."

With a smile of trust, I close my eyes and instantly feel soft warmth surrounding me from my head to my toes.

I open my eyes, all I see is darkness, but the sense of protection and security touching my arms, toes, back, and skin everywhere else is so strong, I gasp and reach out to feel what I can't see. "Feathers," I whisper in awe.

Slowly the outside lights splinter through the darkness. I can see Ethan and we're standing in my room with the door still closed. How did he do that? I can't help myself, I lean over and touch one of his massive wings. "They're beautiful." Ethan shudders, then sets me down on my feet.

As I stare, he folds his wings against his back. "This is how you got my dad out of that hotel room undetected, isn't it?"

He nods. "I can pass through walls on my own. It makes it easier to dispatch an Inferi to Under while the person is sleeping. But my raven wings allow me to bring a person with me too if I wish."

I've been wondering how Danielle snuck in my room that night. Walking through walls is a whole lot easier than picking locks. "Does it hurt?"

He shakes his head. "At first it felt all kinds of weird, but now it just feels natural. When I wish to walk through a wall, I can." While he's talking, his wings grow smaller. Once his wings completely disappear, I point past his shoulder to where they just were.

"That's exactly what I felt every time I was in your dreams. The protective shield I told you about that pulled me out of harm's way so many times? It was your raven wings."

Ethan's jaw hardens. "It was my Corvus protecting you."

I tilt my head and smile. "You can call on your wings when you need them, which is pretty amazing. Are you finally accepting your Corvus?"

He shrugs. "I use his abilities when it suits my needs." A grin flashes. "Like when I want to impress my girlfriend."

Laughing, I walk into his arms and kiss his jaw. "Every part of you is beautiful."

Ethan runs his fingers over the tattoo on my shoulder. Tugging my bra strap down, he kisses my bare skin. "I'm so incredibly lucky to have you in my life."

"Back at you." I kiss his jaw, while I tug on the button of his jeans, impatient for him to shed them quickly.

As he moves his warm mouth to my other shoulder, I unzip his pants and start to push them down, but he grabs my hips and yanks me close, locking my hands between us.

"Impatient?" he teases.

I take advantage of the position and turn my hands around. Touching him through his jeans, I tease back, "If you wanted my hands there, you only had to ask."

Ethan laughs, then sits down on the end of my bed with me straddling his lap. Cupping my neck, he pulls me in for a deep, arousing kiss. I flatten my palm against his jaw and curl my tongue slowly along his, showing him how much I want this.

Ethan grips my waist tight, and then he starts tugging on my clothes just as fast as I yank on his. The sheets suddenly feel so much softer against my bare skin as he leans over me and presses a sensual kiss to my neck while sliding his bare leg between mine.

The sensations that exchange between us when we touch are beyond words. My fingers trail up his hard biceps, then I thread them into his hair, pulling him down to me.

Ethan's kisses turn deeply passionate, his touches tenderly aggressive and demanding. Every stroke builds in possessive intensity, seeking a deeper, closer intimacy. I'm so caught up, I tug on his hair to get his attention and pant, "I'm going to combust without you."

Ethan kisses my neck and whispers, "Not this time, Sunshine," as his hand curves around my thigh. Lifting my leg around his hip, he locks my body intimately against his hard one and slowly eases inside me. My breath catches and I dig my nails into his shoulders, but he bends close and starts to sing a couple of lyrics from Together 'Til in my ear. His deep baritone jacks my pulse even higher as we begin to move to the soulful beat, finding our perfect harmony.

When Ethan's hand slides inside mine and he holds our hands tight against the bed, I arch into him and welcome the crescendo of his powerful emotions as love, loyalty, and devotion roll through me, one after the other. Holding him close, I tremble through every forceful wave while echoing my own promises back with just as much intensity.

As our breathing slowly evens out, Ethan gathers me close and presses a tender kiss to my temple. "I didn't think it was possible to love you more, but being with you like this is beyond…" He swallows and exhales. "It's indescribable."

I nod and slowly lace my fingers with his. "In case it wasn't clear, you just got my 'forever kiss.' I love you too." When he smiles, I lay my head on his chest and settle against him with a happy sigh.

I've just closed my eyes for a second when Ethan's low chuckle rumbles against my cheek and I quickly lift my head. "What?"

He clasps my waist and quickly pulls me across his chest until we're nose to nose. "I'm not going to waste a single minute of this alone time with you. Don't plan on getting much sleep tonight, Sunshine."

As his hands slowly begin to massage their way up my back, I press a kiss against his sexy mouth. *This is what it feels like to be branded, consumed, and thoroughly worshiped.*

Nara

My whole body aches, especially my shoulder. I roll over and rub it, thinking I must've pulled a muscle last night. I start to snicker, but realize Ethan's still asleep, so I smother my laugh and look over at his tousled bedhead with an amused smile.

Watching him sleep makes me want to run my fingers through his thick, dark hair. Sighing, I move to my dresser and grab some underwear, a pair of yoga pants and a zip-up jacket. Every muscle protests my movements, but it's a happy ache, the hard-earned kind you don't want to fade away too quickly. A hot shower will ease the soreness in my shoulder.

After I'm done with my shower, I step out of the tub into the steamy room, tucking a towel around my body. Just as I pick up my comb to run it through my hair, a cool breeze blows across my bare shoulder.

Suddenly the fog in the mirror clears up in a single circular spot, then quickly fogs over once more. I stiffen my spine. It might be too moist in here to feel the electricity in the air, but I know Fate's cold presence.

"What do you want?" I hiss.

Words start to form in the fog on the mirror as if drawn by an invisible finger.

He's
The
Master
Corvus

My green eyes widen before the letters completely fog over once more. "Who is?" I whisper.

Ethan

My stomach pitches and my gaze narrows as Ethan's name starts to fog over. "You're lying!"

He

Needs

To

Know

"How do you know?" I ask in a low voice, but suddenly the heaviness in the room is gone.

Once I've pulled on my clothes, I still shiver as I walk out of the bathroom. I instantly seek out the sunlight shining in my window. I turn my back to its bright rays splaying across my carpet and desk and soak in its warmth as I watch Ethan sleeping.

How am I going to tell Ethan this? Is it even true? Or is Fate screwing with me once more? But why would he do that? He definitely looked scared when Ethan threatened him. I can't deny Ethan had been powerful as he faced Fate. Even *I* felt that.

My gaze travels over Ethan's face. He looks so relaxed in his sleep. Does he already know he's Master Corvus, but he hasn't told me? Tension creeps into my neck, making my shoulder ache all over again.

I roll my head from one shoulder to the other, trying to work out whatever tense muscle is causing my soreness. As I reach up to press my fingers over the curved edge, digging into the sore shoulder muscle, I turn and my gaze snags on all the purple marks I'd made on the map on my desk.

I'd added the other places I was able to cross reference while at the school library. So far, the pattern is holding true to Madeline's theory. In an area where an unusual natural event occurs, not long after that, something happens: a man-made or natural structure is damaged, or an entire street's power is completely drained, or an inexplicable energy surge blows out a power station. The list goes on and on. To anyone else, these events wouldn't have any connection.

While I stare at the information and try to figure out how it can be helpful, my shoulder starts to itch. I reach under my jacket to scratch it and feel an edge roll under my finger, as if I'd gotten sunburned and my shoulder is peeling.

I push my jacket down and look over my shoulder. It's definitely not a string from my jacket. Pinching the rolled edge of skin between my thumb and forefinger, I peel off the dead piece of skin. Except it's not my skin, it's a piece of the feather's vein. I quickly glance at Ethan, then take my arm out of my jacket to slowly pull the feather away from my shoulder blade. It tingles a little but doesn't hurt.

Tugging my jacket back up, I lay the white feather against my trembling palm and run my fingers across the soft vane. I can't believe I can hold it. It feels like the black feather Ethan had left me before, strong but soft. And now that I can see it up close, the shaft end definitely has a jagged, tooth-like edge along one side.

I gently run my finger across the sharp points and wince as a bead of blood surfaces. Leaning across the desk, I move to grab the box of tissue on the other side when my gaze is drawn to the map once more.

Bright lights dance in my eyes like a residual flashbulb response. I blink a couple of times, but the spots don't go away. When I glance toward the wall, they finally recede, but as soon as I look down at the map, they reflect right back in my eyes.

I blink when I see a red dot where one glowing spot had been a second ago. I look at my hand and the feather is sitting in it like a pen. Frowning, I glance at the feather's tip. My finger has stopped bleeding and the tip of the feather is stark white. *Where did the red ink come from?*

But the spots continue to pop up no matter how many times I blink. Is this how really bad migraines start? I just want them to go away. Before I realize it, I've touched the feather to every single place on the map where I'd seen a bright glow. It's like I can't stop until I douse every glowing spot.

When I'm done, I set the feather down and study the map. *What do the red spots represent?* As I ponder the widespread red across the globe, the back of my hand itches, so I rub it across my nose while I chew on my bottom lip. None of the red dots overlap. But do they somehow connect to the purple marks I'd put on the map earlier? Or are they totally unrelated?

I glance to my right, intending to pick the feather back up and study it more, but it's gone. Panic seizes my chest, and I squat to see if it fell off the desk. Nothing. My worry ramps and I quickly move to the mirror to see if the feather I took off at least left an impression behind.

I gasp when the tattoo is back on my shoulder blade, but this time the very top of the feather is black; the dark color quickly fades into gray and then back into white. It's as if the tip has been dipped in ink and only a little of the ink bled down the vane.

"What's wrong?"

Ethan's suddenly alert voice draws my attention.

I turn and tug my jacket lower so he can see my shoulder blade.

He quickly pulls on his jeans and then turns me so the sun shines on the feather. His warm fingers brush against my skin. "Was it like this when you woke up?"

"No." I gesture to the map and tell him what just happened.

Ethan's expression hardens as he pushes his hand into his front pocket. He hasn't even looked at the map, but something is bothering him.

Clasping my hand, he draws me over to the bed and pulls me into his lap. "What is it?" I ask, my stomach tensing. The serious look on his face is worrying me. Is he going to tell me he's the Master Corvus now?

Ethan lifts my hand, then kisses the tip of each finger. When he reaches my ring finger, he slides something on it. I smile that he's putting the silver ring that matches his back on my finger. "You swiped that from my memories box as well, huh?"

He reaches in his other pocket and then slides his ring back on his finger too. Locking our hands together, he glances down at them. "This is why I was gone for a while yesterday."

When I shake my head in confusion, he twists my ring around until I see the new symbol he'd had added; it's the raven yin-yang symbol.

"I drove to three jewelers before I found someone willing to do it while I waited. What better place to add a symbol that protects you from demon possession than on the rings you had made for us?"

I kiss him on his jaw, enjoying his scruff against my lips. "Even though you don't need it, you had it put on yours too?"

"It's a matching pair. Of course I had it added." His smile fades as he cups the side of my face. "I'll do everything I can to protect you, even if that means giving up seeing you in my dreams. Right now there's a faceless Inferi running around out there who knows who we are. I won't take a chance with your safety. Please don't ever take this off. Protecting your soul is more important than seeing a day ahead."

I lay my hand over his on my cheek. "I won't. I promise."

"Good." Tension eases from his shoulders as he glances toward my desk. "So what have you plotted out over there?"

I stand and tug him to look at the map. "Remember the night after the dance when I showed you the video of that airplane accident from when I was a child?"

He rubs the back of his neck. "I remember being surprised we could both see the veil tearing open the sky, considering our abilities are different." Lowering his hand from his neck, his eyes light up. "Did you ask your dad about it?"

I nod. "I showed Dad a couple videos in the hospital, but he didn't see it." I gesture to the purple marks I'd made. "I've only mapped a few, but some of these marks are events that occurred in our world that resulted in veil thinning. Other purple marks are my guesswork based on natural events coinciding closely with inexplicable accidents." Shaking my head, I continue, "But I have no idea what the red dots mean."

Ethan stares at the map for a full minute before his fingers tighten around mine. "We need to shred, or even better, burn this."

My gaze jerks to his. "Why? Don't you think we should try to figure out what all this means first? Like if my purple marks in any way correlate? We at least *know* what those represent."

Ethan expels a tense breath. "I'm pretty sure I know what the red dots are."

"You do?"

He nods and points to the eastern coast of the United States, right around where our state would be. "That's me."

Heat drains from my face, and I grasp the edge of the desk to stay upright. "Are you telling me I just mapped out the location of every single Corvus in the world?"

Ethan nods, his expression grim. "I don't know how you could know this information—I only recognize myself. But a buzz hums as I stare at the other dots like it always did when Danielle was near, so my gut is telling me these are Corvus."

"How can *I* know where all the Corvus are when you're the Master Corvus?" I ask, my voice quivering.

Ethan's gaze jerks to mine. "I'm *not* the Master Corvus. What makes you say that?"

I want to bite my tongue for letting it slip like that. I grimace and gesture to the bathroom as I tell him about Fate's visit.

Ethan's face grows stony, then he points to the map. "There's your proof. I couldn't have mapped all those, Nara, because I don't know them. I sense them while staring at them, but that's what Corvus do, they sense other Corvus. I don't know what new games Fate is playing, but don't buy into his bullshit."

As he runs a hand through his hair, tension reflecting in his gaze while he studies the map, I say, "Why do you want to destroy this map?"

Ethan reaches over and smooths his hand down my damp hair. "I'm sorry if I sounded harsh. I just don't like Fate screwing with our heads." Nodding to the map, he says, "This information is too dangerous. Can you imagine what demons could do if they got their hands on it?"

Understanding dawns and I dip my head in agreement. While Ethan begins to fold the map, I run downstairs.

Grabbing a metal bucket from the garage, I head back into the kitchen. Just as I pull open the kitchen drawer to retrieve the matches, I see someone standing in the garage door I'd left ajar.

Before I can scream, the blond man holds a finger up to his lips.

There's no point asking how he got in my garage. He'll probably disappear in an instant anyway, so I ask the most important questions. "Who are you? Why are we so important to you?" My heart thunders.

He shakes his head. "You can't destroy the map yet."

I scowl. "I refuse to listen to anything you have to say unless you answer my questions."

When a superior look crosses his face, as if he knows what's best, I stare him down.

"Let's just say I have a vested interest in your success."

Dodging my question amps my stubborn meter. "That's not an answer." I hold up the matchbook and raise my eyebrows.

He expels a disbelieving laugh, then bows slightly. "I knew you'd make a great strategist. I'm Michael."

His name echoes in my ears, resounding and larger-than-life. As I wince against the thunderous sound of his real voice, realization curls my stomach inward. I can't believe I threatened the archangel responsible for kicking Lucifer out of heaven with a book of matches. I drop the puny weapon and blink at him, unsure what to say.

"Are you going to listen to me now?" he asks, golden eyes studying me with a mixture of pride and amusement.

All I can do is bob my head.

"Don't discount your work, Inara. Go back upstairs and study it, then destroy it."

As what he says sinks in, I realize Michael would know if Fate was telling the truth. "Is Ethan the Master Corvus?"

Michael's mouth sets in a hard line. "I want to kill Fate myself for meddling."

"Is he?" I ask, my hands shaking. "Why did Fate tell me?"

"Yes, Ethan is," he says on a sigh. "Fate told you because he's scared. He sees the Master Corvus not knowing who he is as a very real threat to his existence."

I'm quaking inside. The implications are huge. What does this mean for Ethan? "Why doesn't Ethan's Corvus know he's the Master Corvus?"

Michael tilts his head. "You need to help him find his way, Inara. He's lost sight of who he is and his true purpose."

I shake my head. "I don't understand. Who does his Corvus think he is?"

Michael offers up a half smile. "Just any other Corvus."

"What happened? How could he not know his own identity?"

He shrugs. "Only he knows that truth. The Master Corvus may not have a fate, but you can take him down the path. Help him find out what happened, so he can find his way back to his destiny. Your world depends on him remembering who he is."

"But if angels can't even talk to the Master Corvus, what makes you think he's going to listen to me?"

"Nara?" As soon as Ethan starts down the stairs, Michael fades right before my eyes.

Ethan walks into the kitchen, his gaze searching the room. "Were you just talking to somebody?"

"You could say that." I walk past him and start up the stairs, my mind spinning.

He's practically kicking at my heels, his deep voice right in my ear, vibrating with tension. "Who was it?"

I flip my hand over my shoulder. "Oh, just the highest ranking archangel and fiercest warrior ever telling me I'm not doing my job right."

As soon as we reach the top of the stairs, Ethan grips my hand and turns me around.

"Your job?" His deep blue gaze searches my face. "Are you an angel, Nara?"

Thank you for following Ethan and Nara's journey!

If you found **DESTINY** an entertaining and enjoyable read,
I hope you'll consider taking the time to leave a review and
share your thoughts in the online bookstore where you pur-
chased it. Your review could be the one to help another reader
decide to read the **BRIGHTEST KIND OF DARKNESS**
Series!

To keep up-to-date when the next **BRIGHTEST KIND OF
DARKNESS** book #4 will release, join my free newsletter
http://bit.ly/11tqAQN

DESTINY
GLOSSARY OF TERMS

Celestial realm - Heaven

Mortal realm - Earth

Under realm - Hell

Veil - a safety zone around the Mortal realm where angels constantly fight demons to keep them from breaking through the veil and entering the Mortal realm

Inferi - a demon who followed Lucifer when he was cast from the Celestial realm, ie a Lucifer demon

Inferni - plural of Inferi

Furia - a lower demon created if a Corvus kills a human who is fully possessed (corrupted) by an Inferi.

Furiae - plural of Furia

Corvus - a human who has been chosen to host a piece of the Master Corvus' spirit. The Corvus' sole purpose is to maintain balance between good and evil in the Mortal realm by fighting demons who possess humans. The Corvus expels the demon from the human, sending it back to Under (if it's a Inferi demon) or killing it for good (if it's a Furia demon).

Master Corvus - a powerful spirit who creates Corvus.

Order - A secret organization that oversees finding newly formed Corvus and assigning a Paladin to help the human adjust to the physical and mental changes he/she will experience as a Corvus.

Paladin - a human, with his/her own special ability, who has dedicated his/her life to the Order to help the Corvus. A Paladin gives the Corvus moral support through a human connection who understands their purpose. The Paladin's goal is to help the Corvus stay grounded to the human world so that the Corvus won't go dark from the demonic evil he/she has to fight on a constant basis.

Archangel – The highest-ranking angel

Other P.T. Michelle Books

Brightest Kind of Darkness Series

Ethan (Prequel ~ Written in Ethan's point-of-view, Ethan is best read after Brightest Kind of Darkness)
Brightest Kind of Darkness (Book 1)
Lucid (Book 2)
Destiny (Book 3)
Book 4 – Coming 2014

ACKNOWLEDGEMENTS

To my critique partners, J.A. Templeton, Trisha Wolfe, Rhyannon Byrd, and Jeri Smith Ready, thank you for helping make *Destiny* the best it can be.

To my wonderful beta reader: Dani Snell, thank you for your amazing support of the Brightest Kind of Darkness series and for your honest and valuable input in helping shape *Destiny*.

To my husband, thank you for being so proud and asking for bookmarks to give out. I promise I'll get some printed.

And to my amazingly adaptive children, who went through an international move with me and pitched in like champs while I finished up *Destiny*. I'm proud that you learned to grocery shop in the city, figured out French food equivalents, and how to cook in Celsius all on your own. Thank you for helping your mom out.

ABOUT THE AUTHOR

P.T. Michelle is the author of the young adult series **BRIGHTEST KIND OF DARKNESS**. She keeps a spiral notepad with her at all times, even on her nightstand. When P.T. isn't writing, she can usually be found reading or taking pictures of landscapes, sunsets and anything beautiful or odd in nature. To learn more about P.T.'s books, visit her at the following places:

Website:
http://www.ptmichelle.com

Facebook:
https://www.facebook.com/PTMichelleAuthor

Twitter:
http://www.twitter/pt_michelle

Newsletter (free newsletter announcing releases and special contests):
http://bit.ly/11tqAQN

DESTINY DISCUSSION GUIDE

What is Nara?

What do you think of the role the Corvus play in the mortal world?

What do you think happened between the Order and the Master Corvus? Do you believe the Order is trustworthy?

What do you think is the difference between fate and destiny?

Do you believe people are destined to be together?

Why do you think Michael brought Ethan and Nara together?

Why do you think Nara was chosen to help the Master Corvus?

Why do you think Patch has a stronger connection to Ethan and Nara than the other ravens?

Why did the Master Corvus forget who he is?

Why did Ethan's sword hurt Nara?

Will Drystan join the Order?

Why did Nara's feather change?

Why did Nara know the location of the other Corvus?

Why has the Corvus always protected Nara?

What do you think happened to Danielle?